P9-DOB-863

Praise for
OUT OF THE ASHES

"[Couch and Galdorisi] understand the inner workings of U.S. intelligence, government, and the military, and tell a frightening and exciting tale about a very new, but also a very old, threat."

—Larry Bond, *New York Times* bestselling author of *Dangerous Ground*

"Thriller addicts like me devoured every Tom Clancy's Op-Center tale. Now they are back, intricately plotted, with wonderfully evil villains and enough realistic military action and suspense to ruin a couple of nights' sleep. Highly recommended."

—Stephen Coonts, *New York Times* bestselling author of *Pirate Alley*

"This thriller procedural packs plenty of pulse-raising action. The open ending promises more to come."

—*Publishers Weekly*

"Op-Center is back with a vengeance! *Out of the Ashes* isn't just a reboot of the Op-Center series; it's one of the best techno-thrillers to hit the shelves in a long time. Dick Couch and George Galdorisi have just raised the bar for military adventure fiction. Suit up, strap in, and hang on, because you're in for one hell of a ride."

—Jeff Edwards, bestselling author of *The Seventh Angel* and *Sword of Shiva*

ALSO BY GEORGE GALDORISI

NONFICTION

*The United States and
the 1982 Law of the Sea
Convention: The Cases
Pro and Con*

*Beyond the Law of the Sea:
New Directions for United
States Oceans Policy*

*Leave No Man Behind:
The Saga of Combat Search
and Rescue*

The Kissing Sailor

*Networking the Global
Maritime Partnership*

FICTION

Coronado Conspiracy
For Duty and Honor

Act of Valor
(with Dick Couch)

Tom Clancy's
OP-CENTER
INTO THE
FIRE

CREATED BY
Tom Clancy and Steve Pieczenik

WRITTEN BY
Dick Couch and George Galdorisi

St. Martin's Paperbacks

This is a work of fiction. All of the characters, organizations, and events portrayed in this novel are either products of the author's imagination or are used fictitiously.

TOM CLANCY'S OP-CENTER: INTO THE FIRE

Copyright © 2015 by Jack Ryan Limited Partnership and S&R Literary, Inc. Excerpt from *Tom Clancy's Op-Center: Scorched Earth* copyright © 2016 by Jack Ryan Limited Partnership and S&R Literary, Inc.

For information address St. Martin's Press, 175 Fifth Avenue, New York, NY 10010.

ISBN: 978-1-250-09210-6

Our books may be purchased in bulk for promotional, educational, or business use. Please contact your local bookseller or the Macmillan Corporate and Premium Sales Department at 1-800-221-7945, ext. 5442, or by e-mail at MacmillanSpecialMarkets@macmillan.com.

Printed in the United States of America

St. Martin's Griffin trade paperback edition / May 2015
St. Martin's Paperbacks edition / May 2016

St. Martin's Paperbacks are published by St. Martin's Press, 175 Fifth Avenue, New York, NY 10010.

10 9 8 7 6 5 4 3 2 1

This book is dedicated to the selfless men and women in the United States military, in the myriad U.S. intelligence agencies, and in the U.S. diplomatic corps, all of whom serve overseas in repeated, lengthy, and often dangerous deployments so we can continue to have the prosperity and security we enjoy in America. They are our silent sentinels and we owe them more than we can ever repay.

ACKNOWLEDGMENTS

Reviving and reshaping a highly successful series such as Tom Clancy's Op-Center was an undertaking that was at once exciting and daunting. It took an extraordinary degree of cooperation, from those with stewardship over the first series to those who had the vision to launch a new series, those who did the heavy lifting to work through the contractual and editorial details of that new series, and those who served as sounding boards in shaping the first, *Out of the Ashes*, and now this latest effort, *Into the Fire*.

There are many people who helped make the new Op-Center series, and this book, live up to our expectations—and especially to the expectations of readers of the previous Op-Center books, as well as our new Op-Center readers. Many thanks to the following, who contributed their time and talent to this effort: Mel Berger, Bill Bleich, Wanda Clancy, Anne Clifford, Ken

Curtis, Melinda Day, Jeff Edwards, Hadley Franklin, Herb Gilliland, Robert Gottlieb, Kate Green, Kevin Green, Jennifer Johnson-Blalock, Brad Kaplan, Krystee Kott, Carl LaGreca, Robert Masello, Laurie McCord, Scott McCord, Madeleine Morrel, Rick "Ozzie" Nelson, Bob O'Donnell, Jerry O'Donnell, April Osborn, Norman Polmar, Sheila Sachs, Matthew Shear, John Silbersack, Charlie Spicer, Scott Truver, Sandy Wetzel-Smith, Ed Whitman, and Anna Wu.

AUTHORS' INTRODUCTION

The setting for *Into the Fire* is Northeast Asia, the center of enormous strife today and the cauldron where the next superpower confrontation could well take place. The issues causing discord in this region go back several millennia, and it is unlikely they will resolve themselves in the next few years. Today's fiction may, in every sense of the word, be tomorrow's headlines. At the center of this story is North Korea. As Adam Johnson noted in the *Reader's Guide* for his Pulitzer Prize–winning novel, *The Orphan Master's Son*, "It is illegal for a citizen of the DPRK [Democratic People's Republic of Korea] to interact with a foreigner." In a nutshell, this helps us understand why North Korea is the most isolated nation in the world and why its decision making is often completely unfathomable. Little wonder *The Wall Street Journal* called Johnson's book "the single best work of fiction published in 2012."

Juxtapose this against the widely heralded initiative by the United States to rebalance the Asia-Pacific region, and you have the compelling ingredients for conflict—you don't have to manufacture them. What North Korea does will continue to bedevil the United States—and the West, for that matter—for the foreseeable future. The Hermit Kingdom remains the world's most mysterious place. As a Center for Naval Analyses study noted, "The Kim-Jong-un regime has not completely revealed itself to the outside world." Not to put too fine a point on it, North Korea would likely qualify as one of the former secretary of defense Donald Rumsfeld's "unknown unknowns, the ones we don't know we don't know."

North Korea is not new to the Tom Clancy Op-Center series. The first book of the original series, *Tom Clancy's Op-Center,* was set in North Korea. The plotline for that book, published in 1995, had renegade South Korean soldiers setting off a bomb in Seoul during a festival and making it look like it was done by North Korea. The plot points of *Tom Clancy's Op-Center* were skillfully manufactured two decades ago, and the reader did not have to work very hard to suspend disbelief. Now, with today's confluence of similar geopolitical imperatives in Northeast Asia—with tensions between and among China, North Korea, Taiwan, Japan, South Korea, and other nations in the region flaring frequently—*Into the Fire* readers will have *no* need to suspend disbelief. What is happening in North Korea today could become the world's worst nightmare tomorrow.

INTO THE
FIRE

CHAPTER ONE

October 26, 0430 Korea Standard Time

The dilapidated, mustard-brown van slowed to a stop in the predawn hours as it approached the checkpoint leading to the housing area where many of the senior officers of the Korean People's Army—the KPA—lived in near-Western accommodations. The exclusive community was south of the Taedong River, close to the KPA's military headquarters in central Pyongyang, North Korea's capital, but far enough away to be suburban by most standards. It was a short ride for these senior military leaders when their staff cars came to collect them for the journey to KPA military headquarters each morning.

But the luxuries and perks afforded these fifty- and sixty-something officers who had clawed their way to the top of one of the KPA's five branches did little to obscure the Spartan, even primitive, living conditions of this nation of 25 million people. Pyongyang residents lived in perpetual misery with perennially unhealthy air, shoddy housing, unreliable utilities, a decrepit health care system, little access to quality food, and virtually none of the amenities most people take for granted. Even the road leading to this housing area was made of cheap asphalt and filled with potholes and ruts that made navigating it a challenge. With a standing army of over a million men, the fourth largest in the world, and over another seven million reserve and paramilitary forces, it was easy to see why there was little money left over to meet the basic needs of the North Korean people.

Two sleepy soldiers manning the wooden guard shack emerged to check the papers of the van's driver. They groused as they stepped out into the below-freezing temperatures. These types of vans, made by the Jianghuai Automobile Co. Ltd. or some other Chinese auto manufacturer, were a common sight in the early morning hours in this neighborhood. The van that was stopped at the guard shack, like the others that made this journey, was most likely bringing fresh fruit, vegetables, and freshly baked bread—things that were an unreachable luxury for ordinary North Koreans—to the household staffs of the senior officers living here. By the time these officers rose, they and their families would have meals prepared for them that would pass muster in most four-star hotels in the West.

As one soldier examined the documents offered by the driver, the other, following standard protocol, moved to the van's passenger side, where he looked down on the sleeping man in the passenger seat. He banged on the window to rouse the sleeper, and, as the man lifted his head, the soldier made a circling motion with his hand, indicating he should roll the window down. The passenger complied while the other soldier continued to shine his flashlight on the sheath of documents the driver had handed him.

Suddenly, the driver grunted, and both men in the van raised pistols and shot the guards in the head. The silencers did their job and muffled most of the noise. Brain matter, blood, and tissue exploded from the back of both soldiers' heads, and they collapsed onto the snow-covered road. Within seconds, three men emerged from the back of the vehicle. They picked up the dead guards and threw them in the back of the van, then used small shovels to rake the snow around to cover the ground where the guards had fallen and to mask the fact there was anything amiss. Their task complete, they jumped into the back of the van as it lurched away and headed for the home of Vice Marshal Sang Won-hong, deputy chief of the general staff of the KPA.

Several hundred meters up a gentle hill, Vice Marshal Sang, his wife, and his three sons slept soundly while their household staff of four busied themselves in their home's expansive kitchen. They piled wood into the cast iron stove to provide extra warmth in the kitchen, cleaned and cooked food, and made preparations for the family's breakfast, which was still several hours away.

Though they were servants and of a lower class in North Korea's society than the family, as live-in help for a senior military officer they enjoyed conditions that made them the envy of most of their countrymen. They bent to their various tasks with energy since they knew they could be dismissed at the whim of the vice marshal or his mercurial wife. One of their fellow workers had been terminated just two months ago and was thrown, weeping, into the alley behind the home.

The van stopped two hundred yards from the house. Five black-clad figures emerged, their faces obscured by ski masks, their hands holding Chinese-made Type 77 semiautomatic pistols with silencers. They moved with purpose and were soon pressed against the outside wall of Vice Marshal Sang's kitchen. A nod from their leader, and they burst into the room.

"Silence and you will not be harmed."

The only man among the household staff, the general's butler, stepped forward. "What do you want here?"

"That's not your business, old man," the leader barked as he pressed the barrel of the pistol to the butler's forehead.

The intruders moved quickly, cuffing the staff with plastic ties and duct-taping their mouths shut. They frog-walked them into the large pantry and slammed the door shut.

"Remember the layout," the leader said. "One bullet to each of their heads, then take everything of value, especially money and jewelry. There will likely be a small standing safe. Carry that away, too."

They dashed up the staircase and split up to cover the bedrooms on the second floor—the general and his wife in their large master bedroom and each of the young boys in their individual bedrooms. The silencers muffled most of the sound as the intruders put one bullet in the head of each victim.

The killing done, the five men concentrated on collecting anything of value in the vice marshal's home. They shoved money, jewelry, furs, and anything else small and movable into large heavy-duty bags. Once they deposited those bags in the van, two of the men returned to carry out the floor safe while the three others removed the artwork from the home's walls.

It was all over in ten minutes. The heavily laden van moved down the hill and toward an unknown destination.

CHAPTER TWO

November 4, 1130 Korea Standard Time

Commander Kate Bigelow sat in the captain's chair on the enclosed bridge of USS *Milwaukee* (LCS-5). *Milwaukee* was the third ship in the Freedom littoral-combat-ship class, the newest class of U.S. Navy ships. It was a 378-foot, 3,000-ton vessel featuring clean lines that provided the ship with a low radar signature. Aboard with Captain Bigelow were some seventy-eight officers and enlisted sailors and a complement of eight civilian technicians. *Milwaukee* called the San Diego Naval Base home and was currently on a forward deployment to the western Pacific, or, in sailor-speak, WESTPAC. The ship was forward-based in Singapore, the U.S. Navy's operating base for its LCS ships of both the Freedom and Independence classes.

In preparation for the upcoming exercise with the United States' Japanese and South Korean allies, *Milwaukee* had called at the Yokosuka Naval Base to participate in the usual pre-exercise briefings and was now just leaving the Fleet Activities Support Base in Sasebo, the U.S. naval facility on the west side of Kyushu, Japan's southernmost home island. Steaming in company with *Milwaukee* was the mine-countermeasures ship, USS *Defender* (MCM-2). Since Bigelow was senior to *Defender*'s commanding officer, she was also in operational command of the two-vessel flotilla.

At Sasebo, *Milwaukee* had an army of Navy civilian technicians and contractor representatives come aboard for three days to tweak the gear associated with its mine-countermeasures module. The LCS ships could be quickly configured for different mission tasking by switching out different mission modules. There was a mission module for surface warfare, for antisubmarine warfare, and for mine countermeasures. These modules had looked good on paper, but their development had lagged well behind getting the lead ships of the class in the water. The mine-countermeasures module was the least technically mature of all the modules the LCS ships carried, so it needed more TLC than the gear on most Navy ships.

Milwaukee's forward and aft mission bays were crowded with conex boxes and shipping containers that housed sonar-towed arrays, unmanned underwater vehicles, and several suites of mine-hunting gear. Among the gear was the AN/AQS-20A underwater towed sonar; the Knifefish surface-mine, countermeasure, unmanned undersea vehicle; the AN/WLD-1(V) Remote Multi-Mission Vehicle; and the Unmanned Surface Sweep System. And as they left Sasebo, eight technicians stayed aboard to continue to tweak the mine-counter-measures gear. None of this pleased Bigelow, but she had learned long ago that her role as commanding officer was not to gripe but simply to get the job done.

Much of this equipment was new or in the testing and evaluation stage of its development. And it was heavy. Not only did the mine-countermeasures module make the ship capable of doing little else but hunting mines, but the added weight elevated the ship's center of gravity. Bigelow, who was acutely sensitive to her ship's movement, was aware *Milwaukee*'s rolling motion was a bit more pronounced and that the vessel held the farthest point in the arc of its roll for just a fraction of a second longer than it used to. The ship was different than it had been before the module was taken aboard.

Kate Bigelow was a graduate of the United States Naval Academy. She had gone to the academy for two reasons: to play lacrosse and to sing. Coming out of Montgomery Blair High School in Silver Spring, Maryland, her two passions had been playing lacrosse and singing in her school glee club and church choir. She was an all-state midfielder and also had a strong voice. Her grades were good if not outstanding, but the academy women's lacrosse coach saw her play and liked what she saw. Lacrosse was a rough sport, even the women's game, and Kate Bigelow, while owning a technically sound game, was not above flattening an opposing player with a legal hit. And Annapolis was but an hour's drive from her home, so her parents could come to her games. So she started for three years on the lacrosse team, beating Army two of those three years, and sang in the Catholic Choir and the Naval Academy Glee Club. Kate had graduated in the upper half of the bottom third of the class of 2002. And while she had never really considered a full career in the Navy as a seagoing officer, two things intervened that kept her from leaving the service. First, she found that she liked U.S. Navy sailors and that she had a knack for leading them. Second, she found command intoxicating. There was nothing like it on the outside, so she stayed in. Since the Navy made it a practice to seek out capable female officers to place in command at sea, her goals and those of the Navy coincided. She had previously commanded an MCM ship like *Defender* that now followed them out of Sasebo.

Milwaukee was her second afloat command, and she relished having another command after this. Oddly enough, many career naval officers did not savor command at sea. There were too many things that could go wrong and derail their chances at promotion. Kate Bigelow was not one of those. When she was assigned staff or shore duty, she was constantly plotting how to get back to sea. When she was at sea and in command, she was always looking for ways to extend her tour in command.

"How 'bout some coffee, Skipper?"

"I can always use a cup of coffee, XO."

Commander Jack O'Connor was the ship's executive officer and two years junior to Bigelow. He had come aboard when Bigelow had taken command, and they had had their differences. The captain was responsible for the operation of the ship, but the XO ran the ship—or, more to the point, ran the department heads, who ran the ship. Bigelow understood this and tried to allow her second-in-command space to do his job. Toward the end of the transit from Singapore to Yokosuka, they had begun to fall into sync and work as a team. Then there had been the pre-exercise conference in Yokosuka several days ago, and that had not gone well. *Milwaukee* and *Defender* were scheduled for an at-sea rendezvous with six South Korean minesweepers for a mine-hunting and -clearing exercise off the west coast of Korea. The officer in charge of the exercise was a senior captain in the South Korean navy. At the pre-exercise conference, attended by all the commanding officers and their execs, O'Connor had spoken out of turn on occasion, and at one point he had encroached on Bigelow's position and the position of the Korean captain. Bigelow had worked with the Koreans before and knew the premium they put on rank and the strict protocols of seniority. Following the conference, Bigelow had taken him aside and quietly but firmly given him an old-fashioned ass chewing. Their interactions since then had been cordial but strained. Bigelow rightly sensed the offer of coffee was a peace overture. She took the proffered coffee, and the two of them made their way out to the exposed starboard wing of the bridge. The wind was coming from the west off the East China Sea, and it had a bite to it.

"Krause, you look like you could use a break and a warm-up," she said to the lookout, loud enough for the officer of the deck inside the bridge to hear. "Why don't you ask the officer of the deck if you can get some coffee for yourself?" She looked in and caught her OOD's eye as well, and he called the sailor into the warmth of the pilothouse.

The two made for an odd couple on the bridge wing. O'Connor was six three and pushing the Navy's height-weight tables. He had played football for North Carolina, a starting guard, but the bulk that served him well on the offensive line was not all that advantageous in the confined spaces of a small combatant. O'Connor had a youthful appearance and clear blue eyes that seemed to obscure his borderline weight issue. He was married with two kids, twin girls, and he wanted to stay in the Navy. He knew if he performed well, he would relieve Bigelow as commanding officer once her tour was done.

But in the U.S. Navy, there was always that "if." Officers could be removed from a position simply because of "loss of confidence in their abilities," a vague clause that had no equivalent in most professions. Beyond that, a less-than-glowing fitness report from Bigelow might not derail him from taking command once her tour was over, but it could put him ashore permanently once his tour in command was complete. That would end his chances for promotion and a long career. Bigelow herself was five eight and as slim as when she roamed the lacrosse fields. At thirty-six, she had outgrown all the girlishness and eased into a quiet command presence that was understated and compelling but still very feminine. She had married one year out of the academy, but the union had lasted only two years, and she had no children. There was a Marine infantry colonel in her life, but he had grown kids and a three-year tour at the Pentagon to contend with. Both welcomed an occasional weekend together, and both put their careers ahead of the relationship.

Kate Bigelow was a careful listener and almost never raised her voice. And she had a knack for judging people as well as leading them. She rightly suspected the reason O'Connor had sought her out. When the lookout was gone, she turned to her number 2 and waited.

"Ah, Skipper, I wanted to apologize again for my conduct at the meeting in Yokosuka. I don't know what I was thinking. Actually, I wasn't thinking. I really want this mine exercise to go well, and it just seemed to me that we were being marginalized by the Koreans. After all, our capabilities are far superior to theirs. Still, it was not my place."

Bigelow measured him. She was still not sure if he truly understood he was out of line or if this was a reaction to O'Connor's knowing full well he and his career were completely in her power. She had, however, seen enough of Jack O'Connor to know her executive officer was not a strong naval officer—adequate perhaps in some ways, but not strong. And it saddened her. She knew it would just make her job all that much harder and the rest of her tour in command less enjoyable. Ships in the U.S. Navy operated best when the CO and XO complemented each other and commanded as a team. Bigelow did not see that happening with Jack O'Connor.

"Very well, Jack, and I appreciate your coming to me like this. But answer me this. If the North Koreans ever do mine the approaches to Inchon, whose mine-clearing ships will be the first on scene?"

"Ah, the South Koreans."

"And what will our primary mine-countermeasure duties be in time of war?"

He paused. She was a step ahead of him, but, to his credit, he was not far behind. "Protecting our capital ships against mines?"

"Exactly. You and I both know that the LCS is pretty helpless in a blue-water hostile environment. Inchon is the likely target of a North Korean mining operation and well within land-based-air and surface-to-surface missiles from the north. So at issue is not how well we can clear mines but how well *they* can clear mines. Of course, we want to evaluate their capabilities and help them in any way we can, but it's their show. If it comes to the real thing, they'll be on their own. They know it, we know it, and Commodore Park and his little flotilla of sweepers know it, okay?"

"Roger that, Skipper."

"And don't forget," she said, lowering her voice, "we have a shitload of untested gear back there, we're undermanned in several critical ratings, and half this crew has never cleared a single mine. We're here to train our crew, test our gear, and do what we can to help the South Koreans."

"Roger that."

"And not to pick a scab, but never, and I mean never, speak over top of me in front of others or in front of this crew. You are welcome to come to me and say what you like behind closed doors. In fact, I count on that; that's part of your job. But never in public. Fair enough?"

"I've got it, ma'am."

After O'Connor left the bridge, she wandered into the

pilothouse and walked over to the tiny navigation cubicle at the rear of the enclosed space.

"What do you have for me, Chief Danforth?"

The chief quartermaster looked up from his screen with its electronic chart and smiled. "I put us right here," he said, pointing to a location on the track of their planned intended movement—or PIM in Navy parlance. "With Uku Jima off to port about six miles and Hirado Jima to starboard some four miles, base course is zero-zero-five at fifteen knots."

"Time to turn?"

"On this course and speed, I make it thirty-six minutes until we come left to our new course of two-seven-six."

"How long until we get to the Cheju Channel?" Bigelow was referring to the broad channel between Cheju Island and the southern tip of the Korean mainland.

"From our next turn, I make it about eleven hours."

Bigelow did the math quickly. That would be about 0300 the following morning. She nodded. "Okay, see that I'm called well before we get into the channel."

"Aye, aye, ma'am."

Bigelow sat down in her chair for a few minutes of peace before she returned to her stateroom and the mountain of paperwork awaiting her. *Milwaukee* had a mixed-gender crew, and that meant there were always matters of fraternization and unwanted, unwise, and illegal sexual conduct. There were issues related to the gear associated with the mine-countermeasures module, and the onboard team of Navy civilians and contractors were pressing her for a meeting to go over *their* problems. For them, it was all about the gear. Her department heads needed some of her time with lists of personnel and mechanical problems. A great deal of this could, and should, be handled by Jack O'Connor, but she still had nagging questions about his abilities. She knew full well she should allow him the space to do his job—sink or swim, as it were. But it was still her ship, and its ability to carry out its mission was on her shoulders, not his. So she was stuck; she had to walk that fine line between trusting him to carry out his duties and seeing to it that the job got done.

And there was the LCS itself, the *Milwaukee*. The critics of the U.S. Navy's LCS program, both in Congress and within the naval establishment, were right in their assessment of the ship's shortcomings. The LCS was basically defenseless. She was a sitting duck for any ship or small craft with surface-to-surface missile capability. Her single gun, the Mark 110, Mod 057 mm BAE Systems cannon, was capable of 200 rounds per minute with 240 rounds in ready-service availability. It could be deadly to small craft that came within five miles, but most of the world's navies, including that of North Korea, had small craft with accurate surface-to-surface missiles that could be fired well outside that range. And they would be operating well within the arc of North Korean land-based air. *Milwaukee*'s RIM-116 Rolling Airframe Missile system was compact and effective against both low-flying aircraft and surface-to-surface cruise missiles. But there was an interface flaw. The RIM-116 had no built-in acquisition capability; it had to be carefully aimed along the axis of the incoming threat. The system that aimed the missiles was the AN/SWY-2 Ship Defense Surface Missile System. When the two systems worked, they worked well. But they didn't always work well. In Bigelow's experience, they produced a missile launch and a missile kill only about half the time.

One advantage *Milwaukee* did have was speed. While it could not outrun a cruise missile or an attacking aircraft, it could make close to forty-five knots with its two Rolls-Royce gas turbines and the two Colt-Pielstick diesels at full throttle and the four Rolls-Royce water jets all online. Yet with the heavy mine-countermeasures module aboard, Bigelow had no idea what her best speed might be, or how her ship would handle at that speed.

And then there was the helo issue. Just thinking about it made her stomach churn. The LCS was designed to embark the MH-60 Seahawk helicopter and the MQ-8C Fire Scout unmanned aerial vehicle. The helicopter and the UAV gave the LCS a tremendously enhanced capability, and she had operated effectively with her helo det before. But for reasons that were still obscure to her, the Seventh Fleet staff and her LCS commodore in Singapore decided not to embark her helo det—neither the Seahawk nor the Fire Scout—for this exercise but to keep the detachment in Singapore. She had tapped into her network to try to find out why, and the most plausible reason she could uncover was that none of the South Korean minesweepers had a helo detachment and thus the Americans did not want to show up their allies. Fine for parades, she mused, not so much for operating in hostile waters. Having the nimble Seahawk aboard armed with a suite of Hellfire missiles always helped her sleep better at night when they were at sea. But it was what it was, she reminded herself. *Deal with it, Kate. You don't want your sailors to bitch, so don't do so yourself when you don't get everything you feel you need or want.*

So, Bigelow thought to herself, I don't really have much of an effective offensive punch, my defense works about half the time, and I don't have an aviation detachment. I probably can't outrun a threat. And in order to make the LCS less expensive and fast, my ship has no armor plating. Everything is electronic and interconnected, so one good hit and we're out of the fight— done. Add this to the personnel problems and crew inexperience, and it was almost overwhelming—almost. Bigelow glanced out the bridge window at the receding coast of Kyushu, and, as she looked over at the LCD screen in front of her officer of the deck, she noted *Defender* was dutifully keeping station behind her. Then she smiled.

I wouldn't trade this for anything.

"You say something, ma'am." She had not noticed Ensign Allie Stockton, the officer of the deck, who had looked over her shoulder from her OOD chair in the pilothouse. Stockton was a Navy ROTC officer from Notre Dame, sharp as a tack.

"I said I think I'll lay down to the chief's mess and see if they have some decent coffee. Then I'll be in my stateroom. Call me after you've come left to the new course, Allie. Otherwise, the standard daylight steaming orders apply."

"Aye, aye, ma'am," Stockton replied. Then, after Bigelow had exited through the rear door of the pilothouse, she announced, "Captain's off the bridge!"

CHAPTER THREE

November 4, 0645 Eastern Standard Time

Chase Williams pulled into an unmarked parking space at the National Geospatial-Intelligence Agency—the NGA—at Fort Belvoir near Springfield, Virginia. The parking lot had been expanded when the location for the revived Op-Center was installed in the basement levels of the NGA. The new lot still had reserved, close-in parking spaces clearly marked for senior NGA staffers. Yet at Williams's insistence, there were none for Op-Center personnel, nor was there any Op-Center logo seen anywhere on the building's exterior signage. A directory of tenant commands at Fort Belvoir did not mention anything about Op-Center. It was still early, and Williams had but a short walk to the main entrance of the building.

There was a reason why Op-Center's very presence at Fort Belvoir was kept secret and why it was housed in a sub-basement of NGA, not in its own gleaming building. Op-Center was a national asset and its director reported directly to the president. It was called into action only when the normal levers of U.S. national security—the military, the intelligence agencies, the many organizations making up the nation's homeland security bureaucracy, or others—could not move quickly enough or were forced by statute or oversight to operate within strict legal protocols. The president had called on Op-Center recently, and they had done just that: operated with speed and precision and well outside legal channels. And they had saved American lives.

Williams made his way through the double glass doors, showed his NGA badge to the guard at the counter, and continued on to a single elevator at the end of a bank of elevators. Just another faceless staffer with a security clearance trudging in to work, which was as Williams wanted it. He punched in his personal access code, and the elevator door hissed open to allow him entry. Following a noiseless, three-level descent, he was deposited in a small antechamber with a single door. After submitting to a retinal scan, he was admitted to the subterranean warren that was Op-Center's main compound.

Williams was sixty-three, six foot tall, and carried himself in a lean, distinguished manner. Yet he was understated and moved with a quiet efficiency that attracted little attention. His dress was closely tailored but conservative, and only the white handkerchief peeking from the pocket of his suit coat suggested a hint of style. A great many senior people in and out of government knew and respected Williams. But no one underestimated him or the confidence President Midkiff now vested in him and his organization.

"Morning, boss."

"Good morning, Anne." Anne Sullivan was waiting for him at the door to his office. It was adjacent to hers, which was larger and better appointed than his own small office. This arrangement was at Williams's insistence. He was the director of Op-Center, but she, as deputy director, ran Op-Center. As a good Navy man, he knew the value of a strong executive officer.

Anne Sullivan was a former GSA supergrade and the embodiment of a Washington insider. Williams counted on her, and she quietly managed the day-to-day administration of Op-Center with dedication, organizational skill, and a certain amount of intimidation. She also knew where all the bodies were buried around Capitol Hill. Op-Center had its enemies, particularly in the Department of Defense. If there were ever a politically motivated campaign mounted to discredit Op-Center, then the ever-vigilant Anne Sullivan would sniff it out early on.

It was Williams's practice to arrive at Op-Center at 0645 sharp, about five minutes after his drip coffeemaker had delivered a strong, full pot of his special Sumatra dark roast. Sullivan was always in the office ahead of him. Following the ritual morning greeting, it was her practice to wait for ten minutes to allow her director to check his messages and e-mail. Then she knocked lightly on his door and stepped inside. Williams handed her an antique porcelain cup and saucer that had been his grandmother's. She took it black, as did he. He then topped off his own Navy messdecks mug, and they got down to business. He thought staff meetings were a waste of time and elected to take the pulse of his organization with a morning briefing from his deputy director. She sipped the coffee appreciatively and tapped on the screen of the security-protected iPad on her lap, then proceeded to brief him on the activity of each Op-Center senior operative.

First there was Roger McCord, Op-Center's director of intelligence and perhaps the most valuable and essential member in the organization. He was fit, bright, and a devoted family man. McCord was highly regarded within the tight-knit intelligence community, and Williams trusted him without question. Op-Center was built on a corporate model where the intelligence and analytic functions were to be kept in house and bolstered by the most advanced technology and capable brains available. This was why McCord's intel shop looked more like a think tank at Google or Amazon than a department of an obscure government agency. On the other end of the Op-Center corporate model was the direct-action component—which was all outsourced. Op-Center had capable and experienced operational planners and logisticians, but they relied on the U.S. Special Operations command or some other DoD or government-strike element when a military or paramilitary response was needed.

Then there were Dawson and Rodriguez. The heart of the operations team were the absent Brian Dawson and Hector Rodriguez. It was their job to contact, nominate, test, evaluate, and interface with these non-

Op-Center action entities and to hold periodic training sessions with them to ensure Op-Center and strike-element interoperability. This kept them out of the office and out from under the direct supervision of Anne Sullivan for several days at a time. Williams knew that in the special-operations-warrior brotherhood they had to mingle. This meant they might even have to linger over a beer at the Green Beret Club at Fort Bragg or over a pile of blue crab at a tavern near Quantico. Williams understood this, even if Anne Sullivan did not.

Sullivan moved on to Jim Wright, a former member of the bureau's hostage-rescue team. His last bureau assignment was with the Special Activities Division at CIA. Normally, the men from the Hoover Building and the men from Langley didn't get on, but Jim Wright was the exception. He got on with everyone, and his contacts in the law enforcement and intelligence agencies were legion. At Op-Center, he was known as Mister Inside.

Duncan Sutherland was the Op-Center supply officer. He was to logistics what Fred Astaire was to dance. The Op-Center plans department was in the capable hands of Richard Middleton. And there was Laura Beall, who, along with Anne Sullivan, served Chase Williams as a political advisor—more specifically, a political spy. What Anne Sullivan may have missed through her former official contacts, Laura Beall picked up at the coffee shops from the congressional staffers and bottom-feeders who swum in and among the power brokers. She was attractive, successful, and very expensive.

Sullivan completed her briefing and looked up. Williams nodded. "Anything else?"

"Just one thing," Sullivan replied. "Since Roger is out of the office, Aaron has asked to be put on your schedule. He says it may be important and asked to see you as soon as it's convenient."

Williams hesitated, but only for a moment. "Tell him it's convenient right now. If he thinks it's important, then it probably is."

Bleich worked directly for Roger McCord, and Williams suspected that had McCord been in that morning, both of them would want to see him. That Bleich did not want to wait until McCord returned to the office told Williams this might indeed be something important.

Aaron Bleich's official title was intelligence directorate, networks assistant, but that was not the half of it. Bleich, at thirty-three, was one of the younger staffers at Op-Center, and his salary was three times that of anyone else in the organization. He was arguably the top video-gaming talent in the nation, which meant in the world. On McCord's recommendation, he was hired at a salary the Government Accountability Office would have considered obscene and illegal. Bleich designed the automated collection algorithms and high-speed data-sorting protocols that set Op-Center apart from other intelligence-collection efforts in or out of government. Through working agreements and occasional outright hacking, Op-Center was privy to the entire spectrum of information collected by the U.S. intelligence agencies. Such a mountain of data would clog all but the most skillful and selective segregation and collation programs. But the computing resources, which amounted to sixty percent of Op-Center's budget, and talents of

Bleich's people, the Geek Tank, as they called themselves, made it all possible.

"On second thought," Williams said as Sullivan rose to leave, "tell Aaron I'll be in to see him." He topped off his coffee mug and followed her out.

The door to the Geek Tank section in Op-Center's warren of subterranean offices was monitored by a palm-print reader and a moniker over the door: ABANDON HOPE, ALL YE WHO ENTER HERE. It was a cultural barrier as well as a physical one. The space was a large open area, with low-walled cubicles, as many as five flat screens per work station, and cables running everywhere. There were posters of Steve Jobs, Albert Einstein, Bill Gates, Stephen Hawking, and RG III on the walls. Among the wall art was a periodic table of the elements and movie posters of *Avatar* and *2001: A Space Odyssey*. A John Legend song drifted across the room. The flat surfaces were cluttered with pizza boxes, empty Slurpee containers, and iPhones and iPads and were punctuated by eclectically dressed, twenty- and thirty-somethings, seemingly lounging and talking rather than working. Most Op-Center staffers seldom entered the space they called the Geek Tank. There was an energy here unlike any other space at Op-Center and unlike anything Williams had experienced in his military or government service. He'd made it his business to know everyone in his organization, so as he made his way through the area to the single glass-enclosed corner office that was Aaron Bleich's, he was able to greet each intel staffer by name. Yet he felt conspicuous and out of place in his starched white shirt and club tie. The dozen or so members of the Geek Tank who were present were attired in blue jeans and T-shirts, with an occasional collared shirt or a pair of polished cottons. Bleich was waiting for him. He was dressed in Dockers and a *Family Guy* sweatshirt and looking a little uncomfortable. The sign over his door read SENIOR HALL MONITOR. "My apologies for my attire, sir. Had I known I needed to see you, I'd not have been so casual."

"Aaron, it's your work we count on here, not how you dress. This is your world, and if you're comfortable, I'm comfortable. Now, what have you got for me?"

Bleich closed the door as Williams took a seat and the Geek Tank leader became all business. "I started to notice things yesterday afternoon," he began. "It's North Korea again, and something's up. It's, well, do you want me to build the watch or do you want to know the time?"

"For now, let's just stick with the time."

Bleich nodded. "As you know, with a few exceptions, they have a pretty inept blue-water navy. Yet they've moved some of their more serviceable vessels from their fleet headquarters at Wonsan on the east coast around the peninsula to the west coast. Over the past two weeks, there has been a slow migration of units south to the DMZ—mostly armor and special-operations units. And there's been an alteration in the frequency and pattern of the testing of their coastal defense and missile guidance radars. There are other indicators as well. On balance, this is nothing new. They're always moving units around, seemingly with no purpose. But this time, we're picking up none of the normal command and control chatter. Between us, the South Koreans, and the Japanese, we have an effective electronic blanket over the North. We generally know about these movements from electronic intercepts, Web-based traffic, and cell-phone activity. This time, there was none of that. It's as if they're using only shielded hard-line communications or couriers. They seem to be prepositioning assets, which we can easily track by satellite, but they're going to great lengths not to broadcast it. It's really weird. If it were business as usual, they'd use the normal communications channels, but they're not."

Williams thought about this a moment. "Is this coming up on anyone else's radar—CIA, DIA, NSA?"

"No, sir. If it were, then they'd at least be talking about it in house."

"And you would know this?"

"Trust me, sir, if there's something being talked about among the analysts at CIA, NSA, the Pentagon, or anywhere else, we'd know about it."

"You mean you've hacked in their internal, in-house communications?"

"Ah, we're starting to get into watch parts here, boss, and well beyond the time of day. But I can go into it if you'd like."

Williams could tell Bleich really *would* like to go into it; it was what he did, and he could do it better than anyone else in or out of government. He demurred but made a mental note to bring it up with Roger McCord.

"Maybe some other time. Is there anything special going on in or around the Korean Peninsula?"

Bleich was expecting this. "We have a major naval

exercise with the South Koreans and the Japanese scheduled to begin in a few days. Most of the activity is in
the Sea of Japan with a shallow-water mine exercise to
take place in the Yellow Sea."

"And you think something's wrong."

Bleich shrugged. "I'm saying this time they're doing
something different with the flow of their command and
control traffic. We did an electronic look-back, and this
is something they've never done before."

Williams was silent for close to a minute. Then he
said, "Aaron, forget about the electronic and communications intelligence, or lack of it, for a moment. What do
you think? What does your gut tell you?"

Now it was Bleich's turn to pause. Aaron Bleich was
an empirical person; seldom did someone ask him for
how he *felt* about something. "Well, sir, this is a little off
point for me. I mean, I'm just a techie."

"And a very good techie," Williams interjected, "but
what do you think?"

"I think they're up to no good, and maybe even something that's not good on a large scale."

CHAPTER FOUR

THE YELLOW SEA

November 5, 0830 Korea Standard Time

Lieutenant Commander Choe Dae-jung was on the starboard bridge wing of the *Won Do* as the vessel stood out from Haeju Naval Base. The two-hundred-foot, six-hundred-ton Soviet-designed corvette had just left a base course of 155 and came right to 185. They were heading almost directly into the gentle swells of the Yellow Sea that were just now shouldering their way into the Haeju estuary. *They may not be so gentle when we get farther out to sea*, Choe thought, *and we are subject to the frequent shifts in wind and weather.* The Yellow Sea could be treacherous in November, much like the Gulf of Mexico in November, only much colder. Of course, it would not be so rough as operating in the Sea of Japan that were home waters of *Won Do,* but it would be uncomfortable enough. His ship had taken on an unusual amount of provisions in Haeju, and that suggested they might be at sea for a while.

Won Do was one of five Sariwon-class corvettes built in the 1960s and 70s in North Korea, which were designed as multipurpose littoral combat vessels. This meant *Won Do* could do a lot of things, but none of them very well. The craft was armed with two twin 57 mm mounts and two twin 37 mm mounts, which gave the ship a heavily armed look, but the fire-control radar, when it worked, was only marginally more effective than the optical pointing systems. Its only air-defense systems were four quad 14.5 mm machine guns that, again, appeared more menacing than they were. Their only effective anti-air weapons were the shoulder-fired Strela SA-7 missiles. Offensively, the craft had little to offer but its ability to sow its thirty-some Chinese-made EM-53 acoustic mines, a mine that could be highly effective in shallow water.

Won Do's only virtues were its relatively good sea-keeping ability and the rugged diesel engines that could move the ship at fifteen knots with a range of 2,600 nautical miles. It was a small ship whose designers had the same mission in mind as the builders of the U.S. Navy's littoral combat ship. But the similarities ended there. The Freedom-class LCS was light, fast, and new; the *Won Do* was heavy, slow, and old. And, like her skipper, the *Won Do* was tired; only the close attention of her faithful crew kept her seaworthy, if not battle-worthy.

Choe Dae-jung was forty-three years old and had been in the Korean People's Army naval force for over half of that time. He had left his family farm to enlist in the navy at sixteen. He had not really intended on a career at sea, but remaining home was not an option. With one younger sister and two brothers, there was simply not enough food. Choe had been hungry all his life and had never known freedom from want until he was posted aboard his first ship. The pay was negligible, but the military kept their people fed, if not well fed, and afforded them a place to sleep. He worked hard and made his way up the enlisted ranks and gained promotion to the rank of ensign at the age of twenty-eight. Like most of his crew, Choe was single and the *Won Do* was home. In this respect, the officers and the seamen of the lower decks were much alike. Except for those infrequent times when the ship was taken into dry dock for hull repairs, Choe was seldom ashore. He was good at his job, and he kept *Won Do* shipshape and ready for sea. He still remembered what it was like to live with hunger every waking moment, and he never wanted to return to that life. He had no idea what he would do or how he would live if or when he ever left the navy, or after he left *Won Do* for that matter. *Won Do* was neither a new ship nor a particularly prestigious command. He had been its captain for five years now; perhaps they would leave him be for another five.

Normally, *Won Do* called the Wonsan Naval Base its home port, as did the other five of the Sariwon-class corvettes. But over the last several weeks, *Won Do* and two of her sister ships had been ordered to make the transit from the Wonsan Naval Base on the east coast of North Korea on the Sea of Japan, around the Korean Peninsula, and to Haeju on the west coast. This in itself was strange and unprecedented. Given the shortages of fuel oil and stores, the corvettes seldom left port, and when they did, they operated in local waters. His sealed orders had been delivered the night before with instructions to open them only after he had entered the Yellow Sea. Choe was torn between repairing to his small cabin just behind the pilothouse or remaining on the bridge until they were farther out to sea. If there was a single compensation to what he considered his maritime indentured servitude, it was being on the bridge of his ship when standing out of port. Choe's brief moment of contentment was cut short.

"Good morning, Captain," a voice called to him from the pilothouse. It was a good deal more blustery on the bridge wing than in the pilothouse.

Choe turned and forced a smile. "Ah, Comrade Ha. Please feel free to join me. The brisk salt air is free to all."

"Perhaps a little later in the day. It would seem, Captain, it is about time to open your orders."

Ha Min-ki was short, pale, and in his late twenties. He had arrived aboard *Won Do* the day before, along with the sealed orders. And he was certainly no seaman. His worn cotton slacks and Western-style cardigan were in contrast to the dungarees and rough wool foul-weather gear worn by the *Won Do*'s officers and ratings alike. He carried orders from their commodore appointing him as the ship's political officer. It became obvious when they got under way this was his first time at sea and that he was clearly uneasy with the motion of the ship.

Choe liked none of this. That he and his ship were

now operating in the Yellow Sea was troubling enough. And they had not been the only vessel to sortie from Haeju. There had been a steady trickle of sailings over the last few days, and there was evidence of other vessels making preparations for sea. The North Korean navy was more accustomed to sitting in port than being at sea, even when operating in the littorals. Now he was saddled with this political hack the day before they sailed. He was a man who, under their system, could exercise a great deal of control over Choe and his ship. All this activity meant something was afoot, something big and perhaps something unprecedented. Choe could only wonder what those idiots in Pyongyang were up to, or just why this young ideologue had been posted to *Won Do*. Whatever it was, Choe suspected it would probably be an ill-conceived and dangerous adventure with little regard for the welfare of his ship or his crew.

"Well, Captain?"

Choe gave him a long stare and then turned to the bridge messenger. "Seaman Hong, why don't you lay down to the messdeck and get Comrade Ha and me a nice bowl of cold kimchee soup and a glass of curdled milk. Something to eat might go well on this fine morning, eh, Comrade Ha?"

Ha paused and took a few deep breaths through his mouth, then disappeared quickly into the pilothouse and down the ladder that led to his small quarters and private toilet. Choe grinned and turned back to the rail of the bridge wing. He glanced at the gyro repeater and saw they were a few degrees off course.

"Steersman, mind your helm."

"Aye, Captain."

As the North Korean mainland slipped astern, Choe Dae-jung made his way to his sea cabin, which aboard *Won Do* was the only personal space, and shucked his bridge coat. The cabin was no more than a closet with a bunk and a little fold-down desk. He opened the small safe bolted to the deck and took out a thin packet that bore the wax seal of the Western Fleet of the People's Army naval force. Choe broke the seal and read his orders. After he read them a second time, he pushed the intercom to the bridge.

"Yes, Captain."

"Please have our guest, Comrade Ha, and the executive officer meet me in the wardroom."

"Aye, aye, Captain."

Choe replaced the orders and locked the safe, then lowered his head. "God help us," he whispered. "God help us all."

Due west of where Captain Choe had opened his secret orders, ships were not sheltered from the winter storm that battered the Yellow Sea the way *Won Do* was protected by the North Korean landmass. The howling storm was intensifying, and the waves were reaching alarming heights. Aboard the Chinese hydrographic vessel *Fen Dou,* the first mate approached the ship's master.

"Captain, this storm is intensifying. It is far worse than was predicted when we left Qingdao two days ago."

"And what forecast have you pulled off the network just now?"

"It's alarming, sir. The winds are predicted to remain at least forty-five knots, maybe more, and the sea state is expected to intensify from seven to perhaps eight in the next twenty-four to thirty-six hours."

The master considered this. The winds and the sea state were marginal already, and sea state 8 would bring waves of ten to twelve meters. Still, he was a professional seaman who had been on ships since he was a teenager. Skillful handling of *Fen Dou* could overcome unfriendly waters.

"As you say, but as you know, predictions are not always accurate."

"Yes, I know that. But we have a vast area to survey. Perhaps we can move to a calmer area on our survey plan—somewhere in the lee of land—and then come back here into open water once the storm abates."

The master had been with this first mate for almost two years and considered him to be one of the best he'd had in his over three decades of plying these waters. But the man was young, had a family, and worried too much. Still, he did not want to dismiss his concerns out of hand.

"Let's see what the weather does in the next six hours. We can decide then, all right? For now, put two extra men on that crane so we can lower the gear into the water."

"Captain, it's getting increasingly dangerous on deck . . ."

"I know that!" the master said, his voice hard.

"You know what safety precautions to take. See that you take them. We have work to do, and we don't have enough time to do it."

The master didn't like scolding his first mate like this. The man was hardworking and loyal to a fault. And his concerns were valid. Truth be told, the ship's captain knew a ship like *Fen Dou* shouldn't be conducting hydrographic surveys in waters as open as the Yellow Sea. But that decision was made in Beijing and was not something that was to be debated in the pilothouse of his ship.

Fen Dou's master had a well-cultivated network, and before he took the assignment to command one of the ships conducting this extensive survey, he did his homework. It was well known China's booming economy was straining its oil and gas supplies, so much so that it threatened to slow down the nation's double-digit economic growth. Ongoing turmoil in the Middle East made depending on that source for its fossil-fuel supply chancy at best.

What was less well known was that North Korea had claimed to have found massive gas supplies on the seabed of Korea Bay and all the way down into the northern reaches of the Yellow Sea. China's leaders were in the process of brokering a deal with North Korea to buy all of this natural gas, but there was a problem. The claims of trillions of cubic meters of gas on the seabed that North Korea said it was going to mine were based solely on North Korean surveys—surveys that were, as yet, unverified.

So China had commissioned a fleet of every Chinese-owned hydrographic survey vessel it could muster to do a rapid survey of these waters to validate the North Korean claims. Time was of the essence since China wanted to seal this energy deal with North Korea before the unpredictable leadership in Pyongyang figured out it could sell this natural gas for more money on the open market and changed its mind. Ships' masters were given areas to search and a deadline for producing their surveys, and they were promised a significant bonus for completing the surveys early.

Fen Dou's master had not only young mouths to feed but also aging parents to care for. He was determined to get his bonus.

CHAPTER FIVE

THE WHITE HOUSE
SITUATION ROOM

November 5, 1000 Eastern Standard Time

Midway through the second year of his term as president, Wyatt Midkiff kept wondering when it would get easier and overseas concerns would abate enough to allow him to pursue his expansive domestic agenda. His administration had been rocked by the bombings of the NFL stadiums during his first year in office and then shocked again the past spring by the reprisal attacks on several malls in the Washington, D.C., area. All told, over two thousand Americans had died at the hands of foreign terrorists for hire on his watch.

The retaliatory strike against Iran had served notice that the United States would avenge attacks on its citizens and actually brought a modest extent of goodwill from most of the Arab nations in the Gulf. They all feared Iran and its desire to dominate the region but didn't have the military wherewithal to take on the Persian state. But there was no denying the United States was not the superpower it once was. And that *too* was happening on his watch.

The previous administration had set in motion drastic cuts to the U.S. military budget, the sequestration debacle had made that worse, and spiraling costs for military weapons and manpower had strained the ability of the U.S. military to maintain the status quo. His predecessor had announced the United States' intent to rebalance the Asia-Pacific region and to move substantial forces to that region to show the nations of that part of the world the United States intended to remain a Pacific power. But military budgets were under strain, and the ability to maintain the existing state of affairs, let alone add forces, was a stretch at best, a fantasy at worst.

For a while it had not mattered. But China's military budget continued to grow at a double-digit rate, and China continued to arm its client states, like North Korea, with modern weaponry. U.S. allies in the region began to ask uncomfortable questions when they saw scant evidence of the U.S. initiative to rebalance the Asia-Pacific region. The hints of greater accommodation with China by even some of the United States' staunchest allies were becoming more evident.

But this meeting of the president's senior policy and military advisors was not about China, it was about North Korea. The Hermit Kingdom was acting increasingly irrationally, and U.S. allies and friends in the region—especially South Korea and Japan— were becoming increasingly worried. North Korean provocations—from capturing the USS *Pueblo* in

1968 to shooting down a U.S. reconnaissance aircraft the next year to North Korea's strident insistence on the need to field nuclear weapons as a defense against "U.S. imperialism" to the sinking of the South Korean corvette, *Cheonan,* in 2010 to others—had been going on for almost half a century. But things had gotten worse under the leadership of North Korea's young, untested, leader, Kim Jong-un.

The faces gathered around the table in the secure conference room in the White House Situation Room were grim. After a nod from the president, his national security advisor, Trevor Harward, opened the meeting. "Mr. President, as you recall, you asked for a constant drumbeat of meetings with your Asia-Pacific intelligence experts. We set up this meeting because there is emergent information we needed to bring to your attention."

"I've been reading your memos, Trevor, as well as the ones Adam has been sending me, but I welcome you bringing everyone together to give it to me right between the running lights." President Midkiff had attended the University of Florida on a Navy ROTC scholarship and had served on naval surface combatants for four years after graduating. He liberally sprinkled his conversation with Navy lingo.

Harward looked toward the director of national intelligence and nodded. Adam Putnam began. "Mr. President, as you know, North Korea is as unstable under Kim Jong-un as it has been at any time in its history since the North invaded the South over six decades ago. Most of what Kim has done has been internal—

like having his uncle and his 'regent,' Jang Song Thaek, murdered in late 2013—"

"I remember reading reports he was supposedly thrown to a pack of hungry dogs and family members were forced to watch," the president interrupted.

"Yes, Mr. President, you're correct, though those reports were not completely verified by the intelligence community. Not only that, but sources we trust tell us, soon after that, Jang's sister, Jang Kye-sun, and her husband were executed."

"As crazy as this all sounds, Mr. President," Harward added, "for a police state like North Korea, none of it should surprise us. Kim was his father's youngest son and came into office with no street creds among North Korea's political or especially its military leadership. He likely figured he would be marginalized by the military unless he took dramatic action to assert his authority. Jang was the perfect target."

"Okay, I've got all that. But now you all are concerned there's a new problem that goes beyond just a young leader trying to consolidate power. Adam?"

"I was coming to that, Mr. President. After getting over the shock of seeing Jang, who was chairman of North Korea's National Defense Commission, murdered by the young supreme leader, North Korea's military came to realize they could influence Kim to take a harder line against the West. Officers who were seen as supporting Kim and who were moderates were forced to retire for health or other bogus reasons."

"I'm not clear yet why we have an imminent crisis," Midkiff probed. He didn't like to keep interrupting his senior advisors, but Putnam tended to take a while to get to the point.

"Mr. President," his national security advisor replied, "as we've briefed you already, North Korea has been shifting ground and naval forces around in peculiar ways that have even Adam's most talented analysts stumped. Overarching all this is the North Koreans' history of engineering provocations to keep the nation's citizens alarmed about United States and South Korean 'imperialism,' and for the past several years things have been pretty much same-old, same-old."

"But not any longer?"

"No, sir. As we have briefed you, these military moves have been perplexing. Coupled with that, late last month, the last senior military leader who was thought to be a moderating influence on Kim, Vice Marshal Sang Won-hong, deputy chief of the general staff of the Korean People's Army, was murdered."

"The report I got said it was staged to look like a robbery, but our intelligence community didn't believe it."

"Yes, Mr. President, but the feigned robbery was clumsily done at best. Sang had been increasingly outspoken regarding the need for restraint and had Kim's ear."

"But if he was a fan of 'restraint,' how did he ever climb that high in the North Korean military? Surely the KPA would have cut him from the herd long ago?"

"You're right, Mr. President," Putnam continued. "Sang only began to do this about two years ago. His call for restraint was short-term and tactical. He was one of the principals who brokered substantial arms imports from China, and he envisioned a ramp up in these arms transfers once North Korea began selling massive amounts of gas reserves from their offshore fields to China. He simply was calling for time for the KPA to learn to use these newer, more sophisticated weapons and adapt their operational plans and tactics to accommodate the new technology—"

"And that got him murdered?" The president interrupted again.

"Yes, sir," Putnam continued. "You know how North Korea's military, reserve, and paramilitary forces suck the life out of the North Korean economy. Their people are increasingly desperate, and recent famines have caused unprecedented suffering. The majority of the KPA's senior leadership think periodic provocations against the United States, South Korea, and Japan are the only way to keep the North Korean people focused on an external threat and not on their own misery."

"They're a police state. Can't they control the message and tell the people what they want them to hear without creating external provocations?"

"Ten years ago, yes, sir. But with the Internet and smartphones, more and more North Koreans are able to connect with the outside world," Putnam continued. "What they learn is so startling to them they quickly spread this word throughout informal networks."

"Mr. President, I think part of Adam's point is just how desperate conditions are in North Korea," Harward added. "There are well-documented reports the North Korean diet has been well south of a thousand calories a day for at least a decade. More recently, some reports have pegged that number as approaching five hundred calories a day. Tens of thousands of people are reported to have starved to death in the most recent famine. We can get you additional information on this if you like, sir . . ."

"No, I get it," Midkiff interrupted. "You're concerned North Korea's military needs to do something provocative against the West to divert attention from what their people have to endure. Tell me what you're seeing and why we need to keep an eye on it."

"Yes, Mr. President." Adam Putnam motioned to one of the Situation Room staffers, and a PowerPoint slide appeared on the large screen display at the far end of the Sit Room.

CHAPTER SIX

November 7, 1030 Korea Standard Time

Commander Kate Bigelow paced *Milwaukee*'s bridge, forgoing the comfort of her captain's chair. She was impatient and knew she didn't hide it well.

They had attended the initial, mid, and final planning conferences for this exercise with their South Korean and Japanese allies. She had put on her dress uniform for all the required social functions that accompanied these exercises, "polite chitchat on steroids," she called them. They had read all the planning orders, operational orders, execution orders, and the like governing the exercise. Her operations officer had subjected her wardroom to countless sessions of "death by PowerPoint," going over all the nuances of this international exercise. But they hadn't done a thing yet!

She tempered her impatience with the geopolitical realities of the situation and reminded herself of the advice her first skipper had given her to "eat your own dog food." Only days ago she had pointedly reminded her exec in time of war that their allies, especially the South Koreans, would be the ones responsible for mine-clearing operations in the waters surrounding the Korean Peninsula. *So at issue is not how well we can sweep mines, but how well they sweep mines,* she had told him. Now she needed to take her own counsel.

It occurred to Bigelow that the South Korean commodore, Captain Park, who was in charge of the mine-hunting and mine-clearing part of the exercise, was maddeningly methodical. He seemed to be more about "process" than about getting anything done. And then there was the multilayered U.S. chain of command, which didn't make things easier. There was commander, U.S. Pacific command—PACOM—the Hawaii-based combatant commander responsible for the entire region. Next there was commander, U.S. forces, Korea—USFK—the U.S. Army four-star general responsible for the almost thirty thousand U.S. forces on the Korean Peninsula. There was commander, U.S. Pacific Fleet—COMPACFLT—another Hawaii-based four-star commander in charge of all U.S. naval forces operating in the Pacific region. Directly under him was commander, U.S. Seventh Fleet—COMSEVENTH FLEET—based aboard USS *Blue Ridge* (LCC-19), home-ported in Yokosuka, Japan. Each level wanted to be kept informed and could weigh in with added direction.

She continued to pace, shaking her head. And those were only the *really* senior masters she had to report to! Under all of them, there was her squadron commodore back in Singapore, in charge of all the LCS ships forward-deployed there, as well as the LCS squadron commodore back at their permanent home base in San Diego. Afloat for this exercise there was the commander of the USS *Ronald Reagan* carrier strike group, the U.S. Navy SOPA—or senior officer present afloat—for the overarching exercise they were a minor part of. And that didn't even include the multilayered South Korean and Japanese chains of command in the region. *Byzantine,* she found herself thinking.

"Captain."

No response.

"Captain?" Bigelow turned toward her officer of the deck, Lieutenant Junior Grade Zack Weaver.

"OOD, what's on your mind?"

"Captain, you wanted to know when we needed to increase speed so we can do the PASSEX with the *Reagan* strike group. We've got her on this screen if you'd like to take a look." A PASSEX—or passing exercise— was a pro forma exercise when ships of the same tactical group, or for that matter different groups, passed each other within visual or line-of-sight radio-communications range. For the junior commander in each PASSEX, there was implicit—and sometimes explicit—pressure to look sharp while they were under the gaze of a senior commander. Kate Bigelow wasn't worried about the PASSEX, but neither did she want it sneaking up on her two-ship flotilla.

"Right, let's do it," Bigelow replied, glad for a respite from worrying about something she couldn't do anything about anyway.

They bent over the electronic display and her OOD

showed her the path that would take *Milwaukee* and *Defender* north to pass close aboard the main body of ships that would be steaming south for the next portion of the exercise. *Reagan* strike group had just spent several days in the Yellow Sea working with ROK air force units out of several bases on South Korea's western coast. She tapped her finger on the display about three-quarters of the way along the route that would take them up into the Yellow Sea.

"Yes, ma'am, you're wondering about the storm that's been hammering the Northern portion of the Yellow Sea and Korea Bay. It's moved west, and the weather guessers are saying it will continue to do so and likely make landfall around Dalian, China, in about thirty-six hours. We'll keep on top of it, though."

"Don't trust the weather guessers, Weaver?" Bigelow said, smiling.

"Not so long as they're living in a warm building at Fleet Activities Yokosuka munching donuts and drinking coffee."

"Ah, Weaver, we need to work on improving your view of humanity," she replied. "But you're right to keep an eye on it. We check with *Defender* to see if they're okay on fuel if we kick our speed up a bit?"

"Yes, ma'am. We're all good on gas."

"Great, give the order. Let's go join the big boys."

Well north-northwest of where *Milwaukee* and *Defender* were steaming to join their exercise, aboard the Chinese hydrographic vessel *Fen Dou,* the first mate was working mightily to carry out the orders the ship's master had given him. He had doubled the number of men on deck heaving on the lines that lowered their survey gear into the water and had made sure they all had safety harnesses to connect them to the ship's superstructure.

He had done all that, but now he was beginning to lose confidence in the master's judgment. The seas had, indeed, intensified to sea state 8, and the master's zeal to continue to do this survey work despite the harsh weather made no sense. Nor had the master taken his advice to move to calmer waters to survey there. He promised himself he would look for another vessel to sign on with next time they were ashore.

"Careful there with that," the first mate shouted to the lead man tending the line and controlling the gear they were trying to swing over the side of the *Fen Dou*. He strained to make his voice heard above the howling wind and the crashing waves. "Slower, slower with the swing, and watch out for the ship's rolls."

The six men on deck tried to comply, but their task was becoming more and more impossible.

"I said slower!" the first mate shouted again at the top of his lungs as he roughly grabbed the lead line tender by the shoulders. "You're about to lose control of it."

Just then, *Fen Dou* wallowed in the quartering sea, and the marginal control the men had maintained over the heavy gear disappeared.

"Watch out!" one of the men shouted.

Momentum and the laws of physics took over, and the gear swung wildly, crashing into the superstructure of *Fen Dou*.

What happened next occurred in the blink of an eye but seemed to take place in horrifyingly slow motion.

The massive survey gear crashed down on deck, pinning one of the deckhands underneath. Instinctively, two of the men tending the support line unbuckled their safety harnesses and slid across the heaving deck to come to the aid of their mate. They grabbed the huge survey gear and tried to lift it off the man who was writhing in agony. They strained to no avail but knew they had to keep trying before the heavy gear crushed the life out of the man. They had no warning when the ship lurched wildly as it was engulfed by a rogue wave. They lost their footing on the slick deck, and the wave swept them over the side.

Shocked, the first mate pushed, shoved, and somehow got the remaining men on deck inside the ship's superstructure. Then he made his way up to *Fen Dou*'s bridge.

"Captain, you saw what happened!" he shouted at the master. But the man seemed frozen in place.

"Captain!"

"I know, I know. We lost two men over the side. Is everyone else all right? I couldn't see everything that happened down there."

"One of the men was crushed by the survey gear. I don't know if he'll make it. But captain, we need to turn around and look for the two men who were swept overboard. They won't survive long in this water."

The ship's master just stared straight ahead and held on to a stanchion to keep from falling over as the *Fen Dou* now bucked wildly.

"Captain, we must turn around!" the first mate

shouted, now only a foot from the master and also holding on to keep from falling down.

"I can barely keep steerageway in these seas. If I try to reverse course, the seas might cause us to broach, and I can't risk that. We'll go down."

The first mate moved to protest but stopped. He knew his captain was right. He said a silent prayer for his lost mates and then left the bridge to see about the injured man, fearing the worst. Three men dead, and for what?

CHAPTER SEVEN

November 8, 1730 Eastern Standard Time

The Blackhawk set down gently just after dark, guided by the lime-green wands of the ground crewman. This UH-60 Blackhawk helicopter had large white FBI lettering blocked on either side of the fuselage, but then it was not unusual for a helicopter with these markings to land at this multipad heliport. This landing facility and this compound on the Quantico Marine Corps Base in Virginia are the home of the bureau's Critical Incident Response Group. This particular pad was the one reserved for traffic serving two of the CIRG's most secret yet most visible action arms, the hostage rescue team and the special weapons and tactics teams—teams similar in capabilities but with slightly differing missions.

Once they were on the ground, the pilot cut the power to the engines and turned in her seat to address the two men in the rear. "My instructions are to wait for you, gentlemen. Do you know how long you will be?"

"That you up there, Sandee?" the larger of the two men spoke into the boom mic of his headset. They had boarded the helo on a touch-and-go at a remote special-operations training facility at Fort Bragg. Because of their priority routing out of North Carolina to eastern Virginia, the flight to Quantico had taken just a little over an hour.

"Yes, sir. Air FBI, at your service." Then she continued in a different tone. "And thanks for your endorsement for this job, Mr. Dawson. I might not be here but for your recommendation."

Sandee Barron, recently Lieutenant Sandee Barron of the U.S. Navy, had been shown the door by the Navy after filing a false flight plan and overflying a friendly Arab nation without permission. The flight, and the loss of a nearly identical helo, a Navy MH-60R, had led to her involvement in a gambit by a rogue Arab prince in Saudi Arabia—an emerging crisis that Op-Center was working to uncover. The Navy's loss was the CIRG's gain. The errant Arab plan was foiled by Op-Center, and then-Lieutenant Barron was a part of it. Op-Center had no need for a helicopter pilot, but Chase Williams had used his influence to see she found a good flying job.

Dawson's laugh carried over the circuit. "We do a little business with the FBI SWAT elements, and we never know when we might be in need of a good helo driver. As for Hector and me, I doubt we'll be heading back before first light tomorrow. If you're back here by zero six hundred, that should be plenty of time."

"Roger that, sir. And just call operations if you need

me before then. Otherwise, I'll be at the transient quarters."

"Fair enough, and thanks for the lift."

The two men made their way from the helo to the waiting black Suburban with darkly tinted windows and several wire antennas sprouting from the roof. There were red and blue flashers thinly concealed in the front grillwork. It had no other markings, but the vehicle shouted "FBI Tactical" loudly.

Brian Dawson and Hector Rodriguez could not have been more physically dissimilar. Dawson was handsome and fair, six foot four and 220, urbane, and carried himself like the career Army officer he had been. Rodriguez, at fifty-two, was ten years older than Dawson, five foot nine, and walked with a bulldog prowl. Yet they both had the same pedigree; they were both Army Green Berets. Dawson had commanded the Fifth Special Forces Group before he had overstepped his limited operational guidelines while on a tour in Central Africa. He was branded a cowboy, though his initiative had in fact saved a friendly regime, and he was put out to pasture. He may have screened for general officer, but probably not. Rodriguez began with the Seventy-fifth Rangers, became a team chief with Third Special Forces Group, and went on to become the command sergeant major at Third Group and the Joint Special Operations Command. Neither of them were unknown in the close world of American military special operations.

The two climbed into the Suburban. They were dressed in light field gear, and each carried a small pack. Once in the vehicle, they were whisked away by a silent driver wearing sunglasses and a communications earbud.

"Sunglasses after dark?" Rodriguez said just above a whisper. "Boss, tell me again why we have to put up with these assholes?"

Dawson smiled. "Well, they're not *all* assholes. And it's the two Ps, Hector—politics and Posse Comitatus." Posse Comitatus was a law enacted in 1878, right after Reconstruction, to limit the use of federal troops to enforce state law. Today it still required a suspension of the law to use federal forces in any domestic law enforcement situation. Op-Center, after a battle with the military establishment, was seconded a direct-action special-operations strike element assigned to the Joint Special Operations Command at Fort Bragg. That element remained under the administrative command of JSOC but could be operationally tasked by Op-Center. It was a platoon-sized unit that trained in readiness at Fort Bragg and could be detached on request by Op-Center, 24/7. But the Posse Comitatus statute precluded the use of this team in the continental United States without a presidential waiver, a procedure that is at best formal, public, and time-consuming.

Months earlier, a CIRG-SWAT element failed to stop a terrorist for hire who detonated small dirty bombs at several shopping malls in the Washington, D.C., area. The terrorist and his intentions were uncovered by Op-Center and passed to the Justice Department with plenty of time to intervene. Bureaucratic inertia within Justice delayed the element's timely response. Hundreds of people were killed and many more contaminated with radioactive material. In the wake of this failure, Op-Center was granted operational control of a CIRG element for domestic work, much as they had been granted OPCON of the JSOC cell for foreign interventions. Dawson and Rodriguez had just left Fort Bragg, where they participated in a readiness drill with their JSOC detachment. Now they were at Quantico to meet their newly assigned SWAT element and observe them in a training exercise. Early on in their assuming control of the JSOC cell, there had been issues with the conventional military and special-operations hierarchy at Fort Bragg; they now expected the same from the CIRG at Quantico.

They stepped into a briefing center that had the Spartan look of a small private aircraft hangar. Along one wall was a neat line of assault packs, short-barreled automatic weapons, and Kevlar helmets—each fitted with the latest generation of night-vision goggles. There were two rows of folding chairs to seat close to two dozen men. Off to one side, there were about that number of men, all dressed in black cotton assault gear, body armor, and rubber-soled jump boots. They had the collective look of a special operations unit, but they were all well-barbered and lacked facial hair. That alone would mark them as a federal tactical unit, but they all had FBI SWAT blocked on the front and back of their blouses. Facing the lines of chairs were a table, a podium, and two whiteboards. An overhead projector looked down on a freestanding screen. The two newcomers were met at once by a tall, officious-looking man with an air of self-importance.

"Good evening, gentlemen," he said without preamble. "I assume that you are Dawson and Rodriguez, but may I see some identification?"

Dawson and Rodriguez exchanged glances and then pulled their ID badges suspended by lanyards from under their tunics. "Would you please remove them?" The two Op-Center officers slowly pulled them over their heads and handed them to the gatekeeper. He inspected each carefully and handed them back.

"And you are?" Dawson asked. As he did, he nodded to Rodriguez, who quietly left them to join the men who were all now watching the inspection ritual.

"I'm Special Agent John Babcock. I've been sent down here from the Hoover Building to act as liaison between Op-Center, the Critical Incident Response Group, and this special weapons and tactics team." Babcock spoke slowly with the assumption Dawson might not be familiar with the abbreviations.

"Liaison, huh," Dawson said with a puzzled expression. "And just what would you be doing as our bureau liaison?"

"Well, Mr. Dawson, since you are new to how we do things here and how we conduct our op . . ."

There was a chorus of greetings and commotion as the SWAT element gathered around Hector Rodriguez. Those who didn't know him or who hadn't served with him had heard of him. All but a handful of the SWAT team members had served with one of the component commands of the U.S. Special Operations Command where Rodriguez was a legend. It was a fraternity reunion.

"You were saying?" Dawson prompted.

"Well, I, ah, as liaison officer on temporary assignment to the unit here, my primary function is to, ah . . ."

"Whoa, hold on here. You're not a *part* of the men assigned to this team?"

"No, and as I tried to make clear, Mr. Dawson, I was assigned by the deputy director for . . ."

"Sorry, John, but the terms of the memorandum of understanding between my director and your director are explicit. This is a compartmented, dual-agency relationship where the interworkings are to be on a strict need-to-know basis. That means team members and team members only are to be present for this briefing and evolution." Dawson suppressed a smile and feigned a serious expression. "John, I'm afraid I'm going to have to ask you to leave."

"What! Me leave? You can't do that!"

Dawson folded his arms and turned from Babcock. "Hector! Hector, get over here and bring the team security chief with you."

"This is preposterous. I'm the headquarters liaison; you can't ask me to leave. It's just, well, you . . . you don't have that authority."

"Look, John, I could call my director, who will call your director—not some deputy but *the* director—and he will call you." While Dawson was speaking, Rodriguez joined them with a large man in black SWAT garb. His bulk was enhanced by his body armor. "Meanwhile, we're burning valuable training time." He turned to the SWAT man, and a flash of recognition spread across his face, followed by a genuine smile. "First Sergeant McGregor," Dawson said as he extended his hand, "it's been a while."

"It certainly has, Colonel. Good to see you again, and it's no longer first sergeant. Just plain Mac will do just fine."

"Mac it is, then, and for me now it's Brian."

"That could take a while, Colonel. Now, what can I do for you, sir?"

"Mac, could you escort Mr. Babcock here from the building and see that no other unauthorized personnel are present while we brief your team."

Before McGregor could move, Babcock took a step back. "You've not heard the last of this, Dawson. You can count on that." And with that, he spun on his heel and left the building.

While this was playing out, another man from the team joined them, a shorter and more compact version of McGregor and similarly attired. He was Asian, fit, serious, and of indeterminable age.

"Mr. Dawson, I'm Special Agent Allen Kim," he said as he extended his hand. "I'm the team leader." He spoke with the precision of someone for whom English is a second language. "I'm also a former Seventy-fifth Ranger and Delta Team leader. I certainly know of you and the command sergeant major. You were a little before my time at Fort Bragg, but they were still talking about you. Welcome to Quantico and Team Whiskey."

"Team Whiskey?"

Kim shrugged. "From time to time we change the names of our teams. The last one was Team Victor, and the next one will be Team X-ray."

Both Dawson and Rodriguez knew about Kim and the team. The FBI and CIRG had not been all that forthcoming with the information, but Aaron Bleich's people had hacked their database and produced dossiers on each team member and on Kim. He was second-generation Korean with a degree in international studies from American University. He was fluent in Mandarin and Cantonese, Korean, and Tagalog. His résumé from the Delta Force was surprisingly thin, which meant that he had probably been involved in operations that were so classified even the Geek Tank failed to uncover the details.

Yet Dawson asked, "Tell me about your team."

Kim paused just long enough to convey that *he* knew Dawson probably already had this information and was asking out of courtesy.

"You and the command sergeant major know . . ."

"Please, Allen," Rodriguez interrupted, "it's Hector."

Kim nodded an acknowledgment. "You and Hector know a great many of them as they are former special operators. Of the non-SPECOP men, four came to us through municipal SWAT programs. Three of my men came from the hostage rescue team to the SWAT side of the house, and two from the crisis negotiation unit. We are a twenty-one-man team, with two eight-man squads in our flyaway element. Unless it looks like a prolonged operation, we leave the two armorers, the comm tech, and the logistics assistant behind, but they are on standby along with the rest of us. They're a solid group, sir, and as good as any unit I've worked with in the military, perhaps even better." Kim paused a moment before continuing. "And speaking of the military side, I'm given to understand that you have a relationship with Mike Volner down at Bragg."

Now it was Dawson's turn to be taken aback, but he quickly smiled in approval. "Well done, Allen," he replied, using his given name for the first time. "If you have some idea of our dealings with Major Volner and his JSOC team, then you can rightly guess why we're here and what we're looking for in our relationship with your team. Why don't you introduce me to your men, and then we can get started. Then I'll try to fill in some of the white space. But"—again the approving smile—"there may not be as much of that as I might have believed."

After introductions, Kim and his men took their seats, and Dawson moved to the front of the room. He eased the podium aside and took a seat on the table. For the next half hour he detailed the organization and charter of Op-Center and the limited nature of the relationship among Op-Center, CIRG, and SWAT. He stressed the nature of their domestic portfolio.

"As many of you know, and which we hope will remain closely held inside this room, we have a working relationship with a JSOC response team. And as you also know, their charter is to operate strictly outside the United States and on foreign soil. Many of you may be wondering why Op-Center has asked for, and been granted at the presidential level, permission to be given operational mission control of this team—a team that operates within the United States or when the lives of Americans are threatened. There is one reason and one reason only, gentlemen: speed. Op-Center has an extremely robust intelligence-collection and analytical arm. There may come a time when the intelligence is so perishable and the operational response so time-critical there is simply no time to notify the Justice Department and the bureau and allow for the normal bureaucracy approvals to click into place."

"Now if it's a hostage taking, when time is on our side, or it's a situation that can be defused through normal channels, then it will be business as usual for you. If our intelligence surfaces an actionable, non-time-sensitive event, then we'll pass that information along to the operations center here at the CIRG and they will deal with it. But when speed is of the essence to prevent a terrorist act or some other loss of life—when there is need of a rapid ops-intel interface or ops-intel fusion—then you will come under our operational control, and we will indeed move quickly. Hector Rodriguez and I will be working with your team leader to establish the on-call standby arrangements and out-the-door procedures that will govern the mission notification and mission-tasking protocols. But I can promise you one thing. There will be very few false alarms or prepositioning drills associated with our relationship. When we call on you, it will be because we have hard information of something extremely bad that is about to happen soon, and it will happen unless you can get there in time to stop it. Okay then, any questions?" There were a few smiles and heads nodding in approval, but no questions. "Hector?"

Rodriguez stepped to the front of the room. "From

time to time, and with ample notice, we will join you in the course of one of your training exercises to familiarize us with your tactics and procedures, and we may even ask you to train to a given situation or mission profile of our choosing. But in no way will we interfere with how you execute a mission. You're all professionals, and you know your job. We may tell you what to do, but we'll not tell you how to do it." Again, nods of approval. "So tonight will be the first of those. Mr. Dawson and I will sit in on your premission briefings, observe the exercise, and attend the hot washup and after-action review. We'll try to stay out of your way, and don't hesitate to individually ask us any questions. And thanks for letting us be a part of your team."

Special Agent Kim took over and briefed the night's training exercise. It was a compound takedown under darkened conditions conducted with live fire. The training facility was a multiroom shoot house with ballistically armored walls to absorb and contain the high-velocity rounds from the SOPMOD M4A1 rifles the team used.

As the training exercise evolved, the team broke themselves down into four four-man fire teams and took turns moving through the compound—shooting silhouette targets that were armed threats and not shooting silhouette targets that represented noncombatants. Kim controlled the actions of his fire teams on their intrasquad radio net with his fire-team leaders directing the action. Without the Peltor sound-canceling communications headsets and night-vision goggles, it was all noise and muzzle flashes. With ear protection and goggles, it was calm tactical chatter and a lime-green-cast laser light show with the teams moving through the compound like well-rehearsed ballet troops. Dawson and Rodriguez had seen this many times before, and they liked what they saw now.

"Hector, these guys look ready to go. You agree?"

"I do. Shows you what a decade and a half of war can produce. These guys have all been there and done that. Kim and the fire-team leaders look especially solid."

At the hot washup, the two Op-Center men expressed their appreciation and approval. Then Dawson took Kim aside.

"You have a fine team, Allen. You should be proud of what you've done here."

"Thank you, Brian."

"And while I envision your operational role to be primarily tactical and kinetic, we may have occasion to want to filter at least some of you into an area undercover. So why don't you and your men relax with the haircuts. And lose the FBI and SWAT logos from your battle dress."

Kim grinned. "Roger that, but we might need a little top cover for that."

"Oh, I wouldn't be too concerned about that," he replied as they shook hands. "I think we can see to that."

At first light, Sandee Barron was waiting for them with the rotors turning. "Welcome aboard, gentlemen," she said as they climbed into the rear cabin, buckled in, and plugged in to the intercom. "Good training evaluation?"

"They were superb," Dawson answered. He knew the

airmen were proud of their ground operators, just as the ground operators liked and trusted their flight crews. "They were everything we expected and then some."

Sandee glanced over her shoulder and smiled behind the mic. "Great. And if something does go down and you need helo support, don't forget to request me by name."

"Count on it, Sandee. Count on it."

CHAPTER EIGHT

BEIJING, CHINA

November 10, 0830 China Standard Time

The leaders of China's state-run businesses typically chose to meet with foreign delegations in one of their opulent headquarters. These venues were more suited to the court of Louis XIV of France than to a country with hundreds of millions of peasants still making barely subsistence wages. For these mostly male, middle-aged bureaucrats, it helped establish a superior image and usually resulted in their being able to broker a business deal that was to their advantage.

This meeting with the North Korean delegation was not held in one of those buildings but in a nondescript office building on the outskirts of Beijing—a location with underground parking and shuttered windows that was selected with secrecy in mind. The meeting was not just about a business deal but about national survival. While the Chinese leaders wanted to have the upper hand in the negotiations, they also knew the North

Koreans they were negotiating with lived in a nation burdened by wretched hardship. For once, the Chinese needed to plead poverty. It was not the time to show off gilded, Versaillesesque buildings.

The Chinese delegation was standing at the entry of the large meeting room when their North Korean counterparts arrived. They had performed this ritual over a dozen times in the weeks-long negotiations with their North Korean neighbors. In any other culture, this ceremonial dance would have been dispensed with long ago. But the heads of both the delegations were under strict orders from their leadership: Secure a deal—or else. Easy to say, much more difficult to execute as the national leaders of both nations had given their chief negotiators almost equally strong expectations as to how hard they should bargain.

Qiang Weidong, leader of the state-owned Assets Supervision and Administration Commission of the State Council, stepped in front of his dozen fellow Chinese delegates and said, "Welcome, comrades, we look forward to another day of fruitful negotiations."

"We do also, Comrade Qiang," General Lee Kwon Hui replied with a neutral bow. "Shall we begin again?"

The delegations were a study in contrasts, the dozen Chinese all civilians, the half dozen North Korean all military. Qiang had extra motivation to make this the last day of negotiations and secure an agreement: China's premier had broadly hinted if there was no deal by today, Qiang's deputy would replace him as head of the group.

The respective delegations sat down on either side of

a long table. There was no preliminary chitchat and no small talk. This was all business.

With the world's largest economy and still one of the fastest growing, the world's largest population, and a rapidly growing military, China's leaders—and especially those leading China's increasingly lucrative state-run businesses—were accustomed to having the upper hand in virtually all negotiations they undertook. But that was not the case on this blustery Beijing morning. China needed what North Korea had, and they needed it desperately. They knew it, and they sensed the North Koreans knew it, too.

China's double-digit economic growth began at the beginning of the millennium and lasted for over a decade. It made China the envy of the world, lifted hundreds of millions out of poverty, and completely changed the character of the nation. China was no longer a country centered on small agricultural communities dependent on subsistence farming but one marked by massive, world-class cities that dominated global manufacturing. And that growth had managed to at least mostly obscure China's increasing list of ills—wretched air and water pollution, widening class divisions, restive minority populations, rampant corruption, and the like. As long as a booming economy lifted all—or at least most—boats, the nation's leaders could keep a lid on most other problems.

But that growth was slowing and threatening to all but grind to a halt over one issue: energy. China's manufacturing economy was straining its oil and gas supplies to the breaking point, and significant renewable-energy

sources were still a future dream. Worse, the forced ur-
banization of hundreds of millions of Chinese from
small farms to high-rise apartments in China's growing
cities created its own spike in energy demand. Turmoil
in the Middle East and the whims of sheiks or mullahs
meant depending on the Arabian Gulf as the main
source for its fossil-fuel supply was becoming bad business and worse strategy. In addition, the fact that this
oil and gas had to make an eight-thousand-kilometer
journey and pass through waters China's enemies could
easily choke off made China realize this was not only a
short-term challenge but also a long-term strategic co-
nundrum.

But a new source of energy—and one that was much
closer to China—offered a solution and maybe even sal-
vation. While North Korea's claims regarding the extent
of these undersea gas resources had not yet been verified by China's government, there were grave concerns
other nations would outbid China for these resources.
Qiang had his orders—negotiate hard, caveat the
multiyear agreement to buy this natural gas with the
requirement for verification by China's Ministry of Land
and Resources, and do whatever else it took to get the
upper hand—but in no case lose this deal.

The morning dragged on into afternoon, and then
into evening. At 2230, Qiang rose and addressed the
North Korean delegation. "Comrades, in the spirit of
mutual cooperation between our two nations, I believe
we have an agreement."

General Lee rose but said little. "My nation accepts
your terms."

The two men shook hands, and the delegations filed out without another word.

Qiang Weidong had done what he was told to do—get the deal. But as he made the short walk to the bus that would take them back to central Beijing, he reflected on a brief conversation he had had with a member of his delegation's support staff on the second day of this extended negotiation. The young woman, a lawyer and an expert on the United Nations Convention on the Law of the Sea, had pulled him aside and told him much of the water and seabed North Korea planned to extract this gas from was either claimed by South Korea or was clearly international water owned by no one. He had waived aside her concerns—that was not something their delegation was supposed to worry about, he had told her a bit roughly. Now he wondered.

CHAPTER NINE

WESTERN APPROACHES TO THE CHEJU CHANNEL

November 11, 1015 Korea Standard Time

"Time to turn?" Kate Bigelow said to her junior officer of the deck as she momentarily leaned into the pilot-house. She was standing on the port wing of *Milwaukee* with her binoculars trained on a nest of fishing vessels operating off the north coast of Cheju Do Island.

"We'll come right to new course two-eight-five in about twenty minutes, ma'am," the JOOD replied.

"Very well."

The transit from Sasebo had been smooth, but the weather in the Yellow Sea could change instantly. The only sure thing was that it would be cold. She had made certain her chief bos'n, who also served as the *Milwaukee*'s first lieutenant, had broken out and inventoried the ship's cold-weather gear before they left Yokosuka. A great deal of mine-hunting and mine-clearing work exposed her crew to the elements, and she knew that when sailors got cold, they got tired. And when they got tired, they got injured. She wanted to return to Singapore with her crew intact. That and completing her mission were her dual priorities.

"What's the latest on the *Reagan* CSG?" Bigelow asked out loud as she stepped into the pilothouse.

USS *Ronald Reagan* (CVN-76) and her escorts—otherwise called the *Reagan* carrier strike group—were now steaming south out of the Yellow Sea, just as *Milwaukee* and *Defender* were entering. The Chinese had recently extended the boundaries of both their air-defense identification zone, or ADIZ, and their claimed exclusive economic zone, their EEZ, well out into the Yellow Sea and the East China Sea—extensions that overlapped those same zones claimed by South Korea and Japan respectively. Within this ADIZ, the Chinese required all air and maritime traffic to check in with their coastal military commands for permission to be in the ADIZ. China's claims were in direct conflict with what America and most other maritime nations held as international waters with freedom of navigation. Since then, American carrier strike groups had routinely—and purposefully—steamed through those areas without the requests for right of passage China demanded. These FON—or freedom of navigation—operations were designed to protest these types of illegal claims and had been going on for decades. But tensions were always highest when conducting these FON ops in waters claimed by China and especially in those claimed by North Korea. Those two nations stood out as having the most controversial—even bizarre—

illegal maritime claims that ran counter to all norms of international law.

Now the *Reagan* carrier strike group was steaming south away from the Chinese mainland and would then swing east around the Korean Peninsula and Cheju Do Island to rendezvous with a Japanese naval element for a maritime exercise in the Sea of Japan.

"Ma'am, our closest point of approach to the *Reagan* carrier strike group will be about six miles at two-six-zero. That will take place five minutes ahead of our next scheduled turn. We start the PASSEX an hour before that and end it an hour later."

"Very well, Sam. When we're at our CPA, have radio send our regards to the CSG staff communicator."

"Aye, aye, ma'am."

That's where the action is, Bigelow thought. She was in e-mail contact with fellow officers and Naval Academy classmates stationed on destroyers and cruisers that had made what they called the Dragon Run—running near the coast of China from the Taiwan Strait north up to the Korean Peninsula. While not at general quarters, they were on alert with all sensors trained on the Chinese mainland, tracking People's Liberation Army aircraft as they shadowed the American ships and made careful inventory of all electronic emissions and communications intelligence. It was as close as it got to steaming into harm's way for units of the fleet, and it was exciting—a step away from the real thing. And here I am, she mused, playing at hunting mines with our South Korean allies. Mine hunting and mine clearing had always been a second-class, underappreciated mission of the U.S. Navy—strictly blue-collar work and well away from the more glamorous open-ocean, blue-water action.

Commander Kate Bigelow knew the blue-water Navy. She had served as a junior officer and qualified as a surface-warfare officer on an Aegis cruiser and had served as a department head on an Aegis destroyer. She knew what she wanted from this woman's Navy, and it was command of a cruiser, one of the Navy's Ticonderoga class of guided-missile cruisers with the Aegis Weapons System. But that was in the future. Ahead would be a shore tour, probably at the Pentagon; a promotion board that would consider her for advancement to captain; a joint tour on one of the unified combatant commander staffs; a selection board that would evaluate her against other high-performing post-commander-command officers; and then, if she were one of the lucky few, command of one of the Navy's diminishing number of Aegis cruisers. The odds were long, but secretly she fancied her chances. There was a saying among naval officers climbing up the ranks: "Command was command was command." Seagoing command happened only two or three times in a career, so she was determined to enjoy it in whatever form it came. That included *Milwaukee*. Indeed, she did relish command of the LCS, but she also saw it as a stepping stone to command of a major blue-water surface combatant.

I'll get there, she said quietly to herself. *Someday, I'll get there.*

"Beg pardon, Captain," the JOOD said. "Did you say something?"

"Sorry, Sam," she replied. "Just mumbling to myself." Then, glancing at her watch she stated, "I'll be in the wardroom for a meeting if anything comes up."

"Aye, aye, ma'am."

Bigelow hurried down two levels to *Milwaukee*'s small wardroom, which served as a conference room as well as the officers' mess. She tolerated no lateness at meetings and was herself careful to be punctual. When she arrived, they were waiting for her—Jack O'Connor; her operations officer, a seasoned lieutenant who would also serve as the mine-countermeasures officer for the exercise; her master chief bos'n, who as first lieutenant would be responsible for most of the topside exercise gear and deck personnel; and Chief Carol Picard, the lone corpsman aboard who would act as safety officer for the exercise.

"Good afternoon, everyone."

"Good afternoon," the assembled crew leaders chorused.

"Okay, Eric, this will be your show. What have you got for us?" Lieutenant Eric Ashburn had recently arrived on board *Milwaukee* fresh from department-head school. But he had been in the Navy longer than anyone in the room, with the exception of Master Chief Crabtree. Ashburn had been an enlisted electronics technician and rose quickly up his rating to first class petty officer. The Navy's STA-21 Program, or Seaman-to-Admiral Program, sought to identify bright enlisted sailors, send them to college, and commission them as officers. It took Ashburn but three years to get his degree in electrical engineering from Georgia Tech. He then toured on an Arleigh Burke–class destroyer as the electronic maintenance officer and came to *Milwaukee* with outstanding fitness reports. In the short time aboard, he had quickly become one of Bigelow's go-to officers. Even Jack O'Connor deferred to him on operational matters. He was smart, even-tempered, and, though he was frail in appearance, Bigelow perceived an underlying strength in the man. Even though he was a chain smoker, seemed to live on coffee, and, Bigelow sensed, something of an old-school Navy sexist, she felt she could count on him. He was, she quickly determined, a thoroughly professional seagoing officer.

"All right, Skipper, here's what we have ahead of us," Ashburn began as he consulted his notes. "We're scheduled to rendezvous with the six South Korean minesweepers late tomorrow afternoon. Once we join up, we'll be under the direction of Commodore Park, and we'll move in a loose flotilla to the exercise area to be on station the following day at dawn. A South Korean auxiliary vessel will have laid a field of practice mines somewhere in the exercise area. They will be bottom mines, and we'll have to find them." He looked up and smiled. "It will be a chance for us to test our mine-hunting sonars and towed arrays while the Koreans watch. If neither we nor *Defender* can find them, then the Koreans will. As you know, the Korean sweeps have very primitive mine-hunting sonars, but Park will see they succeed where we fail."

There were smiles around the table. Everyone there had some experience operating with the South Koreans, and they all knew they never failed—it was a matter of face. If the Americans could not locate the mines, they would readily admit it, and the failure would be a part of the lessons learned from the exercise. That was not the South Korean way. Both Park and his minesweeper captains knew the exact location of the mines and, if called upon, would conduct their own search and somehow manage to succeed, even with their dated gear. It was just the way it worked.

"How about clearing the mines?" O'Connor asked. "Hard to fake not being able to clear what you somehow managed to find."

"That will be a little more difficult," Ashburn replied, "but at some point in the exercise the practice mines will be declared neutralized and brought to the surface by command activation. But that's really not our concern. Our job is to find, classify, and clear. Now, let's get down to business."

Ashburn highlighted the main stages and key execution points that were to take place over the course of the four-day exercise. Commodore Park, aboard one of the Korean minesweepers, would be the OTC, or officer in tactical command, but much of the exercise would be directed from *Milwaukee* by Ashburn and his watch teams in *Milwaukee*'s mission control center. Most of the physical activity would be in the mission bays, where her master chief bos'n and his crew would be deploying and retrieving their mine-hunting gear. It was dangerous, wet, cold work, especially at night. Chief Picard would serve as safety observer and tend to any injuries along the way. Seldom did a mine exercise go off without at least some minor injury, which was a major concern for Bigelow. It would be no less dangerous in the unpredictable waters of the Yellow Sea in November.

Jack O'Connor would have, at least in theory, the least to do during the mine exercise, or MINEX. His job was to run the ship and to ensure the underway steaming watches were manned and alert. He was responsible for the ship's work and normal shipboard routine, but those tasks were largely in the care and management of the ship's junior officers, chief petty officers, and senior petty officers. Bigelow herself had no additional duties, assigned or otherwise, except that of commanding officer. As such, she owned it all. Over the course of the next several days, she would doze fitfully for no more than a few hours each afternoon in her bridge chair, drink gallons of coffee, and wear out a path between the bridge and the mission control center. In this harried, sleep-deprived state, she would often be greeted by a passing sailor in a cramped internal passageway.

"Afternoon, ma'am," or "Good day, Captain."

And she would invariably answer with the sailor's name. "Hey, Jones, how are you today," or "Good morning, Smith. How's everything down in the mission bay?"

It was during these times of increased operations tempo, when she had had little sleep and the weather had turned ugly, that she knew she really loved her job.

CHAPTER TEN

November 11, 1815 Eastern Standard Time

Allen Kim swung the rental car into the vacant parking space at the Green Beret Club at Fort Bragg. It was happy hour, and he had to circle the parking lot twice before he found a spot. Kim made his way to the door and stepped inside. He was dressed in khaki slacks, a blue oxford shirt, and a corduroy sport coat. He was noticed by no one. The club was open to all ranks and branches, active and retired, so it was crowded by a great many soldiers in uniform and civilians, many of whom were former Green Berets or active-duty special operators, and many who were not. It was crowded but not overly noisy, as those gathered were generally male, military, or ex-military. Most were crowded around the bar in the center of the single large room. There were flat-screen TVs with sports, but this was not a sports-bar crowd. Their sport was combat, and the coin of their realm was war stories. Most of the tables and booths on the periphery of the bar were occupied, but Kim spotted a single table in the corner and made for it. He ordered a beer and quietly observed the scene around him. There were those who came to the Green Beret Club to be with their own kind and talk of past deployments and wars and those who came to just sit and drink alone. Allen Kim, for all outward appearances, seemed to be one of the latter.

A short time later, Major Mike Volner stepped into the club, and, like Allen Kim before him, his entry was quiet and passed unnoticed. He stepped to one side, surveyed the room, and immediately spotted Kim. He was dressed in jeans, a cotton pullover, and a Windbreaker. Seeing a few soldiers he knew, he carefully skirted the room as he made his way to Kim's table. He offered his hand as he took a seat.

"Allen, it's been a while."

"It has, Major."

"It's Mike now. I hear you're a team leader up there at Quantico. Congratulations. Now you get to make the big bucks and still have fun."

Kim returned his grin. "Not sure what passes for big bucks in the D.C. area without the variable housing allowance and combat pay you guys in the military get, but it's a living. And it is fun. How have you been?"

"Couldn't be better. I have another year in the job, and if I'm lucky I'll be able to stretch it into eighteen months. That's the problem in the military. If you're in for a career, you have to move around, and there's no way to sidestep the staff jobs and Pentagon duty."

Kim nodded appreciatively. That was why he got out.

He liked the tactical work, but neither the prospect of endless rotations overseas nor the reality of being desk-bound for two to three years at a crack appealed to him. The FBI Critical Incident Response Group work and SWAT duty had been a perfect choice. His travel was limited and he could remain in a tactical element—at least for the foreseeable future. Like the field agents, he could choose his track. He could remain with the CIRG and stay in the field, but his advancement would be limited. Or he could step into the normal special-agent career path and try to move up the line. For now, he wanted to stay where he was. Mike Volner didn't have that option; for a military officer, it was move up or move out.

"You know, Mike, there is another way. Not a better way, but a different way."

Volner nodded. "I suppose you're right, but somehow I just don't see myself as a federal agent, even if I am carrying an assault rifle. It wouldn't be the same. I guess I'm just a soldier. At least the guys up the chain of command have all walked in my boots, or at least most of them have. Not sure I could take orders from someone who's not been there and done that."

Kim took a measured sip of his beer. "Well, that's what I wanted to see you about. I guess in some ways you're doing a little of that right now with Op-Center. You know my team has been assigned as their domestic action arm. What can you tell me about them?"

Volner paused to frame his answer. It was not an issue of security since both of these men were cleared for the most sensitive top-secret material. Brian

Dawson himself had briefed Volner on the role of CIRG-SWAT element being seconded to Op-Center. And Volner had history with Allen Kim; Kim was a new man to the JSOC Army special missions unit well after Volner had arrived. Kim was assigned to another team, but his reputation was solid. He was known as a reliable operator and a combat leader. A good many special operators, SEALs, Rangers, Green Berets, and special missions–unit veterans had left their service component and gone to the FBI. There was a good deal of kidding by those who remained in uniform about the federal SWAT boys—obtaining hall passes to train, getting permission slips to kick in doors, and Miranda-izing some dirtbag before you could shoot him—that kind of thing. But the facts were that, for the most part, they were the same men tactically doing much the same thing. Their mission sets were different, their area of operations was different, and their rules of engagement were different. Otherwise, the mechanics of how they did their business was much the same.

"You've met Brian Dawson and Hector Rodriguez?" Kim nodded. "Well, what you see is what you get. Both of them have been around the block more than once. They know what can and can't be done, and they know when it's important to go on a dangerous mission and when it's *really* important to go. They've upgraded our communications and callout protocols, but they've not messed with our team operating routines or our standard tactics, techniques, and procedures. We've been called out on two no-go operations and one time for the real thing. They gave us the mission and let us run with it. Can't ask more than that."

"No, no you can't," Kim replied. He was quiet for a moment, then continued. "I've thought about this since they came to Quantico to brief us and observe one of our training exercises. I'm not seeing any problems with this, but I want to be sure I'm not overlooking something. One of the reasons I came down here was to ask you if you see any downside to their taking operational control of your team. Am I missing anything?"

Now it was Volner's turn to pause before answering. "Just this. I knew these guys would not be coming to us with a targeting mission on some lowlife al Qaeda operative or even a senior Taliban leader. Or some nutcase with a suitcase bomb in Mumbai. When they come to us, I knew it would be because something really bad is about to go down, and the normal, through-channel action arms either can't handle it or can't get there in time. The guys in my team think this is really cool because it's another chance to put their guns in the fight. But they also know it could be extremely dangerous. And they're right." He again paused and lowered his voice. "I don't think the shot callers at JSOC would send us on a one-way mission, but I'm not sure I can say the same for Dawson and his organization. They're standup guys and they wouldn't do it on a whim, but Op-Center gets involved when the stakes are big, and failure could cost a great many lives. They will do what has to be done. They've not said as much, but they know it, and I know it. And I've made sure the guys on my team know it.

If it's really important, we could be a fire-and-forget part of their solution. So, my friend, this is not like serving a high-risk warrant or going after a hostage in a convenience-store robbery that's gone wrong. They'll call you when time is short and the situation is critical—a situation that could get some or all of your people killed. Just so you know."

Allen Kim did in fact know. He and his element leaders had talked about this, and the "why us?" question had come up. They had, as had Mike Volner, concluded that if they got the call, it would be because the bureau could not get a regular CIRG-SWAT team there in time or would not send a team since it was simply too risky. Kim and his team had agreed to work with Op-Center for the same reason that Mike Volner and his team had. It was, Kim concluded, a chance to use their unique skills to make a difference when it really counted. Now Mike Volner had just confirmed it.

"One more thing, Allen. I know your aviation arm is an important asset to all of you with the CIRG. You've got a fairly new pilot with your Blackhawk unit. Her name's Sandee Barron. We worked with her the last time we were called out for an op. She's good people and a hell of a pilot. You get in a tight spot, you want her in your corner."

"She is new, but I've heard about her already. She's making her bones, and my senior pilots think she's on track to become an impact player. But I take your point. I'll make sure she is on the A team if and when Op-Center calls on us."

There was another issue Kim wanted to raise with

Volner. It was not like the CIRG teams and the military special operators never trained together, but there had never been an ongoing, cross-training program in place. A good many senior military special-operations leaders saw the CIRG as poachers of their talent pool. Kim rightly guessed the nature of the tasking for his team and Volner's team would come from the same source and might well be focused on a similar threat. Their communications would be identical and their assault tactics nearly so. Issues of collateral damage and risk to noncombatants would fall more heavily on Kim, but Volner had those same concerns. They could learn a good deal from each other. And there might come a time when Kim's team would be called on to operate overseas and a domestic threat could arise that could only be managed with the help of Volner and his team. It made sense they establish a working relationship and establish a measure of interoperability.

"Mike, Hector Rodriguez suggested we conduct some joint training. Maybe you could come up to Quantico for one day a month and we could come down here for the day. That sound doable?"

Volner thought about it, but not for long. "Why don't you come over to the JSOC compound tomorrow and let's try to put something together. I think I can sell it to my boss, and if I can't, Op-Center seems to have the pull to make it happen. How about on your side?"

"I was turned down flat when I took it up to my higher headquarters, but a funny thing happened when I told Hector about it. The next day, my boss called me and said I had a green light."

"Yeah—funny thing," Volner replied with a grin. "Let's order some chow and another beer. I'm starving. We can work this out tomorrow morning."

Kim raised his hand to signal for the waitress.

CHAPTER ELEVEN

IMPERIAL PALACE,
BEIJING, CHINA

November 12, 1030 China Standard Time

China's president had read the reports, but he wanted to hear the results of the negotiations with the North Korean delegation directly from his handpicked man. Qiang Weidong, leader of the state-owned Assets Supervision and Administration Commission of the State Council, sat anxiously in the outer office of China's paramount leader. Qiang paused to consider the immense power the man held. While his presidency was a largely ceremonial office, with limited powers, as general secretary of the Communist Party of China and chairman of the Central Military Commission, he was the most powerful person in China, perhaps in the world.

After waiting for almost a half hour, Qiang was ushered into the president's office. "Comrade Qiang, good morning and welcome. I apologize for having you wait; other matters intruded. You have exceeded our expectations in these negotiations. I am mindful that while they are our brothers, our North Korean neighbors can be difficult and even unpleasant to work with. You showed great fortitude brokering this agreement."

The two men exchanged a few more pleasantries, and then Qiang launched into his summary of the negotiations. After a time, Qiang finished his report and had answered all the president's questions when one of the president's aides entered and reminded him he had another meeting.

"Thank you again, Comrade Qiang. Know that you have done an important service for our nation."

"Again, it was my honor, Mr. President."

The arms-for-energy deal China's Qiang Weidong and his North Korean counterpart, General Lee, had hammered out was welcome news to China's supreme leader. While some senior generals in the People's Liberation Army did not favor giving some of their newer and more technologically advanced weapons to a neighboring nation with a track record as an international pariah and a leader who was mercurial at best, crazy at worst, it was a trade-off that worked to China's advantage.

China's civilian leaders realized their superpower rival across the Pacific was not only weary from over a decade of conflict but was dramatically reducing its military arsenal. Not only that, but, as America's recent actions in the Middle East had demonstrated, the United States seemed incapable of focusing on—let alone dealing with—more than one crisis at a time. Afghanistan was all but ignored while the United States went into Iraq to topple Saddam. The crisis in Syria was completely overlooked while the United States "led from behind" in the attack on Libya. And so it went to the present day.

China was slowly, but persistently, working to marginalize U.S. power, presence, and prestige in the western Pacific. From China's aggressive territorial claims over the Diaoyu, or Senkaku, Islands in the East China Sea to China's claims to the totality of the South China Sea—an area the size of India—to the Chinese ADIZ in the East China Sea, China was expanding its sphere of influence throughout Asia. And most troubling was that China backed up those territorial assertions with forceful maritime and aerial encroachment in areas that had traditionally been judged uncontested. In addition, China had made it increasingly clear that it did not intend to compromise with its neighbors in order to settle these disputes. China's leaders had, if anything, hardened their position over time.

While these Chinese moves caused the United States to protest diplomatically and to send its increasingly vulnerable naval forces to signal disfavor over Chinese assertions and incursions, America never really *did* anything. This was because China's neighbor did things that alarmed America even more. China supported North Korea because strategically it was far better to have them pull Uncle Sam's beard. That way, China could have all the rewards with virtually none of the risk.

Thus, a North Korea armed with modern weapons could be an effective surrogate, but only with an implicit understanding that if they poked the Western superpower in the eye with a sharp stick, China would stand behind them if the United States threatened military retaliation. Add to this the U.S. alliance with South Korea and the tens of thousands of American military personnel stationed in South Korea, and the stakes increased dramatically. As one of China's leaders famously said, "If North Korea didn't exist, we would have to invent it."

That said, China did not give North Korea carte blanche. Through means subtle and more overt, North Korea's political leadership—and especially its generals—knew how far they could push America and where the limits were. Much of this knowledge of "how much was enough and how much was too much" when their ally confronted the United States became known to China by way of extensive hacking of U.S. military databases and U.S. intelligence agency communications. China knew how long the leash was, and the North Koreans knew it, too. And now that the ink was dry on the arms-for-energy deal, the leash had become substantially longer.

China's president had given North Korea's leader a long leash this time for one reason and one reason only—the energy reserves on the floor of Korea Bay and the northern Yellow Sea. And it was now more than just poking the United States in the eye. The armistice that ended the Korean War in 1953 had settled land boundaries firmly, but not so at sea. The Northern Limit Line extending from the Korean coast west into the Yellow Sea had been hastily drawn by the United Nations to keep South Korean and North Korean naval vessels apart—and to some extent it had worked. But in 1999 North Korea had declared the more southerly Inter-

Korean Military Demarcation Line, vastly increasing the oceanic area it claimed it controlled.

South Korea and the United States had protested vehemently against this North Korean claim, and until now it was all political and diplomatic posturing and mattered not a whit. But now it *did* matter. If North Korea was to keep its part of this deal and deliver the vast energy reserves on the floor of the Korea Bay and northern Yellow Sea to China, it needed undisputed claim to those waters. What South Korea thought didn't matter. China's president knew if the North said the sky was blue, the South would say it was green. But America was a different matter. The United States needed to accede to the Inter-Korean Military Demarcation Line so the North could mine the seafloor of the West Sea— the Koreans' name for the Yellow Sea. The North Korean president told China's leader that he had a plan to force the United States to accede to the North's sea claims. He would have something to trade the United States in return for its accession to his country's claimed maritime boundaries. China's president had agreed to his plan. Now it was in motion.

"Aaron!"

Aaron Bleich looked up from one of the four LCD screens on his desk and saw Hasan Khosa standing in his doorway. "What's up, Hasan." The twenty-eight-year-old former wunderkind that McCord and Bleich had recruited from eBay was one of the Geek Tank's most low-key members—McCord kept chiding Bleich to check the second-generation Pakistani's blood pressure to see if it registered at all. The look on his face told Bleich instantly something was amiss.

"Easier for me to show you than tell you," he replied. Khosa walked up behind Bleich, leaned over him, and grabbed the mouse. "I just sent you a blast," he continued, opening the link and clicking rapidly, opening one window, then another. If Bleich had an MVP, it was Khosa, and he sat in rapt silence as the younger man populated his screen with information.

"We've been getting hints and snippets this was going to happen, but there was nothing concrete—until now. You can see from this satellite picture here," Khosa continued, wiggling the cursor over a spot on the screen, "North Korea is trying to mask it with a fleet of fishing boats, but they are massing naval assets near Nampo."

Khosa paused to let the Geek Tank leader absorb what he said. "And here, this is an infrared picture, as you can see, and it shows the movement of huge numbers of troops in an armored convoy from their camps here and here to positions just north of the DMZ . . ."

"And let me guess," Bleich interrupted, "you picked it up on infrared only because they hide them in the daytime?"

"Exactly."

Hasan Khosa continued, showing Bleich more and more alarming indications North Korea was planning some sort of military operation. Finally he stopped.

"When are we going to take this to Roger?"

"Right now!" With that, the two men made a beeline for Roger McCord's office.

CHAPTER TWELVE

THE YELLOW SEA

November 12, 1115 Korea Standard Time

"Message from the Korean commodore, ma'am." It was the leading radioman calling on the IVOX, the interactive voice exchange phone, the primary internal comms net on the LCS as well as on most U.S. Navy ships.

"It's just 'the commodore,' radio. What do you have for me?" Kate Bigelow replied.

"Ah, yes, ma'am. From the commodore: 'Keep station smartly.'"

"Acknowledge message and thank you."

She looked over to the OOD, who looked up from his screen showing the radar display. She merely shrugged. They were on station or very close to it. It seemed, Kate mused, station keeping was more important than locating mines. Since *Milwaukee* and *Defender* had met up with the six Korean minesweepers sixteen hours earlier, they had been maneuvering in the exercise area in what seemed to be a command and control exercise.

Commodore Park had been ordering his vessels and the two American ships around like a fleet battle admiral. Kate knew that for these small vessels steaming in the open sea for several days was an exercise in itself, and much of their presence there was just being at sea with their South Korean allies. Still, she had to wonder if he was riding close-herd on her just because she was a woman. Park had not been nearly as directive with the captain of *Defender,* who was male, as he had been with her. And their adherence to their assigned station had been the same. *Defender*'s skipper was good, but then so was she. Kate Bigelow had long ago stopped taking offense at all but the most blatant sexist treatment. When it came to performance, she knew she could hold her own and then some. But this commodore was, for this exercise, her senior officer. He didn't write her fitness report, but for the time being, she was under his orders.

Milwaukee, Defender, and the Korean minesweepers were operating some seventy miles west of Inchon and forty miles south of the Yeonpyeong Island group. These islands, of which only two were inhabited, had been awarded to South Korea under the terms of the ceasefire that put the Korean War on hold. This placed the MINEX ships in international waters, south of the Military Demarcation Line, or maritime border claimed by North Korea, as well as the Northern Limit Line established by the United Nations. In times past, U.S. and South Korean ships had challenged this maritime border and steamed up to the U.N.-established line, but then those were fleet combatants, not a poorly armed mine-hunting flotilla. This exercise was being conducted in waters that were considered international by all parties—at least until North Korea came up with another bizarre maritime claim. They were also waters that were the sea-lane approaches to Seoul and Inchon, which were the likely areas where the North Koreans would sow their large inventory of mines if war ever erupted. They had rendezvoused with the South Koreans the previous afternoon and were scheduled to begin mine-hunting operations later that day. Knowing she would be continually on the bridge for the exercise, Kate was about to go back to her stateroom for a short nap when Lieutenant Ashburn approached.

"Morning, Skipper." Bigelow had a good read on her people, and she could tell Ashburn had something on his mind.

"Morning, Eric. Something up with the gear?"

"I wish, ma'am. I just got this in from Seventh Fleet." He held out his iPad with a message on it. She took it but focused on him. "Seems that there's an unusual amount of naval activity in and around the Haeju naval complex. It looks like a number of North Korean naval vessels are putting out to sea or getting ready to put to sea. Seventh Fleet staff duty officer says there's nothing urgent here, but I thought you'd like to know."

She took the tablet, read it, and handed it back. "What's your take, Eric?"

Ashburn shrugged. "I don't know, Skipper. Now that the *Reagan* strike group has cleared the area, maybe they think it's okay for them to leave safe harbor. Maybe the supreme leader wants some of his ships to watch us hunt mines. It wouldn't be the first time they crowded us during an exercise."

Bigelow considered this. "Send a priority message to Seventh Fleet asking them to keep us advised on North Korean naval-unit locations and movements."

"Yes, ma'am. Do you want to info Commodore Park on this?"

"No. For now, let's keep the South Koreans out of this."

Aaron Bleich was huddled with two of his analysts. It was 1815, but there was a burst of traffic that began around 1600 that had held their attention. The two analysts were playing with Op-Center proprietary software that performed a continuous sweep of all U.S. intelligence collectors and more than a few belonging to the Chinese, including the Chinese Ministry of State Security. They also monitored the traffic coming out of the State Security Department of North Korea. Some, but not all, of the Chinese and North Korean chatter could be deciphered in-house by Bleich and his Geek Tank. Bleich had alerted Chase Williams that he might have something for him by early evening, and Williams made sure not to leave the building.

"What do you think?" Bleich asked his lead hacker, a twenty-something who owned two felony convictions for busting into corporate databases and would probably be doing time right now had Aaron Bleich not pulled him back from the dark side and put him to work.

"The land-based, unit-communication anomalies are

still in place. Units are still moving, but there is an absence of communications chatter between the People's Army headquarters in Pyongyang and the field units. Given how hierarchical they are, this in itself is strange. The only radio chatter we're now picking up is from their naval headquarters at Nampo. The transmissions are all coded, and we're working on that, but they are decidedly short in duration."

Bleich gave this a moment's thought. "Okay, keep me informed." He stepped away and took the cell phone from his belt. All Op-Center staffers had their cell phones imprinted with a secure, limited-range transmission channel for internal use. He keyed a number that was answered on the second ring.

"What do you have, Aaron?"

"Nothing definitive, boss, but there are too many North Korean units moving, both on land and at sea, for this to be a routine military-training exercise. And they're still observing a near communications blackout. The only transmissions going out are to naval units, and those units responding are at sea. All traffic is short and coded."

"You mean short as in orders to execute a previously planned standing order?"

"That is a definite possibility. But something's up; as of yet, we just don't know what."

"I see. Will you be staying with this?" Chase Williams asked.

"Absolutely. I will have a rotating watch team on this, and I'll not leave the tank here until this thing sorts itself out, one way or another." Williams said nothing for several moments, prompting Bleich to see if he was still there. "Sir?"

"Have you backfilled Roger yet?"

Bleich hesitated a moment, realizing he had gone right to Op-Center's director before looping in his boss. Williams was gently nudging him to remember to do this. "No, sir, not yet, but I will immediately."

"Good. Thanks for this and keep me informed as things progress. In the meantime, draft up an intelligence summary, run it by Roger, and have him pass it to our liaison at the Pentagon."

"Understood, sir."

Williams rang off, paused for only a moment, and then hit a coded number on his cell phone.

"Boss?" Brian Dawson knew something was up, and he too had made no move to leave his desk at Op-Center.

Moments later, he was in Williams's office and they were planning their next move. It did not take them long to agree on what needed to be done. Fifteen minutes later, just as he was finishing dinner and preparing to help his daughter with her homework, Major Mike Volner got a call from Dawson. Shortly before midnight, Volner and his JSOC team lifted off from Pope Army Airfield in a C-17 bound across the North Pole for Kadena Air Base on Okinawa. Brian Dawson and Hector Rodriguez were already on an extended-range G-5 that, after a refueling stop at Elmendorf Air Force Base in Alaska, would meet Volner's C-17 at Kadena. On Aaron Bleich's recommendation, they had taken along one of his analysts to serve as a communicator and an on-site intelligence presence. The JSOC element was armed to the teeth with a flyaway communications package and contingency equipment. Dawson and Rodriguez had only their field gear and iridium satellite phones, but the analyst had a small communications suite with a real-time voice and data link to Bleich and Op-Center. The three also carried presidential warrants that allowed them to go where they wished and do what they wanted to do on any American military installation. It also bound any regional commander to, within reason, give them whatever they asked for. Williams and his team at Op-Center would be in constant communications with the two aircraft.

His teams in motion, Chase Williams began to compose one of his infrequent POTUS/Eyes Only memos to the president. *We were a bit slow out of the chute sending our JSOC team downrange when the crisis broke in the Middle East and we almost let the president down. I'm not going to let that happen again,* Williams found himself thinking.

Shortly after the two Op-Center aircraft reached cruising altitude, *Milwaukee* and *Defender* began to look for mines while the six South Korean minesweepers steamed smartly about in formation. Commander Kate Bigelow began her long vigil on the bridge, and her crew began to work port and starboard mine-hunting watches, twelve hours on duty, twelve off. And every hour on the hour, Commodore Park radioed to see if they had located any mines.

CHAPTER THIRTEEN

THE YELLOW SEA

November 12, 1530 Korea Standard Time

Lieutenant Commander Choe Dae-jung stood on the bridge wing of the *Won Do* and thought about what he was about to do. All that day, as they moved cautiously to their assigned operational stations, Choe had prayed his orders would be rescinded. He tried to remember the last time he had prayed, or when the supreme leader and his military advisors had done anything this drastic or this stupid. It seemed like every year or three, there was a skirmish between North Korean and South Korean patrol craft, with the North Korean boats invariably getting the short end of the exchange. The Republic of Korea boats were simply better. The single notable exception to these South Korean–dominated exchanges was the 2010 sinking of the ROK corvette *Cheonan*. It was believed to have been sunk by a North Korean midget submarine, but blame for the loss of the ship was never confirmed. The fingerprints of North Korea were all over the incident, but China and Russia blocked any censure of Pyongyang by the United Nations. Forty-six South Korean seamen were lost when *Cheonan* went down. But what the *Won Do* and her two sister ships were being asked to do was nothing short of an act of war.

"Well, Comrade Choe, are we prepared to execute our assignment for the glory of our nation and the supreme leader?"

Choe looked at the bundled form of Ha Min-ki, *Won Do*'s recently assigned political officer. It was cold, overcast, and *Won Do* was steaming in a mixed seaway with an uncertain motion. Yet Ha now seemed immune to the conditions, buoyed by the prospect of the task before them. Clearly, Ha seemed to have no idea of the risky course of action on which they were about to embark or the perils that might await them at the hands of the South Koreans and the Americans. At that moment, Ha represented all that was wrong with his nation and his nation's leaders. And he hadn't a clue about the dangerous situation his ship and his crew were about to enter upon. A part of him wanted reach out and choke this pompous political sycophant.

"Comrade Ha, we are about to commence operations per our instructions. This does not require your presence on the bridge. Please return to your stateroom."

"But . . . but I have every right to be here to witness this historic event."

Choe considered this. "Perhaps. But I am still captain of this ship, and your presence on my bridge is at my discretion. You will return to your quarters, and you will stay there, or I will have you forcibly removed and taken there."

Choe took a step toward him, and Ha stepped back. "This is outrageous. I will comply with your direction, but be assured that your actions and disrespect will be passed along to my superiors. I will see that you are removed from command."

"So noted," Choe replied coldly. "Now get off my bridge." *And you may do what you will after this,* Choe mused, *if we're still alive. Won Do* was now some twenty-five miles west of Inchon and fifteen miles east of the Korean-American mine flotilla. The weather was freshening with the wind building from out of the southwest, bringing moist, warmer air out of the South China Sea, along with a blanket of fog.

Choe sighed and then gave the orders that would, in concert with the other two Sariwon-class corvettes, sow a string of acoustic mines that would deny entry to, or an exodus from, the approaches to the Han River and the city of Seoul, as well as the port of Inchon. As with many North Korean seagoing professionals, Lieutenant Commander Choe was not among the most politically astute members of his military. Nonetheless, he knew he was committing an overt act of war.

The three corvettes began their mine-laying operations in the late afternoon and continued into the evening. Mines were as much a psychological weapon as a kinetic one. Once it was known that there was an active minefield in the area, few sea captains, military or civilian, would want to steam in those waters. As for the South Korean navy, which had some very capable patrol craft and Western-armed destroyers, they would effectively be sealed in port.

Just after dark, two *Najin*-class frigates slipped their moorings at the North Korean naval base at Haeju and made their way slowly out into Haeju Bay and took a southeasterly heading for the Yellow Sea. Once into open water, they turned south to a heading of one-seven-zero at a speed of twelve knots, keeping a distance of three miles between them. At this course and speed, they would be taken by any orbiting reconnaissance satellite to be two merchantmen leaving the Port of Haeju on routine transit.

The North Korean navy was primitive by Western naval standards, but if there were two vessels that might hold up in an encounter with the more modern navies of Japan, South Korea, or even the United States, it was these two frigates. There were four of them built in the 1970s in North Korean yards. Two had been laid up and cannibalized for parts to keep the two active warships afloat. They were 330 feet long, displaced 1,600 tons, and had a complement of 180 sailors. Both were armed with a recent version of the CSS-N-2 Safflower missile—a variant of the Chinese Silkworm surface-to-surface missile. The frigates were also armed with an array of four-inch and two-inch guns, making them no match for a Western destroyer but capable enough when it came to non-missile-armed patrol craft or minesweepers. Both frigates, *Najin Three* and *Najin Four,* had just completed an overhaul at the ship-repair facility at Haeju, so most of their systems were operational, or as operational as two dated frigates could be. Unlike older North Korean naval vessels like *Won Do,* they were identified by their hull numbers rather than individually named. As a result of their recent yard period, both could make their flank speed of twenty-six knots. As they entered the Yellow Sea, the two ships turned to divergent courses. *Najin Three* came right to a course of 180 that would bring her to the west of the South Korean island of Yeonpyeong. *Najin Four* came left to 140, a course that would take the frigate well east of Yeonpyeong Island and between the South Korean mainland and the American-Korean mine-hunting flotilla.

There was also a flurry of after-dark activity on the Ongjin Peninsula of North Korea. Long-range coastal artillery crews took up their positions. Yeonpyeong Island was at the extreme range of their guns, but every few years, the North Korean batteries shelled Yeonpyeong, and the South Koreans answered in kind with their American-made 155 mm self-propelled artillery. These exchanges resulted in a few deaths and casualties and reminded both sides that, while they may have signed a cease-fire accord some sixty years ago, they were still at war.

Aboard the Seventh Fleet flagship, USS *Blue Ridge,* Lieutenant Hugh Risseeau studied the intelligence summary that the petty officer of the watch had handed him. It was filled with North Korean troop movements and a seemingly unusual number of North Korean naval-unit sightings. Risseeau was fairly new to the Seventh Fleet staff. He was by trade a surface warfare officer with a specialty in communications and was now assigned to the Seventh Fleet as one of the staff communicators. About every ten days, he took his rotation as the staff duty officer, which was where he found himself now. The activity in North Korea seemed out of the ordinary, but he had no real basis for comparison.

"Hey, Senior Chief O'Gara, have you seen this intel summary?"

O'Gara had been on staff for close to two years. He was rated as an operations specialist, and he did have a basis for comparison.

"I did, sir, and there's a lot more activity than I've seen since I've been here on staff."

"What do you make of it, Senior?"

"Hard to tell. With the North Koreans, you never know whether they're getting ready for war or just posturing to blackmail the international community into giving them more food and fuel. But for all that movement, there's been very little communications activity."

Since one of the major responsibilities of the Seventh Fleet was the defense of the Korean Peninsula, all intelligence regarding North and South Korea was to be routed to the Seventh Fleet staff. The intel now being processed came from a variety of electronic intercepts, satellite data, and open-source media collected by the NSA, CIA, the National Reconnaissance Office, the Eighth Army G-2 section at Yongsan Garrison, and Seventh Air Force Intelligence S-2 at Osan Air Base. The information flow was comprehensive and continuous, but it contained none of what Op-Center had passed to the Pentagon, nor any of their early assessment of the mounting danger. Most of what Risseeau and O'Gara were seeing was classified secret traffic but carried the routine routing of "monitor for future developments." Whatever was brewing would have a direct bearing on a great number of American service personnel. There were some twenty thousand troops in the Eighth Army and eight thousand airmen in the Seventh Air Force.

"So, Senior Chief, what about these three corvettes that seem to be operating along the approaches to the Han River and off Inchon?" Risseeau had pulled up a chart on the big desktop flat screen that showed Seoul, Inchon, and some forty miles west-southwest into the Yellow Sea. "Here's where they were last evening, and here's where they are now. They seem to be moving in some sort of an extended formation, close in but still in international waters."

O'Gara studied the presentation for several minutes. "Your guess is as good as mine, sir, but, best I can tell, they seem to be conducting some sort of mine-laying exercise. It'd make sense as we're conducting a MINEX with the South Koreans just west of them. But I've never seen them operating this close to shore. It's probably nothing, sir, but we're not going to get much more out of these satellite passes. If we really want to know what they're up to, we're going to have to request a low-level reconnaissance pass."

"You mean from the *Reagan* air wing?"

"Tell you what, sir," he said with a grin. "Why don't

we just pass this requirement over to the Seventh Air Force in Osan. Get a couple of those Air Force flyboys off the golf course and have them do the flyover. Give them a little honest work for a change."

CHAPTER FOURTEEN

November 12, 2230 Korea Standard Time

Milwaukee and *Defender* continued to operate in the mine-exercise area, deploying their gear throughout the night. They were mine hunting, not mine clearing. *Defender* was equipped with embedded high-frequency, high-resolution, target-classification sonars. *Milwaukee* was similarly outfitted with the equipment that comprised its MCM module. They were basically mapping the bottom of this portion of the Yellow Sea and cataloging minelike objects. *Defender* was a bit more proficient at the task since this was its sole mission. The data collected by each vessel was transmitted, collated, and displayed on a bottom-contour flat-screen image. A team of analysts on both ships worked to sift through the information to identify and classify what might be a mine and what might be man-made junk or natural rock formations.

Every few hours, Kate Bigelow made the trek from

the bridge back to the mission control center—what she had grown up in her career calling the combat direction center—which contained both her ship's-company control team and the specialized team of operators who came aboard to control and monitor the gear that was part of their mine-countermeasure module. There, she was briefed by Lieutenant Ashburn or one of his leading petty officers. She timed these visits carefully, wanting both to be informed and to show a command interest in their progress, but not wanting to be disruptive. The work was going well despite the weather. A front had just blown in from the East China Sea, reducing the visibility to a half mile. There was a heavy overcast and a strong promise of fog. The sea state was moderate with waves three to four feet, but, with a steady ten-knot wind from the southeast, it was bound to get worse. Unless it got really bad, the weather just made their work uncomfortable, not impossible. Like modern-day farmers, they tilled their field, in this case the sea bottom, with the precision afforded them by an extremely accurate GPS running fix. Anything they found and marked on their bottom topographies, they could return and find at a later date.

And they were finding mines. Each hour *Milwaukee* sent a status report on confirmed exercise mines found or objects classified as minelike to Commodore Park on his flagship. Park acknowledged the reports but seemed more intent on the formation and station keeping of his South Korean ships. Just after midnight, Jack O'Connor found his captain on the bridge. She was well bundled and sitting in her bridge chair. Her eyes were closed, and she was on the edge of sleep when O'Connor moved to her side holding his iPad. Before he could speak, her eyes snapped open.

"What you got, XO?"

"I'm not sure, but it can't be anything good." O'Connor knew Bigelow liked to be briefed by her officers. Rather than handing her the iPad, he continued, "Seventh Fleet is telling us there are three North Korean corvettes now between us and the approaches to the Han River and Inchon, and they seem to be conducting some sort of a mine-laying exercise. That, plus two of their frigates—their only two operational frigates—have just sortied from Haeju. One of our low-orbit radar surveillance satellites caught them in Haeju Bay heading for the northern Yellow Sea at about twenty hundred—some five hours ago."

"Where are they now?"

"They don't know. We'll not have another satellite pass until about zero eight hundred. A section of F-16s are being scrambled out of Osan at first light to check out the three corvettes."

Bigelow held out her hand, and he passed her the iPad. She studied it for several minutes.

"Want to call off the MINEX?" O'Connor asked. Bigelow didn't answer, still studying the message. After a minute, she looked up.

"Not yet. See this is passed to Commodore Park immediately. And get me a rundown of whatever we have aboard in the way of intel on the capabilities of both the corvettes and the frigates. I want to know how fast they are and how they're armed. See that information is passed around to the department heads and is a pass-down item for senior watch standers."

"Aye, aye, Captain, right away," he said, and he left the bridge.

Kate Bigelow sat lost in thought for several minutes. The captain of *Defender* would have this same information as well, and she would want his opinion on these developments. It seemed there was just too much activity on the part of the North Koreans and too little intelligence coming in from communications intercepts and electronic sources about just what they were up to. Though she was well bundled against the cold sea air, the hair on the back of her neck was starting to bristle, and she was getting goose bumps. She reached over to the IVOX and punched in the button for the mission control center.

"MCC, bridge."

"MCC, aye, ma'am," came the reply from a watch stander who recognized her voice.

"Is Lieutenant Ashburn there?"

"Roger, ma'am, wait one."

A moment later, "Ashburn here, Skipper."

"You saw the last from Seventh Fleet?"

"Yes, ma'am, I did."

"What do you think?"

"I don't like it. There's a lot we don't know, and we've got a ton of gear over the side. If something comes our way, there's not much we can do right now."

There's probably not a lot we can do about it anyway, Bigelow thought. "How long will it take to bring everything aboard and get it secured?"

Ashburn paused, and then said, "Maybe ninety minutes."

"Okay, let's keep hunting, but I want all gear aboard and stowed by first light."

"Aye, aye, ma'am."

Kate then called the skipper of *Defender* and told him what she intended. He agreed with her course of action and said he'd have his gear aboard and stowed by dawn as well. Bigelow then called Commodore Park to keep him informed. He did not agree with her assessment or her decision. In his limited English, he ordered her to continue with the exercise—that no North Korean vessel would dare interfere with South Korean vessels in international waters. She tactfully reminded him the North Koreans had done just that, and fairly recently, but he was adamant. The MINEX would continue. After she broke the connection, she pondered his order to continue mine hunting. *But he doesn't have his movements severely restricted by gear in the water and a crew working in worsening weather.* O'Connor was back on the bridge and had heard the exchange between Bigelow and their commodore.

"So what do we do, Captain? Continue on?"

"I think not," she replied. "Get a message out to Seventh Fleet and info the *Reagan* strike group and *Defender.* I will be suspending both ships' participation in the mine exercise until the intentions of the North Koreans become clear."

"Uh, Captain, if this turns out to be just more posturing by the North, you're going to get a reprimand for going against the orders of Commodore Park."

Bigelow shrugged. "It will in all probability be just posturing on their part, Jack, but it's my call. The safety of the ship and the crew comes first. It could be different in time of war, but not now, not for an exercise. We'll not go back to hunting mines until this gets sorted out."

"What do we tell the commodore?"

Bigelow smiled. "I'll deal with that when the gear is aboard. Now, get that message out."

She watched O'Connor leave the bridge, back through the pilothouse on his way to radio. Then she frowned. *Is he ready to command this ship—and make the right decisions once I step down?* She put that thought out of her mind for the moment—but knew she would need to return to it in time. Then she eased herself from the chair and elected to go back to the MCC.

Behind her, just after she'd stepped from the bridge, the JOOD said, "Captain's off the bridge."

While *Milwaukee* and *Defender* were thrashing about in the early-morning hours in the Yellow Sea, Chase Williams was having lunch at his desk the day before. Shortly after Dawson, Rodriguez, and Volner and his JSOC team headed toward Okinawa, Williams and Sullivan adjusted their watch teams to accommodate the time difference between Washington, D.C., and the Korean Peninsula. Korea was fourteen time zones away—and on the other side of the international date line—from Washington. It was important that Op-Center's watch teams were mindful of this difference and manned appropriately at the right times. Williams was looking ahead, anticipating Op-Center's next actions, when there was a loud, insistent knock on his door. He didn't need to look up to see who was there.

"Come in, Aaron!" Williams said as he rolled the last bite of his sandwich in a napkin and pushed it aside. He looked up and could see Bleich was alarmed. "Talk to me," he continued as he motioned for him to sit down.

"It's the North Koreans," Bleich began without preamble, and then quickly added, "I just briefed Roger, and he told me to come see you immediately."

"Good," Williams replied, smiling. *My Geek Tank leader is a quick study*, Williams thought. *I never thought I'd count on someone this young for so much.*

"First, their comm channels were strangely quiet," Bleich continued. "Now they're extremely active, especially the chatter coming from their naval headquarters. What bothers me is they have an unusual number of their larger warships at sea. The strength of their navy is their fleet of patrol boats and their submarines. The patrol boats are crude and dated, but they're simple to operate, and they have a lot of them. Their subs are coastal boats with limited range but well suited to coastal maritime defense." Williams had spent over three decades in the U.S. Navy, had risen to four-star rank, and he knew all this, but he declined to interrupt his Geek Tank leader. "The threat posed by their patrol boats is their surface-to-surface missile capability. They're designed to engage and sink other surface craft. The same with their subs and their torpedoes. But they're all in port. Now they have the best of their corvettes and frigates at sea. Except for the Silkworm-type surface-to-surface missiles carried by their frigates, these are gunships. They're a threat to no one, but . . ."

"To no one," Williams interjected, "but a lightly armed mine-hunting flotilla."

"Exactly," Bleich replied. "If I had to bet, the North is plotting something that has to do with American and South Korean minesweepers. And given all the land-based military movement, it's something big. My guess is the North is going to move against the ships of that mine exercise, either as a primary objective or as a diversion for some ground action along the DMZ."

"And if the ships are the target," Williams asked, "what's your best guess of what they might be up to?"

"Well, if they just wanted to sink one or two of those ships, they'd have a lot better luck with their missile-patrol boats or one of their submarines. I think they want to make a capture at sea and take some hostages—a ship or some sailors, or both."

"The *Pueblo* again?"

"Just conjecture, boss, but that would be my guess."

Williams considered this. Op-Center did not fight engagements at sea, but it did plan for the odd contingency and operate where major-military action was deemed inappropriate or unwise.

"Are Brian and Hector on the ground yet?"

"As of about fifteen minutes ago."

Even though their G-5 had to make a fueling stop in Alaska, they set down at Kadena thirty minutes ahead of the C-17 carrying Mike Volner and his JSOC team. The big Globemaster III had twice made rendezvous for aerial refueling, but it was much slower than the Gulf-stream. Per the request from Op-Center, the two aircraft were directed to a small hangar on a remote part of the airfield. Once the aircraft were parked, Brian Dawson, Hector Rodriguez, their Geek Tank analyst, and the twelve-man JSOC contingent, with their five-man support team, unloaded their gear into the small hangar and made themselves at home. This included a small but capable communications suite, cots, a field kitchen, and a generous variety of operational gear. They were a self-contained element, prepared to do just about anything and to wait for as long as it took.

As the last of the gear was unloaded, a blue Chevy Suburban pulled up to the hangar. It was 0300. The base was quiet except for the whine of the jet engine run-ups coming from a maintenance hangar across the field. The front passenger door opened, and an aide leaped out to open the rear door for the base commander. He was dressed in long-sleeved Air Force fatigues with bloused boots. There were silver eagles perched on his collar points as well as on his utility cap. He looked at the C-17, an aircraft that came and went daily from Kadena, and the Gulfstream, which was a rarity. He made no move toward the hangar but waited by the car. His was a courtesy call, but it was also a curiosity call. Brian Dawson was alerted to the Suburban's arrival by the sentry posted at the door. He walked over to the Suburban.

"Good morning, Colonel. My name is Brian Dawson, and I'm the element leader of this contingent."

"Colonel Bost here, Dawson," the colonel said neutrally. "Welcome to Kadena."

Dawson stepped away from the Suburban, motioning Bost to follow.

"Colonel," Dawson said in a quiet voice, "we are a special-operations contingency force that reports to an organization called Op-Center that answers directly to the president. I'm sure you've been given our clearance and operational mandate." Bost nodded. "There's something brewing in the Yellow Sea that may or may not come to a head and may or may not require our attention. In all probability, we'll just sit here for seventy-two hours or so, pack up, and then go home. If we get tasked, it could be anytime, day or night, and then we will move quickly. That's about all I can tell you. We're completely self-contained, and we should be out of your hair one way or another within just a few days."

Bost again nodded. "Thank you for that. My aide will give you an on-base contact number that's good twenty-four/seven. If you need anything, just call that number. And if there are any problems, have them call me." He offered his hand, which Dawson took. "Otherwise, good luck."

"Thank you, sir."

Moments later, the Suburban and the colonel were gone. If he resented their presence or felt neglected because he had been told so little, he had the good sense or good manners not to show it.

When he reentered the hangar, Dawson was met by his staff analyst, who also served as a communicator. "Sir, I have a real-time, secure voice link established with Op-Center. It's a lot clearer than the Iridium satellite phone."

Jesse Carpenter was the Geek Tank's utility infielder. He was not a programmer, but he could set up and manage a computer network, and he knew just about all there was to know about military and corporate communications. He also had a good grasp of military intelligence and intelligence analysis. Carpenter had a degree in mathematics from the University of Phoenix online, as well as a master's degree. He was a self-starter and prided himself on being such. Bleich had hired him away from NSA, where he was considered a rising star. Jesse Carpenter was thirty-five, five ten, a hundred and sixty pounds, and extremely fit. As an enlisted soldier, he had served with the Seventy-fifth Ranger Regiment and the Fifth Special Forces Group, where he qualified as an 18-Delta medical sergeant and an 18-Echo communications sergeant. Hector Rodriguez said he was as useful as a Leatherman tool and as handy as a pair of pants.

"Sir," Carpenter continued, "I've got us set up over in the corner of the hangar, where there's a little privacy. I've tested the comm link. We're up, fully operational, and Mr. Williams would like you to call him as soon as it's convenient."

"Thanks, Jesse. Great work." *I know the boss knew what he was doing sending us downrange just in case,* Dawson found himself thinking, *and I've got good men here with me trained and ready to go on hot standby. But for the life of me I can't conjure up a scenario where they'd be able to get their guns in the fight.*

Just before 0400, about the time the crews of *Milwaukee* and *Defender* began the cold, wet work of retrieving their mine-hunting gear, two F-16Es with extended range tanks lifted off the runway at Osan Air Base, made their way out over the Yellow Sea, and turned north. Both were two-place aircraft but differently configured. One carried an AN/ASD-11 Theater Airborne Reconnaissance System pod attached to its centerline station. The second was riding shotgun and carried a complement of AIM-120 air-to-air missiles. Each aircraft carried five hundred rounds of 20 mm ammunition in their M61A1 Gatling-gun system that, at six thousand rounds per minute, gave each F-16E a brief but lethal five-second squirt. Just before takeoff, Senior Chief Ed O'Gara managed to get one of the pilots of the reconnaissance bird on a secure line and told him what he was looking for on a visual pass.

The two North Korean captains who now commanded *Najin Three* and *Najin Four* had been selected for their seagoing experience and their political reliability, of which the latter took precedence. Their mission, as Op-Center's Aaron Bleich had rightly guessed, was to capture one or both of the American ships in what the North Koreans claimed to be their waters. *Najin Three* was to take a station just west and south of Yeonpyeong Island to block the American escape to the west and south while *Najin Four* would make for a station southeast and south of Yeonpyeong with the intention of herding them north, closer to the coastline of North Korea.

Both captains knew it was a bold and dangerous plan—and one likely concocted by military bureaucrats and political sycophants in their air-conditioned offices in Pyongyang. And both knew failure was not an option for either of them.

The Yeonpyeong Island group had a curious history and geographic location. Yeonpyeong was situated off the North Korean coast and south of the United Nations–created Northern Limit Line. Yet Yeonpyeong Island and a smaller inhabited island of the group, Soyeonpyeong Island, were located north and inside of what the North Koreans called the Inner-Korean Military Demarcation Line. The North allowed ferry service between Inchon and the two islands through a maritime corridor that ran approximately north and south through the Yellow Sea to the island group. Except for an occasional exchange of artillery between the Yeonpyeong Island garrison and the North Korean coastal batteries, the arrangement had worked for more than sixty years. And the Chinese seemed to permit it as well. It was not unlike their own aggressive history regarding the Taiwanese islands of Quemoy and Matsu off the coast of China.

Now, with the Americans operating at sea close by and just south of the Military Demarcation Line, Pyongyang saw this as a chance to change the calculus. With the capture of an American ship in waters they claimed, the North Koreans hoped to see South Korean forces removed from Yeonpyeong and the islands returned to North Korea—along with an extension of North Korean waters into the Yellow Sea to include the recently discovered oil and gas deposits. The attention and leverage gained by the capture of USS *Pueblo* in January 1968 was not lost on the North Korean leadership. It was still considered one of the great victories of the People's Republic of North Korea. They knew the premium the Americans placed on POWs, and they wanted to bring this about again. What they would ask the Americans for in return for the precious U.S. POWs should matter little to a nation on the other side of the Pacific, they reasoned. As the sun began to turn the low-hanging fog over the Yellow Sea from black to a dark, dirty gray, both frigates were on station. When word came from the People's Army Naval Headquarters, *Najin Three* began to move west at twenty knots, while *Najin Four* made for the Korean-American mine flotilla at flank speed.

The two F-16Es found the *Won Do* and her two sister ships just after first light. Per their orders, the corvettes had set up a picket line with twenty miles between each of the three ships and just west of the arc of their minefield. There they were to await further instructions. Their standing orders were to allow any South Korean vessels to pass by and enter the minefield. They were to warn off or take under fire any American warships that attempted to escape east through the mines.

Since *Won Do* was the southernmost of the three pickets, the F-16Es found it first. Lieutenant Commander Choe Dae-jung watched the two aircraft flash past, one after the other at two hundred feet off the surface. After a second pass, they disappeared into the overcast, headed north. Choe's crew was on full alert. His two missilemen were ready with their Strela-2 shoulder-fired surface-to-air launchers, but the two fighters were moving way too fast for the infrared homing device of either Strela to obtain a lock. Much to Choe's relief, they zoomed off unmolested. The next corvette received the same basic treatment, but on the third ship, a trigger-happy missileman fired his rocket. The missile had a weak signal, so the rocket went ballistic after its intended target juked away from the flight path. But the F-16s did not keep moving this time; they turned to fight. Twenty mm rounds from their internal cannon ripped into the superstructure of the unarmored corvette. After two gun passes, the cries of dying crewmen echoed within the ship and rendered several passageways slick with blood. And there was fire—not a fire that would completely disable the corvette, but one that created enough smoke to asphyxiate several more crewmen. In a matter of seconds, eight North Korean sailors were dead with that many again dying from shrapnel wounds. The first blow had been struck.

On clearing the third ship, the two F-16Es headed for Osan with their reconnaissance pod full of images and electronic intelligence. The second pilot in the recce F-16E called back to his base with the information Senior Chief O'Gara wanted most. He reported the mine racks of all three ships were empty. This information was quickly passed to O'Gara at Seventh Fleet. He confirmed again that satellite imagery from the day before showed the racks to be full. The corvettes had indeed mined the waters west of Seoul and Inchon.

Op-Center was not on the Seventh Fleet distribution list for classified intelligence traffic, but with the computer-generated sifting of the Geek Tank's electronic eaves-dropping programs, they had the information within minutes of Senior Chief O'Gara's receiving it. Fifteen minutes after one of the F-16Es reported the empty mine racks on the North Korean corvettes, Aaron Bleich was in Chase Williams's office, even as the Op-Center director was reading an electronic copy of the F-16E transmission to Seventh Fleet on his desktop computer. It was 0930 in Washington.

"What do you make of it, Aaron?"

"It would appear that the mines and corvettes are an attempt to block our ships and the South Korean ships from returning to port, either by way of the Han River or to Inchon."

"Not entirely," Williams replied.

"Sir?"

"The corvettes are too widely spaced to intercept many, if any, of the South Korean or American ships. And the minesweepers, both the Korean sweeps and *Defender,* are wooden ships and designed to be able to move relatively freely in a minefield. Only *Milwaukee* is at high risk from the mines." Williams was silent for a moment, then continued as if thinking out loud. "Perhaps the corvettes and the mines are there to serve a dual purpose—to keep *Milwaukee* from escaping to a friendly port and to prevent the South Koreans from coming to the rescue. Their frigates and destroyers, not to mention a very capable patrol-boat force at Inchon alone, are enough to overpower just about anything the North can put to sea. Only a minefield could keep them in port."

"What about our air assets at Osan and Kunsan? Can they intervene?"

"They could," Williams smiled ruefully, "but it's not that simple. Our ships and the South Korean ships are well within the coastal air defenses of North Korea. China has given them some pretty sophisticated stuff, and the Russians have sold them the best they have. You've been reading their mail, Aaron. You know they're in a high state of readiness. Our fighters can protect the ships, but we're going to lose some aircraft in the process. I'm reaching back a ways to my time as PACOM commander, but as I recall they have a wide array of anti-aircraft missiles. They have the full range of Russian SA-class missiles—from the SA-2 up into the teens to the SA-17. And they have the S-25 Berkut and the Strela-10 to boot. But let's not trust my memory. Get me an order of battle of what they might have in the way of air defense. Meanwhile, I need to make a call."

After Bleich left, Williams tapped a number on his secure phone console, one he had committed to memory, not to speed dial. It was answered on the first ring.

"I need to speak with the president . . . no, it absolutely cannot wait until morning."

Back at his desk, Aaron Bleich's fingers flew over his keyboard. He was determined to get the Op-Center director the information he needed ASAP. And he wanted to do it quickly, for he felt he had an equally urgent task. *I walked into the director's office, he asked for my assessment, and what I gave him didn't answer the mail completely. That won't happen again. I'm better than*

*this. I need to get smarter on the capabilities of our
ships and game the likely scenarios if shooting starts.*

"You shock me, Commander," Commodore Park said in
his broken English. "I specifically told you that I wanted
the mine exercise to continue without interruption. You
have disobeyed my order—my direct order." Park had
called on the open bridge-to-bridge circuit, which was
line-of-sight, unencrypted, and on the bridge speaker.
The anger in his voice was plain to Jack O'Connor,
the OOD, and all the bridge watch standers. As it was
an open circuit, it could be heard by those on the bridges
of *Defender* and the other Korean minesweepers. But
Park was not done. He launched into a tirade, called Bigelow a coward, and threatened court-martial. While he
was in full rant, a sailor ran onto the bridge from radio
and thrust an iPad into Bigelow's hand. She motioned
O'Connor to her side to read it with her. It was flash
precedence, the most urgent of all military traffic.

"Commodore, stop right there!" Bigelow barked into
the handset, and a chagrined Park fell silent. "I've just
received a message from Seventh Fleet saying the North
Koreans have mined the waters off the Han River and
the Port of Inchon. The report also indicates two of their
major combatants put to sea last night and may be in our
area."

Park knew his minesweepers were defenseless.
"Wha—what are you going to do?"

Bigelow hesitated, but only for a second. "I'm going
to request continuous air cover and clear my ship for

surface action. I recommend that you do the same. Bigelow, out."

"Jack, sound general quarters. OOD, find Mr. Ashburn and have him report to me here on the bridge." Then she took up the handset for the secure comm link to the bridge of the *Defender*. "*Defender, Milwaukee,* over."

"*Defender* actual, here, over."

"You get all that, Tom?" Lieutenant Commander Tom Welch was commanding officer of *Defender,* a University of San Diego NROTC graduate, and a capable MCM skipper.

"I did, ma'am. What are your instructions?"

"Let's start moving south at twelve knots with you in the lead. I don't want to abandon the sweeps, but we need to get some sea room from them just in case. I'll ask Osan for some air cover—and meanwhile get your best people on your surface-search radars."

"Roger that, ma'am. Turning to zero-eight-zero at twelve knots. Good luck, Captain."

"Same to you, Tom. *Milwaukee,* out."

Moments later, Eric Ashburn was on the bridge, helmet strapped into place, life jacket on, and his trousers tucked into his boots—proper general-quarters dress.

"Eric, get a message out to Seventh Air Force at Osan and request immediate and continuous air cover. Tell them we'll be moving south from the exercise area. Info Seventh Fleet and *Reagan* strike group."

"Got it, Skipper." And he was gone.

Bigelow had just clipped the chin strap on her battle helmet and was shrugging into her life vest. Both were embossed with COMMANDING OFFICER, on the front of the helmet and the back of the vest.

"Bridge, MCC," came the call on the IVOX phone. MCC—mission control center—was the tactical and electronic nerve center of *Milwaukee*. On previous classes of U.S. Navy ships it was called either the "combat information center" or "combat direction center." During general quarters, Bigelow might be in the MCC, or she might be on the bridge—it all depended on the threat and the tactical situation. She could direct the ship's operations from either location. For now, she chose to be on the bridge.

"Bridge, aye," the OOD replied.

"Bridge, we have a surface contact twelve miles at one-seven-five true. It's coming straight at us at twenty-six knots."

Shit, now what? Bigelow beat the OOD to the IVOX phone. "What's your evaluation, Chief?" The watch officer was a chief operations specialist and a good one. Bigelow recognized his voice.

"I'm showing a Square Tie air search radar and a Pot Head surface-search radar, Captain. Got to be a *Najin*-class frigate and it's coming hard."

Bigelow looked off to the south, knowing the North Korean frigate was still below the horizon, especially in this weather. Again, *shit*. She was considering her options when the IVOX phone on the bridge squawked again.

"Bridge, combat, Chief Jones again. You there, Captain?"

"Right here, Chief."

"Ma'am, I have *another* paint on yet *another* Najin-class frigate. At first I thought it was an echo, but it's definitely a second frigate. She's west of us and on a heading of zero-eight-five at twenty knots—no, make that twenty-five knots. She's putting on speed."

Double shit. Warships were no longer referred to as "she" and "her." But Chief Jones was old-school, and Bigelow didn't really care. What she did care about was the unfolding trap the North Koreans were about to spring. Instantly, her mind's eye captured the full implications of the tactical situation. And she immediately knew she had but two choices—run or fight. Running was the simplest solution. *Milwaukee* could easily outrun these frigates, even with her heavy MCM package. And even with the minefield to the east and North Korean waters to the north, there was enough seaway to the west to maneuver and stay out of potential gun range of the North Korean frigates. But *Defender* couldn't run, at least not fast enough. The flank speed of the MCM ship was fourteen knots. The South Korean minesweepers, not quite that. They could scatter, but the two frigates would run them down like wolves on a pack of sheep on the open prairie. There was one and only one course open to her, or one course open until she could get air cover. She turned it over in her mind once again, but saw no other option.

"OOD!"

"Yes, ma'am."

"I want to see the weapons officer and the operations officer here on the bridge, ASAP."

"Aye, aye, ma'am."

Bigelow's eyes locked on Jack O'Connor's for a brief instant as she reached for the secure bridge-to-bridge net with *Defender*. His mouth was open and he looked like a deer in the headlights. She turned her attention to the handset.

"*Milwaukee* actual to *Defender*. You there, Tom?"

"Right here, ma'am."

"Do you have the North Korean frigates?"

"Yes, ma'am. We just picked them up."

"Okay, these are your instructions. I want you to come left to a course of zero-eight-zero and run east for that minefield. Commodore Park is on his own, but I will recommend he do the same. Those frigates'll not follow you into a minefield."

"Understood, ma'am, but it's too far. With their speed advantage, they'll run us down."

"No, they won't, Tom. *Milwaukee* will see to it."

"I don't see how . . . Hold on, Kate. You can't do this. No way!"

"This is the only way. Do you understand your orders?"

"Yes, but . . ."

"No buts, Lieutenant Commander Welch. Do you understand your orders?"

"Yes, ma'am."

"Then execute them. Good luck, Tom. *Milwaukee*, out."

She made a similar call to Commodore Park. He understood the tactical situation as well as Bigelow and had turned his ships east. "Thank you, Commander Bigelow. God willing, we will see you in port in Inchon."

"God willing, Commodore," she replied and broke the connection.

Jack O'Connor, Eric Ashburn, and Ensign Grace Montgomery were waiting for her on the port bridge wing. Montgomery was her weapons officer. It was a lieutenant junior grade billet, but she had been aboard for fifteen months and had proved her worth as the ship's gunnery officer. When the previous weapons officer had been rotated ashore, Bigelow had fleeted her up to the job. Grace Montgomery was a slightly built woman who looked younger than her twenty-three years. In her battle helmet, she looked like a kid playing war. Bigelow stepped over to meet them on the bridge wing.

"Okay, Roberts, take a coffee break," she said, dismissing the port lookout. When he was gone, she turned to the others. "We don't have a lot of time, so I'm going to make this quick. We're going to put ourselves between *Defender* and the closest frigate and shield *Defender* while it makes for Inchon. Eric, have the chief quartermaster put us on a course to keep us between that closest frigate and *Defender*. Then I want you supervising the watch team in MCC. This could turn out to be a game of chicken or the real thing, but let's let them make the first move. They radiate us with a fire-control radar, then we light them up. They shoot; we shoot. But we let them make the first move. Gracie?"

"Yes, ma'am."

"That gun of yours ready to do business?"

"Yes, ma'am. My gunner's mates have run their prefiring checklists, and the fire-control techs have the radars calibrated with the gun. We're ready to shoot."

"Very well. Let's hope it doesn't come to a shootout, but if it does, we're counting on you. Questions? Okay, let's get to it." She motioned O'Connor to wait while the others went to their stations. "Jack, I want you to make a tour of the ship and make sure all stations are manned and ready. Make sure Chief Picard has the wardroom fully converted to a surgery suite and ready to receive casualties. Then I want you in MCC with Eric as well. Eric will run the show, but I need you there to back him up. I'll also want you to ensure Seventh Fleet is kept informed of whatever takes place. If this turns into a surface action, I'm going to want to be on the bridge."

"Captain," O'Connor said in a low voice, "you can't be thinking about a surface action with these frigates. They have two 100 mm guns and four 5 mm guns—*each!* We have a single 57 mm gun. We have no business mixing it up with them. We're totally outgunned."

Bigelow regarded him carefully. "What would you have me do, Jack?"

"Negotiate. Talk to them. Anything but challenge them like this. If we provoke them, they'll fire on us, and we have one lousy gun." As he spoke, a messenger from radio came up and handed Bigelow an iPad. She took it, scanned it quickly, and typed in a quick acknowledgment.

"Thank you," she said to the messenger. Then, turning back to her executive officer, "Well, Jack, it seems the shooting's already started. One of those corvette minelayers fired on a section of our F-16Es, and they fired back." She lowered her voice a notch. "Look, I'm not looking to make this ship a martyr, and we will do all we can to avoid a confrontation. But we're in international waters, and those sailors on the *Defender* are helpless. Their best offensive weapon is a fifty-caliber machine gun. I'll not abandon them to the North Koreans."

O'Connor took a step closer, making the mismatch in their sizes more apparent. "What about us? What about the sailors aboard *Milwaukee*?"

"XO, don't think I've forgotten about them for one minute. But this is a United States warship, and our duty is clear. We'll stand with *Defender*. Now, get with the program, Jack. You do your job, and I'll do mine."

O'Connor stiffened, but took a step back. "Aye, aye, Captain," he said, and left the bridge.

Bigelow looked around and saw that the bridge GQ watch section was at their stations and in battle gear. Then she looked out to sea to the south. The weather was worsening, and the cloud cover was now down to three hundred feet, making it difficult for the air cover she had requested.

Staff officers and senior enlisted personnel were now streaming aboard USS *Blue Ridge* as it sat pierside in Yokosuka, Japan. The Seventh Fleet commander had ordered the *Reagan* battle group to head back toward the Yellow Sea at best speed. The staff intelligence section had shed no new light on the situation except to note that the North Koreans had mined the northern portion of the west coast of South Korea and that aircraft from the Seventh Air Force had disabled a North Korean corvette. Now word had just come in that two North

Korean frigates were bearing down on an American–South Korean mine-hunting flotilla of eight ships—eight extremely helpless ships.

Vice Admiral Edmond Bennett had been in the Navy for twenty-six years. He was new to the Seventh Fleet, having come from a two-year tour in the Pentagon. Before that, he had commanded the *Carl Vinson* carrier strike group. He was a solid, seagoing officer; an efficient administrator; and, like all naval officers who rose to three-star rank, a capable politician. And he knew a nasty encounter at sea brewing when he saw one. He was discussing the matter with his chief of staff and his intelligence officer, both senior Navy captains, when Lieutenant Hugh Risseeau interrupted.

"Excuse me, Admiral, gentlemen, but you wanted to see anything new about the North Koreans in the Yellow Sea." He handed Bennett a hard copy of a message. The admiral studied the sheet for several minutes and then passed it to his chief of staff, who then read it with the intelligence officer looking over his shoulder.

"This originated from an outfit called Op-Center," the COS said. "I'm not familiar with them. Who are they?"

"And they seem to feel strongly," the intel type offered, "the North Koreans are looking to capture one of our ships. Seems a little far-fetched to me."

Ed Bennett was now more worried than he had been at any time since the crisis broke. He was far enough up the military food chain to know who Op-Center was and, more importantly, who was running it. As such, he was inclined to take the capture scenario at face value.

Bennett, like every line officer at Seventh Fleet, or the entire Navy for that matter, knew the limitations of the littoral combat ship. And on his desk, he had a listing of the speed, armament, and combat capabilities of the *Najin*-class frigates. On paper, the LCS was terribly overmatched, the MCM ship slow and essentially defenseless. But capabilities only told a part of the story. Sometimes it was not how big the dog in the fight but how big the fight in the dog. In this case, what was the combat readiness of the crew, and how good was the captain?

"COS, get me a file on the skippers of our two ships over there, and I'm specifically interested in the skipper of the LCS."

"Right away, Admiral."

After they had left, Bennett asked for a line to the Pentagon operator. It took routing through several exchanges, but in a little less than ten minutes, he was put through to Chase Williams.

CHAPTER FIFTEEN

November 13, 0645 Korea Standard Time

The dustup between the U.S. Air Force F-16Es and the North Korean corvette triggered the initial alarm bells to ring and ring persistently up and across multiple chains of command, from the Republic of Korea Navy (ROK Navy) command to the Japanese Maritime Self-Defense Force (JMSDF) to multiple U.S. military commands. Those alarm bells intensified when the reports of the hostile actions of the *Najin*-class frigates hit the intel feeds. For the United States' allies in the area—the Japanese and especially the South Koreans—those alarm bells were on steroids. Commodore Park minced no words in alerting his ROK Navy chain of command, and the panic in the voice of their on-scene commander got the full attention of watch standers at the ROK Navy headquarters in Gyeryong, South Korea. From there, the reports rocketed up to the headquarters of the Joint Chiefs of Staff of Republic of Korea in Seoul.

General Kwon Oh-Sung, Chairman of the South Korean Joint Chiefs of Staff, arrived at his Seoul military headquarters and made a beeline for his chief of staff amid the growing chaos of their watch floor.

"Has the situation changed since you reached me at my home?"

"No, General. Navy headquarters is passing all reports from Commodore Park on scene up to us after they receive them. His ships are all steaming east at best speed."

"What about the American ships? Are the North Korean frigates still threatening them?"

"We're . . . we're . . . not exactly sure. Commodore Park has been reporting on the status of his six-ship flotilla but hasn't reported specifically on the *Najin*-class frigates since his initial report they were inbound towards the two American ships."

Kwon considered this for a moment. He didn't know Park personally; an ROK Navy captain was too far down in the food chain. But he did know his flag-officer counterparts in the ROK Navy. "Armchair admirals," he called them when he was alone with his fellow ROK Army officers. With 160 ships, almost 100 aircraft, and over 75,000 personnel, the ROK Navy was sucking an enormous share of South Korea's military budget away from the army and air force.

And for what? North Korea's navy was little more than a joke in his mind. No, the threat from North Korea was the more than one million active and over seven million reserve and paramilitary forces under arms that could swarm across the border at any time. What was the ROK Navy going to do to blunt the assault across the DMZ? Hell, they couldn't even protect their own ships. They let the North Koreans sink the ROK corvette *Cheonan* in their own home waters. General Kwon knew when the real fight came, the navy would be on the sidelines.

The Joint Chiefs of Staff of Republic of Korea was modeled on the United States Joint Chiefs of Staff, but General Kwon's responsibilities set him apart from his American counterpart. The American chairman was charged with providing advice to the U.S. president and secretary of defense but had no operational control over U.S. military forces; Kwon had operational control over all military personnel of the ROK armed forces. In a crisis, he was in charge, and he had no intention of abdicating that responsibility or surrendering any of his authority.

Kwon turned to the officer manning the command console. "Colonel, contact our navy command center. Tell them I want all on-scene reports from Commodore Park piped directly to this command center, not forwarded by them. Understood?"

"Yes, General."

"Contact General Jeong. Tell him to scramble a flight of KF-16D's from Seosan Air Base. Then have him call me here immediately after that."

"Yes, General. What orders do you want me to give them once they take off?"

Kwon was simmering. They were in the middle of a crisis and a full-bird colonel was asking a question a private should be able to answer.

"Look at a map!" Kwon shouted, startling everyone

in the command center. "You know where our ships are. You know where the American ships are. You know where the North Korean frigates and corvettes are. Tell them to head north by northwest and await further instructions. I want our fighter jets over our ships, and I want them there now!"

As the watch team scrambled to carry out the chairman's orders, radios crackled in the background and watch standers updated electronic status boards. General Kwon Oh-Sung had served well over three decades in South Korea's military. Almost thirty-five years on hair-trigger alert. He had less than a year before his tour as chairman of the South Korean Joint Chiefs of Staff would end—and, with it, his military career. His legacy wouldn't include standing idly by while his nation suffered another humiliation.

"Major," he bellowed at the nearest watch stander.

"Sir!"

"I wish to speak with Admiral Cho immediately. Then I want you to arrange a conference call with my five operational commanders. Do it now!"

"Yes, general. And General Green is on the line holding for you."

General Kwon paused for a moment. General Everett Green was the commander of all U.S. forces in Korea.

"Tell General Green I am busy. I will call him when I have a few minutes to spare."

"Yes, General."

Just over one hundred miles north of where General Kwon Oh-Sung was trying to take control of the situation he faced, General Lee Kwon Hui sat at his desk at North Korean military headquarters in Pyongyang and stewed. He had roughly dismissed his staff and told them he didn't want to be disturbed under any circumstances. Now he just sat—and he worried.

He had recently returned to Pyongyang after his weeks-long negotiations with his Chinese counterparts. There, he and his delegation had received congratulations from North Korea's political and military leadership for their successful arms-for-energy negotiations. Then, unexpectedly, he was granted a private audience with North Korea's supreme leader, who had showered him with praise and given him a medal. That was all good—and well deserved, Lee thought—allowing himself a bit of self-congratulation. But as he rose to leave, the supreme leader's parting words still rang in ears, "General Lee, you have done your job and now we must do ours. We will own the Korea Bay and the Yellow Sea. Fateful days are ahead."

What fateful days? Pumping gas from the sea bottom for the next several decades? That was of no concern to a military man. What *did* concern him was what else was happening—events that were playing out in the dispatches that had crossed his desk and the rumors he was hearing from his military colleagues. The murder of Vice Marshal Sang Won-hong, deputy chief of the general staff, had started it all—but that was just the tip of the iceberg. There had been a dramatic series of firings and advancements in the North Korean military hierarchy over the past several months, and the top military leaders were all generals who had extreme enmity toward the West and especially the United States. Now there were massive troop movements and naval shifts that were puzzling and concerning. *Own the Yellow Sea. What was that all about?* Lee wasn't senior enough to be party to any of the meetings and conversations that would explain all this—and he felt isolated and out of the loop. But he could change that. He knew whom to contact to find out what he wanted to know. His fingers flew over the keyboard of his secure computer. Once he had fired off several messages, he also had a phone call to make. For that call, he needed complete privacy.

Chase Williams had just returned to his office from briefing the president. He had presented Op-Center's assessment regarding the developing situation in the Yellow Sea. The president was both cheered and frustrated: cheered because Williams was able to provide him with critical information his Geek Tank had generated, but frustrated because neither his intelligence nor military leaders could come up with the same information—at least not with the same fidelity or granularity.

Williams placed a call to Brian Dawson, who answered it on the second ring. "What's cooking, boss?"

"How's Kadena, Brian?"

"Oh, it's a tropical garden spot, that's for sure," Dawson replied with only a hint of sarcasm in his voice. "Any tasking for us for the situation with North Korea yet?"

"No, not yet. But I'm glad you all are downrange. The shooting's started with North Korea, and it looks like we're about to have a standoff at best—a shooting war at worst—at sea. I'll keep you posted in real time, but right now it looks like the North's hell-bent on attacking one of our ships—most likely USS *Milwaukee*—it's a littoral combat ship—and maybe trying to capture the crew. We're still trying to come up with the 'why,' and I've got Aaron and his team going full tilt. When I know more, you'll know more."

"Roger that, boss; we're good here. Any other words of wisdom?"

"Yes, as I've advised you before, don't let Hector talk you into a game of cribbage."

As the line went dead, Dawson marveled at Williams's ability not to be debilitated by a crisis.

But Chase Williams was not sanguine he had yet done enough. It troubled him, and troubled him deeply, that he didn't know why North Korea was doing this—and why now. He wanted to know; no, he *needed* to know. He eased himself out of his chair and headed for the Geek Tank.

CHAPTER SIXTEEN

Commander Kate Bigelow had brought *Milwaukee* to a heading of one-five-zero and a speed of ten knots. They were bow-on to the nearest North Korean frigate that was at twelve thousand yards and closing fast. She had maneuvered her ship to present the smallest radar signature to the North Korean frigates. The South Korean minesweepers had taken *Defender*'s lead and were making best speed due east for Inchon. They were still in sight but hull down and probably out of radar contact with the North Koreans.

Bigelow stood on the starboard outside wing of her bridge. Under her battle helmet she wore a headset and boom mic that connected her to her mission control center. With the foul-weather jacket and life vest worn over her coveralls, she looked like a preschooler ready to play in the snow. She had not needed her XO's warning to tell her she was outgunned, but if it came to a fight, she was not without advantages over the two frigates bearing down on them. The first was that their 57 mm BAE Systems Mark 110 gun was probably better than anything aboard the frigates. They had more and bigger guns, but not a better one. Secondly, *Milwaukee* was built with flat-angled topside areas that gave it a low radar signature. The North Koreans would have a much more difficult time ranging her with radar than she would them. And, finally, there was speed. They'd not done a full power run with the MCM module aboard, but she felt *Milwaukee* held something close to a ten-knot speed advantage. She hoped it would be enough.

Kate Bigelow spoke into her boom mic and called the watch stander at the Main Propulsion Control and Monitoring System—the MPCMS for short—a console inside the bridge and right behind the OOD and JOOD consoles. The senior petty officer manning the MPCMS kept tabs on *Milwaukee*'s unmanned engineering plant. Now that they were at general quarters, her chief engineer had stationed himself right beside the MPCMS operator.

"MPCMS, Captain."

"MPCMS, aye. Chief engineer is here with me, Captain."

"Okay, Steve. Ready to answer all bells?"

"Yes, ma'am," her CHENG replied. "Everything is online, and we can give you all we have." All he had was a great deal—two Rolls-Royce MT30 gas turbines and two Colt-Pielstick diesels driving four Rolls-Royce water-jet propulsion units.

"Understood and thanks. Captain, out."

She then turned to her comms officer. "We patched in?"

"Yes, ma'am. We've been monitoring their bridge-to-bridge circuit, and it's on your handset."

Bigelow paused. She was about to make the most important radio transmission of her naval career. With steel in her voice, she began. "North Korean frigate, this is the United States ship *Milwaukee*. We are conducting a military exercise in international waters. Please state your intentions, over."

There was a long pause. Bigelow could imagine them looking for an English speaker and wondering about a female voice coming from an U.S. Navy warship.

"American navy ship. This is the captain of *Najin Four*. You are not in international waters. You are in the waters of the People's Republic of Korea. You are ordered to stop and prepare to be boarded for inspection."

Kate called her OOD. "Come right to two-seven-zero and make turns for twenty knots."

"*Najin Four*, this is *Milwaukee*. May I know why you wish to board us, over?" She felt the ship heel to port in the turn and surge ahead as she waited for the reply.

"American warship. You are in our nation's sovereign waters. You will stop immediately and prepare to be boarded and inspected."

Kate stepped through the hatch and into the pilothouse. She looked at the LCD display in front of her OOD. The nearest North Korean frigate was just under ten thousand yards away, well within gun range—hers as well as theirs.

"Bridge, MCC." It was Eric Ashburn's voice in her

headset. "Now that we're broadside to them, they're painting us with their surface-search radar. They're also searching for us on their Drum Tilt fire-control radar."

"Roger that. Let me know when they have us locked up." Then, into the handset, "*Najin Four,* this is *Milwaukee.* Once again, please state your intentions. We are steaming in international waters."

Bigelow was playing for time, allowing the mine-sweepers a few additional minutes to make good their escape. She was now steaming in the opposite direction of them and hoping the two frigates would converge on *Milwaukee* and allow the sweeps to leave unmolested.

"American warship, you are in waters that belong to the People's Republic of Korea. You will stop for boarding and inspection. This is your last warning."

Before Kate could answer, "Bridge, MCC. They have a lock on us with their fire-control radar, and both frigates have altered course. They're converging on us!"

"MCC, bridge, roger." Then to the OOD, "Continue right to two-eight-zero and make turns for twenty-eight knots." The good news, Kate thought, is they've turned their attention to us; the bad news is they've turned their attention to us. Back on her headset, "You with us, Weps?"

"Weapons here and standing by," came the childlike voice of Grace Montgomery.

"Light them up and prepare to fire on my command."

"Emitting now and will prepare to fire on your command," Montgomery echoed.

Milwaukee had a recently installed modification of the Saab Sea Giraffe fire-control radar that had not been fully tested. It would certainly let the North Koreans know they had been locked on by a sophisticated radar, but would it get shells on target? Time would tell. Fortunately, Montgomery and her gunner's mates had proved themselves proficient with their gun's optical systems—at least during gun drills.

"Fire control locked on and tracking."

"Very well," Bigelow replied. "Eric, they still following us?"

"Still with us, Skipper."

At twenty-eight knots, *Milwaukee* could just stay ahead of the two converging North Korean frigates. Bigelow knew she could outrun them at any time, but she needed to keep them in range, and *Milwaukee* in their range, to draw them north and away from the fleeing minesweepers. *Once those sweeps are at a safe distance,* she thought, *we are so out of here.* But that would keep her in harm's way for at least another three hours. A lot could happen in three hours. *And where is that damned air cover?*

"Bridge, Weps. Bridge, Weps, over."

"Bridge here. Go ahead, Gracie."

"I have a visual on the enemy. We are under fire! I have gun puffs from their main battery!"

"Roger that, Weps. Battery released. Return fire, return fire, break. You copy this, Jack?"

"Copy, Captain."

"Inform Seventh Fleet and Seventh Air Force we have been fired on by a North Korean frigate and are returning fire."

"Captain, you sure you really want to—" It was Jack O'Connor's voice.

"XO, get that message out ASAP! When that's completed, would you please come up to the bridge."

The OOD looked up at her. "Ma'am, from the lookout on the hangar. We have splashes in the water, one on the port quarter and two on the starboard quarter."

"Very well."

Then on her headset she heard, "Bridge, Weps. We seem to have found the range and have bracketed the frigate. We may have even hit it." Her voice was calm, even measured. "But the fire-control radar's crapped out, and we are now engaging visually with radar ranges generated here in MCC."

"Very well, Gracie. Keep at them, steady and slow." Bigelow sighed. This was unfortunate but not unexpected. That's why Montgomery had worked her gun crew on shooting with a visual solution and radar ranges.

"Okay, Willie," she said to her general-quarters officer of the deck, a lieutenant junior-grade from MIT and the Officer Candidate School in Newport, Rhode Island. "We're now shooting visual. You know what to do."

"Roger that, Skipper," and he began to dial in a series of speed and course changes. This had also been worked out in advance, and Bigelow knew she could rely on her OOD to maneuver the ship properly. He was the smartest officer on board, and this complex maneuvering of the ship came easily to him.

For now, there was nothing for her to do but wait and worry. *Milwaukee*'s gun was forward on the fo'c'sle and could not shoot back through the ship's superstructure. So with her speed advantage, the ship would follow a zigzag course that would keep them ahead of the twenty-six-knot frigates but allow their only gun to engage the pursuing enemy. These same restrictions applied to the optical gun director that could not see back through the baffles created by the ship's mast and stack. But this maneuver made for noise and discomfort with the gun shooting back and close to the exposed bridge wings. It was not too bad in the pilothouse, but on the bridge wings it was deafening. They were running at close to forty knots and approximately thirty degrees left, then right, of a steady course of their pursuers. The OOD knew to adjust the course so the gun would bear and at a speed to keep the ship at nine thousand yards from the closest frigate—the maximum effective range of their gun. The gun could fire 220 rounds per minute, for a short period of time. The ship carried close to 1,100 rounds of various types, but 90 percent were high-explosive rounds. Her weapons officer knew to conserve ammunition to make good their escape yet to keep the North Korean frigates in *their* range to keep them following *Milwaukee*. All this should work, Bigelow reasoned. The North Korean frigates were following, and each passing moment put *Defender* and the South Korean minesweepers that much closer to safety. And the periodic change in course and speed was creating problems for the frigate gunners. *Yeah, this will work,* Kate told herself as she watched a 100 mm shell from one of the pursuing frigates splash a few hundred yards to port and just ahead of them, *unless we take a hit and can't keep this up.*

As President Wyatt Midkiff entered the White House Situation Room, his national security advisor, Trevor

Harward, was at the doorway to meet him. "Anything more since you called me, Trevor?"

"No, Mr. President. When I called you in the family quarters, I'd just arrived here and was beginning to assess the situation. The North Korean frigates were ordering *Milwaukee* to stop and prepare to be boarded." Harward paused and looked at his watch. "About twelve minutes ago, our LCS began taking fire from one or both of the frigates . . ."

"Taking fire!" the president exclaimed. "They weren't bluffing?"

"No, evidently they weren't," Harward replied as he began to walk toward the Sit Room watch floor. The president followed.

As they entered the small Sit Room watch floor, the Sit Room director, a Navy captain, signaled everyone there with the exception of his watch standers to clear the room.

"Mr. President, you can see the display here on your right," Harward began, aiming at the display with a small laser pointer. "Our ship, *Milwaukee,* is in international waters here in the Yellow Sea. The two North Korean frigates, here and here, have taken her under fire . . ."

"Has our ship been hit yet?" the president interrupted.

"No sir, not yet. *Milwaukee* has about a ten-knot speed advantage over the North Korean ships, so right now she's trying to return fire enough to threaten the frigates, stay a bit ahead of them, and count on the North Korean fire not being accurate enough. We know from earlier reports the skipper of the LCS is intent on distracting the North Koreans to give our mine-counter-measures ship, *Defender*—as well as the six South

Korean minesweeps—time to move east towards Inchon, where they'll be protected by South Korean units."

"How long will that take . . . until the other ships are safe, I mean?"

"Captain?" Harward asked, turning toward the Sit Room director.

"Mr. President, it's hard to say exactly. South Korea has substantial naval assets in and around Inchon, but of course they are trapped due to the mines those three North Korean corvettes sowed west of the harbor approaches. The South Koreans are scrambling aircraft to protect their minesweepers."

"And *Defender* and *Milwaukee* also, right, Captain?" Harward interrupted.

"Yes, sir, although we have no way of knowing that for certain."

"I assume our ship is seriously outgunned?" the president asked of no one in particular.

"Yes, sir," the Sit Room director replied. "At this stage it looks like *Milwaukee*'s captain is using speed and maneuver until Seventh Fleet or Seventh Air Force or other U.S. assets can either take out the North Korean frigates or drive them away."

"Is there any other help nearby? South Korea? Japan? I understood this was a multinational exercise."

The national security advisor gave the Sit Room director a measured look to ensure the man didn't respond.

"We're checking on that, Mr. President," Harward replied, then paused. "A moment in one of the conference rooms, sir? I'm sure the captain will keep us informed of developments. In the meantime, he'll put the tactical picture up in the conference room and we can follow it as we talk."

The president paused. "Certainly, Trevor, lead on."

Wyatt Midkiff was mildly annoyed Harward was pulling him out of the Sit Room abruptly. But he had worked with him long enough to know there must be a reason.

"Trevor?" the president began once they were seated in the conference room. The same tactical picture they saw on the watch floor was also displayed on the large LCD display at the front of the conference room.

"Mr. President, I thought some privacy would be best for the moment. The situation is confusing right now, but we will eventually get it sorted out. Of course, we're worried about our ship that has been taken under fire and for the lives of the captain and her crew."

"Her?"

Harward smiled. "We can talk about the changes that have occurred in the Navy since you served, but, yes, Mr. President. *Milwaukee* is commanded by Commander Kate Bigelow. She's been in command for almost fourteen months, and this is her second ship command. Right now, she appears to be doing everything possible to take evasive action while still, apparently, trying to distract the North Koreans long enough for all the sweeps to escape. As you know, Mr. President, those ships are basically defenseless."

"I know that, Trevor, but all I want to know is what we can do to help *Milwaukee*. Is there something intensely private about my trying to get a simple answer to that question?"

"Mr. President, we—and I mean the Secretary of Defense, the Secretary of State, and my staff—feel strongly we must only use U.S. forces to come to the aid of *Milwaukee*. North Korea's intentions are unknown. On the surface, it appears they just want to embarrass us—maybe even with an implicit okay from the Chinese—and disable or even capture *Milwaukee*. But maybe there's more here than meets the eye." Harward paused before continuing, measuring the president, trying to determine how he was processing what he was telling him.

"Go on, Trevor. Tell me more."

"We've briefed you recently on some of the major North Korean troop movements as well as the murder of Vice Marshal Sang Won-hong, deputy chief of the general staff of the KPA. Other moderates within their military hierarchy have been forced out for bogus reasons. For all we know, they could be baiting the South Koreans into attacking those frigates and then use that 'aggression' by the South to start a major military crisis on the peninsula, maybe even an invasion . . ."

"I take your point," Midkiff interrupted. "But we have American lives on the line. If your counsel is to make this a U.S.-only show to relieve our LCS, what are we doing about it—I mean right now?"

Harward placed his tablet—which already had a large-scale operational display pulled up—in front of the president and began to describe the U.S. response.

Aboard *Najin Four*, the captain was urging his chief engineer for more speed and his gunners, who were pouring forth a tremendous volume of ineffective fire, to shoot better. *Najin Three,* which for some unknown reason had a slight speed advantage over his ship, had drawn abreast of *Najin Four* and taken station a quarter mile to port. The captain of *Najin Four* was senior, and he had ordered his sister frigate to hold its relative position and not advance. Both captains knew they must find a way to stop the American ship. If it were to escape, then all this careful planning would be for nothing. More than that, the supreme leader and his senior generals of the Korean People's Army would think nothing of killing a sea captain who failed in his duty—along with his entire family. *So I must not fail.* The captain of the *Najin Three* was thinking much the same thing.

Back aboard *Milwaukee,* Jack O'Connor made his way to the bridge and stood next to Kate Bigelow. "You want to see me, Captain."

"You bet I do, XO," and she motioned her executive officer over to step out onto *Milwaukee*'s starboard bridge wing.

Once out on the bridge wing, Bigelow moved to within a foot of her exec. "All right, Jack," she began in a low, menacing voice. "Here's the deal. I'm going to talk, and you are going to listen without interruption. We're in a fight, and you directly challenged my orders on an open internal circuit. A lot of people on that circuit heard you, and by now it's all over the ship. How could you?" O'Connor started to reply, but she raised her hand to silence him. "Listen to me and listen carefully. We don't have time for this shit. You're supposed to run this ship, and I'm supposed to fight it. Right now, it's all about the fight. So what now? I want you to agree to go back into MCC and do your job per my instructions and keep your mouth shut regarding my decisions. If I want your input, I'll ask for it. Or I will have you escorted to your stateroom and put under guard." O'Connor just stood there, unable to hide his shock. "So if you agree to do as I've asked, I want you to step back, give me a parade-ground salute, and a loud, cheery, 'Aye, aye, ma'am.' Then get your butt back into MCC. And if you don't agree, I want to know it right now. I'm going to put you in hack and under guard. So what's it going to be, Jack?"

After only a moment's hesitation, he stepped back, rendered a salute, and said, "Aye, aye, ma'am!"

"Very well, XO. Carry on." And she turned her back to him and brought her glasses up again to inspect the two pursuing frigates.

While the situation was tense in the White House Situation Room, it was frenetic in command centers across multiple time zones. The need for information up, down, and across various chains of command was insatiable. Watch standers sorted through typically conflicting reports, fielded endless demands for information from their commanders, pulled information up on large-screen displays, and updated information on status boards.

Once conflicting information was sorted out and the operational and tactical picture stabilized, it became clear the fastest way to come to the relief of *Milwaukee* was to call on the Seventh Air Force. Army General

Everett Green, commander of U.S. Forces in Korea, picked up the command net and called Seventh Air Force Headquarters at Osan Air Base. Soon, units of the Fifty-first Fighter Wing were on the move.

Aboard *Milwaukee,* Kate Bigelow again looked at her watch. They had been running and gunning for close to two hours, and she was beginning to think they just might make it. She had just told the OOD to open the range to the North Korean frigates to 10,500 yards—the outer limit of their effective gun range, yet it would probably put them beyond the operational gun range of the North Korean frigates' 57 mm mounts. It was their 100 mm guns that worried her. One of their 57 mm rounds had crashed into the rear portion of the helo deck, but it had been a dud. Nonetheless, it had cut through a cable tier, a freshwater line, and had scared the hell out of one of the repair parties in an internal passageway. The round had made it through to the lower engineering spaces and had seemingly caused no further damage. But it had come to rest only after bouncing off one of the water-jet units. The unit continued to function but was now emitting a slight vibration. Another round, presumably a 100 mm high-explosive projectile, had landed close aboard to starboard and detonated. The explosion had damaged a seam on *Milwaukee*'s hull, and they were now taking on a small quantity of seawater, but it was nothing the pumps couldn't handle.

Grace Montgomery and her gun crew now had both frigates under fire, lobbing a few shells at one, then shifting to the other. She had reported hitting both ships, but they were still coming. Bigelow knew the frigates, being older and more primitive, could probably absorb more punishment than *Milwaukee*. Being newer and faster had its disadvantages. The LCS was built light and with a thin skin to increase speed. Its dependence on electronics, fiber optics, and computers made it more vulnerable to gunfire. And the LCS was not a true surface combatant. It was built to be versatile and to work close to shore and in restricted waters, but with blue-water Navy protection. It was never designed to slug it out with enemy frigates.

Suddenly, the whole ship rocked as a 100 mm round slammed into the helo hangar. *Milwaukee* seemed to shake it off and charge ahead, but they had been hit and hit hard.

Bigelow stepped into the pilothouse and stood behind the sailor manning the Main Propulsion Control and Monitoring System console. Her chief engineer was already there. "What's your status, Steve?"

Job one was to run, and speed was a priority. An engineering casualty would end it all. The reply was several long seconds in coming. "We seem to be intact, Skipper. Probably cracked a few fittings, and our rover is checking everything, but both diesels and both turbines are running within specs."

"Understood. Let me know if anything changes." The gun was still firing, so she assumed they were all right. "MCC, bridge. Everything okay there?"

It was Ashburn. "We lost a few displays, and one of our surface radars is down, but nothing we can't do without until it gets fixed."

Knowing her assistant engineer for damage control, or damage control assistant, would call her with a status update when he received a report from one of his on-scene damage-control parties, Bigelow paced the bridge impatiently. The DCA was a seasoned chief petty officer and had been in the Navy for over two decades. He could also be taciturn when pushed, so she waited. Then the call came.

"Bridge, DC Central."

"Bridge, go ahead, Parker."

"Cap'n, that round went into and through the hangar space, continued down into the mission module, and detonated right in the middle of the module. There was no one there, so all it did was fuck up a lot of MCM gear—beg pardon, ma'am. Some of the conex boxes holding a bunch of the mission module gear have a few shrapnel holes in them, but the mine gear took the brunt of the explosion. I'm glad I'm not signed for that gear."

"Any casualties?"

"One of the storekeepers took a little shrapnel, and there are some bumps and cuts. Doc Picard is attending to them. We dodged one this time, Skipper. How much longer?"

"I don't know. As long as it takes. Parker, let me know if there's any additional damage I should know about."

"Yes, ma'am. DCA, out."

She turned her attention to the screen in front of her junior officer of the deck, who was also in charge of navigation. "Skipper, we're now about fifteen miles south of Yeonpyeong Island, and we're running out of sea room. If we get much closer to the coast of North Korea, we'll come under their coastal batteries. If we're going to do an end run around these guys, we better do it soon." Bigelow glanced at her watch. They'd managed to keep on the run and keep the frigates in pursuit for just over two and a half hours.

"Okay, let's pass just to the southeast of Yeonpyeong, and then we'll swing west and make a dash to get out of range of these two clowns." She looked over to where her OOD was strapped into his chair. "Willie, when you come left for your next zig, hold that westerly heading and come up to full speed."

"Aye, aye, ma'am."

Milwaukee was still firing, but for the last several minutes there were none of the waterspouts around the ship there had been earlier. What was going on with the North Korean frigates? *Have they given up?* Bigelow wondered.

"Bridge, MCC."

"Bridge, aye. Go ahead, Eric."

"Captain, something's up. Both ships have shut down their surface- and air-search radars, and they've quit shooting. Skipper, you know this could mean"—and they both said it together—*"Missile launch!"*

Bigelow swung her binoculars around to the frigate on the starboard quarter just in time to see a blossom of white smoke from the solid rocket booster. It quickly flamed out, and the liquid-fueled rocket engine took over. Clearly, it was a big missile, and she watched it climb, nose over, and head for her ship. The missile was an old, first-generation cruise missile: a Safflower CSS-N-2. Its pedigree flashed through her mind—initial inertial guidance, then active radar homing on terminal, twelve hundred pounds of high explosive, Mach .8. That means it will be here in thirty seconds—now about twenty.

"Left full rudder; weapons officer, fire chaff, fire chaff; sound the collision alarm," but she knew there was time to do none of those things.

"Bridge, MCC. I have monopulse active radar on final. That missile is locked on to us!" Ashburn's voice was still conversational but with a hint of urgency.

After the second gong of the collision alarm, the Safflower cruise missile slammed into *Milwaukee*'s helo hangar. Because of the light skin of the hangar, the twelve-hundred-pound warhead, which could have broken the back of the ship, did not detonate. But as it passed through the hangar, the liquid fuel tank in the missile ruptured. Most of the propellant in the nearly full tank passed through the hangar along with the missile body, but not all of it. Enough spilled into the hangar and the weather decks to set the after part of *Milwaukee* ablaze.

The impact of the missile was like a loud clap of thunder. Bigelow felt the ship heel to starboard in a turn as the ship carried a full left rudder. Instinctively, she called out, "Rudder amidships!"

"Rudder amidships," the OOD answered, as if nothing had happened.

But something had. Bigelow stepped out to the starboard bridge wing to look down the flat metal side of the ship and saw that the whole aft portion of her ship was in flames. She felt *Milwaukee* begin to lose speed and rightly assumed they no longer had the two gas turbines online—only diesel power. With just the two diesels driving the four water-jet propulsion units, the ship would not be able to outrun the North Korean frigates. But that was now the least of her worries.

"Damage control, bridge, this is the captain. What do you have for me?"

"Bridge, DC central." Even now, there was a laconic tone in her damage control assistant's voice. "I have firefighting parties moving to the scene, but we have a lot of structural damage and a lot of fire. I have no idea whether or not we can control this fire. When I know, you'll know, Cap'n. Any chance we can slow down to keep the wind from driving these flames?"

"Not for a while. Do what you can, Parker, and keep me informed."

The gun on the fo'c'sle barked out another round, so at least they could still shoot. She turned to her chief engineer, still standing behind the sailor on the MPCMS console. "Engineer, what's your status?"

After a moment, he said, "We got problems, Skipper. That last hit further opened up that seam from the previous hit. We're taking on water, both from the rent in the side of the ship and water from the firefighting. The pumps aren't going to be able to stay up with this much water. My gas turbines are offline from the shock, and I'm getting a bad vibration from the port inboard water jet. If it gets any worse, I'll have to shut it down. Skipper, this ship wasn't designed to take this kind of punishment."

"Understood, Steve. Do what you can to keep us running and afloat. I'll get us out of this just as soon as I can."

She stepped back out onto the starboard bridge wing and glanced back along the side of the ship. The flames didn't seem as bad as they were a few moments ago, but they were still visible and spawning clouds of black smoke.

Bigelow moved right behind her JOOD, who was looking at the navigation display. "What's our nearest land?"

"Captain, it's the Yeonpyeong Island group. Closest land is Geodo or Little Yeonpyeong Island. We're about eight miles due south of it."

"Very well. Give the OOD a course to make for that island."

"Aye, aye, ma'am."

His national security advisor had constructed a short list of calls that needed to be made and made urgently. President Midkiff had called the president of South Korea and urged a hands-off approach to the crisis. The secretary of defense and secretary of state had called their respective counterparts in Japan and South Korea and had done the same. On the uniformed side, the U.S. chairman of the Joint Chiefs of Staff had called his South Korean Joint Chiefs counterpart. Now that those calls urging inaction had been made, it was left to the United States' theater commander to protect *Milwaukee* and keep the Navy warship from being captured or sunk by the North Koreans.

"You fool," the captain of *Najin Three* said over his secure circuit to the captain of *Najin Four*. "Our orders were to disable the American ship and either tow it into port or at least make the crew prisoners." He was junior to the captain of the *Najin Four,* but he was still of the same rank. And he would answer just as severely if they failed.

"What would you have us do," the senior captain replied, "let them escape? Would you like to explain *that* to our masters in Pyongyang? See, the American ship is on fire. Now we can overtake them and," he added with a chuckle, "offer assistance under our terms."

"But what if it explodes or sinks, then what?"

"We will deal with that if and when it occurs. Meanwhile, we will close on them and offer to help. I will come alongside to port. I suggest that you approach from starboard. We have them now."

The captains and crews of the two North Korean frigates were so engrossed in their closing on the American ship they failed to notice four black dots that dropped carefully from the overcast some three thousand yards astern of the frigates. The dots separated into pairs. The lead pair fell astern of one frigate and the second pair the other. Then each pair separated, one dot in the lead, the other in trail. As they closed on the frigates, the dots sprouted wings, and then huge air intakes for the jet engines mounted to the rear and high on their fuselages. By the time the radar operator on *Najin Four* saw the dots on his scope, a lookout on *Najin Three* reported there were four aircraft directly astern and closing fast. They were U.S. Air Force A-10 Thunderbolt II ground-attack aircraft from the Air Force Fifty-first Fighter

Wing at Osan. By coming in low and directly behind the two frigates in their radar blind spot, they had arrived virtually undetected.

The A-10 is an ungainly, heavily armored aircraft built around a GUA-8/A 30 mm Gatling-type cannon that can issue expended-uranium, armor-piercing bullets at a rate of seventy rounds per second. The Warthog, as it is affectionately known by the pilots who fly it and the ground troops who appreciate it, is a tank killer. Three inches of tank armor present no problem for the Warthog. The quarter-inch steel-plate construction of the two North Korean frigates was like punching through paper with a .22 caliber bullet. The bullets from each lead A-10 clawed into the aft superstructure of its assigned frigate and took down the masting and all the communications and radar-antenna arrays. The frigates were now deaf and blind. The trailing A-10s came in from behind at a slightly steeper angle and sent expended-uranium projectiles deep into the machinery and engineering spaces of the vessels. Both frigates began to lose headway. Then, recovering from their first pass, the Warthog pair that had just raked *Najin Three* from stern to stem wheeled around to set up a firing run on *Najin Four*. The other pair came around for a head-on pass at *Najin Three*. This time, the A-10 pilots sent their rounds into the lightly armored forward gun mounts, shredding the gun crews. Then, lifting their noses slightly and with a gentle kick of the rudder, first left and then right, they destroyed the bridges of the two ships, killing both captains and nearly all the bridge watch standers.

The carnage was unimaginable, the chaos complete. The ships lost internal lighting, and most of the emergency battle lanterns were disabled. When the damage control and medical teams began to move about the ships, they had to work through twisted corpses and dismembered body parts to get to the wounded. The ships and a third of their crews would never sail again.

The three Sariwon-class corvettes fared no better than *Najin Three* and *Najin Four*. They were ordered to remain on picket duty near the edge of the minefields they had sown. That order proved fatal. Each received a Tomahawk cruise missile dead amidships that broke each ship in half. They sank within minutes. Many crewmen perished on impact. Others died in the sealed tombs of their compartmented battle stations, feeling the air pressure increase as water poured into their sinking ship. Some died when a bulkhead gave way and they quickly drowned. A few made it to the bottom of the Yellow Sea and died slowly as they breathed the last of their trapped air. Those lucky enough to be blown overboard were taken by the relative mercy of a cold-water death. Almost all were taken by surprise. Only Lieutenant Commander Choe Dae-jung, who spent more time on his bridge that the other corvette captains, saw the inbound missile that took out *Won Do*. His last conscious thought was why it had taken the Americans so long.

Aboard *Milwaukee,* Kate Bigelow was standing by her bridge chair in the pilothouse and dealing with damage reports and the fire that still burned unabated on the aft part of the ship. Her chief engineer and his damage-control assistant had confirmed they could either deal with the fire or deal with the flooding, but not both. The pumps could either get water to the fire-fighting teams or dewater the ship—one or the other. *Sink or burn,* Bigelow thought, and as she did, a plan formed in her mind.

She turned to her chief engineer. "Steve, get that fire under control and give me as much speed as you can. We're going to run for shore."

"Aye, aye, ma'am."

As she turned, her XO was there with a grim smile on his face. "Come take a look at this, Captain."

They made their way out to the port bridge wing, where he pointed to the two frigates on the horizon. Through their binoculars, they saw neither frigate was making a bow wave and one of them was issuing a dark shroud of smoke.

"The Air Force finally got here," O'Connor said. They watched as the A-10s flashed overhead, waggled their wings, and disappear to the east. "So now that we might not be shot out of the water, and before we sink, I recommend that we begin abandon-ship procedures. It's the sensible thing to do."

"Perhaps. For now, we stay with the ship, Jack. You said you visited the Naval Academy once when they were trying to recruit you to play football. Remember that flag on the far wall of Memorial Hall at the Academy?"

"You mean the 'Don't Give Up the Ship' banner."

"That's the one. Make all preparations to abandon ship, but not now and not until I give the order."

"But Captain . . . ," and he got no further. The look on her face all but told him she neither needed nor wanted any rationalization from him.

"Aye, aye, Captain." And he left the bridge.

She stepped back into the pilothouse and stood behind her OOD. "How far, Willie?"

"The main island is about six miles dead ahead."

"Very well." She looked ahead and saw a trace of land on the horizon under what seemed to be a flat band of haze or smoke. On the screen in front of her OOD, the speed indicator showed fifteen knots—now fourteen. She turned toward her chief engineer, still standing behind her MPCMS console. "Steve, status report?"

"Good news and bad news, Skipper. The fire is not out, but we're bringing it under control. But with the rent in the hull and the fire-fighting efforts, we're taking on a lot of water. It won't be too much longer until the entire plant is underwater."

"Steve, I need another half hour at this speed. Can you give it to me?"

"No guarantees, Skipper, but we'll do our best."

"Understood, but let me know if things change. I need that time and that speed."

She turned around, took two steps, and eased herself up into her bridge chair and took a deep breath, aware that while the bridge watch standers were tending to their duties, they frequently looked in her direction. They knew that their ship was dying and that she held their fate in her hands. A messenger appeared by her elbow. He was the bridge messenger, a young seaman she had sent to the ship's wardroom turned surgery suite. During general quarters or action stations, the wardroom was converted to an aid station to marshal and treat casualties. The seaman peered out with wide eyes from underneath his battle helmet, and his color wasn't good. *None of this is good,* Bigelow thought.

"What do you have, Robbins?"

"Sir, er, ma'am, Chief Picard sends her respects. So far, we have eight dead and about a dozen wounded. She has converted the ship's office into a makeshift m-morgue and is using the officers' staterooms f-f-for wounded who have been treated." He took a breath and started to speak, but fell silent. He was white as a ghost, and there was a sheen of sweat on his forehead.

"It's okay, Robbins, you're doing fine. Just tell me what the chief said." Bigelow laid her hand gently on the sailor's shoulder. *He's just a kid,* she found herself thinking, *I was still at the Naval Academy when I was his age.*

"She said that four of the wounded are critical and cannot be moved. The others c-can be moved, but she recommends th-they not be. And she says there are more wounded coming in . . . ma'am."

"Good report, Robbins. Go stand over there; I may have another job for you." She was digesting this casualty report when Lieutenant Ashburn's voice burst into her ears.

"Bridge, MCC."

"Go ahead, Eric."

"There is an artillery exchange between South Koreans on Yeonpyeong Island and the North Korean coastal batteries. We may not want to attempt a landing there."

"Very well, stand by." She slipped from her bridge chair and stepped behind the junior officer of the deck. "What are our options, Dennis? I need to park this ship just as soon as I can." She did her best to keep her tone light, but there was an urgency not lost on her JOOD.

"Well, if we don't make for the main island, there is Chedo Island that's a little closer. But there's no harbor there, or not one that could handle us."

"Not looking for a harbor, Dennis. I need a good beach gradient where I can get this ship hard aground before we sink."

He cast her an incredulous look, then turned back to the LCD display and the navigation picture in front of him. "Then I don't recommend Chedo as it has a steep gradient and a lot of submerged rocks offshore."

"How about this one?"

The JOOD peered closer. "Kujido Island." He pulled up another screen and read the navigation summary. "Good gradient and no offshore obstacles. And it's uninhabited." He quickly pulled up a local guide to mariners on another screen. "Used to be a crab-processing plant there, but it was abandoned some time ago. About three hundred yards long and a hundred yards across the northern tip. It looks to be an emergent sea mount. It's about a mile and a half south of Yeonpyeong Island. Might keep us out of the artillery fan of the North's coastal artillery."

"Let's hope. Give me a course to the southern tip of that . . . what's it called?"

"Kujido."

"Right. This is the captain," she announced to the

pilothouse. "I have the con." Kate Bigelow reached over her OOD's shoulder and dialed in a course to point *Milwaukee* toward the little speck of land in the northern Yellow Sea. Then she picked up the handset to the 1MC, the ship's general announcing system.

"This is the captain speaking. In a few minutes, we are going to beach the ship on a small, uninhabited South Korean island. I'll put us ashore as gently as I can, but prepare for the impact of the grounding. We'll stay with the ship as long as we can, but we may be forced to abandon ship at any time and go ashore. You've all performed splendidly, and I'm proud of you. For right now, remain at your stations, do your duty, and this will all be over soon. God bless each of you and God bless *Milwaukee*. That is all."

The fire was all but out; however, *Milwaukee* was noticeably down by the stern when Kate Bigelow nudged the LCS ashore on the southern tip of Kujido Island. While she did her best to touch her ship down with bare steerageway, the sound of metal grinding on rock was deafening and unnerving. As the ship scrapped the bottom of the seafloor, it sounded to her as if the hounds of Hades were being released. Only one of her two diesels still functioned. The ship ground to a halt at a forty-five-degree angle to the rocky beach, port side to, and took on a permanent fifteen-degree list to starboard. The stern, still in deeper water than the bow, continued to settle into the seabed. With her ship hard aground, Bigelow left her OOD in charge of the bridge and, in the company of Master Chief Wilbur Crabtree, began an inspection of her ship. Her first stop was the wardroom-surgery suite, where Chief Carol Picard and the corpsmen tended to the wounded.

Aboard the Seventh Fleet flagship, USS *Blue Ridge,* pierside in Yokosuka, Japan, Vice Admiral Ed Bennett stared at the cryptic message on his computer screen. It read:

> *HARD AGROUND ON THE SOUTHERN TIP*
> *OF KUJIDO ISLAND. SHIPBOARD FIRES*
> *EXTINGUISHED AND MAINTAINING*
> *AUXILIARY POWER. SURFACE SEARCH*
> *RADAR AND MAIN BATTERY FUNCTIONAL;*
> *ALL OTHER SYSTEMS NOT OPERATIONAL.*
> *EIGHT DEAD, SEVENTEEN WOUNDED,*
> *THREE MISSING. WILL REMAIN WITH SHIP*
> *BUT MAKING ALL PREPARATIONS TO*
> *ABANDON SHIP AS SITUATION DICTATES.*
> *BIGELOW COMMANDING.*

Bennett then flicked to another message from Seventh Air Force that detailed the downing of two A-10 ground-attack aircraft over the Yellow Sea by Chinese-made North Korean air-launched PL-8 missiles. The PL-8 was not a terribly sophisticated missile, but then the Mach 3.5 missile didn't have to be to take down a relatively defenseless A-10. And it served to remind the fleet commander of the dilemma facing him with the stranded *Milwaukee.* Any aircraft sent to relieve the crew of *Milwaukee* would be flying into one of the most deadly air-defense envelopes in the world. If there was to be a rescue, it would be seaborne rescue—a fleet action. And when ships moved into an area contested by land-based air, the fleet often ended up on the short end of the exchange. It was true for *Pueblo* in 1968 and it was true for *Milwaukee* now.

He pressed the button on his intercom. "Yes, Admiral?"

"Tell the chief of staff I want a meeting of all department heads in the conference room in five minutes."

"Aye, aye, sir."

"And have ops contact *Ronald Reagan* strike group ops officer. Get them headed for the Yellow Sea at flank speed. I'll have more for the strike-group commander. Have him contact me on the battle net."

"Yes, sir."

Chase Williams had not left the Op-Center command center since his watch team alerted him that a U.S. Navy combatant was in a running gun battle with North Korean ships. Reports were coming in too quickly for him to pause and reflect on the wisdom of sending Brian Dawson and Hector Rodriguez, as well as Major Mike Volner and his JSOC team, downrange the day before, during the early stages of the unfolding crisis. As he monitored the situation, he reflected on his former uniformed career and, specifically, his three years as the Pacific Command commander. He knew the geography and the order of battle of the forces involved. But he did not yet know how *Milwaukee* was faring in the duel with the North Korean ships, nor did he know the intentions of the North Koreans. So he had no way of yet knowing how Op-Center might be able to help or if it could help at all.

Some of that uncertainty was clarified as Roger McCord and Aaron Bleich appeared, seemingly out of nowhere. "Boss, we have something for you," McCord began.

"I'll take anything you fellas have."

"Aaron?" McCord prompted.

The Geek Tank leader stepped next to Williams and held up his secure iPad, showing him the message that had appeared on the Seventh Fleet commander's screen minutes ago. "We just got this off the Seventh Fleet JWICS net. Looks like *Milwaukee* is hard aground on Kujido Island in the Yellow Sea . . ."

"Hard aground? Make me a little smarter on where Kujido Island is, Aaron."

Bleich scrolled his iPad as he pulled up the geographic display. "Here it is, boss. It's part of the Yeonpyeong Island group." Bleich continued, "It's about fifty miles west of Inchon . . ."

"How close is it to North Korea?" Williams interrupted.

"Less than eight miles, sir."

"I wonder what the hell the skipper was doing there." Williams mused to no one in particular.

"We've been following the live radio feeds," McCord interjected. "When the North Korean ships appeared on scene and made for the ships in the mine-hunting exercise, *Milwaukee*'s skipper took on the two North Korean frigates so the South Korean ships and one of ours, the MCM ship *Defender,* could make good their escape.

The *Milwaukee*'s only option was to run to the north. Tactically, it seems she did the right thing."

"She?"

"Yes, sir," McCord continued. "*Milwaukee* is commanded by a Commander Kate Bigelow."

Williams paused to consider what his intel team had just told him. Then he was all action. "Okay, Roger, Aaron, good report. Aaron, let's turn up the gain on what I asked you to do a little while ago. I want you both to get upstream of the immediate action reports and deep dive into why North Korea attacked these ships and what else they may be up to. Brian is the senior man downrange, so I'd like to have him give us his assessment. I don't know if we'll get the call on this one yet, but let's alert our JSOC team at Fort Bragg and let them know we may need additional assets to support Major Volner and the team he has in place."

As his team moved to carry out his instructions, Chase Williams left the watch floor and headed for his office. He had calls to make.

Roger McCord followed Aaron Bleich back to the Geek Tank, and now the two men sat in companionable silence, considering the task ahead. Then McCord spoke, "The boss has given us a big assignment. Given what we know now, we have to get out in front of this and find out why the North Koreans did this."

"He started me working on this a little while ago," Bleich replied, "and it's not just the 'why,' but the 'why now?' And why did they seem to want to attack *Milwaukee*? Why not the Korean minesweepers or *Defender*?"

"That's what we need to know. Could be that they just wanted an American ship. Could be that given the poor weather conditions, *Defender* just got taken for another Korean minesweeper. But until we find that out, we're operating with one hand tied behind our backs."

"It would seem to me," Bleich continued, "the North Koreans are trying to precipitate a crisis to put our forces in the region in check. Taking an American crew hostage would do that. But why? What do they want from us? Or the South Koreans?" Bleich knew it was his job to find the answers to these questions, not McCord's. He also knew he had to amp up his game. And for the first time he could remember in the longest time, he worried about failure.

CHAPTER SEVENTEEN

KUJIDO ISLAND IN THE
YEONPYEONG ISLAND GROUP

November 13, 1615 Korea Standard Time

Kate Bigelow stood on the bridge of *Milwaukee* in relative silence. With the main engines shut down and the big forced-draft blowers quiet, there were only the faint vibrations from the generators. And there was the creaking of the hull. As the stern of the ship continued to settle into the seabed, the hull and the superstructure were being stressed in such a way that they issued a continuing series of squeaks and groans. It was at once eerie and unsettling. Her chief engineer had said they would continue to settle and that there was little chance that the ship would roll onto its side like the Italian cruise liner *Costa Concordia,* but there were no guarantees. No LCS had ever been beached in this fashion and at this angle. Already, there was a slick of diesel and gas-turbine fuel surrounding the stern of the *Milwaukee. My ship is broken,* Bigelow admitted to herself. *But it had done its job—fought off two frigates and brought us to the relative safety of this islet.*

"Captain, engineer." Bigelow was no longer on her headphones, and now communicated with other spaces in the ship over the IVOX system, which, miraculously, was still working.

"Captain, aye. Go ahead, Steve."

"Skipper, I'm down here in the plant surveying the damage. I can give us power for no more than a half hour. The water's creeping up on the auxiliary generator, and it'll soon be offline. We're working to cross-connect with the two portable gensets, but they will not be able to carry the load of the guns and the radars. About all we'll be able to give you are lights and power to the bridge, MCC, and radio central. Sorry, Skipper."

"Okay, Steve, but I want you to give priority to the wardroom and the forward officer staterooms, where we're caring for the wounded. And let me know when you're ready to shift the load to the portables."

"Yes, ma'am. Engineering, out."

Bigelow took in a quick inventory of her situation. As when the ship was in a running gun battle with the frigates, there was not a lot for her to do at the moment. The department heads, the junior officers, and the senior petty officers were seeing to the care of the ship, the care of the wounded, and the many details that would accompany the welfare of the crew, should they remain aboard or have to abandon ship. She had been to Korea several times, and the weather was always like it was today—bad. The temperature was forty-two degrees and would get close to freezing before morning.

The blowing sea mist and the low ceiling were projected to continue for the next several days. She was most concerned about the next twelve hours. They had been sending situation reports out to Seventh Fleet every half hour. That made three since she had run *Milwaukee* aground. Her attention was captured by a bulky figure entering through the rear hatchway to the pilothouse. He was swathed in foul-weather gear, and there was an unlit cigar clenched in his teeth. A knitted watch cap was pulled low across his forehead.

"Master Chief, how was your shore leave?" Right after the grounding, Bigelow had sent her navigator and command master chief, Master Chief Wilbur Crabtree, ashore with two sailors from the combat systems department to scout the island. She had no intention of abandoning ship for this piece of rock, but then she had to inventory all her options and plan for alternative courses of action. That, too, was part of her job description.

"Well, Skipper," Crabtree began, removing the stogie from his mouth. As an afterthought, he pulled off the watch cap to reveal a bald stubble. "I can see why no one's living on this piece of turf. Its gravel and volcanic rock with scrub brush, lichen, and a lot of seagull shit. Just over the berm, there's a concrete structure that looks like it was an old fish cannery. It's cold, wet, and deserted, but the structure is rock solid. Looks like some kind of World War Two coastal-bunker complex. It smells gawd-awful. I'd hate to spend the night there. It's damp as hell and cold as a well digger's ass, excusing the language, ma'am."

Bigelow considered this. She knew the master chief was from West Virginia and a small mining town near Martinsville. He would know the temperature of a well digger's ass. "Let's hope none of us have to spend the night there, Master Chief. But if we were to have to, I want you to begin assembling everything we might need to do just that. And if it comes to it, we'll have to take our wounded with us, so let Chief Picard know that as well."

"Aye, aye, ma'am. Oh, and from what I could see from the top of the small rise on this end of the island, it looks like the big island off to the northeast is under shore-battery fire from the mainland. Lots of smoke. And it seems they're shooting back as I could hear artillery fire. Near as I could tell, it was outgoing."

"Thanks again, Master Chief. Carry on."

After he left the pilothouse, she dialed up the IVOX. "Radio, bridge."

"Radio central, aye, ma'am."

She recognized the voice of her chief information technology specialist, who was the senior rating in the ship's communications center. "Petty Officer Matheson, how're you making out there in radio?"

"As well as can be expected, Skipper. We came off-line after the missile strike for about fifteen minutes, but we're now transmitting and receiving on all normal frequencies and guarding those same freqs as we were before the hit."

"Good to hear. Now I want you to prepare for what might happen if for some chance we lose the load or can't get power to you."

"Roger that, ma'am."

"And, Matheson, I want you to start thinking about what you might want to take along if we're forced to abandon ship. If that happens, I will still need to communicate, and I'll want to talk on an encrypted basis. Got that?"

"Skipper, are we going to abandon ship?"

"Not yet, but if we have to, it will be critical that we have secure comms with Seventh Fleet, the *Reagan* strike group, and commander, U.S. Forces, Korea. Think you can manage that?"

There was a pause. Then, "Not sure, Skipper, but I'll do my best. And that best may just be an encrypted Iridium satellite phone."

"That's fine; I'll take your best. Just make sure I can talk, talk secure, and there's someone on the other end who can hear me. And make sure we have plenty of battery backup."

"Aye, aye, ma'am."

"Oh, and how are we for the destruction of crypto equipment and classified documents?"

"The combat systems officer and I began assembling the docs and the gear right after the North Koreans opened fire. The incendiaries are in place and await your orders. Might burn the ship up along with it, but all classified materials will be disposed of completely."

"Thanks, Matheson. Let's hope it doesn't come to that."

Fifteen minutes after she rang off with radio, the first North Korean artillery shells began to land on the north side of Kujido Island.

* * *

At the Pentagon, it was morning, and hundreds of staffers on the Joint Staff had been working at a frenetic pace since the first shots were fired in the Yellow Sea. There were many differing opinions as to how to rescue the LCS crew. The Joint Staff had heard from the subordinate regional commanders, and none of them had a ready plan for quick action. Those that might work put forces at risk from North Korea's deadly inventory of antiship and anti-air missiles *and* risk the lives of *Milwaukee*'s crew. The Joint Staff debated the pros and cons of an expeditious rescue versus one that might have a higher probability of success. When the chairman of the joint chiefs asked the Pacific theater commander for a rescue plan to extract the LCS crew, he was told there simply wasn't one; the crew would have to hang on indefinitely. The chairman considered this, then pulled in a small cadre of his closest advisors to consider how to tell the president and the secretary of defense their senior military advisor had no options for them.

But beyond giving his political masters the grim assessment, the chairman of the joint chiefs of staff had an equally difficult task. The president, the secretary of defense, and the secretary of state had all spoken with their South Korean counterparts and felt they had been successful in urging restraint and convincing their close ally to let the United States rescue its own crew. He was much less successful in his discussions with General Kwon Oh-Sung, chairman of the South Korean Joint Chiefs of Staff. Kwon reminded him that the North Korean ships had attacked a flotilla of ships under South

Korean command. Kwon had even called him "hesitant" and had all but given him an ultimatum to rescue the crew or he would have his South Korean forces do it. Most troubling, the last two times he had tried to call his South Korean counterpart, Kwon refused to take the call because he was "too busy with operational matters."

Eight hundred miles due south of where *Milwaukee* sat stranded on Kujido Island, Brian Dawson pushed himself away from the table in his makeshift office in hangar 17 at Kadena Air Base, Okinawa, with a sour expression on his face. "Think I need to stretch my legs a bit," he announced to no one in particular.

"Me too," Hector Rodriguez, who was seated across the table, said, adding, "and I'll be available if you need another lesson."

"Yeah, right." Dawson snorted. Rodriguez had just taken three games of cribbage from him, and one of those was a skunk. They played for a nickel a point, and it was starting to add up. Worse, he knew Chase Williams would find out about this and remind him he had cautioned him against taking on Rodriguez.

The JSOC team and their gear were strewn about the hangar in an orderly fashion, and the team members were well into their isolation protocol. They would not communicate with the outside world, nor would the outside world, namely friends and family, communicate with them until they were tasked with a mission or recalled. The operators and the support cadre were variously reading, sleeping, or working out in the makeshift gym they had created in the corner of the hangar. For food, there were multiple cases of MRE rations, but these were veteran special operators, and most of them had brought along their own stores of food and drink. And they were ready. On a moment's notice they could be kitted up and out the door. And since the nature of a potential mission was still undefined, they could be out that door and undertaking any number of operational configurations.

"Hey, Mr. Dawson, I mean Brian. Mr. Williams would like to speak with you and Hector. I have him standing by on a secure VTC link."

Dawson and Rodriguez followed Jesse Carpenter to the small cubicle he had set up, which functioned as the Op-Center detachment communications center. It was Williams's policy to have a video teleconferencing ability whenever possible, even at a forward operating base. There, they found Chase Williams waiting for them on a twenty-eight-inch, flat, high-resolution LCD screen. He was sitting at his desk at Op-Center headquarters looking at *his* screen and into the small camera eye set into the top of the casing just above the screen.

"How are things downrange?" Williams asked. "You all up and running okay?"

"As you might expect, sir," Dawson replied. "We have our own space, and we're pretty much self-contained. The locals are curious but compliant. Mike Volner and his troops are standing by to stand by, as are we. Any more news?"

"The good news is *Defender* and the South Korean minesweepers managed to reach Inchon safely. The *Mil-*

waukee is hard aground on Kujido Island. A flight of A-10s out of Osan managed to severely cripple both North Korean frigates, but they managed to splash two of the A-10s, so we have a real shooting war going. Admiral Bennett, the Seventh Fleet commander, is reluctant to bring his ships to within range of North Korean land-based air since they have overwhelming airpower on that part of the Korean Peninsula to say nothing of a highly sophisticated air defense. And I agree with him. We'd be feeding his strike group into a shredder. So, for now, that LCS and the crew are on South Korean soil, but they are, in effect, hostages of the North Koreans."

"Can the North Koreans get to our people?" This time it was Rodriguez.

"Perhaps," Williams responded, "but we will make it hard for them. The main Yeonpyeong Island is well fortified by 155 mm artillery, capable of reaching the mainland and covering the island where *Milwaukee* is aground. Admiral Bennett will soon have an airborne combat air patrol at the limits of the North Korean SAM envelope. And we will have constant drone surveillance of the area before long. If the North Koreans come out with any kind of surface force, we'll know about it and can respond."

"So it's a Mexican standoff," Dawson said. Williams nodded on-screen. "But, boss, *why* are they doing this? This is a big gamble, even for the wacky North Koreans."

"That's something we're working on, Brian. We'll keep looking for what's behind all this. For now, the crew of *Milwaukee* are hostages, not POWs. If we can find out why they tried to capture them in the first place, it might help us to get them out of there. And if you have any bright ideas, I'd like to hear them."

After Williams's image faded from the screen, Dawson, Rodriguez, and Carpenter sat in silence. Then Rodriguez rose and stepped over to the coffee service Carpenter had laid out in his small cubicle. It was an expensive drip-grind setup, complete with a custom dark Sumatra blend.

"Not bad, Carpenter," he murmured as he sipped it carefully, "not bad at all." Then, turning to Dawson, he asked, "So, what do you make of all this?"

"I don't know," Dawson replied, helping himself to some coffee. "Kim Jong-un is crazy, but he usually does crazy things for a reason. But whatever it is, there doesn't seem to be a play for us. It looks like it's going to be a blue-water Navy show and it's going to get messy." He paused in reflective silence, then said, "Jesse, this is damn good coffee. We need you with us on these flya-ways more often."

Carpenter shrugged off the compliment, and, after another thoughtful silence, he spoke quietly. "Sir, I mean Brian, if I understand this right, the crew of the Navy ship is, in effect, hostage to the North Koreans and are, in all probability, just pawns in some game." Both Daw-son and Rodriguez nodded. "And if there were some way we could sneak them safely off that island, then it would be a game changer, right?"

"That's right." He now had their full attention.

"Well, I don't know if I mentioned it, but I have a brother in the Navy. He's an officer and a team leader with the SEALs. Specifically, he's with the SDV team—

the team that operates their SEAL delivery vehicles. And I don't know if you know this, but they have a detachment here, over at the White Beach Naval Facility. Now, it's just a thought, but here's an idea on how we might pull this off."

Carpenter spoke for the next ten minutes with Dawson and Rodriguez drinking in every word. "So there it is," he concluded. "It's just an idea, but it just might work. And most of what we will need is here on Okinawa or can be staged here. If you can find me a jeep, I could run over there and check it out."

"Even better," Dawson said, taking out his cell phone, "let's see if we can find us a helicopter. I'll even go with you. We'll let Hector hold down the fort here and guard the coffeepot."

Rodriguez frowned but said nothing. He did go for more coffee.

From Pacific Command headquarters on down, there was feverish activity to move assets into position to support all political and military options. The primary at-sea operational force was the USS *Ronald Reagan* carrier strike group, now steaming at flank speed for the Yellow Sea and Korea Bay. The USS *Bonhomme Richard* with a Navy–Marine Corps expeditionary strike group sortied from Sasebo, Japan, with an augmented Marine Corps–battalion landing team. Selected submarines in the western Pacific were being rerouted for the Yellow Sea and the Sea of Japan. On the U.S. west coast, additional strike groups made preparations to sortie and head for the area.

CHAPTER EIGHTEEN

KUJIDO ISLAND IN THE
YEONPYEONG ISLAND GROUP

November 13, 1830 Korea Standard Time

From the starboard bridge wing of *Milwaukee,* Kate Bigelow watched as the two big Zodiacs, under the supervision of Master Chief Wilbur Crabtree, shuttled personnel from the ship to the rocky shore. There were bundles of supplies in each shuttle, but the priority was on the crew. Once they were safely ashore, they could send back teams to gather provisions—if the ship was still there. *Milwaukee* had a fifteen-degree starboard list, which made getting people and supplies over the side a little easier. Ashore, there was an orderly file of the ship's company in helmets and foul-weather jackets making their way across the gravel beach and over the berm to the abandoned cannery.

An hour earlier, artillery rounds began to drop around the island and had begun to range closer to *Milwaukee.* For a while, none had come closer than two hundred yards, but the whistle and boom of the incoming shells terrified the captain and her crew. For these sailors, it was their first artillery barrage, and it was terrifying. Then a round landed on the beach just twenty yards off *Milwaukee*'s port quarter, sending a wave of rocky shards pinging along the side of the ship. No one was hurt, but everyone on the weather decks dove for cover. Only the threats of Master Chief Crabtree and the senior petty officers got the crewmen up and moving again. That was when Kate Bigelow decided it was too risky to remain aboard *Milwaukee*. She had to move her crew ashore to the abandoned cannery.

Now on the port wing of the bridge, Bigelow felt the pressure wave of the shell and singing of rocks as they rippled along the side of the ship. She was rooted in fear, afraid to move, afraid to breathe. *My God, I can't take this.* She might have remained there immobile longer had her XO not appeared at her elbow.

"Status?" she managed, trying to sound normal.

"About three-quarters of the crew are ashore, including most of the wounded. There are two Chief Picard says just cannot be moved. She's asking to stay behind to tend to them. I told her we'd make that determination when the rest of the crew was off the ship. When everyone's in the shelter ashore, the master chief will begin the supply-shuttle runs."

"Very well. How're things ashore, Jack?"

"It's pretty Spartan, but the structure is solid reinforced concrete, like it was built to withstand a tsunami or something. The crew's scared, Captain, and this artillery is not helping."

O'Connor's reminding her of the crew seemed to

bolster her. "We're all scared, Jack, including me. I want you ashore and at the cannery organizing things there. You'll be in charge until I get there. And, Jack, good job in getting things prepared and everyone off the ship."

"Understood, ma'am. I'll see you ashore." And because it somehow seemed the thing to do, he offered her a salute, which she returned. "Good luck, Captain."

"And to you, Jack. I'll be off with the last shuttle. Hold down the fort until I get there."

The artillery rounds continued to fall. It was only a matter of time before they caught one of them. *I'm on my own,* she thought, *and help is not going to be arriving anytime soon.* Now that they were hard aground, leaving the ship for cover ashore was their only option.

There was little left for her to do on the bridge. The ship was dead but for the battery-powered emergency internal lighting. One of the portable generators was being wrestled ashore while the other was still aboard to service the wardroom turned casualty center. She had just left the pilothouse, headed for the wardroom, when an enemy artillery shell struck the bow just forward of the 57 mm gun. The explosion unseated the gun mount and blew off a portion of the port bow. Those still on board and moving about the ship, like Kate Bigelow, were thrown to the deck by the impact. For those few still aboard, all was darkness and terror.

While Kate Bigelow struggled to her feet and shakily made her way on down to the wardroom and what had become the surgery suite on *Milwaukee,* the Air Force H-60 Blackhawk helicopter carrying Brian Dawson and

Jesse Carpenter set down gently on a vacant stretch of concrete near a corrugated metal building at the end of the pier in the early evening hours. It was a nondescript building like many along the waterfront at the White Beach naval complex. What *was* different was that this building had unusually large hangarlike sliding doors. The sign at the personnel entrance read SEAL DELIVERY TEAM ONE, OKINAWA DETACHMENT.

"Sir, you want us to keep turning or shut down?"

"Go ahead and shut her down, Captain," Dawson said into the intercom mic. "We might be a while."

Before they left Kadena for the short ride to the Navy base, Dawson had managed to get a call through to Chase Williams, who in turn put in a call to the duty officer at the U.S. Special Operations Command at MacDill Air Force Base in Tampa, Florida. At selected operational, component, and geographic combatant commands, Williams had protocols set in place that any request, within reason, would be executed immediately with follow-on notifications through normal command and administrative channels. The U.S. Special Operations Command was one of those commands.

The duty petty officer stepped outside the hangar entrance to meet the helo's arrival. He was dressed in swim trunks, sneakers, and a utility blouse and cover. He came to attention and saluted.

"Afternoon, sir. We just got a call from higher headquarters to expect you. The detachment commander, Lieutenant Denver, is over on the other side of the base. I just spoke with him, and he'll be here in a few minutes. Would you like to come inside?"

The open bay of the hangar was bathed in florescent lighting. The painted and polished concrete floor looked like something out of a high-end NASCAR mechanic bay. There were tool trolleys with sliding drawers, stands of metered test equipment, and an intricate overhead traveling crane system. In the middle of the hangar on custom designed mobile cradles were two fat black torpedolike minisubs, complete with bow and stern planes, and two propellers bisected by a finlike rudder. They were just over twenty feet in length and had the look of slumbering hippos.

"These things look a little small," Dawson said quietly to Carpenter.

"Not these, sir. These are the Mark 8 boats. They're the wet, tactical submersibles. We want to see if they have one of the advanced dry minisubs available."

"There's my officer," the SEAL petty officer announced. "Give me a minute to brief him, and he'll be right with you."

Following what Dawson and Carpenter took to be an animated discussion between the two SEALs, the detachment commander approached them. He was dressed in faded blue jeans, a 49ers sweatshirt, shower shoes, and tattered ball cap with an unreadable logo.

"Gentlemen, I'm Lieutenant Tom Denver." He offered a firm handshake to both. "Excuse the attire, but I wasn't expecting you. My petty officer tells me that you're here with command blessing, both from the U.S. Special Operations Command and the Naval Special Warfare Command. But it might help if you tell me just who you're with and how you think we might be able to help you."

The two SEALs and the two Op-Center men retired to a corner of the hangar, where Dawson and Carpenter were offered coffee. The four sat on folding chairs around a pedestal table. Denver and Petty Officer Collins drank bottled water while Dawson gave them a crash course on Op-Center, an update on the situation in the northern Yellow Sea, and the plight of the crew of *Milwaukee*.

"So we have a stranded crew under the guns of the North Koreans," Dawson concluded, "with no way to rescue them without a major and costly fleet action, and that action just might put them at further risk. Jesse here thought you might have a clandestine way to get to the island and rescue them, but"—he looked at the Mark 8 submersibles—"I'm not sure these craft are capable of meeting our needs. Do you have anything bigger?"

Denver was quiet for several moments and then turned to his petty officer. "Collins, could you go over to the nav locker and dig out a chart of the northern Yellow Sea?" Then he turned to Dawson and Carpenter. "You're right; the Mark 8s are too small and too cold for what you have in mind. But we do have another option. There's the Advanced SEAL Delivery System, or ASDS. It was a program to develop a dry minisub for use by SEALs—a boat that had a range and on-station loitering capability well in excess of the wet submersibles. The program was canceled due to cost overruns and reliability issues. The boat was, and is, a maintenance pig. We kept a single boat from the program to use as a test bed and to work on technologies that could support future dry-submersible craft and operations. It's still a prototype boat, but we've got most of the bugs worked out. But it's a dry boat, and it can carry up to twenty SEALs or, in this case, twenty evacuees."

Dawson looked around. "But where is it?"

"It's in a hangar on Ford Island in Pearl Harbor." The disappointment showed on Dawson's face, but Denver continued. "But the boat, in theory, is air transportable by C-17. And Kadena has the longest runways of any base in the Pacific. The ASDS can be piggybacked on a Los Angeles–class nuclear submarine. Can we use the ASDS to evacuate the LCS crew on that island? Maybe. Collins and I and the ASDS crew from Hawaii have some serious planning to do before we can give you an answer to that. There are a lot of ifs and maybes that have to be worked out. One of those is the getting it here and the other is the availability of a Los Angeles–class submarine to get the ASDS to the operational area." Denver paused, looking from Carpenter to Dawson. "You two seem to have a lot of pull; you sure got my commanders to move quickly enough in getting you cleared and into our facility here. Think you have the juice to whistle up a C-17 and a nuclear attack submarine?"

Collins arrived with a chart of the Yellow Sea, and the four of them pored over it. "In answer to your question," Dawson replied, "if you think there's even a chance you and your ASDS can get that crew off that island, then you'll get your aircraft and your submarine, and you'll get them sooner rather than later."

At the White House, President Midkiff met nearly non-stop with his national security staff and his senior military advisors. For the moment, there was nothing to do but stage military assets, pursue answers through diplomatic back channels, and prompt the United Nations Security Council to convene an emergency session. Around the table, there was much hawkish sentiment to "do something" to North Korea but still no solid plan to rescue the LCS crew. Politically, the president felt cornered.

At Op-Center, the Geek Tank was working at top speed around the clock; empty pizza boxes and a littering of aluminum soda cans documented the all-out effort they had begun the evening before. Williams and his senior staffers digested the raw data from a variety of intelligence-community feeds, the OC analytic product, and communications from the LCS and military commanders near the scene. Williams continued to press his staff for answers: why this, why now, what's next, and who's behind it all? Aaron Bleich remained silently camped in front of his computer searching for answers. After hours of painstaking search, a single name fluttered across his screen: North Korean General Lee Kwon Hui. Bleich sensed he might be onto something, and now he was out to prove it.

CHAPTER NINETEEN

KUJIDO ISLAND IN THE YEONPYEONG ISLAND GROUP

November 13, 1915 Korea Standard Time

It had taken several moments for Kate Bigelow to drag herself to her feet, and a few more to recall just where she was going. She was in the main ship's passageway, and the explosion that had just rocked the ship had thrown her against the bulkhead and then to the deck. After a quick inventory, she pronounced herself bruised but unhurt, save for a four-inch shallow cut in her forearm that oozed blood—messy but not serious. Then she remembered she was on her way to the wardroom and continued aft in that direction. As she made her way, she took out her AN/SRC-59 Motorola XTS 2500I transceiver.

"Damage Control, this is the captain. What just happened?"

"Ma'am, we took a hit up forward of the gun mount. Believe that part of the ship is evacuated, but we have a repair party on the way there to check for damage and personnel."

"Copy that and keep me informed. Captain, out."

She stepped into the wardroom and quickly surveyed the area. Chief Carol Picard, the ship's corpsman, was tending to two patients, one on the makeshift surgery table and another on a nearby folding cot. Another sailor, a female operations specialist, was helping her. Neither patient was conscious, and both were connected to IV drips. The place smelled of alcohol and disinfectant.

"How are they, Chief?"

"Captain, you're bleeding. Let me tend to that." After a brief inspection, she said, "You're going to need stitches for that."

"Give me a compression bandage to stop the bleeding and bind it up." Picard started to protest, but Bigelow cut her off. "Now, Chief, and be quick about it."

Picard worked quickly with birdlike gestures, and while she was at it, the other sailor helping her, a junior petty officer, came in. "All of the wounded are ashore, Chief, oh, excuse me, Captain. These patients are the last two."

"Then get yourself ashore, Johnson," Picard replied while she wrapped Bigelow's arm with an elastic bandage to hold the compression pad over the wound. "These people can't be moved, so I'll have to stay with them."

"Belay that, Johnson!" Bigelow interrupted. "These two patients will have to be moved ashore." Then, to Picard, "Chief, get these people ready to move. I'll get a couple of the combat systems officer's people to help you with the transfer."

Bigelow pulled the Motorola from its keeper on her belt and was about to key it when Picard grabbed her arm. "Captain, you can't do this. These two are badly burned and suffering from smoke inhalation. They'll die if we try to move them."

"They'll die if we don't, and I need you ashore." The force of her grasp was unnaturally strong. Bigelow looked at her sharply. "Get them ready to move; that's an order." Neither of the two junior sailors assisting Picard moved. "Now!"

While they prepared litters for transporting the two wounded crewmen, Bigelow took out her transceiver. "Master Chief, this is the captain. Where are you?"

"I'm just about to reboard the ship, ma'am, and I have two of the ops officer's bos'n mates with me. We'll be making a sweep of the ship to make sure we don't have any stragglers. The XO is making a head count at the cannery. We're still short a few people."

"Okay, send one of your teams on a sweep. I want you and two of your people here in the wardroom ASAP, copy?"

"Uh, roger that, ma'am. We'll be there in just a few minutes."

She turned to where the two junior sailors were working. "Johnson, carry on with what you're doing. Chief, please step over here."

"Captain, I really need to . . ."

"Over here, Chief, and right now."

Picard sighed and moved away from one of the patients. She was not wearing a helmet and pushed a strand of hair from her forehead as she complied with her captain's order. Again, a self-conscious, birdlike movement, and her hand was shaking slightly. Bigelow clamped her by the elbow and guided her to a corner of the makeshift surgery suite. She then spun her a quarter turn and looked her directly in the eyes. The chief corpsman's pupils were so dilated she could see but a small band of brown iris before the color gave way to white.

"What have you been taking, Chief?"

"Captain, I don't know what you're talk—"

"Stop it, Chief!" she hissed. "Stop it right now. Shipmates have died and more might die. I've no time for this. What are you on?" The grip on her chief's elbow tightened.

"I've been up for nearly two days now. So I may have taken a little Dexedrine to keep me going, and maybe something a little stronger to help me through all this. I've been doing the job, and I can still do the job."

"God damn it, Chief. Now of all times! Get yourself topside and into the next boat going to shore. When you get to the shelter, report to the XO."

"Captain, I can still . . ."

"No, you can't. Get the hell out of here." When Picard made no move to leave, Bigelow took a step closer to her. "Now, Chief Picard. Move!"

The chief corpsman left without another word. Petty Officer Second Class Randy Johnson couldn't help but follow the exchange. He watched Picard leave and looked to Bigelow.

"You're in charge now, Johnson. Get these people ready to move. When Master Chief Crabtree gets here, get them ashore as best you can."

"Aye, aye, ma'am."

Bigelow stationed herself by the starboard access

hatch, where the Zodiac shuttles made up to the side of the ship. She got there just in time to see a Zodiac loaded with stores and Chief Picard cast off and begin to make its way around the shattered bow for the beach. Meanwhile, she gave orders to those ashore and those few still on board and monitored the exodus onto the island. Shells continued to fall around the ship, but most were more than a hundred yards off. But they kept coming. A short while later, her master chief, the two bos'n mates, and Johnson reached the hatchway from the wardroom. The unconscious patients, strapped to the litters, were lowered over the side to a waiting Zodiac by the two bos'n mates. Then they joined the litters in the boat and made for shore. Only Crabtree remained.

"Captain," the master chief said in a low voice, "it's time for you to go."

"Is everyone off the ship?"

"We're still checking, but begging your pardon, Captain, you're done here. You're needed ashore with the crew."

She hesitated, but only for a second. "Very well, Master Chief. Don't be too long yourself."

"No longer that I have to be, ma'am."

The Zodiac shuttle came alongside, and she scrambled down the Jacob's ladder and into the craft. Before the craft cleared the bow, she looked back in time to see her command master chief toss her a salute. They were out of sight before she could return it.

At the Korean People's Army headquarters in Pyongyang, General Choi Kwang, marshal of the KPA, sat behind his massive desk and read the report an aide had just handed him. At age sixty-four, he had clawed his way to the top of the KPA and was the senior military man in North Korea, leading the largest military organization on earth. Kim Jong-un trusted him and had given his blessing to the operation to capture *Milwaukee*. But Choi had failed.

Choi had roughly dismissed his staff and now sat alone with his number 2, Chung Su-yong, vice marshal of the KPA. Months ago, when the supreme leader and his political sycophants came up with this half-assed plan to capture the American ship and its crew, it was Chung who had protested most vehemently. Choi remembered Chung's words as if he had spoken them yesterday: *Even if we take the ship's crew hostage, the Americans will never agree to our territorial-water claims. Those claims our political leaders are making are just too outrageous.*

But Choi's job as marshal of the KPA was not to question orders that came from Kim Jong-un but to execute them. *Execute them or I will be executed*, he mused. Now their plan had come undone, at least for the moment. One foul-up after another, beginning with the idiot captain of *Najin Four* firing the cruise missile at *Milwaukee*. What part of the order to capture the ship didn't the navy fool understand?

But it had gotten worse when the KPA coastal anti-aircraft batteries had shot down two of the American aircraft. He hadn't authorized that, either! Did this mean they were at war with the Americans? Yet that wasn't his concern at the moment. The supreme leader hadn't called him, but one of the leader's underlings had—worse than if it had come from Kim himself. The man had made it abundantly clear: Failure was not an option. Pluck the LCS crew off Kujido Island and get them to North Korean territory—and do it quickly.

Choi lifted his head from the report and looked at his number 2. "It's a press report from South Korea. Our 'friend,' General Kwon Oh-Sung, Chairman of the South Korean Joint Chiefs of Staff, has just announced South Korea is going to a full-war footing and mobilizing its reserves. Just what we need!"

Chung realized that, despite their massive military spending, forty percent of the population under arms, huge arms support from Russia and China and all the rest, North Korea was no match for their South Korean adversary, let alone a South Korea allied with America and maybe even other nations like Japan. It was his job to find a way out of this, or it would cost him his job and his life. "Marshal," Chung began, "above all else, we dare not disappoint the supreme leader. I think we need to address our problems one at a time."

"Go ahead, I'm listening."

"First of all, there's the South Koreans. We all know Kwon is a warmonger. What he says about them going to a war footing is not surprising on several counts. First, it's still not clear to the South that *Najin Three* and *Najin Four* didn't go after their ships too—"

"But they didn't!" Choi interrupted.

"Yes, clearly that wasn't the plan. But the way it was executed by our navy comrades sowed enough confusion it could be taken as an act of war. Then there's the buildup along the DMZ. We've done that before, but never in such numbers and in such a threatening manner."

"But that was all designed as a feint. To distract them and the Americans from our actual plan to capture the LCS ship."

"Marshal, I know that and you know that and our political masters know that, but, in hindsight, I think you can see why it sowed confusion in the South. Aren't they really reacting the same way we would in a similar situation?"

Choi was beginning to understand his subordinate's logic. "That's all well and good, but we still have this crisis our politicians have pushed us into, and it's our job to fix it."

"I think all this talk of war with the South is subsiding already. They don't really want war, in spite of Kwon's bluster. I think you'll see he'll be reined in and all this will subside."

"We'll see what the next twenty-four hours bring," Choi groused. "But what about the LCS crew? We still need to take them hostage and do it soon, or the supreme leader will have us in prison, and God help us and our families." There was genuine fear in the marshal's voice.

"General, we have been working on that." Chung produced a thick manila folder. "Now, here is what the staff has come up with as the best option to do just that." With that, the younger officer laid out the folder's contents on Choi's desk and the two men began to pore over the details.

The ride from ship to shore was less than two minutes. On the pebbly beach, there were boxes of supplies, stacks of blankets and bedding, cases of bottled water, and small crates of MREs. Individuals from the crew were making their way over the steep rock-beach berm, grabbing a load, and heading back up and over the berm to the shelter. Bigelow grabbed a crate of MREs, a good forty-pound load, and began to churn her way up the slope, slipping every other step on the gravely surface.

"Cap'n, you don't need to be doing this," said a sailor coming down to the water's edge for another load. "Let me help you with that."

"I got it, Sanders. You go on and get another load."

As she crested the hill, she glanced back at her ship, and, for the first time, she almost lost it emotionally. *Milwaukee* now had a more pronounced starboard list. Its bow looked like a twisted aluminum beer can, and the aft part of the ship was black and scarred from the missile strike. It was a gut-wrenching sight, but there was more. A single flag fluttered from the ship's masthead. Someone had thought to hoist the third-substitute pennant to the port yardarm. The flying of this black-and-white flag meant that the commanding officer was ashore.

"You okay, Captain?" It was a sailor coming up behind her with yet another box of MREs.

"I'm fine, Perkins, but thanks for asking. Let's get this chow to our new shore facility." After another quick glance at the ship and a waterspout that marked the landing of an artillery round, just long and very wide, she followed the newly worn path to the cannery.

The abandoned cannery had the look of a pillbox of the type that dotted the coast of Normandy in France.

It was a two-story structure with 2,500 square feet per floor. The faded gray building was everything Senior Chief Crabtree had said it was—cold, damp, and massively built. From a distance, it had the look of a mausoleum from a previous century. The weathered, reinforced concrete walls and ceilings were intact and looked to be their best chance for protection against the North Korean artillery barrage. The crew had taken refuge in the ground level, leaving the second story and second-story roof as a potential barrier against a direct artillery strike. There was only the purr of a gasoline-powered generator and the occasional *krump* or a shell impact to disturb the silence of the building. Bigelow dropped her box of rations with others piled by the sheltered entrance and stepped inside.

Bundled figures moved amid the multiple shadows cast by strings of bare-bulbed lights that lined the walls. It was a large single room marked by three rows of pillars that supported the ceiling and the upper story. Under the direction of the senior petty officers, the crew was clearing out the remnants of old boxes, lumber, work-station tables, and debris. The only evidence of automation from when the structure served as a crab cannery was two canning machines that had been moved off to one side. Someone had thought to bring brooms and dustpans, and several sailors from the ship's ops department were working to get the top layer of grit from the floor. There was little talking among the crew, which was unusual for U.S. Navy sailors at a distasteful task. But then this was a crew fighting for survival.

Her XO met her as she entered the building. "Captain, welcome ashore. We're doing what we can to make this place habitable, but let's hope we don't have to be here long. How's the ship?"

"The ship is history, I'm afraid. The engineering spaces are flooded, and I don't want to think about the hull damage from the grounding, let alone the shelling and missile strike." She inventoried the quiet chaos around her. "Jack, you've done a great job in a very short time. In addition to keeping our people safe, warm, and fed, there's not much else we can do." She motioned him to one side, where they could have a measure of privacy. "Our job now is to protect this crew until help arrives, and who knows when that might be? I want you to give priority to the wounded and, until further notice, work through Petty Officer Johnson."

"Johnson? What about Chief Pic—"

Bigelow raised her hand to intervene. "Chief Picard got into the medicine cabinet and is high as a kite. When and if we can get her down, she may be of help. Until then, say nothing of this to anyone else and work through Johnson. Now, I've got to get a call through to Seventh Fleet and see when cavalry might arrive. We good with this?"

O'Connor hesitated, then asked, "Any idea when we might get some help?"

"None whatsoever, but then that's not your concern right now. Taking care of the crew is. Okay?"

"Aye, aye, ma'am."

She found Petty Officer Matheson, who had his portable comm gear laid out on a blanket along one of the interior walls and under the glow of a stringed light. He was bent over equipment like a Buddhist monk over a prayer wheel.

"What do you have for me, Matheson? Can I talk?"

"Yes, ma'am, after a fashion. I have only one portable radio and it's an AN/PRC-150, which is good for HF and VHF transmission and reception, but not really compatible for talking with the fleet and the people we want to communicate with. I'm using it to scan for any local military traffic, and if it's not encrypted, we can listen in. Our best contact with the outside world is by satellite phone and our commercial Iridium 9505 encrypted sat phone. Before we left *Milwaukee,* I sent a message to Seventh Fleet with our number here, and they gave me theirs. Here's the phone, and here's the number into their comm center."

She took the handset, which was about the size of her Motorola but with a fixed, fat, stubby aerial, and the three-by-five card with a thirteen-digit number. "Just dial 'em up?"

"That's it, Skipper. Wait until you get a dial tone, which means you have a bird within range, which is no problem here since we're not that far from Seoul. You might have to step outside to do that. Then dial away."

Bigelow stepped out into a drizzling rain and around to the east wall of the building with a clear view toward the sky above Seoul. It was a wireless major city with more than one communications satellite parked overhead in synchronous orbit. She waited a moment for the dial tone to click in and dialed. It was answered on the second ring.

"Seventh Fleet communications central. Petty Officer Graham speaking. How may I help you, sir or ma'am?"

"Graham, this is Commander Bigelow, captain of *Milwaukee*. Let me speak to the watch supervisor, please."

"Ah, Commander, you're captain of the what?"

"*Milwaukee,* Graham, *Milwaukee*. The ship that is getting the shit beat out of it as we speak. Now get me your supervisor."

"Uh, roger that, ma'am. Wait one."

After another moment, "Captain, this is Senior Chief O'Gara, the watch-section supervisor. Good to hear from you, ma'am. Can you hear me all right?"

"I hear you five-by, Senior Chief. I need to speak with the COS."

"Understood, ma'am, and he's expecting your call. Please stand by while I patch you through. And good luck, ma'am. We're all pulling for you."

"Thanks, Senior. Standing by."

Following a short delay, there was an audible click as the call was rerouted. Then a voice came through with a slight echo that told her she was on speaker.

"Captain Bigelow, this is Vice Admiral Bennett. Are you able to hear me?"

"Loud and clear, Admiral."

"Good. Captain, I'm here with, among others, my chief of staff, my operations officer, and my logistics officer. We've followed your plight with a great concern for the safety of you and your crew. We know your current location, but not much else. It would help us a great deal if you would brief us on your current status."

And she did. She spoke for close to five minutes on the condition of *Milwaukee,* the condition of the crew, and concluded with their dead and wounded. For the next five minutes, she answered their questions. Then the fleet commander summed it up.

"Captain, it pains me to tell you the strongest Navy in the world cannot come to your aid immediately, at least not without risking you and your crew. And then there's the North Korean cruise-missile envelope we're going to have to deal with. We're working on diplomatic and military options, but I have nothing to offer in the near term. You're just going to have to hang on there as best you can."

"I understand, Admiral. My immediate concern is the artillery. If you could do something to get them to stop the shelling, that would help a great deal. Or there may be no pawn for you or anyone else to worry about."

"Understood, Captain, and be assured we'll do our best. Bennett, out."

After the fleet commander rang off, Senior Chief O'Gara came back on, and they agreed to an hourly comm check and status update. As she lowered the Iridium phone, she took a deep breath and let it out slowly. While briefing the admiral and being questioned by his staff, she had remained poised and professional. It had been a struggle, but she had done it. Now, in a barely audible voice, she let out a long string of nautical profanity and four-letter words like the sailor she was.

"Beg pardon, ma'am?"

It was the roving sentry making his rounds. He had just rounded the corner of the building. He was armed with a 9 mm sidearm and an M14 rifle. He was a seaman and, Bigelow guessed, no more than nineteen.

"Nothing, Seaman Bedford, just talking to myself. Carry on."

"Aye, aye, ma'am," and he moved past her.

When she returned to the southern entrance of the building, she saw Master Chief Crabtree toiling up the shallow rise with two cases of bottled water under each arm. He set the water by the door and turned to her.

"Captain, we've made our final sweep of the ship and accounted for everyone, including Lieutenant Ashburn. I'm sorry to have to tell you this, Skipper, but he was killed when that last round hit the bow of the ship. We found him at the base of the ladder coming down from MCC. He must have fallen when the shell hit. His neck was broken. I'm sorry, ma'am."

She nodded imperceptibly, suddenly struck by the terrible unreality of it all. The fight with the frigates, the missile strike, the grounding, the artillery, and then this godforsaken place. *And now I've lost my best officer. What next?*

An artillery round landed a hundred yards to the north on the ridge of the island but close enough for them to feel the shock wave.

"Uh, Skipper, it's probably a good idea for you to get inside." When she made no move, he said, "Ma'am, let's go inside."

"Good idea, Master Chief. Go make your full report to the XO, then tell him I'd like to have a word with him."

"Aye, aye, ma'am."

That there were no U.S. ships or aircraft that could enter the area was not quite true. A single Predator drone flying out of Yakota Air Base in Japan had just taken station over the Yeonpyeong Island group. It would shortly be joined by another Predator, and, within hours, a Global Hawk drone flying out of Nellis Air Force Base in Las Vegas. All were armed with Hellfire missiles.

Wham!

Aaron Bleich burst into Chase Williams's office unannounced, with Roger McCord in tow. Williams had the door to his office half-open, and Bleich rushed in so quickly he slammed the back of the door against the office wall. That brought Anne Sullivan from her adjacent office.

"Aaron? Roger?" Williams said, looking up from his chair.

"Boss, I've got it. I've got it!"

"Got what, Aaron?" Williams asked, motioning for them to sit at the small table next to his desk. As they sat, McCord put his hand on Bleich's arm, encouraging him to slow down and repeat what he had told him moments earlier.

Bleich exhaled deeply and then began. "Well, boss, I know you usually want me to just tell you what time it is, but this time I think I need to build you a watch."

"Should I send out for pizza?" Williams asked.

"I don't think it will be that complicated," McCord replied. "Aaron and his team have been in overdrive since you asked us to find out why North Korea tried to capture *Milwaukee*'s crew, and I think he's run it to ground."

"Good, I'm listening."

"It's like this sir," Bleich began. "I knew we'd have to collate raw data from multiple sources to get to the bottom of this. But at the end of the day, it was basically a process of elimination in narrowing the field to just a discrete number of sources. We suspected a massive energy-for-arms deal that was cooking between China and North Korea, even though they tried to keep it a secret. There were these talks between Chinese and North Korean delegations in Beijing and just too much activity going on in Korea Bay, the Bohai Sea, and the Yellow Sea. The real puzzler was the number of Chinese survey ships crisscrossing the area and operating in marginal weather conditions. We asked ourselves, Why? In addition to that, we know how hierarchical the North Koreans are, so we put a special focus on communications going into and coming out of Pyongyang. Then there was the military buildup along the DMZ and, of course, the movement of naval forces we briefed you about before *Milwaukee* was attacked. And then . . ."

Bleich *was* building Williams a watch, and McCord could see the frustration beginning to eke across his face. "Aaron, I think you've set it up for the director beautifully. Now tell him about General Lee."

"Right, I was coming to that. Well, it's like this, boss.

The head of the North Korean delegation in those talks I told you about, a General Lee, is actually a pretty junior guy. Yet he was brought back to Pyongyang and given a medal by Kim Jong-un. The fact he got a medal was all in the open media, although the North Koreans were opaque as to why. But after that happened, I decided to focus on what Lee was doing after he returned . . ."

"Suspect none of *that* was open-media-source stuff," Williams interjected.

"No, and that kind of gets into building the actual watch parts. But Lee made a number of calls and had an active e-mail exchange going with several senior members of the KPA. Again, as a junior guy he was not privy to a lot of high-level deliberations, but I guess he was just curious. He reached out to senior officers he knew to try to get to the bottom of what the supreme leader had said to him when he gave him his medal . . ."

"Which was?" Williams pressed.

"I've been able to hack some of Lee's e-mails and cell-phone calls. After giving him his medal, Kim said words to the effect of 'owning' Korea Bay and the Yellow Sea and about 'fateful days' being ahead."

"Isn't that just typical North Korean bluster?" Williams asked.

"It would be, sir, except in one of his conversations Lee told a senior colleague there was a major caveat in the deal he had worked out with the Chinese. Before the deal went into effect and they got some modern military hardware we know they coveted, North Korea had to guarantee they had the sole right to exploit those energy resources on the seabed. And I think I'm a bit out of my wheelhouse right here, so I'll let Roger take over for a minute."

"Boss, you know from your Navy experience the United States guards its rights of freedom of navigation as zealously as we do just about any rights, save basic human rights. You probably participated in freedom-of-navigation ops during your seagoing days . . ." Williams nodded, so McCord continued. "You also know that the issue of who owns what in the Yellow Sea is about as confused as it gets anywhere at sea. I'm sure you recall all the controversy and churn over the Northern Limit Line, the Inter-Korean Military Demarcation Line, and all those unresolved issues left over from the Korean War."

"I do recall them, and not fondly."

"Rich Middleton and I checked with our contacts at State and DoD, and we did our homework. The North Koreans have a problem delivering clear title to the waters where those oil and gas reserves seem to be located. And now they're using the threat of war and American hostages to try and gain concessions, especially from us and from the South Koreans. Aaron's work all but proves it." McCord now turned to Bleich. "Aaron, you want to pick it up from here?"

"Well, it's like Roger said, boss. It seems pretty clear that North Korea's political leaders, all the way up to Kim, thought this would be an easy win for them, especially given the kind of concessions the United States has made in the past on things like their developing nuclear power. If they could capture the crew of the *Milwaukee,* they reasoned the United States might deal mineral rights to the seabed under Korea Bay and the northern part of the Yellow Sea to get our people back."

Williams paused to consider this. "Aaron, first of all, great job in tracking this down. Roger, now that we know all this, what do you think the North Koreans' next move is going to be?"

"I think it means, given the stakes involved, North Korea is going to pull out all the stops to get that crew on the island any way they can. They're in deep, and Pyongyang is in all likelihood prepared to go in deeper."

"I agree with your assessment. Well done, again. Now, I've got to get a note off to the Oval Office. Stay on top of this, Aaron."

CHAPTER TWENTY

Captain Ben Crowley had taken the C-17 Globemaster III to the end of the runway and spun it around in a tight pirouette. Then he reversed the thrusters of the four Pratt & Whitney PW2040 engines to back the aircraft up to where his wheels were on the very edge of the tarmac. He was going to need every inch of the 4,000-foot runway and every knot of the westerly 17-knot wind coming in off the Pacific. Fully loaded with 171,000 pounds of cargo and 180,000 pounds of fuel, the Globemaster needed 7,800 feet of runway to take off. But it was not fully loaded. The Advanced SEAL Delivery System and associated gear and personnel in the cargo bay weighed 125,000 pounds, and they carried but 20,000 pounds of fuel, enough to get them airborne and to cruise altitude, where a KC-135 flying fuel bowser was waiting for them. Still, Crowley knew he had a 215-ton aircraft and only 4,000 feet of runway to get it off the ground. Both he and his copilot again went through their preflight checklists. They were as ready as they could be.

"Ford Island tower, this is Air Force seven-two-six heavy. Request permission to take off."

The response was immediate. "Roger, seven-two-six, you are cleared for takeoff. Good luck."

Yeah, right, Crowley thought. He looked over and nodded to his copilot, who then advanced the four throttles to their stops. When the four Pratt & Whitneys were shrieking at full power, he released the brakes, and they began their roll. Both pilots' eyes flicked between the airspeed indicator and at the shrinking length of runway before them. With seven hundred feet of hardstand left, he picked up the nose and felt the aircraft shudder and hesitate, and then they were airborne. His copilot immediately took in the gear, and they watched the airspeed indicator creep ahead as they began to climb away from Oahu. It was not until they were well out over water that they began to bring in the flaps.

"Piece of cake," the copilot said over the cockpit intercom, trying to sound casual and almost succeeding.

Yeah, right.

The ASDS was a sixty-five-foot-long, sixty-ton dry submarine that was crewed by a pilot and a navigator. It was designed to be carried piggyback on a Los Angeles–class or Virginia-class submarine to the operational area. From there, it was to be launched from its mother sub with sixteen fully loaded Navy SEALs. It had a speed of eight knots and a range of 125 nautical miles. The original program called for six of these craft.

Because of technical issues and massive cost overruns, the program was canceled. Only two of the craft were built and one of those sank in deep-ocean waters during sea trials. This left only one such boat, the one that was now winging its way west in the belly of the Globemaster.

The ASDS took up almost all the cargo space of the big transport. Just forward of the bow of the craft were assorted flyaway boxes of test equipment, service modules, and spares. Two men strapped into bench seats on one side of the fuselage were conspicuous in that they weren't attired in blue coverall flight suits like the rest of the crew. Both wore desert-pattern fatigues and bloused boots. One wore lieutenant's bars on his collar points, and the other a fouled anchor and stars of a master chief petty officer. Both had SEAL tridents over the name tags above their left jacket pockets.

They were an odd pair. The master chief was big and bald with a salt-and-pepper push-broom mustache. He had a shuffling, bearlike appearance and did in fact move about with a slight limp. As a first class petty officer, he had been one of the first Navy SEALs into Afghanistan after 9/11. During a firefight near Kandahar, he was shot multiple times through the legs. The engagement left him semicrippled and facing separation from the Navy when he managed to talk himself into a tour of duty with the SEAL delivery team. There, he learned the intricacies of underwater operations and the subsystems of the team's submersibles. He quickly made himself indispensable. And while he could no longer keep up with a SEAL squad on land, he now moved like a ballerina underwater. The underwater choreography required to launch and recover SEALs from a submerged submarine was now what he did, and he did it well.

Except for the SEAL trident on his chest, the lieutenant would never be taken for a Navy SEAL. He was of average height, slightly built, and had almost feminine features. In the rigorous basic SEAL training, he managed to survive because he was a good swimmer and an outstanding runner, having placed in the top ten in the NCAA cross-county finals. His first active deployment in 2009 as an assistant SEAL platoon officer did not go well. He was well liked by everyone, but he was tentative and ineffective as a combat leader. So he was assigned to SDV Team 1, where he was then sent to the required advanced diver schools and, after that, into SDV pilot training. Some people are born to fly, and this lieutenant would have been one of them. He found his stride as an SDV pilot. The intuitive nature of navigating in a dark, liquid vacuum and balancing the delicate buoyance systems of a minisubmersible came easily to him. He was a natural. Just as the master chief was the best systems man at SDV Team 1, this lieutenant was far and away the best pilot. At the team, they were known as the pilot and the mechanic.

Once safely airborne, the lieutenant took out a five-dollar bill and handed it to the master chief. He took it without looking and stuffed it into the pocket of his blouse.

"Thank you, sir. Told you we would make it."

The lieutenant shrugged. "It was still an even-money bet. But how would you have paid off if we'd crashed?"

"We'd have at least made it to the water and crashed

at sea. And you know full well master chiefs walk on water. I'd have carried you ashore and paid up."

The lieutenant pursed his lips as he considered this logic. "But of course," and they settled into a companionable silence, save for the whine of the engines, as the big cargo plane clawed for altitude and its rendezvous with the tanker.

The original manning of the ASDS called for two pilots. One was to be a Navy submarine-qualified officer and the other a Navy SEAL. Now that there was but one boat, the driving chores would be handled by these two SEALs. This lieutenant and this master chief were the most experienced ASDS pilots in the Navy. Basically, they were the only ASDS pilots in the Navy. They were both competent with the Mark 8 boats, but they represented the corporate knowledge when it came to the larger and more complex operations of the advanced SEAL delivery system. It would require other SEALs and technicians to marry the ASDS to its parent sub and a crew of SEALs and divers to launch and retrieve the craft. The personnel for those duties could be drawn from the SDV Team 1 platoon on Okinawa.

After refueling and reaching a cruise altitude of 42,000 feet and a cruising speed of 450 knots, one of the aircrew came to the two Navy men and offered them each a box lunch. The lieutenant accepted his, while the master chief waved the airman off. And while the lieutenant picked through an assortment of dried chicken wings, a hard-boiled egg, a bologna sandwich, and a small bag of chips, the master chief took a Philly cheesesteak from an insulated carry-on bag. It was smothered with Dijon mustard, horseradish sauce, and grilled onions. The smell filled the bay of the Globemaster. He tucked into it with relish. A half hour later, they were both sound asleep.

While the two SEALs slept, it was early evening and all was quiet at a small command module at Nellis Air Force Base just outside Las Vegas. That was about to change. A young second lieutenant recently out of the Air Force Academy was monitoring the approaches to the North Korean naval facility at Haeju from an altitude of 58,000 feet. Actually, that was her vantage point, not her physical location. She was the Global Hawk's controller, seated comfortably in an air-conditioned space while the outside temperature still hovered in the mid-eighties. It was still dark in the Yellow Sea, and there were multiple layers of clouds between the Global Hawk and the surface of the ocean. It was a dirty night on the water, one that made those who wished to remain undetected safe. Yet with her forward-looking infrared sensor pod, the young lieutenant watched as two patrol vessels emerged from the naval port and made their way into Haeju Bay. On reaching the mouth of the bay, they turned south and came up to forty knots. They were now clearly headed for the Yeonpyeong Island group some forty-five miles away. She was not the only one who saw this. Analysts in the intelligence section at Seventh Fleet in Yokosuka and at the National Security Agency were privy to the download from the Global Hawk. She signaled for her supervisor.

"What've you got, Allison?"

"Major, it looks like two patrol craft have just sortied from the Haeju Naval Base. My bird is in position and armed. I'm ready to drop on your authorization."

"All right, stand by and continue tracking."

The major turned to a bank of phones at his watch station. He was about to pick up the handset that was a dedicated secure link to Seventh Fleet, but it rang before he could reach it.

"Nellis control, Major Duncan, speaking."

"Major, this is Commander Rich Sargent at Seventh Fleet Operations. Through your Global Hawk downlink, we're seeing two patrol craft from Haeju entering the northern Yellow Sea. You have them?"

"Roger that, Commander. We have them, and our bird is armed." Duncan knew he hadn't the authority to hit these boats, but the man on the phone did. "What are your instructions?"

"Major, we have IDed these as Shershen-class torpedo boats. If they come within twenty-five miles of the Yeonpyeong Island group, lethal force is authorized by the commander, Seventh Fleet. If they get that close, sink 'em."

Duncan repeated the order and the authorization and added, "If they reach the twenty-five-nautical-mile mark, we will make the drop." Then he stepped back to his controller.

"You get that, Allison?"

"Yes, sir. If those boats get within twenty-five miles from the island, we go to war."

They said very little as they watched the two craft continue south in the Yellow Sea. It took them just over twenty minutes to reach the twenty-five-mile range. The major continued to study the ghostly IR video presentation for a few more seconds, and then said, "You are cleared hot. Drop authorization is granted; weapons free."

"Roger that, sir, weapons free."

The lieutenant slewed a cursor slaved to an airborne laser on the Global Hawk onto the lead craft. She quickly received a tone from the warheads of the specially modified Hellfire missiles. Both missiles indicated their eagerness to seek out any target illuminated by the laser. The designers of the Hellfire assumed the target would be a tank or a bunker or a structure. But the Hellfires themselves didn't really care. For them it was all about the reflected energy from a laser beam. A moment later, one Hellfire dropped from the left under-wing pylon of the Global Hawk and began its descent. Two seconds later, a second Hellfire left the right pylon, following its brother down. Each in turn fired its rocket motor. The 2.6-second burn time accelerated the missiles to Mach 1.4. The young lieutenant kept the laser cursor on the lead enemy craft. It took close to twenty-five seconds for the first missile to travel the ten miles from the Global Hawk to the first patrol craft. She placed the laser well abaft of the bow so the warhead struck just forward of amidships. With the flair of the initial strike, the controller immediately slewed her laser designator back to the second boat, again just forward of amidships. The second Hellfire obediently turned for the second boat.

Aboard the two Shershen-class boats, there was none of the orderly exchange that had taken place at the Nellis control facility or the Seventh Fleet headquarters. It was a sledgehammer blow. One Hellfire took the lead boat in the pilothouse, killing the helmsman instantly. The patrol-boat skipper and the lee helmsmen were instantly blinded by the flash and had their eardrums imploded by the concussion. Both were rendered unconscious and shredded by shrapnel carried through from the roof. Both would live, but both would carry visible scars for the rest of their lives. The Hellfire is an antiarmor weapon, so most of the force of the explosion is linear and carried through the main deck to the keel, where most of the force of the warhead was absorbed by an auxiliary generator. This bought them time. The men in the troop compartment were shaken but unhurt and began an orderly evacuation of the sinking boat.

The second Hellfire struck just behind the pilothouse in the troop compartment of the second boat. One soldier was decapitated and another had his arm severed at the shoulder. The expended warhead passed through to the keel, where it opened a gaping hole in the craft. There was no orderly evacuation here. Following the flash of the impact, blind and wounded soldiers began to grope their way across the blood-slick deck for the escape hatches. In the ensuing panic, only a few made it out. As the second Shershen boat sank, clawing and screaming soldiers clogged the way out, dooming those behind them

"Nicely done, Lieutenant," the major said. "Very nicely done."

The second lieutenant and her major, along with those

at Seventh Fleet and NSA, watched as several life rafts were inflated and a great many blurred figures scrambled into them—far more figures than were needed to man two fifty-year-old torpedo boats. The two boats were packed with a commando force, the remnants of which were now slowly making their way back to the north. One of the boats sank immediately while the other remained afloat for another hour, then it, too, was gone.

"Well, Allison, how do you feel about your first two kills?"

She thought about this a moment. It was not, she thought, all that different from her training—it was still a video game, and she said as much.

"Well, maybe," Duncan replied, "but you don't get a DFC for playing video games."

A Distinguished Flying Cross, she mused. She shook her head, *Only in this woman's Air Force.* Then she took her Global Hawk back up to Haeju Bay and began to search the area for more surface contacts.

If there was one boat in the undersea fleet of the U.S. Navy that was said to have been snake bit, it was USS *Greenville* (SSN-722). She was a Los Angeles–class nuclear attack submarine and just shy of her twenty-first birthday. But the boat had packed a great deal of misfortune and controversy into those twenty-one years. In February of 2001, she was operating off Oahu with several reporters on board. In an emergency surfacing demonstration, the sub had come up under the Japanese fishing boat the *Ehime Maru,* sinking the vessel and killing nine of the crew, a crew that included four teenagers. Then, scarcely six months later, *Greenville* found herself aground while entering port on the island of Saipan. The damage to her rudder and propulsion intakes, while minor, required the boat to be dry-docked. Only six months later, the submarine collided with USS *Ogden,* a Navy amphibious ship, during a personnel transfer in the Gulf of Aden. The collision resulted in a rent in the side of the *Ogden,* spilling thousands of gallons of fuel into the Gulf. Since that time, *Grenville* had served without mishap and with distinction, earning high marks for readiness and tactical proficiency. But no matter; the boat was considered something of a Jonah by submariners around the fleet.

Greenville was returning home to Pearl Harbor following a ninety-day patrol. The crew was homesick, and the boat was ready for an in-port restricted availability and some minor but much-needed maintenance. They were west of Japan when the boat came to periscope depth and slowed to lift its communications mast. It was only near the surface for a few minutes to collect the burst transmission that contained several days of message traffic. Amid the many routine and a few priority messages, there was one that trumped all others.

TOP SECRET: FLASH PRECEDENCE
From: Commander, Submarine Force Pacific
To: USS *Greenville*
Subj: Operation Immediate
You are hereby directed to make for the White Beach

Naval Facility on Okinawa at best speed, repeat best speed, for a classified mission tasking. There you are to remain submerged offshore and await further orders. Following an acknowledgment of these orders, observe communications blackout.

TOP SECRET: FLASH PRECEDENCE

Commander Allen Baumstark was attending to paperwork in his small stateroom, anticipating hearing from his wife in the "famlygram" that accompanied these normally routine communications downloads. This one would be loaded with family news for the homeward-bound crew. He was in tune with his boat and had already felt her return to cruise depth and accelerate to her transit speed of twenty knots. Suddenly, his lead comm tech burst in.

"Excuse the interruption, sir, but you better look at this," he said, and handed him a hard copy of the transmission.

Baumstark studied it for a moment. "Christ on a crutch. What now?" After a moment's reflection, he took the handset from the wall-mounted communications box and cranked the small handle. It was already set for the control room.

"This is control."

"Control. This is the captain. Return to periscope depth and prepare to raise the comm mast for an outgoing transmission."

"Uh, aye, aye, Captain."

He scratched out a brief cryptic reply.

TOP SECRET: FLASH PRECEDENCE
FROM: USS *Greenville*
To: COMSUBPAC
Subj: Receipt of OP-IMMEDIATE
Am in receipt of your last and making best speed as
directed. Baumstark.
TOP SECRET: FLASH PRECEDENCE

He handed the message to the tech, then called him back
and added a line to the message he had written, "Please
advise *Greenville* wives and families as situation al-
lows."

He again called the control room and told his officer
of the deck to pass word to the executive officer, the
chief engineer, the navigator, and the COB (chief of the
boat—pronounced "cob," as in "corncob") to meet him
in the wardroom. Unlike the wardroom on *Milwaukee,*
Greenville's wardroom was more like a stockbroker's
cubicle. By the time Baumstark had finished briefing his
key senior leaders on what little he knew, *Greenville*
would be on a course of 250 at two hundred feet at a
speed well in excess of thirty knots. That alone made
them uncomfortable. Submariners are listeners. They
rely on their ability to hear in the same way that blind
animals rely on smell. At this speed, they were deaf, but
at this speed, they would be off the White Beach Naval
Facility in eighteen hours.

"I know this is going to be difficult for the crew,"
Baumstark concluded, "but we wouldn't be tasked like
this if it wasn't important."

"Don't worry about the crew, Skipper," the XO replied. "They know it has to be some kind of real-world mission tasking. You can count on them."

"Think it has to do with this business with North Korea?" asked the navigator.

"Perhaps," Baumstark replied, "but we're headed for Okinawa, not the Yellow Sea."

"Any idea why they might want us?" the chief engineer asked.

"Haven't a clue. I guess we'll find out when we get there." But he did know, or at least he thought he might. "Thanks. I'll let you return to your duties. When I know something, you'll know something." But at this speed there was no chance of any contact with the outside world. "COB, you want to stay back for a moment?" The COB had been on board longer than anyone else and knew more about *Greenville* than any member of her crew, including her captain.

"Sir?" He was a master chief petty officer and had spent more than fourteen years of his twenty-six-year Navy career *underwater*.

"You thinking what I'm thinking, COB?"

"I think so, Skipper. Could be that we were just the closest boat, but I don't think so." Both of them knew *Greenville* was one of the few Los Angeles fast-attack boats that had carried the ASDS. "We got nothing to do for a few hours. Let me get together with a few of the old hands and we'll start thinking about this—just in case."

The Globemaster chased the sun across the Pacific but could not catch it. It landed a few hours after dark, as planned, and was directed to a section of tarmac adjacent to the hangar occupied by the JSOC flyaway element. Brian Dawson waited with Lieutenant Denver while the big cargo plane taxied to where they stood watching. Denver had shed the blue jeans and sweatshirt and was now in fresh desert-pattern fatigues, cap, and bloused boots.

"How many SEALs will be with the minisub?" Dawson asked.

"Just two."

"Just two?" Dawson echoed.

"My guys will see to getting the ASDS deplaned and over to pierside. And about half of them will go aboard to serve as deck crew for the launch and recovery of the boat. But the two who will see to the actual operation of the ASDS are very special SEALs."

"Tell me more," Dawson prompted.

"Master Chief Harlan Mecoy has been at the team for more than twelve years, and he knows just about everything there is to know about the ASDS. He's the corporate knowledge. He will supervise the launch and recovery of the boat. Once away from the parent sub, he will then serve as navigator and copilot for the boat. He will basically be in charge of the operation start to finish. In short, he's the best there is. We call him the mechanic because he will direct the preparation, loading, launch, and recovery of the ASDS.

"Your pilot is Lieutenant Bill Naylor. Billy has only been with SDV One for two years, but he's the best there is at what he does. Nobody can drive an SDV or an ASDS better than him." Denver had come to know

Brian Dawson and knew of his Special Forces background. "Think of all the helicopter pilots you've known at the 160th Special Operations Aviation Regiment. Can you name one or two MH-60 pilots you would ask for by name if you had to go in on a really hairy mission?" Dawson nodded. "Well, at SDV Team One, Billy Naylor is that pilot."

The aircraft was met by the entire Okinawa detachment of SDV Team 1. The SEALs and their support technicians swarmed aboard the C-17 and set about the business of easing the ASDS from the fuselage of the big aircraft and preparing it for land travel. Mecoy and Naylor made their way over to where Dawson and Denver waited. Introductions were made, and they all retired to the hangar. There they were joined by Jesse Carpenter, Hector Rodriguez, and Major Mike Volner. Over coffee and a detailed chart of Kujido Island, they went over the operation—as Dawson and Rodriguez envisioned it and as Mecoy and Naylor would have to execute it. Mike Volner and Jesse Carpenter figured into the scheme, but it was all about the ability of the ASDS and its operators to make it happen.

"So that's how we see it unfolding," Dawson concluded, "but the question is, Can you execute it? Is this doable, and can you do it?"

All eyes were now on Master Chief Harlan Mecoy. He permitted himself a small smile and took a sip of coffee.

"All these years, we've been waiting on a mission for the ASDS. And all these years, I thought it would be some secret harbor penetration or sneaking a squad of SEALs into a denied area and waiting offshore while they scrambled over the beach to execute an important covert operation. And now that it's finally here, it's a lifeboat mission. But saving those American lives is probably more important than anything else I may have had in mind. Getting in close enough with the parent sub may present problems, but I don't see any problem with making the operational runs, do you, Lieutenant?"

"If we can get the boat prepped and the big sub can get us on station," Naylor replied, "I can fly the mission."

"So to answer your question, sir, it's doable, and we can do it. But the successful execution is all in the details. Keep in mind this is a complex prototype system and we have to anticipate the operational and mechanical problems that are sure to arise. And we have a ton of work to get done if we're going to get aboard the parent sub and away from the pier before the sun comes up and Chinese satellites are overhead." The master chief took out a notebook and began working his way through a series of details that included the slow, sixteen-mile journey from Kadena to the pier at White Beach, the mobile crane services on the pier that could handle a sixty-ton submersible, and the estimated time of arrival of *Greenville*. After another fifteen minutes of discussion, they broke from the meeting. There was indeed much for all of them to do before sunrise.

"Major, let's take a walk outside for a few minutes," Dawson said as he and Volner left the others.

Commander Kate Bigelow had been sleeping fitfully on a mattress pad brought from the ship when she was suddenly fully awake. She pulled on a layer of foul-weather gear that by now was exceedingly ripe. Something wasn't right, and she instantly knew what it was. The shelling that had been with them since they abandoned *Milwaukee* had suddenly stopped. That was certainly a welcome change but somehow ominous in its sudden cessation, like a two-day storm that had suddenly blown itself out. She was grateful for the reprieve but wondered when it would begin again. Or was the quiet a prelude to some form of waterborne or aerial attack? Nonetheless, she was aware of the break in the shelling within only minutes of the last round dropping. She immediately sought out Master Chief Crabtree. Like her, he wondered if the break in the barrage might signal an attack from a North Korean army contingent. To her relief, Crabtree had just doubled the roving patrols about the cannery complex, not that they could do much if there was such a move against them. It would be dawn in a few hours, so they made a slow circuit of the interior of the building while most of the crew slept. The crew had segregated themselves into small enclaves that reflected their watch sections aboard ship. They had fallen into something of a schedule that, while not shipboard routine, was of some comfort to those who had grown used to daily military procedures.

Just after dark the previous evening, the master chief and a work party had returned to the ship on yet another scavenging mission.

"Skipper, there's not much left that is of any use to us. Of course, it would be helpful if we knew how long we'd be here. Food is not an issue, given our stock of MREs and the canned goods we've taken out of the galley. In about another three days or so, fresh water will start to be a problem. To stay ahead of it, and as long as the artillery holds off, I'll send a working party back out to replenish our empty containers each evening. Our freshwater holding tanks are down to about a third—that is, those that weren't damaged by gunfire. I've been rotating the personnel in the working parties. I give them each a few minutes to go to their personal lockers and get what they might need ashore. And, uh, Skipper, we've moved our dead shipmates into the cold-stores locker. It's . . . it's not a pretty sight, them stacked in there like that. For now, it's cool if not cold, but there's not much else we can do."

"No, there isn't," Bigelow replied. She was silent for a moment, then said, "What about that other portable generator?"

"It's ashore and we're holding it as a backup. Fuel is an issue, so we're only using one. I hope it doesn't come to that, but we've got fuel for about another four days, and then that's it. No more power."

"Thanks, Master Chief." He turned to go, but she called him back. "What's she look like? I haven't wanted to be away from here and the radio. How's *Milwaukee* holding up?"

"Well, ma'am, she looks to have been hit several more times. There's been no more fire, but the damage from the missile hit is pretty apparent. It's, well, it's a sad sight. She's got a twenty-degree starboard list and is well down by the stern. Skipper, *Milwaukee* is the crew here in this concrete bunker; it's no longer that hulk out on the beach."

"I hear you, Master Chief. And thanks—thanks for everything."

Just after first light, Bigelow was making a slow circuit around the facility, chatting with individuals and groups of crewmen. No matter how many times she did this, and she did it often, they still had questions. And now, more than ever, they looked to her for answers— answers and leadership. She was speaking with a group of gunner's mates when Jack O'Connor rushed up and interrupted.

"Excuse me, Captain, but there's something you should hear on the radio." She followed him over to where Petty Officer Matheson had set up their makeshift shore-based radio central.

"What do you have, Matheson?"

"Ma'am, I tuned into this about twenty minutes ago. It's on the international-distress frequency, and it's a UHF / line-of-sight transmission, so it's probably not reaching anyone but us. It's repeated every five minutes with a time interval between each transmission for a reply. It's not a recording but an English speaker reading the same message each time—I'm sure of it. Wait, here it comes again.

This is a message for the crew of the American ship now stranded on Kujido Island. This is the Democratic People's Republic of Korea and we are most concerned for your welfare. After your shipwreck on this island, you must be in need of food, water, and medical aid. A humanitarian rescue mission sent by the People's Republic has been turned back at sea by your government. Our only concern, however, is for your welfare. Ask those in your government and the aggressors in Seoul to allow for us to bring you aid. I say again, our only concern is for your welfare. Please acknowledge this transmission. And please let us come to your aid.

"That's it, Captain. The same message every five minutes or so."

"Okay, Petty Officer Matheson, call Seventh Fleet Operations and let them listen to the next transmission using the Iridium sat phone. We'll see what they think of this. Meanwhile, I'll want to in no way let them know that we are even hearing that message."

"Aye, aye, ma'am."

"And tell Seventh Fleet that we have no intention of taking them up on their offer, but some fleet guidance would be appreciated." She left Matheson with O'Connor at her elbow.

"Captain," he said quietly once they were out of earshot, "do you think this is a good idea? The North Koreans have a beef with South Korea, and we seem to be caught in the middle of it. Shouldn't we at least consider it? Chief Picard says we could lose one, maybe two more people if we don't get some help."

Bigelow measured him. "Jack, the North Koreans shot the shit out of us at sea and pounded us here on this rock. You really think they want to help us?"

"I know it's risky, but we're in a tough spot here. We

have wounded; we're stranded here; and it seems our own Navy either can't or won't help us. We've done enough; this crew's done enough. I think it's time we put their welfare first. If there's a chance to get them some help, we need to take it. I mean, we should at least talk to them."

"Okay, Jack," she began in a measured voice. "Your concerns are duly noted. But first of all, I don't trust the North Koreans or their crazy leader. The crew of *Pueblo* didn't fare so well, and I don't see them being any nicer to us. Secondly, you're forgetting the second paragraph of the Code of Conduct: 'I will never surrender of my own free will. If in command, will never surrender the members of my command while they have the means to resist.' No, Jack, they're not offering to help us; they're asking us to surrender."

"What's the difference?" he persisted. "You said it yourself, we have no means to resist. We're hiding in a fish factory with a bunch of sailors who are by and large technicians, not infantrymen."

"Listen to me, Jack. As long as we hold up here, we deny them the ability to parade us on TV as captive war criminals. We deny them the leverage of holding Americans as prisoners of war. As long as we can hang on here, we *are* resisting. And as long as I'm in command, or until directed otherwise by higher authority, we'll do all in our power to continue to hang on here, is that clear?"

"Yes, that's clear."

"That's clear what, XO?"

"That's clear, Captain."

"Thank you." She brushed past him and headed for where the wounded were being cared for. It was time she took up a matter with her chief corpsman.

General Choi Kwang, marshal of the KPA, burst into his command headquarters. The destruction of Shershen-class torpedo boats by an American drone, if that's what it was, had shown their intel was imperfect at best. One of Kim's subordinates, this one even more junior than the first, had called to tell him of the supreme leader's displeasure. He told him there would not be another failure. That was more than an ominous sign; it was a prelude to a death sentence. Immediately after that call, Choi had his driver take him to his quarters on a false pretext and told his wife to begin preparations to leave the country. He summoned the senior naval officer, Rear Admiral Reeh Sun-oh to his side.

"Admiral?"

"General, the Americans surprised us with what we believe was a drone strike. Though we lost both of our patrol boats, most of their crews and almost all of the commandos were able to escape. Other naval vessels have picked them all up. We estimate they will arrive back in Haeju in about—"

"Stop! I don't need an after-action report of yet another failure by your naval forces. How many ways can you find to screw things up?"

His number 2 stepped in to try to defuse the situation. "Marshal, Admiral Reeh has another plan."

Choi valued Chung's counsel and above all his loyalty, and he didn't want to treat him poorly or cause him to lose face in front of this admiral. But he had endured enough half-baked plans and heard enough pathetic excuses. "I think not, General Chung." Now he turned to the navy man, and the full fury of the moment exploded. "Admiral Reeh, you are relieved of your duties. Leave this command center immediately."

"Yes, Marshal," was all the man could say.

"General Chung, get me the senior navy submarine commander at headquarters as well as the Special Operations Force officer. This time, we will go with my plan."

After speaking with her supply officer regarding daily rations, Kate Bigelow finally made her way to what was now their land-bound sick bay. She moved from cot to cot, taking a moment with each of her wounded crewmen. Three were sedated, and two of those three were still critical. One of the wounded had died during the previous day, and he was zipped into a body bag and taken back aboard *Milwaukee* to be with the rest of their fallen shipmates. That was the tenth crew member who had perished. Chief Carol Picard followed her commanding officer on this circuit at a respectful distance. Then the two of them stepped off to one side.

"Okay, Chief, where are we on the condition of our people?"

"Well, ma'am, the two still in critical condition will probably die unless we can get them to an urgent-care-type facility and get them there soon."

"How soon?" Bigelow interjected.

"Within twenty-four hours, forty-eight at the outside.

As for the others, under these conditions, only time will tell. Most will continue to gain ground unless some infection beyond the reach of our antibiotics sets in. There's always that chance. This place is not a good patient-recovery environment. It's a petri dish, ma'am. The sooner we can get them out of here, the better off they'll be."

You can say that for all of us. Bigelow was silent for several moments while she considered this. "Very well, Chief, this is about all I can tell you. I don't know when or how we're going to get out of here. We could catch a break and the medevac helos from Osan could show up at any time, but I wouldn't count on it. I'm not getting a lot of direction or information from the powers that be. For now my job is to hold on here, report changes in conditions and our situation here up the chain of command, and await events. Your job is to do your level best to care for our shipmates for as long as it takes. I wish I could tell you more, but I can't. Meanwhile, we carry on as best we can. Keep the XO advised of any changes and come straight to me if there's an issue he can't resolve, clear?"

"Yes, ma'am." Bigelow had been watching Picard closely during the exchange so she was ready when her chief corpsman continued. "And ma'am, about what happened aboard ship and my, well what I had taken . . ."

"Chief, let's not go into that. We will talk about it later, but not now. I told you I'd give you a second chance, not out of charity but because I need you and, more importantly, my crew needs you. There won't be a third chance. I need you, and these patients need you. It's my sense you're straight now, is that correct?"

"Yes, ma'am."

"Then do your job. What you did was wrong. You know it, and I know it. I can't say that what took place will not come back on you, but a great deal of how that will be viewed will depend on your performance from here on out, okay?"

"Yes, ma'am."

"All right, then. Carry on."

As she turned from Picard, a young seaman came rushing up. "Captain, Petty Officer Matheson needs you. He has Seventh Fleet on the line."

It was but a few steps over to where her communications petty officer was waiting. He held the Iridium satellite phone with one hand over the speaker end.

"It's Seventh Fleet Ops, ma'am. They asked for you directly." She took the handset and headed for the door, both for the privacy and the better reception.

"This is Commander Bigelow."

"Captain, this is Commander Sergeant at Seventh Fleet Ops. How're you doing there, ma'am?"

"Well, we're cold, wet, tired, and getting sick of MREs. I've got wounded that need more attention than we can give them here. And my senior medic tells me that two of my crewmen will be dead within forty-eight hours—perhaps sooner—if they don't get better care. Past that, we're holding on. So, Commander, what have you got for me?"

"First of all, we are going to ask you to do just that—hold on for just a little longer. Last night the North Koreans tried to slip a commando team onto your island by small craft. One of our drones spotted them and sank both boats. So as for their concern for your welfare and offer of help, well, we think that's a lot of crap. Our intel shop and the agencies up the line believe the attack on your ship was all about taking hostages. And we think that's why they stopped the shelling; they want you alive. It's the *Pueblo* all over again. But you've managed to outrun them and, so far, out-think them. We now have the *Reagan* strike group sitting off in the Yellow Sea, out of range of their land-based air and their cruise-missile envelope. So it's a standoff. We will not let anything get to you, and yet we can't risk sending the carrier strike group north without risking ships and the safety of your crew. But we do have a plan."

Bigelow listened for several minutes, and she liked what she heard. It was not the six or eight H-60 Blackhawk transport helos she was hoping for, but it was at least something.

"So, Captain. When the submarine is on station, you will be getting a call on this line from a Mr. Brian Dawson. It will be his people coordinating the operation, and you'll take your direction from him. Your wounded will be moved first, then the rest of the crew."

"We'll be ready, but who is this Dawson and who is he with—some special operations outfit?"

"We don't really know, but it's some kind of special, quasi-government operation. And they have support from across the DoD spectrum and from the president. But they do seem to know what they're doing. Meanwhile, is there anything you need medical wise that we can help you with? We have a new Predator drone coming on station about every eight to ten hours. We can get you about forty pounds of medical resupply in precision airdrop if that will help."

"Let me check with my corpsman and see what we need. I'll get back to you. When do you think this rescue craft might get to us?"

"They will be on station in about twenty-four hours, but we will have to wait until after dark to begin making transfers. But, again, Dawson will call you when he and his submarine are on station. Good luck, Captain."

"Thanks. Bigelow, out."

CHAPTER TWENTY-ONE

KUJIDO ISLAND IN THE
YEONPYEONG ISLAND GROUP

November 15, 1215 Korea Standard Time

Commander Kate Bigelow had taken a full hour to digest the possibility of a submarine rescue, and a minisubmarine rescue at that. At first the prospect of what Seventh Fleet operations officer had proposed to her seemed farfetched and more than a little complex. But the more she fully understood the risks associated with any kind of air- or surface-rescue effort, she had to admit this might be their best option—perhaps the only option.

She huddled her department heads and senior enlisted leaders for a briefing. In addition to Jack O'Connor, there was Master Chief Crabtree, her chief engineer, navigator, weapons officer, and her new operations officer. She sorely missed having Lieutenant Eric Ashburn among this group of senior advisors. His good counsel and quiet leadership would have added to her confidence. She told them of the planned rescue and how it was to take place.

"Timing is everything," she told them, "and we have to assume the North Koreans or the Chinese will be watching us, so all movement between here and the ship will have to be done at night. The staging for this will be the starboard stern quarter of *Milwaukee*. At the earliest, we'll begin transfer operations just after sundown tomorrow evening. That means we will have to move the wounded and a portion of the crew to the ship before sunup tomorrow morning. That also means we have a lot to do between now and before the sun comes up tomorrow. Master Chief Crabtree will break the crew up into increments for evacuation; we'll move the wounded first, and I'll work with the master chief to come up with a sequence for the rest of us. Commander O'Connor will supervise the movement from here to the ship and coordinate things from aboard ship. I'll remain here and be among the last to leave." She pushed through a list of assignments and did her best to answer questions. After the meeting broke up, Chief Picard remained behind.

"Captain, Gary Radcliffe and Beth Hefner are simply too weak to be moved. If we try to move them, we'll kill them. I'll volunteer to stay behind with them and take my chances with the North Koreans. It's their only chance, ma'am."

"Chief, my inclination is to say no; we all go together. But let me give it some thought, and thanks for your willingness to stay back with them. Meanwhile, make

preparations to move all our wounded to the ship by
midnight tonight."

Later that afternoon, Kate Bigelow assembled the entire crew near the makeshift sick bay so those being
cared for there could hear as well.

"You've all probably heard talk of getting off this
rock," she began, "and it's true. We have a plan in place
to get us out of here." There was a weak round of applause and cheering, but they quickly quieted to hear
what more she had to say. She went on to outline the
general details of the rescue. "This will be a phased
withdrawal," she concluded, "and your division officers
and chiefs will give you direction on where to be and
when. This will be a lengthy and complex operation, and
we'll be doing it at night and as expeditiously as possible, so that means we work as a team and stay professional. Shipmates help shipmates, right?"

"RIGHT!"

"I've also been told that there may be Chinese ISR
drones or spy satellites in the area and passing information to the North Koreans. So stay inside unless the
normal course of your duties has you outside for routine work. The idea is to look like we're going to remain
here while we get ready to leave. So let's get this done
and go home."

USS *Greenville* had gotten under way just before dawn
that morning and had been running north for ten hours.
With the ASDS clamped to the hull just behind the sail,
the boat was straining to make thirty knots. It was like

a sleek dolphin trying to race through the water with a beach ball tied to its tail. Designed for speed and silence, it now had neither. To the crew of *Greenville,* the boat seemed to wallow a bit as it made its way through the water. There was an audible hiss as the water passed asymmetrically over the after part of the hull and a disconcerting rumbling from the ASDS that carried through the hull. *Greenville* was made to go fast; the ASDS wasn't. All this noise made the veterans of the Silent Service a bit uneasy. Yet, for the most part, the crew knew why they were making a speed run with an ASDS clamped to their submarine and welcomed the opportunity for a real-world mission. It certainly beat quietly boring holes in the ocean on a training exercise or even searching for Chinese or Russian submarines in the Sea of Japan. While *Greenville* thrashed her way north toward the western tip of Chejudo Island, a half dozen men crowded around the wardroom table.

"These aren't the most comfortable waters to operate in," Commander Allen Baumstark offered as they pored over a chart of the waters around Kujido Island, "but if we launch the ASDS at periscope depth and can maintain steerageway of three knots, then we can get you to within about ten miles of that island—maybe a bit closer."

"Ten miles will be just fine," Master Chief Mecoy said. "How about the transfer of personnel coming off the island?"

"Given the possible coverage from shore-based or airborne radars, I'd like to get no closer than fifteen miles to the south. Especially since we'll have to be dead in the water for the transfer. We'll only partially surface to take the LCS crew aboard, but my sail will still be fifteen feet or so in the air. How long will we be exposed?"

Again, Master Chief Mecoy, "It could be anywhere from fifteen minutes to a half hour. And on each trip, the first thing over the side will be a battery-charging pigtail and the last thing that will be disconnected before we make for the island for the next run. Our Achilles' heel is battery life. Every little bit helps."

Baumstark looked to Dawson. "How many personnel will be going in on the first run?"

"Jesse Carpenter and I will be going in, and we'll have two or three waterproof cases with equipment. How about you, Major?"

"I'll take everyone I brought along," Volner replied. "There'll be eight of us, and we'll be going in heavy with weapons and about seventy pounds of gear per man. We'll probably come out a lot lighter."

"And I've decided to send along my medical officer," Baumstark continued. "My last from Seventh Fleet is that there are several seriously wounded sailors that are going to be brought aboard the ASDS. He'll be needed, but only on the first run. So that's eleven that will board the ASDS from here, and perhaps twelve or so wounded and a few others on the first run back. How many can you carry, Master Chief?"

"Hard to say with the wounded and their condition. Probably not a lot more. Past that, we'll try for about twenty per trip, but we've never had that many aboard. We'll just have to wait and see. And you can make that twelve on the first run into the island. Lieutenant Denver will ride the ASDS both ways to help with the transfer."

"I have a question," Volner said. "Where are we going to put all these people?" This was not Volner's first time on a submarine, but his previous experience was with USS *Michigan,* a Trident-class ballistic-missile submarine that had been modified to support special operations missions. It was almost three times the size of *Greenville.* Compared to *Michigan,* the Los Angeles–class boats were sewer pipes.

Baumstark grinned. "It will be a little crowded, but we'll make it happen. And that's why we have *Santa Fe.*"

"*Santa Fe?*" Volner asked.

"That was another piece of information we received on our last communications check. We'll have some help on this mission."

Volner considered this. *I know we've got to get the crew off this rock. They're counting on me, Mr. Williams is counting on me, and Mr. Dawson is counting on me. I've worked with SEALs before, but it's been on land—not in a submarine and a submersible like this. Can I really control this mission and bring this crew— and my men—out alive?*

While *Greenville* sped north, blind, deaf, and putting a lot of noise into the water, USS *Santa Fe* (SSN-763) was silently making her way into the northern Yellow Sea at ten knots. Also a Los Angeles–class boat, it was carefully sniffing along the proposed track of the

Greenville to make sure there were no enemy submarines lurking about and to be on hand to handle some of the evacuees from *Milwaukee*. And neither of the boats assigned to this rescue mission were without teeth. In addition to a large number of torpedoes, each of them was equipped with twelve Tomahawk cruise missiles housed in vertical launch tubes mounted just forward of their sail.

On Kujido Island, a buzz of excitement and anticipation had overtaken the crew of *Milwaukee*. There was, in reality, little for them to do, but the officers and senior petty officers kept them busy to pass the time. They had been told they could bring nothing—no bag, backpacks, or carry-ons. Space would be at a premium, and they needed to be prepared to move quickly down boarding ladders and through a narrow hatchway. Personal effects were to be limited to medicines and a few articles of personal hygiene stuffed into pockets. They were to dress warmly, but no bulky clothing. In scarcely five hours, they would begin moving the wounded back across the beach to the ship along with about a third of the crew. The rest would follow the next evening when the actual evacuation began.

Kate Bigelow continued to make periodic rounds and spent a moment or two with each crewman. And each hour, she checked in with Seventh Fleet Operations. All seemed to be in order for the planned rescue, although for reasons that were not given, the parent sub, which she now knew to be USS *Greenville,* was not going to be on station off Kujido Island until late tomorrow afternoon. That was cutting it a little close, but she was assured that it would be there and that the physical evacuation would begin on schedule.

"Captain, Chief Picard would like to see you in sick bay." It was Petty Officer Third Class Horace Matthews, one of the more medically knowledgeable crew members Picard had pressed into service to help her with the wounded.

"Very well, Matthews," she said, and they made their way across the concrete enclosure to where the wounded were being cared for. She found Chief Picard standing over a blanketed form that had the sheet pulled up over the head and shoulders. Picard stood with her arms folded, seemingly unaware of Bigelow's presence. She waited in silence a moment with her chief corpsman before she spoke.

"Who?" she asked quietly.

"Petty Officer Gary Radcliffe." Bigelow took her by the elbow and with more than a gentle tug, led her away from the still form on the ground. "I did everything I could, Captain, but this cold, this place; damn it, he never had a chance. I didn't even have the right meds to ease his pain. When's it going to end, Captain? And how are we going to get the rest of these people down to the ship and into this submarine or whatever it is that's supposed to be coming for us?" Bigelow now had placed her hand on her shoulder in a soothing gesture, but she was closely observing her. "And no, I'm not taking any meds myself, damn you! Sorry, Captain, it's just . . ."

Bigelow now had a hand on each of her chief's shoulders, and she was in fact looking for signs Picard was taking something. She saw nothing. "Look, Carol, we asked for none of this, but here it is and here we are. Everything that has taken place, those who have died, including Petty Officer Radcliffe, and those who may yet die, are my responsibility and mine alone. I'm the captain. I have to do my job, and I have to depend on you to do yours. Now I want you to continue to prepare these people for transport." Picard started to protest, but Bigelow silenced her with a firm stare. "We will leave no one behind, and that's my final decision. Those ship-mates who are dead we'll come back for another time. I'll have Master Chief Crabtree get Radcliffe to the ship so he can be with the others. I want you to focus on those who still need your care. Okay?" Picard nodded, but she seemed to be looking past her. Bigelow shook her gently. "I said, okay, Chief?"

"Aye, aye, ma'am."

"Good. I'm counting on you."

She turned to go and found Jack O'Connor waiting for her on the edge of sick bay. He had a sour look on his face.

"What's up, XO?"

"I heard about Radcliffe. It's a shame. You know he has a wife and three kids back in San Diego." Bigelow did in fact know that, but she was not going to let Jack O'Connor take her there.

"There's someone at home waiting for all of us. The loss of Radcliffe is a tragedy, for his family, for me, for you, and for his shipmates. That doesn't alter what's ahead of us and what we have to do."

"But respectfully, Captain, what is it we *have* to do?

The North Koreans have offered to help us; if we'd taken them up on that offer, we might have saved Radcliffe. And this proposed submarine rescue is not going to be easy. And I know about that dry minisub the SEALs use. It's an untested prototype system. Are you sure this is worth the risk? And who thought this one up? Sorry, Captain, but I don't like this."

Bigelow waited a full fifteen seconds before responding. "Jack, I don't care if you don't like it. I'm not sure I like it. But all that's beside the point. This is our duty. It's our duty to get off this island, out from between the North Koreans and our fleet. I'm in command, and we'll do our duty to the best of our ability, period. Now, you don't have to like it, but if you're not prepared to back me one hundred percent and execute my orders, then I better know that right now. So how's it going to be, Jack? Are you prepared to execute my orders without question?"

O'Connor hesitated a moment longer than he knew he should have before answering. "Yes, ma'am, I will follow your orders."

"Very well." She took a half step closer and continued in a quieter voice. "And when and if you have command at sea, I hope you have an executive officer who shows you a lot more support and loyalty than you've shown me." She paused a moment before continuing. "Now I want you to go with the wounded and first lot of the crew to be evacuated. I'll send Master Chief Crabtree with you. You'll wait the day out there in the mission module deck and then begin the loading at dusk tomorrow when that minisub gets alongside. Any questions?"

"No, ma'am."

"If there are, you'll know where to find me. I'll be over with the last of the crew to leave the island. Now, you better get your people ready to move out. Good luck, Jack."

"Uh, good luck to you, Captain."

The wounded of *Milwaukee* now numbered thirteen. A number of those only slightly injured in the surface action and artillery shelling had been patched up and returned to duty. Eleven had been killed in the attacks or died of their wounds and would remain on board the ship until they could be reclaimed along with what was now the hulk of *Milwaukee*. The thirteen wounded were now back aboard the LCS and resting as comfortably as possible in the vessel's mission bay. The ship's enginemen had brought one of the portable generators back aboard and had powered up several space heaters. It was not warm, but they had taken the bite out of the wet Yellow Sea winter chill. There was just enough fuel to last the day. Two of the casualties were highly sedated and another four had injuries that rendered them incapacitated due to their pain meds or splinted limbs. The other seven were semiambulatory but would need some assistance in any evacuation effort.

Another twenty crew members had reboarded the ship with the wounded. Seven of those twenty were civilian technical representatives. The eighth tech rep had been killed in the exchange with the North Korean frigates. These twenty would assist with getting the wounded over the side and then be the next increment of evacuees.

Still on the island were forty-two crewmen and the captain of *Milwaukee*.

"XO, Master Chief, are you there?" Kate Bigelow was speaking into her Motorola transceiver.

"XO here, Captain."

"Master Chief Crabtree standing by."

"Everything all right there?"

Jack O'Connor answered. "We're all secure and the wounded are resting as comfortably as possible. The spaces smell of gasoline and burnt rubber, but we're setting up a portable blower to get some fresh air in here. We have a long day ahead of us, but we'll make the best of it. And we'll make a point of staying off the weather decks. Any word from our rescuers?"

"I don't expect to hear from them directly until later this afternoon. When I hear from them, you'll hear from me. If anything comes up, give me a call. Captain, out."

While the crew on *Milwaukee* did what they could to be comfortable and await events, those ashore moved in and out of their concrete refuge at will. The roving patrols were visible, and they had started a burn pile some fifty yards downwind from the building. Inside, they continued to make preparations to abandon the building under cover of darkness that evening.

Orbiting at thirty-five-thousand feet overhead was a lone Lijian, or Sharp Sword, Chinese drone. The unmanned aircraft had stealth design features and bore a striking resemblance to the American X-47 stealth drone. The Lijian was a prototype aircraft and did not yet have an infrared capability, and the ducting that served the turbofan engine was such that the U.S. airborne radars circling over the South Korean mainland had no trouble tracking it. There was talk of shooting it down, but not until it served its purpose, which was that of reporting to its Chinese controllers the Americans were still hunkered down in the abandoned cannery on Kujido Island.

CHAPTER TWENTY-TWO

THE WHITE HOUSE OVAL OFFICE

November 14, 1030 Eastern Standard Time

Wyatt Midkiff knew it wouldn't be a pleasant encounter, but he needed to ensure that his Op-Center director and his national security advisor were on the same page—that's why he had insisted on the meeting. The tension between the two men was well contained but still just under the surface. Williams knew Harward had supported the defense secretary and the chairman of the Joint Chiefs in urging immediate, decisive action against North Korea for attacking *Milwaukee*. Close to a dozen U.S. Navy sailors had died, and more were wounded. Worse, North Korea was trying one plan after another to snatch the crew off the island and hold them hostage.

But the president had the final word, and Williams had convinced him to play for time and let him try to rescue the crew with the ASDS. Now they were just hours away from executing the plan. Midkiff needed consensus.

"Chase, we've read your memos, and I've back-briefed Trevor on our most recent phone conversation. You have an update on USS *Greenville* and on *Milwaukee*'s crew on Kujido Island?"

"I do, Mr. President. First, regrettably, another *Milwaukee* sailor has died, bringing the total dead to eleven. And it is good we are close to extracting the crew. Commander Bigelow reports at least one sailor, and perhaps another, will likely perish within the next twenty-four to thirty-six hours if we don't extract them from that freezing rock soon."

"How cold is it there on Kujido Island?" Harward asked.

"It creeps up to about forty degrees by early afternoon but then plummets to below freezing at night. The medical packet we air-dropped about eight hours ago helped, and the captain and her chief corpsman have all the antibiotics and other medical supplies they need for the moment. But there's nothing we can do about the exposure the crew is dealing with except to get them off that island."

"I've got that, Chase," the president replied. "Now tell us more about the rescue and about *Greenville* and the other assets you've got close to the scene."

Williams powered up his secure iPad and began to walk them through the plan.

Chase Williams's spectacularly successful naval career and his success in winning the confidence of the president in being appointed Op-Center's director were not achieved by second-guessing himself or by letting himself become immobilized by a crisis. But while he confidently walked the president and Harward through the rescue process, he thought, *Will this plan really work?*

The day and evening of the planned rescue seemed to drag by. Those huddled aboard the grounded *Milwaukee* had little to do but try to stay warm and pass the time. Those who could sleep did, but most were too keyed up with the prospect of a rescue to do more than nod off for a few minutes. All were dreaming of a hot shower and a fast-food burger with fries. Under Master Chief Crabtree's direction, one of the culinary specialists had gone to the galley and was able to activate one of the gas-fired shipboard grills. Though the ship was at a severe starboard list, she was able to put together a broth with a few vegetables and deliver a round of hot soup. It did much to cheer her shipmates.

On the island, the rest of the crew did what they could to maintain a routine. They kept up a roving patrol and burned trash at the downwind site a short distance from the cannery. The only sign of conflict was the ongoing artillery exchange. The North Korean coastal guns on the mainland and the South Korean 155 mm artillery on Yeonpyeong Island kept up an intermittent duel that crashed and echoed just a few miles northwest of Kujido Island. While the crew of the *Milwaukee* both ashore and on board were somewhat content to pass the time as best they could, their captain was not.

Kate Bigelow paced about the disused concrete

cannery, becoming more impatient by the hour. During each of her scheduled Iridium sat-phone calls to Seventh Fleet Operations, she asked about the progress and location of the rescue submarines, and each time she was told that all was on schedule. On a recent call, when she further probed, the watch officer did admit it had been more than eight hours since *Greenville*'s last comm check. Following the 1700 call, Bigelow was struggling with great difficulty to remain calm. She told herself a great many people and a great navy were doing all in their power to help her and her crew. But she was exhausted, and the crushing responsibility of extracting her crew from this concrete hell was almost overwhelming. There was nothing for her to do but put on a positive face, make her rounds, and do what she could to keep up the morale of her crew. *Or are they keeping up my morale? Each one I meet seems to have a smile and a good word for me! God bless these fine sailors; I simply must find a way to get them out of here and to safety.*

"Hey, Captain," Petty Officer Matheson called from across the large central room. There was some urgency to his voice, bringing Bigelow at a run. "Some guy named Dawson. He asked for you by name." She grabbed the Iridium and made for the door, again for the privacy and the reception.

"This is Captain Bigelow."

"Captain, this is Brian Dawson here aboard USS *Greenville*. Was it you who called for a taxicab?"

"Damn straight, Dawson, and it's good to hear your voice. Where are you and"—she just couldn't help herself—"*who* in the hell are you, anyway?"

"Captain, I'm the guy who's going to get you off that island. Right now, we're about ten miles south of your position. And you can call me Brian, Cap'n. The ASDS, or minisubmarine, will be leaving *Greenville* in just a few minutes to come for you. Are your people ready to make the transfer?"

"As ready as we can be, and our wounded will be first."

They talked for another five minutes before Dawson rang off. Bigelow returned the Iridium to Petty Officer Matheson feeling better than she had since the two North Korean frigates appeared on the *Milwaukee*'s radar in what now seemed like several months ago.

Aboard *Greenville*, Brian Dawson left the sub's communications station and made his way aft to the ASDS. *Greenville* was indeed a little more than ten miles south-southwest of Kujido Island. The submarine was at periscope depth with her comm mast extended and was making three knots—just enough to hold depth, which was a challenge for the planesman with the weight of the ASDS on the parent sub's back.

Aboard the ASDS, Lieutenant Bill Naylor was at the controls with Master Chief Harlan Mecoy at his side. They were going through their prelaunch checklists. In the rear of the minisub, Major Mike Volner and seven heavily armed members of his team sat quietly awaiting events. Collectively, they maintained a practiced impassivity that only veteran special operators can do on the eve of a mission tasking. Along with the JSOC team was a single medical officer who, though a qualified submariner, had the apprehensive look of a doctor used to a much larger submarine. With him was Jesse Carpenter, along with several waterproof cases of electronic and communications gear. Also aboard were Lieutenant Tom Denver and Petty Officer Collins to help get the wounded aboard from the LCS. Collins was a last-minute addition for this first run to help embark the wounded. Under normal circumstances, *Greenville* would be in deeper water for an ASDS launch, and at a lower speed, and there would be SDV SEALs outside in the water to help get the ASDS safely away. But not at this speed.

Brian Dawson scrambled up through the pressurized collar that served to mate the ASDS with *Greenville*. As he did so, Master Chief Mecoy was there to meet him and drop the hatch to seal the minisub from the outside. The main portion of the ASDS was comprised of three compartments: a forward compartment for the pilot and copilot/navigator, a center compartment that housed the docking collar that also served as a "moon pool" entrance for the launch and recovery of swimmers under water, and a rear compartment for troops. These three compartments were connected by access hatches and accounted for the first two-thirds of the sub's length. The after portion housed the batteries and propulsion unit. Once Dawson was aboard, he followed Mecoy forward to where Naylor was preparing to undock from the mother ship and strike out on their own.

"You guys ready to break away and do this?"

"Just say the word, Mr. Dawson," Mecoy replied as he slid into his control station.

"Then make it happen, Master Chief—and it's Brian."

"Roger that, Brian." Then to his lieutenant he said, "Ready, sir?"

Naylor just nodded, neither speaking nor taking his eyes from the displays in front of him. Master Chief Mecoy tended to the mechanics of unlocking the docking collar. The ASDS was held to *Greenville* only by the residual pressure differential between the lower boarding hatch of the ASDS and the escape trunk of the parent sub, as well as the external sea pressure. Naylor flooded this small space with seawater while blowing air into the ASDS ballast tanks and making turns for three knots. It was a neat piece of watermanship and airmanship. The ASDS separated from *Greenville* and rose to the surface like a buoyant sausage. Naylor immediately turned away from *Greenville*'s base course, flooded his ballast tanks, and dove his boat. He took the ASDS to the planned cruise depth of fifteen feet and took a heading for Kujido at the little boat's max speed of eight knots.

Looking over Mecoy's shoulder, Dawson could feel little. The boat rolled slightly in the Yellow Sea chop, but there was no sensation of motion once Naylor had it on a steady course, speed, and depth. There was only the slight vibration of the seventy-horsepower motor that pushed them through the dark waters.

"So how do you know when we get there?" Dawson asked.

Mecoy turned his head and motioned him closer. "This is not a sophisticated craft," he whispered. "We have an inertial navigation system, but the lieutenant flies this as much by intuition as by instruments. He'll feel his way to get us close to *Milwaukee*. Then he'll make the final approach visually using the port periscope." He further lowered his voice. "It's all on him to get us there. But he's the best there is." He turned back to monitoring the dials and gages in front of him.

Sensing he was only a distraction, Dawson made his way aft to check on the others. As he made his way back through the docking compartment to the troop compartment, he realized that the entire operation rested on the talents of this quiet, baby-faced lieutenant. Brian Dawson prided himself on not being a worrywart, but now he was having the same thoughts Mike Volner was having.

CHAPTER TWENTY-THREE

KUJIDO ISLAND IN THE
YEONPYEONG ISLAND GROUP

November 15, 2245 Korea Standard Time

Master Chief Crabtree had come out and positioned himself just behind the coaming that led out onto the flight deck. It was here that he had a good vantage point along the starboard side of *Milwaukee* from amidships aft to the stern. It was a cold, quiet evening with the wind slackening from what they had experienced earlier that day. As darkness continued to settle over the island and the grounded ship, he thought he saw a mast appear in the water, but it quickly disappeared from view. It came and was gone so quickly that he was not sure it was ever there. But then he wasn't thinking all that clearly. He'd just had a confrontation with Commander Jack O'Connor about the staging of the wounded for transfer. Crabtree had wanted to move them to where they could quickly be lowered to the rescue sub. O'Connor had overruled him. "We're not even sure that sub is going to be here.

If and when it does, we'll move the wounded. Not until then."

Crabtree had almost called Captain Bigelow, but going over his executive officer's head ran contrary to what the master chief knew and liked about the Navy. The tension between the skipper and the XO was well known to Crabtree and was becoming apparent to most of the crew. It was not a good thing, to be sure, but Crabtree was not willing to jump the chain of command, at least not yet. Then suddenly, a dark form mushroomed at the starboard side of *Milwaukee* some twenty feet from the stern. A hatch opened just forward of the middle of the vessel, and three figures poured out. One tossed a grappling iron over the rail to hold the ASDS close alongside *Milwaukee,* then quickly scrambled aboard. The other two moved fore and aft, each carrying a half-inch mooring line. The forms on deck quickly made the black tube secure forward, then ran back to secure its stern. The ASDS now rested gently on the fenders Crabtree had put over the side earlier that morning.

Moments before, Lieutenant Bill Naylor had brought the ASDS to a dead stop just fifty yards from *Milwaukee*. Then, taking a sighting on the starboard quarter of the LCS with a periscope that had low-light-level capability, he quickly judged the distance to the ship. He then downed the scope and proceeded to bring the ASDS gently alongside the ship. He knew his craft and his boat that well.

Now that the minisub was made up alongside, more dark figures poured from the hatch and swarmed aboard. The first of them were, once again, dark forms, but these were heavily armed men with assault packs, body armor, night-vision goggles, and weapons. They scattered about the ship and took up security positions. The few who saw Crabtree waiting a step behind the coaming paid him no heed. Then a form dressed like the others but without an automatic weapon, assault pack, or body armor moved onto the deck. Like the others, his face was painted black and he carried only a sidearm—a .45 caliber automatic. The boarding had taken less than a minute.

"Ahoy there, *Milwaukee*," he announced in a quiet, confident voice. "Anyone home?"

Crabtree stepped forward and saluted. "Command Master Chief Crabtree here. And you are?"

"I'm Brian Dawson, command master chief. I'll be orchestrating your redeployment from the garden spot. Is Captain Bigelow about?"

"She's still on the island, Mr. Dawson. Our wounded, my executive officer, and a part of the crew are be-lowdecks waiting for the word to begin the transfer."

"Then we better get cracking, Master Chief. We've a lot to do and not a lot of time to do it."

The transfer of the wounded took close to an hour. The first of the wounded had to be brought aft to the after-mission bay of the LCS, something Dawson im-mediately noted should have been done earlier. The critically wounded had to be lashed into Stokes litters and lowered out the side of the mission-bay door to the ASDS. Then they had to be unlashed and gently lowered through the top hatch, into the locking collar compart-ment, and aft to the troop compartment. All this re-quired multiple hands and a great deal of coordination among the *Milwaukee* crewmen and the ASDS SEALs. Aboard the minisub, *Greenville*'s medical officer tended to each as they came through the troop-compartment hatch, dispensing meds and starting IVs. It was almost after midnight before the ASDS was loaded and ready to leave the LCS. In addition to the thirteen wounded crewmen, they were able to take only two additional members of the crew. On direct order of Commander Bigelow, Commander O'Connor and Chief Corpsman Picard were those two. Only Picard objected to this initial boarding. Lieutenant Denver remained on board *Milwaukee* while Petty Officer Collins stayed aboard the sub. As the ASDS took on the added weight of the passengers, close to three thousand pounds, only a skillful reballasting effort by Lieutenant Naylor kept the top of the craft awash during the transfer. Once loaded, the ASDS cast off, submerged, and made its way back to *Greenville,* a run of close to two hours.

Once the ASDS reached *Greenville,* it was quickly made up alongside. Because the parent sub had its afterdeck just above the surface, a brow was put over making the unloading much easier than had been the vertical drop from the LCS to the ASDS. It took twenty minutes to get everyone onto *Greenville,* allowing for twenty minutes of battery-charging time. Air hoses were also put over to top off the ASDS ballast and breathing air. Then it was away and headed back for Kujido Island.

Mike Volner split his force into two fire teams. Four of his men would remain aboard *Milwaukee,* where they would take up firing perches on the upper portions of the superstructure. The other three, along with Volner, made their way ashore in the Zodiac, which had just delivered another increment of the LCS crew back aboard their ship. Dawson and Carpenter also went ashore. While the JSOC men took up security positions around the cannery, the two Op-Center men stepped inside. They were met immediately by the captain of *Milwaukee*.

"You must be Brian Dawson," she said, extending her hand. "Commander Kate Bigelow. I can't tell you how glad I am to see you, sir."

On entering the cannery, Dawson felt like he was entering some kind of medieval dungeon. He was immediately taken with the dampness and the stench of too many people kept in close quarters for too long a time. It was a cramped, depressing, unhealthy place. His first glance at Commander Kate Bigelow told him he was dealing with a courageous lady who was not too far from her breaking point. But when he made eye contact with her, he came up with another calculus. She was a leader who might be tired and beaten down, but she would never be broken. He reflexively took her hand with both of his own.

"Captain, you've made a gallant stand here. But now I think it's time to get you out of here. I have a security team that will take over from your people. When you're ready, I think it's time to get all your people back aboard your ship and ready to move out."

A short distance away, Jesse Carpenter didn't have to be told what to do. He immediately found Petty Officer Matheson and began to set up his gear. While he did that, Kate Bigelow directed the evacuation of the cannery. Brian Dawson was never far away. The ASDS returned at 0345 and was able to take off eighteen members of the crew, including all the tech reps. This time it made for *Santa Fe,* which had closed to six miles southwest of the island. That left forty-three on board *Milwaukee* plus the eight-member JSOC team, the two Op-Center personnel, and a single SEAL lieutenant. If they were quick, they could possibly get one more pickup in before sunrise. The last run or runs would have to be done in the daylight.

In the weeks since he had met with the handler, Seung Min-jae had been a blur of activity. He told his professors at New York University that his mother was dying of congestive heart failure and that he needed to return to North Korea to arrange for her care. He also had to see to the welfare of his two younger sisters, one of whom was autistic, and his younger brother. Only then could he return to the United States and continue in his prelaw program. Seung was a bright student and something of an extrovert, a ruse he had quietly cultivated in his two-plus years at this American university. His teachers, as well as the NYU school administrators, had bent over backward to accommodate this smart, eager young North Korean student. One of his professors had even quietly asked other teachers and students for donations so Seung could pay for his airfare from New York to Pyongyang as well as his train fare from the North Korean capital to his family home along North Korea's northwest coast.

It was all a lie, but a lie that served its purposes. Seung dropped his classes and moved from his apartment into the safe house—a fourth-floor walk-up, one-bedroom apartment in a decaying rent-controlled building in New York's Murray Hill neighborhood. Seung lived in these cramped quarters with his four partners, three men and one woman, all students at other local universities. Now the five of them were together and fully focused on what might come next. The handler had made it clear to Seung Min-jae that they might never be called upon to carry out their mission. Yet if they were, they would be national heroes and their families would be well cared for. If they didn't, they would return to their studies and await another assignment. Two weeks after they had begun camping in the apartment and evolving their plan, one of the other men began to complain about the uncertainty of the assignment. Seung had asked him to walk outside with him. Once on the street, Seung guided him into an alley, where they had a one-way conversation.

"You will never question me or the supreme leader again. We were selected from among thousands of equally acceptable candidates whose families had the high honor of putting them forward for this worthy undertaking. You will recall I personally vouched for you and Major General Hwa recommended you to the marshal. Do you understand what will happen to your family if you fail in your duty?"

"I . . . I am . . ." The man began to reply, but Seung cut him off.

"Shut up, you fucking coward. You will do what I tell

you to do, when I tell you to do it, and how I tell you to do it, is that clear?" Seung barked, and as he did, he grabbed both of the man's shoulders and roughly slammed him against the brick wall in the alley.

"Yes," was all the man could say through his whimpering.

"Good, now go to the market and get us food for tonight."

As the man retreated down the alley to do Seung's bidding, the leader of the sleeper cell paused to ask himself the same question the man had asked him. When would they be called upon? One week after giving him his assignment, the handler produced a 1998 Honda Odyssey minivan for their use. The tired-looking vehicle was designed to blend into the background in New York City's chaotic, constantly snarled traffic. But it had not spent much time in the city. The handler's instructions had been explicit regarding where they were to buy the explosives and other materials they needed for their assignment. They had ranged as far west as northern Ohio and as far south as eastern Kentucky to carry out their duties and make their purchases. Then they had carted all this up to the already-cramped apartment, and now they slept with enough explosives to level several city blocks. They would need that much to destroy the building that was to be their target. The handler told Seung he would be informed what his target was to be "in due course," but he did reveal that their safe house had been selected for its proximity to their intended target. Seung was well aware of the news and knew his country and the United States were in a shooting war. Though he dared not say it to the others, Seung himself was beginning to wonder when they would be called upon to act.

After receiving the eighteen crewmen from the ASDS, *Santa Fe* took up a patrol station west of Kujido Island. *Greenville*'s sister was on a heading of 030, making a mere two knots and listening intently for any surface or submarine activity between the North Korean mainland and the island. It was about to leave station and take a southeasterly heading to join *Greenville,* which was about to take on board yet another ASDS passenger load, when the lead sonarman heard something. He listened for another several minutes to connect what he was hearing to what he was seeing on his visual waterfall display.

"Control room, sonar. I have an underwater contact at zero-one-five, range nine thousand yards."

"Sonar, control, can you classify it."

The sonar tech recognized his captain's voice. "It sounds like a submarine blowing ballast, Skipper. And if I had to guess, it's a sub that has just surfaced."

When it comes to underwater acoustics, no one is more practiced or vigilant than the U.S. Navy. Navy submariners have always prided themselves on having the quietest submarine technology and the best underwater listening capability. But this superiority applied only to nuclear-fleet submarine operations. The one hole in their game was finding the quieter diesel submarines. Good as they are, U.S. nuclear submarines have a difficult time finding these smaller submarines when they're operating inshore and running on batteries. And *Santa Fe* would not have found this one had it been more careful in blowing air into its ballast tanks to surface—that and the fact that this submarine was all but a museum piece. The captain of *Santa Fe* knew immediately what he had to do.

"Come to periscope depth and get the communications mast up ASAP. Meanwhile, get me a firing solution on that contact and prepare to put fish in the water on my command."

There was a flurry of activity aboard *Santa Fe,* but all was disciplined and professional activity—quiet and purposeful.

Two miles north northwest of Kujido Island, a Romeo-class North Korean submarine had just surfaced. This one had a large walrus nose that rose from the deck almost as high as the sail. It was a Romeo variant officially classed as a PZS-50 but known in the submarine community as the Ugly Romeo. It had more piping and valves than a Kuwaiti oil terminal. The Romeo was large as far as diesel boats went, displacing close to two thousand tons submerged. Of an ancient Russian design, this Chinese hand-me-down had been modified by the North Koreans to support the landing of special operations teams. From a deck hatch abaft the bulbous nose and another in the forward part of the sail, dark forms poured out like rats from a flooded sewer. They quickly sorted themselves out, produced four inflatable rafts,

and put them over the side. After installing outboard engines, thirty-two commandos piled in and turned their
small craft south. They had just cleared the side of the
submarine when an orbiting Global Hawk drone, alerted
by a burst transmission from the *Santa Fe,* spotted them.
But this Global Hawk was unarmed and could only report what it saw back to its controllers.

Aboard *Santa Fe,* the captain was handed a message
from one of his communicators. It was brief and to
the point, and he permitted himself a quiet smile. Then
he turned to his weapons officer.

"We still have a solution on that target?"

"Yes, sir, at least the general area. Sonar says the contact may have just submerged. They've now classified it
as a Romeo-class boat."

"A Romeo, huh. How about that. Recheck your solution and shoot. Two fish, slow run to target."

"Aye, sir. Understand weapons released, two fish,
slow run to target."

Moments later, two Mark 48, Mod 7 advanced-
capabilities (ADCAP) torpedoes left *Santa Fe* about
ten seconds apart. The Mark 48s were of a basic design
that was fifty years old, almost as old as the prey they
sought. But they were light-years ahead in technology
and design modification. Both were instructed to make
their way through the Yellow Sea on a given bearing
for a given distance. When they got there, they would
then execute a helix-type search pattern with their active sonars. Anything they found in the water they would
immediately attack and kill. While the two torpedoes

made their run, *Santa Fe* turned southeast to take station and await the return of the ASDS.

While the two American Los Angeles–class boats went about their business, they were not alone. A Chinese Type 093, Shang-class submarine had slowly and carefully made its way into the area and was monitoring events as they unfolded. It was no small thing to backdoor an American nuclear boat in open water, let alone two, but the Shang-class had done it. It was China's best boat, and it was skippered by her best captain. The sonar operator aboard did not detect the launch of the two Mark 48s from the *Santa Fe,* but he did pick up the underwater explosions as both fish found the Ugly Romeo. Had he been more experienced or his equipment more advanced, he would not have put it down to rounds falling short from the coastal artillery barrage.

The North Korean Romeo died quickly and violently. Seconds apart, the Mark 48s crashed into the amidships section of the old submarine and cut it in half. Those in the control-room maneuvering rooms died instantly. Those aft in the engineering spaces and after-torpedo room drowned quickly as the Yellow Sea poured into the aft portion of the sinking sub. But the bulbous bow of the Romeo had enough buoyancy to pop to the surface before it, too, filled with water and slipped below the surface. But five crewmen, all ratings, managed to escape with minor injuries. They clung to an old, deflated life raft; none had life vests. They were drenched in diesel oil and looked like survivors of a World War II U-boat sinking. But their good fortune was only temporary. One by one, the cold took them, and they slipped quietly away. By morning there was only the rumpled raft and an oil slick.

The ASDS had just returned from the *Santa Fe* and made up to the starboard stern quarter of *Milwaukee*. Dawn was fast approaching as twenty-two more LCS crew members scrambled aboard. With two excursions under his belt, Bill Naylor felt he and the ASDS could take a few more passengers. Before the personnel transfer, some bulky equipment, including a large, heavy canvas bag weighing upward of 125 pounds, was wrestled back aboard the ship.

"What the hell's this," growled Master Chief Crabtree as he and Lieutenant Denver hauled it up to the deck of the LCS.

"Something the major wanted," Petty Officer Collins replied. He was making the runs with the ASDS while Denver remained on board *Milwaukee* to work that end of the exodus. When the last of the LCS crew were aboard, Collins ducked into the hatch and dogged it shut, and the ASDS was away with its third load of evacuees.

"Let's get this thing out of sight and get below," Denver offered. "I've a feeling things are going to get a little lively before too much longer."

Earlier that morning, Kate Bigelow and Brian Dawson had been alerted that North Korean commandos were about to land on the northern shore of Kujido Island. This was not good news, but they could now at least be ready for them. And their numbers were dwindling. With the last twenty-two from the crew away on the ASDS, there were now twenty-one from *Milwaukee,* counting her captain, eight from the JSOC team, and three others—Lieutenant Tom Denver, Dawson, and Carpenter—left to evacuate. All were now aboard *Milwaukee,* but they were ready to welcome the North Korean contingent that had just invaded sovereign South Korean territory.

General Choi Kwang, marshal of the Korean People's Army, allowed himself a tight smile. He had tried to let his subordinates come up with a plan to capture the LCS crew stranded on Kujido Island, but they had failed and failed miserably. He even allowed himself a bit of self-congratulation for his foresight. In his previous position as vice marshal of the KPA, he was the one who had made sure the Chinese hand-me-down Romeo-class submarine was retrofitted to carry commandos.

Now the Ugly Romeo, as Western navies dubbed it, had accomplished its mission. It had secretly delivered the team of commandos to Kujido Island, where they would soon take the LCS's crew captive and ready them for transport to North Korean territory. When his commando team leader had radioed the headquarters in Pyongyang and announced that they had landed on Kujido Island unopposed, a quiet cheer rose from the command center. Choi knew success was close at hand. He needed these American sailors in his grasp on North Korean territory. Then and only then would the supreme leader be pleased with him. General Choi liked to think of himself as fearless. Yet when the prospect of failure began to stare him in the face, he knew that he, his wife, and his two teenage daughters would spend the rest of their lives in one of the North's infamous rehabilitation camps. He knew about life in the Chongjin concentration camp, as well as in those like it, in northeastern North Korea near the Chinese border. The thought filled him with dread.

And once he had accomplished this mission, he knew he had to turn his attention to the other task the supreme leader had assigned to him. He had delegated this undertaking to his protégé, Major General Hwa, and had Hwa giving him almost daily updates since he had activated the cell several weeks earlier. Choi was well connected enough politically to anticipate it would not be long before the supreme leader would seek retribution for what the Americans were doing.

But that was not his immediate concern. He needed to hear from his commando team leader again—and soon.

The focus of the North Korean commando element was the cannery. Two men were sent to the beach to put eyes on the hulk of the *Milwaukee,* but the balance of the force made for the cannery. The structure had a carefully blocked rear door and front entrance served by a makeshift door of hinged plywood. The windows were covered with blankets, but there was evidence of lights burning inside. A generator purred by the side of the building with a heavy power cord that snaked in through a window. A radio played South Korean music from within. From the perspective of the North Koreans, it was an unsuspecting enemy camp. They moved in quietly and set up for a classic compound assault. There was a security element, a blocking element, a command and control element, and an assault element. The commando leader waited until there was just enough light for his men to clearly see their targets.

"On balance, they don't seem to be too bad," Mike Volner said in a professional tone. "That's just about the way I'd do it."

"What are they waiting for?" Brian Dawson asked.

Volner leaned forward to adjust the tough-book computer screen. "Not all of them have night-vision goggles. I think they're waiting for more daylight. Don't forget: They want prisoners, not casualties."

Not fifteen minutes earlier they had tossed a hand-launched Raven drone from the flight deck and put it into an orbit around the cannery at about one thousand feet. Its low-light video feed gave Volner and Dawson a clear picture of the North Koreans' movements.

Suddenly, the van of the assault element, some eight men in all, kicked in the plywood partition and stormed into the cannery. Nothing happened for several seconds, then there was a blinding explosion from within. Greeting those first men in the door was an arc of three command-detonated claymore mines that literally shredded them. Six were killed outright, while another two would soon bleed to death. Then more claymores skillfully attached to the sides of the building began to cook off in sequence, tearing into those exposed supporting elements. Within ten seconds, fully half of the North Korean force was dead or incapacitated. Yet the

North Koreans, like the special operations professionals they were, carried on. Men with lungs pierced and
useless limbs helped those more seriously hurt to a more
comfortable position while they bled out. There were
few cries for help or from pain; they were a stoic and
disciplined lot. Those uninjured or slightly wounded re-
distributed ammunition and looked to those officers
and sergeants still alive for direction. Yet none of them
moved with the same élan and sense of purpose as they
had when they came ashore.

Back on *Milwaukee*, the JSOC snipers, well placed
on the bridge wing of the pilothouse and on the signal
bridge, each took a shot. They were armed with Stoner
SR-25 semiautomatic sniper weapons, but neither needed
a second shot. The North Korean commandos sent to
watch the ship were center-punched and died where
they lay in their observation posts.

"Help! This is Commander Bigelow, captain of *Milwaukee*. We are under attack from the North Koreans.
They are overrunning our compound. We will soon be
taken prisoner. Can anyone hear me? We need help,
please! This is Commander Bigelow. We can't hold out
much longer!"

It was Kate Bigelow's voice, and it was indeed being
broadcast in the clear of a UHF emergency channel, but
she was no longer on the island. This and two other calls
for help had been recorded by Jesse Carpenter and were
now being transmitted remotely from a radio hidden on
a shallow rise some sixty meters from the cannery. On
the ground below, the wounded leader of the commando
element was crouched beside his radio operator, trying

desperately to make communication with his mainland headquarters. But an Air Force EC-130H electronics-warfare aircraft orbiting over Inchon, South Korea, was putting a great deal of electronic energy into the air, blocking all frequencies but that one coming from the radio with Bigelow's recorded message. Realizing his radio was useless, the commando leader quickly searched the cannery and found it empty. Isolated and with only half his force effective, he immediately turned his attention to *Milwaukee*.

Above the island, the Chinese Lijian drone had just taken station at a leisurely twenty-five thousand feet. Its controller was bringing the cannery and *Milwaukee* into partial focus. Then sun was just up, but patches of low fog still obscured much of the island. Yet the weather was improving. The prospect of further clearing promised a good day of visual observation, but that was still perhaps an hour off. Meanwhile, unknown to the Lijian drone or its controller, a single F/A-18E Super Hornet from USS *Ronald Reagan* was on patrol just sixty miles south of Kujido Island. The Lijian was the reason it was there. The Super Hornet could not see the drone with its radar, but the E-2D Hawkeye aircraft, also from *Ronald Reagan,* could. The Hawkeye, a further ten miles to the south, passed along the range and bearing of the drone to the pilot of the F/A-18E. Moments later, two AIM-120D AMRAAM air-to-air missiles dropped from the under-wing pylons of the jet. The drone was well within the missiles' one-hundred-mile range. Accelerating quickly to Mach 4, it took the AMRAAMs less than thirty seconds to cover the distance. It was not until they were within ten miles of the Lijian that the two birds acquired the drone on their active radars. But their vector was good, and they had to alter course and altitude only slightly. One missile cut the Lijian in half, and the second, knowing it now had one of two options, tore into the larger section of the wreckage. In the control bunker on the Chinese mainland, the Lijian controller looked away from his scope for just a second. When he looked back, there was nothing but electronic snow.

The plan Chase Williams had outlined to rescue the LCS crew was moving forward, and the Op-Center director had dispensed with his POTUS/Eyes Only memos to the president. He now called the president on a secure comm line whenever the situation warranted. The president had canceled all his appointments and spent his time shuttling between the Oval Office and the Situation Room. Now he sat in the Oval Office with his national security advisor. Williams had just called, and the president had Harward listen in on this latest update.

The situation could not have been more complex. Trevor Harward had become a fixture at the president's side, discussing options, weighing alternatives, determining which allies to consult and which ones would have to wait for later. Other than the imminent rescue of *Milwaukee*'s crew, the other bright spot was that, for the moment, cooler heads had prevailed and common sense seemed to have replaced bluster. It did not appear that South Korea was going to preemptively attack the North in retaliation for North Korea's moves against

Kujido Island. The president had personally appealed to South Korea's president, and his counterpart had, in turn, reined in General Kwon Oh-Sung, at least for the moment.

But that was where the good news ended. The United States and North Korea were at war by any definition of the term. Soldiers and sailors on both sides had died and, given the marshaling of forces, more were likely to die. Worse, now China had entered the picture. While China's premier had personally assured the president China had no intention of interfering with the rescue of the LCS crew, he had made it clear activity in the northern Yellow Sea was clearly within China's sphere of influence. "China," he contended, "has rights and historical interests going back several millennia." The premier had even obliquely mentioned his willingness to rein in North Korea's leader, but Midkiff knew the chances of this happening asymptotically approached zero.

"I don't know if we'll get the entire crew off the island, Trevor," the president offered. "It looks like every time we do something, North Korea ups the ante. We could still lose part of the crew, and this entire situation could spin out of control."

Harward found himself in the unusual position of defending Op-Center. "Mr. President, Chase has his best people on scene, and I think we have a better-than-even chance to extract the entire crew. The North Koreans haven't thrown anything at them yet they can't handle."

"I know, but it's clear they want our people and they want them badly, even though we've made it known in every way possible way we're not going to support their seabed claims under any circumstances. We've even hinted to them, as well as to the Chinese, we know why they felt the need to extend their territorial-water claims. It just makes no sense they are still trying to keep us from extracting our crew."

"If we were dealing with almost any other nation, I'd agree with you, Mr. President. But don't forget that this is North Korea and that China needs what they have. And if we retaliate against the North in any substantial way, it might play into China's hands. They could move in and claim the disputed area for themselves or pretend they're establishing some sort of protectorate. If you look at it from that standpoint, it's not too much of a stretch to understand why they are playing this the way they are."

As the president paused to consider this, his secretary came in to tell him that Chase Williams was again calling on the secure line. "Put him through, please."

"Chase, I've got Trevor with me on speakerphone. What do you have for us?"

"Mr. President, I don't have a great deal more to report since we spoke a short while ago. We've turned back the initial North Korean commando attack, and Admiral Bennett's submarines have sunk the North Korean submarine that deposited them on the island. We've killed many of the commandos on the island, but not all. It's still a standoff with the rest of them for the moment. I'll keep you updated as I hear from my people on the island."

"Yes, Chase, please do."

"There's more, Mr. President. As you know, I've been working closely with Admiral Bennett to neutralize the North Korean air and maritime forces until we get all our people back. But we do know the Chinese have been secretly providing them intelligence. We did take out a Chinese Lijian drone that was anchored over the island, but only when it was able to visually scan our rescue effort in the daylight. And my people here at Op-Center have just learned they were also downloading data to the North Korean special operations compound at Nuchonri Air Force Base. You should have all this through your normal military reporting channels."

"We knew of the drone, Chase." It was Harward who replied. "But this is the first we've heard of the North's special operations connection to Chinese intelligence."

"As you can appreciate, Mr. President, it's one thing to take out a Chinese drone, especially since we're virtually certain there are no fingerprints that can tie the shoot down directly to us. But it will be another if we get in a shootout with a manned Chinese asset."

"I know that all too well, Chase. I'm assuming anything we do to another Chinese asset will be strictly in self-defense."

"Absolutely, Mr. President. That's all I have for now, sir. I'll report again once we have the next batch of the crew off the island."

"Godspeed, Chase," the president replied as the line went dead.

"That was reassuring, Mr. President."

"It was, Trevor. So where were we?"

"Sir, that's about it regarding rescuing our hostages, but you did say you wanted an update on our efforts to censure the North Koreans at the United Nations. I've got our ambassador standing by in New York for a call anytime. Shall I get her on the line?"

"Yes, please do."

For those aboard *Milwaukee,* it was a waiting game. The North Korean commandos, what was left of them, were trying to work their way from the cannery to where they could make an assault on the ship. But the JSOC-team snipers owned the high ground, and each time the commandos crept close enough to even put eyes on the LCS, they came under fire. The Raven had been pulled into a higher orbit with the growing daylight, but Mike Volner still had a visual command of the beachhead. It was a standoff, and, unless the commando unit could be reinforced, any assault of the ship was doomed to failure. Volner and Dawson knew this, as did the leader of the North Korean commandos. It was a standoff that might have gone on indefinitely but for a strange turn of events. One of the commandos had a cell phone that found a hole in the EC-130H's electronic blanket. The commando leader was able to get through to his command and tell them what he would need to successfully attack the ship and take the crew hostage.

The captain of the Shang-class Chinese submarine was not entirely sure what the two American submarines were up to, but his orders were to find out. All submarines have signatures, and veteran sonarmen have learned to distinguish between classes of submarines and even individual subs. He knew he had two American Los Angeles–class boats operating nearby, but there was a third acoustic signature with which he was totally unfamiliar. Periodically, one or the other of the American boats would activate a beaconlike underwater transponder, as if it was attempting to mark its position. Then there was what seemed to be a third craft in the area that was electronically very noisy. According to the Chinese sonar technicians aboard, it appeared this third submarine was emitting navigation-sonar transmissions. But the emissions were beyond anything they could classify.

Not wanting to guess wrong or appear unknowledgeable to his superiors, the captain came to periscope depth and raised his communications mast. He reported only that the two American boats, and possibly a third, were maneuvering south and west of Kujido Island—nothing more. He was ordered to press in closer to determine what the Americans might be up to. This sketchy and imprecise information was immediately passed to the North Koreans.

But the Chinese submarine running at periscope depth for the time it took to transmit its message and receive instructions had not gone unnoticed. It had lingered near the surface just a few minutes too long. The sky high above the northern Yellow Sea was now a debris field of orbiting satellites, with more being repositioned each day to cover the crisis. The submarine had been seen by a keen-eyed Key Hole KH-12 high-resolution satellite, and that sighting had been confirmed by a Lacrosse 2 radar-imaging satellite. Both relayed their findings to the NSA. That information was immediately relayed to Seventh Fleet and to *Santa Fe* when it surfaced to receive what it hoped would be its last complement of the *Milwaukee* crew.

Yet with the daylight, there was no hiding from Chinese surveillance satellites. And since time was more important than stealth and the risk of detection by North Korean coastal radar, *Santa Fe* had closed to within four miles of Kujido Island for this final transfer. It was indeed spotted on the surface by an orbiting Chinese surveillance vehicle. But unlike the flow of information from NSA to Seventh Fleet to the operational units at sea, this sighting was processed by one bureaucracy and only grudgingly made available to another. This critical piece of intelligence would not arrive at the headquarters of the Shenyang Military Region of the People's Liberation Army until later that afternoon. It was the Shenyang Military Region that was responsible for the northern Yellow Sea.

Greenville, too, still had another load of refugees to retrieve and a minisub to recover and make fast to her hull. It had closed to within six miles of the island. But the *Santa Fe* was now a free, fast-attack, hunter-killer sub, albeit a very crowded one.

At the North Korean special operations compound at Nuchonri Air Force Base, some forty miles northwest of Kujido Island, a North Korean colonel did something most uncharacteristic for a senior military officer in his army; he made a decision without going to his superior to ask permission. He was experienced enough to know his superior would have to ask *his* superior and that the moment would be lost. In that case, his men on the contested island and their objective of capturing the American crew would be lost. The fact that he would be blamed for the failure, whether he acted or not, helped him to come to this decision. His commando team's assault on the island had started well. The submarine had successfully delivered them to the island, where they landed unopposed. They had located the American sailors in an abandoned building and had stormed the building successfully, or so he was led to believe. They had picked up radio broadcasts from the American ship's captain, a woman, if that could be believed, who said they were being overrun. It seemed that his commandos had been successful. But since then, nothing! His commando team leader was under strict orders to check in hourly and report his progress, both to him and to military headquarters in Pyongyang. But that call had been long overdue. When a call finally came, it was not by radio but by cell phone. The assault had been a trap, and half of the commando force was out of action. It was from this cell-phone call that the colonel learned of the setback and what still might be done to overcome the American crew that had now reboarded their ship for a final stand.

His quick-reaction force was standing by, and the flight crews were on alert status. All he had to do was give the order, which he did. Moments later, two Russian-made MI-24 Hind helicopters lifted off and streaked at low level for the island. Each carried a dozen commandos, but these men were armed differently. In addition to their normal combat load and AK-56 assault rifles, each carried an RPG-89 grenade launcher and several rounds of grenade ammunition. As for the Hinds, they had a dual mission. They were to serve as troop transports and as attack helos. Their primary mission this day was to deliver their cargo to the island. Then they were to remain on station to support an assault on the ship.

The Air Force AWACs aircraft orbiting over Seoul picked up the helos shortly after they lifted off from Nuchonri. But at their top speed of two hundred knots, they were barely twenty-five minutes from Kujido Island. Alerted by the AWACs and half a world away, two Predator drone controllers saw the inbound helos just as they cleared the coast. By then, they were but fifteen minutes from a touchdown on the island. Both Predators were armed with Maverick missiles, but neither could engage a moving airborne target. All they could do was arm their missiles and track their targets. The two helos touched down several hundred yards from the cannery about fifty yards apart. The commandos were able to clear the aircraft and safely make for cover, but the aircrews had no chance. One was turning on the ground while the other had just lifted into a hover when the Mavericks slammed onto them, creating two giant fireballs that were clearly visible to the JSOC snipers on *Milwaukee*.

Several decks below the sniper perches, Brian Dawson and Mike Volner were joined by Kate Bigelow to watch the new batch of commandos disperse across the island. They moved in pairs, so no raining death from the sky could get more than a few of them in a single strike. The Raven drone had long since expended its on-station time and was allowed to drop into the sea. A Global Hawk with a downlink created by Jesse Carpenter had been brought down to fifteen thousand feet and now orbited the island. The presentation on the small computer screen was not as precise as that of the Raven, but then the distance was much greater.

"Well, this kind of ups the ante," Dawson said. The North Korean commandos had fanned out and were moving like a troop of rats to the island's southern strip of beach. The RPG launch tubes were clearly visible on their backs. "Can we hold them?"

Volner didn't answer for several moments as he made a professional assessment of the video presentation. "Yeah, maybe, but it will be a close-run thing. A lot will depend on their orders. They probably think all of the crew is still aboard. Are they here to take hostages, or are they here to kill us?" He leaned in and continued to study the screen. Neither Dawson nor Bigelow spoke. Both knew from here on, no matter what happened, Major Mike Volner would be in charge. "Okay, this is how we're going to play this. I want all your people ready to go when that ASDS returns. Keep them well to the starboard side of the ship as close to the skin of the ship as possible. I want everyone in flak jackets and helmets. Those RPGs will go through the skin of this ship like it isn't there. If the warheads have any kind of a delay, one of them could get through. I'll need two of your gunners and one of your deck people to help me defend and delay what's going to come at us in short order." He looked to Dawson. "I'll be occupied keeping them off the ship. Let me know when that ASDS gets alongside and then again when you and everyone but my people are aboard."

"Are we going to be able to get everyone on board?" Bigelow asked.

"Don't worry about that right now. You just focus on getting your people and yourself aboard. Our job is to keep them off the ship until that ASDS is loaded and away."

The ship suddenly shook as a rocket-propelled grenade slammed into the port side of *Milwaukee*. It was a solid hit, opening yet another gaping hole just below the pilothouse. But the shooter paid for it with his life. Rather than ducking for cover, the commando couldn't help but watch the impact of his rocket. One of the snipers quickly traced the rocket trail back to the missileer's firing position. He was lying prone on the beach berm just down from the bow of the ship. The JSOC marksman took him with a head shot.

The call with his United Nations' ambassador had, at least for the moment, cheered the president and reminded him why he had selected her for the assignment. While there was no chance of getting a Security Council resolution to censure North Korea for attacking *Milwaukee,* as China would certainly have vetoed that effort, the General Assembly was another matter. Japan, South Korea, Indonesia, Malaysia, and other Asian nations had had their fill of North Korea's intransigence. Under her leadership, they had joined America in a coalition of the willing to censure the Hermit Kingdom. North Korea's aggression and violation of international norms would be fully exposed in the General Assembly. And once the LCS crew was safe, the president himself was going to address the United Nations.

The ASDS arrived back at the *Milwaukee* midmorning to find a ship under siege. Volner had partially offset the commandos' use of the RPGs by mounting two of the ships .50 caliber machine guns fore and aft, where they could rake the beach with their heavy fire. They were manned by two of the ship's gunner's mates. But automatic-weapons fire from the beach and the RPGs had forced them to periodically abandon these partially exposed emplacements. Now one of the gunners had been wounded, and his gun was inoperable. But only once had the North Koreans tried to cross the beach. The machine-gun fire and precision shooting of the JSOC team had driven them back. But the one operable .50 caliber still in action was beginning to overheat, and Volner's men were now rationing their ammunition. Both the commandos and defenders knew it was but a matter of time until the North Koreans were able to cross the beach, put grappling hooks over the bow, and board the ship.

"Mike, this is Brian," Dawson said over the team tactical net. "The last of the crew is just now boarding the ASDS. I'm here with Captain Bigelow. What's next?"

"Get aboard. I'll send the remaining gunner down to

you. I want no one aboard but me and my team. Let me know when you have everyone else aboard the ASDS."

Kate Bigelow refused to leave the deck of *Milwaukee* until every member of her crew was in the minisub, including the two gunner's mates, Jesse Carpenter, Lieutenant Tom Denver, and her boatswain mate chief petty officer, who had been tending the ship's Zodiac that was now tied off on the side of the LCS. It was a tight fit, but they crammed everyone aboard, with pilot Bill Naylor fighting to control the buoyancy of his overloaded craft. Brian Dawson sat on the hatch coaming of the ASDS and slipped through just ahead of *Milwaukee*'s captain.

"Mike, Brian here. We're ready to shove off. Sure you don't want a ride? Room enough to squeeze in one or maybe two more." There was another flurry of gunfire coming from the shore, and it was a moment before Volner replied. "They'll be aboard any minute now, Brian. Get the hell out of here. With any luck, I'll be aboard *Greenville* before you."

"Good luck, Mike."

"And you, Brian." And he was gone. *Now it's up to me,* Mike Volner said quietly to himself. *Just cover their escape. Once they're gone, you can get out yourself. But cover their escape!*

Dawson closed and secured the hatch, then nodded to Master Chief Mecoy. A moment later, the ASDS slipped from the side of the LCS for the last time. Still tied to the side of *Milwaukee* was the last Zodiac. But the previously mounted OMC twenty-five-horse outboard that was clamped to the transom had been jettisoned for a 110-horsepower Mercury that was purring impatiently at idle. The main and cross tubes had been topped off so they were now rock hard.

Each member of Mike Volner's JSOC team knew exactly what he was to do. One at a time, they dumped their magazines on rapid single fire, turned, and raced along a predetermined route to the waiting Zodiac. The first man there stowed his weapon and took charge of the outboard engine. Then, one at a time, they made the edge of *Milwaukee*'s aft mission bay and the open mission-bay door, and Volner directed them over the side. They came in the sequence he had expected, but number six did not appear. When the last man, his senior sergeant and a burly veteran, arrived, Volner knew he probably had a man down.

"Carson, Volner here. Where are you?" Volner and his sergeant heard a mic being keyed, but there was no voice transmission. "Carson, this is the major. Are you there?" Nothing. He turned to the man at the outboard. "In sixty seconds you go, with or without us, clear?"

"Clear, sir!"

I'm not leaving without all of my men! Volner raced along the route the last man should have taken, followed by the big NCO. Up a deck and in an interior athwartships passageway just inside the port skin of the ship, they found him. As Carson turned to leave his fighting position, he had taken a round under the ear, and it had unhinged his jaw. He was unconscious, and there was a lot of blood, but he was breathing. They discarded his weapon, and Volner helped the wounded man to a fireman's carry over the sergeant's shoulder. Then they turned and ran. Volner, a step behind, chanced to look down a port-side fore-and-aft running passageway and saw two armed men in black, ninjalike attire. His weapon was still slung so he instinctively snatched a fragmentation grenade from his vest and tossed it at them. He had nearly caught up with his sergeant and called "fire in the hole" when the blast crashed behind them. But they were now ninety degrees to the blast alleyway and escaped back across the passageway to the bay that led them back to the Zodiac.

It had been closer to two minutes than sixty seconds when the three of them reached the tethered inflatable. The man at the outboard was where Volner had left him, but two of the others had taken up security positions, and the fourth tended the little craft's mooring line. The two on security quickly collapsed back in and were over the side in seconds. They handed down the wounded man, and the others literally dove into the boat. The man at the tiller in the coxswain's position popped the big Merc into gear, and they tore away from the side of the LCS. While they sorted themselves out, the rest of Volner's exit strategy began to unfold.

The controller of the orbiting Global Hawk, on seeing the Zodiac leave the side of the *Milwaukee,* bid the drone to signal *Greenville,* which was patiently waiting with a raised communications mast. Shortly after receiving the coded transmission, a fire-control technician aboard *Greenville* closed two firing circuits on his firing panel. First one and then a second Tomahawk land-attack missile leapt from their vertical-launch tubes just forward of the submarine's sail. Following their precisely programmed instructions, they nosed over and flew straight for *Milwaukee,* each at an altitude of no more than fifty feet. Just before they reached the ship, they climbed to a terminal attack altitude of three hundred feet and detonated exactly over the ship—again the one, then the second.

Aboard the Zodiac, the JSOC medic tended to the team's wounded comrade as best he could while the others clung to the spray tube of the pounding craft. Volner looked back across their wake to the LCS. There were waterspouts as the North Korean commandos took up firing positions along the deck. There were now a dozen or more of them aboard, most of them shooting at the fleeing Zodiac. Then came the crash of the airburst over the LCS. The force of the blast sent a pressure wave across the weather decks of the ship. It did little additional damage to the battered ship, but it swept the North Korean commandos who were topside away like grains of sand being blasted by a garden hose. Those inside were knocked from their feet, and those who didn't go down from the first blast did so from the second.

Volner took stock of his team and his boat. They'd taken no hits, and the tubes appeared to remain firm. And the engine screamed with effortless power. He crawled forward to where his medic and his team sergeant were working on the wounded Sergeant Carson.

"How's he doing?" he shouted over the roar of the outboard.

"If we could slow down a bit, sir," his team medic said, "I think I can get a pressure bandage in place and stop the bleeding."

Volner again looked back at *Milwaukee*. They were well out of range, but the sooner they got to *Greenville*, the better. Yet he estimated they were making close to thirty-five knots. The ASDS was doing no more than nine. He motioned for his coxswain to slow down.

The Shang-class submarine was moving toward *Greenville* at three knots and at a range of just over two miles. It was bow-on to the American boat and at its best speed for passive listening. The sonar operator aboard the Chinese boat sat concentrating, pushing his earphones tightly against the sides of his head so he would miss nothing. He had heard the two missiles leave *Greenville*, but, because they were launched close to the surface and there was a great deal of surface-chop noise, he didn't know what they were. He had never heard an American cruise-missile launch, nor had the simulators where he received his sonar training prepared him for the real thing. All he really knew was that this was a loud, unfamiliar noise coming from an enemy submarine that was not only an extremely quiet adversary but one who took great pride in that silence. And there was the issue of the transponder-like pinging that in fact was a homing beacon for the ASDS. Suddenly, his face contorted in pain, and he ripped the earphones from his head. He dropped them to the deck and clamped the heels of his hands over his ears in an attempt to ease the ringing in his head. The force of the screech he had just experienced was all but debilitating.

Less than two thousand yards off the port bow of the

Shang-class sub, USS *Boise* (SSN-764) had just lashed the Chinese boat with a highly focused active sonar pulse. A few seconds later, USS *Santa Fe,* hovering about the same distance off the starboard bow, did the same. The two pings rippled through the Chinese boat and were heard by all, especially the Chinese captain.

"Sonar room, this is the captain. What is happening? What does this mean?"

The sonar tech's ears were still ringing, but he reflexively answered his captain. "Sir, this is most certainly the work of an American attack submarine. And since there were two such pings that came from different directions, two American attack submarines. They are in front of us and between our boat and what must be a third American submarine."

Once Seventh Fleet became aware there was a Chinese nuclear submarine in the area, it had notified both *Greenville* and *Santa Fe.* Then the fleet commander ordered *Boise* to detach from the *Reagan* strike group in the central Yellow Sea and proceed north to join her sisters. While *Greenville* worked out the details of the last extraction and the covering action with its Tomahawks, *Santa Fe* and *Boise,* too, using *Greenville* as bait, planned and executed this acoustic ambush.

While the captain considered his options, two more loud pings, one from *Boise* and one from *Santa Fe,* reverberated through his boat. If he was in fact considering some other course of action, the second set of audio calling cards from the Americans put that to rest.

"Left full rudder," he said to his helmsman. Then to his officer of the deck, "Make turns for fifteen knots and lay in a course that will take us back to Northern Fleet Headquarters at Qingdao."

Within the hour, all personnel from the ASDS and the Zodiac were packed into the crowded hull of *Greenville*. It took another hour to get the ASDS secured to the afterdeck of the mother sub. Then *Boise* and an equally crowded *Santa Fe* proceeded to escort *Greenville* back south to the protective skirts of the *Reagan* strike group. And thanks to the skill of the *Greenville*'s medical officer, Sergeant Carson was sedated and resting comfortably and no longer in critical condition.

CHAPTER TWENTY-FOUR

November 17, 1430 Korea Standard Time

The marshal of the Korean People's Army sat huddled with his number 2, Vice Marshal Chung Su-yong, at KPA headquarters in Pyongyang. They had failed and failed miserably, and neither man dared speak of what might be ahead for them or for their families. And despite his vast array of political and military connections, General Choi Kwang was unable to learn of the supreme leader's reaction when his aides had told him all the Americans were off the island and could no longer be used as bargaining chips. He could only imagine, but he imagined the worst.

He had just been given his new assignment: Contact General Hwa and tell him to contact a senior member of their U.N. delegation in New York. That man had all his normal diplomatic duties but was also Hwa's conduit to the handler. The fact that the supreme leader had entrusted him to do this rather than going directly to Hwa himself did give him some slight hope he might salvage something from this ill-fated mission. But upon reflection, Choi knew this was but a rationalization. His fate was already sealed. All he could do was try to get his family safely out of the country. That would be difficult since he had every reason to believe they were already being watched by North Korea's state security forces. Difficult, but not impossible, and he had already set that plan in motion. Now he had to carry out his orders. He trusted Chung enough to seek his counsel.

"You know what the supreme leader wants us to do," Choi began, "and that General Hwa is the instrument. But I dread making that call."

Chung was careful with his reply. He trusted Choi—up to a point. Yet he wasn't certain where this conversation was going or whether this was to be a ploy where Choi was going to try to make him the fall guy to save his own skin. "Marshal, I understand completely," Chung answered carefully. "If Hwa carries this through and they are successful, the Americans will almost surely retaliate, and we'll lose more than just a few troops."

Choi paused to consider the man's response. Chung was good, but he was a consummate bureaucrat who had advanced in his career more for his administrative and technical skills than for his soldiering. The loss of their submarine with all hands; the complete annihilation of their first contingent of commandos, followed by the second; the loss of the Hinds and their crews; and, most recently, the final battle on the island all added up to more than "just a few troops." On the positive side, he knew Chung's career path had imbued him with good political instincts, and he needed to leverage them now. "General Chung, I trust your counsel, and I am just trying to anticipate questions General Hwa might ask. Why is the supreme leader ordering this attack?"

"Marshal, I have thought about it. While we can never be certain, consider this: We knew full well that, whether this attempt to seize the LCS crew succeeded or not, the United States would move to censure us in the United Nations for two reasons. One, the obvious one, for attacking their ship in international waters. But the other one would be for our attempt to extend our maritime claims. We need to have unopposed claims to the seabed if we are to—"

Choi interrupted. "Yes, but that's all political. Why are we in the military even involved?"

"Marshal, you yourself have pointed out to our nation's leaders more than once how antiquated our military equipment is becoming. Our political leaders want us to have modern military equipment, but they can't pay for it. The recent debacle of trying to capture the American crew is but a demonstration of that. But now China wants our energy resources, and our political leaders want the modern arms and money, but mostly modern arms."

"All right, I'll give you that, but I still don't understand what he hopes to accomplish in attacking the building, especially *that* building."

"This is only a guess, but I will tell you it's an educated guess based on what my political contacts are telling me. I think by attacking and attacking there, the supreme leader intends to tell the world that we will do whatever it takes to make good our claim on the territorial waters off our coasts. We need to make it clear to the international community we intend to mine that seabed and what the rest of the world—especially the Americans—think be damned. And now that the American president is scheduled to address the United Nations and condemn us, I think the supreme leader wants to deny him that pulpit. That's probably why he wants this attack done now. You recall how absorbed Americans become when their territory is attacked. Look what happened in September 2001. They will be so immersed in mourning their losses they'll all but forget we attacked their ship and are making these claims."

"I see your logic, but I am dreading the consequences. Will you give me some privacy so I can call General Hwa?"

"Of course, Marshal," Chung replied as he rose to leave.

General Choi called to summon Hwa to his office. He dared not speak of this over the phone, even a secure phone. He did not have his adjutant place the call, as was his custom. He wanted as few of his fingerprints on this madness as was possible.

The day before General Choi Kwang made this fateful call, USS *Greenville* and USS *Santa Fe* had arrived in Okinawa with the LCS crew. The *Ronald Reagan* carrier strike group had escorted them the entire way. The vice president, the chairman of the Joint Chiefs of Staff, the PACOM commander, and Vice Admiral Bennett were there to meet them. Accompanying this assembly of senior officials were military medical personnel, chaplains, and grief counselors. After only a few hours on the Japanese island, the LCS crew was loaded aboard specially outfitted medical-evacuation C-17s to begin their 4,800-mile journey from Okinawa to Hickam Air Force Base in Hawaii. The president wanted them on American soil ASAP. There, after being debriefed by military intelligence as well as by professionals from several three-letter agencies, they would be united with their families, which were being flown to Hawaii for a brief reunion. After that, there would be a welcome-home parade in *Milwaukee*'s home port of San Diego.

That would be the joyous part. It would soon be followed by memorial services for the *Milwaukee* crewmen who perished during the ordeal. Compounding the sadness, there would be no bodies to intern. The bodies left aboard had been incinerated. There was talk of refloating the hulk that was the *Milwaukee*, much as the USS *Cole* was salvaged and returned to service after it was attacked by terrorists. But at the direction of the president, a barrage of cruise missiles from Seventh Fleet surface combatants was launched at the grounded LCS. It was burned to the waterline.

Now that the LCS crew was safely on American soil, President Wyatt Midkiff was free to do what he knew he needed to do. The Joint Staff was working to come up with an appropriate military response, but for now the president was most focused on his speech at the United Nations.

Just when General Choi Kwang thought nothing else could go wrong, something did. When he called General Hwa's office, the general's assistant told him Hwa was "indisposed." Choi lambasted the colonel and demanded to speak with Hwa's number 2. He got a brand-new brigadier general he didn't even know personally, and he, too, was evasive about where Hwa was. Choi was furious. He told the man to find him, find him now, and have him return his call. The supreme leader had told him when he wanted this action taken, and until he could track down Hwa, Kim would continue to simmer. That prospect filled him with dread and put him on the edge of panic.

At that moment, Hwa was with his mistress in one of the KPA's "hospitality houses," kept solely for just such liaisons. He had left strict instructions not to be disturbed except under the most compelling circumstances. For his brand-new brigadier, this was one of those moments. He dialed Hwa's private cell phone from the secure phone in his command center. The call caught Hwa at an awkward moment. He disentangled himself, grabbing the phone on the fourth ring.

"What is it?" he barked.

"General, sir . . ." the brigadier stammered. "Marshal Choi just called. He says it is most urgent and for you to call him immediately. I think he wants you to come to his headquarters right away. Shall I send the staff car to you at, ah, your location?"

Hwa didn't know whether this was just another routine summoning to Choi's office or something more important. He looked across his companion's body to his uniform that lay strewn over the floor. He liked this woman because she played rough, but the foreplay had taken a toll on his clothes, especially his heavily medaled coat. He knew one look at his rumpled uniform blouse and the marshal would know precisely what he had been doing when he was supposed to be at his office.

"No, I will take care of this myself," Hwa snapped as he ended the call.

Hwa shook his companion and sent her into the bathroom to clean up. Once she closed the door, he punched Choi's office number into his cell phone.

The marshal's adjutant answered the phone. "Marshall Choi's office. Colonel Muk speaking."

"Colonel, this is General Hwa. I need to speak with General Choi."

"I think he is expecting your call, but he wishes you to come to his office. Are you en route, General?" Muk was an efficient and officious gatekeeper who was well-practiced at anticipating his boss's demands. He phrased what he said as a summons, not a question.

Sitting there in his boxer shorts, Hwa exploded. "You don't need to know whether I'm en route or not, Colonel. That's way above your pay grade. Is the marshal in, or not?"

"Yes, he is."

"Then tell him I'm on the line."

The officious gatekeeper wasn't going to let some major general step all over him like this. Rather than just buzz General Choi on the intercom, he strode purposefully into the marshal's spacious office.

"Major General Hwa is on the line, General. Apparently he's not en route here yet."

"Why not?"

"He did not say, sir, but he seems quite agitated. Shall I put him through?"

"Yes, put him through now! And close that door behind you."

Choi was simmering already when Hwa came on the line. But when Hwa was terse with him, he exploded. "Where are you? I demand that you come to my office immediately!"

"It is just not possible, General. I can come in—in about two hours—but not right now."

"Are you disobeying a direct order? I'll have your rank for this. Get here now, at once!"

"That is not possible, General. Now what is it you wish from me?"

Choi felt his head was about to explode. He knew the supreme leader would have *his* rank, and likely a great deal more, if he didn't get this done. Covertness and all this security crap be damned, and he said what he had wished to say to Hwa in person over the phone.

"It is not what I want, you fool," Choi shouted. "The supreme leader wants you to unleash your people in New York. Their objective is the building of the United Nations. You have your instructions. Get it done, damn you!" And he slammed down the phone.

* * *

Now it was Hwa's turn to worry. He anticipated the supreme leader would want to move and move quickly. He dared not question his orders, but these things didn't happen with the snap of a finger. He had worked with, coached, and all but micromanaged Seung and his team, albeit through a cutout to Seung's handler. It was a well-thought-out and well-crafted plan and one that would leave no fingerprints indicating this had been orchestrated by the Hermit Kingdom. But that would happen only if it was executed with precision.

But now these fools were meddling with his plan and asking for the impossible. Didn't they understand the meticulous preparations and the volume of explosives that had to be moved into position? People and equipment had to be staged and the times of normal vendor deliveries had to be coordinated. A successful operation like the one they were planning depended on timing and a great many small but important details. He would do his best, but he would have to take shortcuts he didn't like.

Trevor Harward had been asking for a meeting with the president since early morning, but Wyatt Midkiff was absorbed with fine-tuning the speech he was to deliver at the United Nations the next afternoon. Harward couldn't blame him. The speech needed to condemn North Korea for the attack on an American ship and all that had happened during the attempted rescue of the LCS crew, but it also needed to do a great deal more. And the United States' allies had to be aligned with what the president would say. *It might well be the most important speech of Wyatt's presidency,* Harward found himself thinking, and he needed to support his boss in that effort.

President Midkiff felt much the same way. There was also the issue of retribution and, with it, the United States' standing in the world. His predecessor had been raked over the coals, appropriately Midkiff thought, for being weak in crises as diverse as Syria, Rwanda, and Ukraine. Midkiff, in contrast, had been elected on a platform of giving the United States more backbone internationally. He had done just that with his actions after the two domestic attacks on the United States earlier in his administration. The attack on USS *Milwaukee* was of a different nature. It was not an attack on U.S. soil but one that took place on the other side of the world. Public opinion polls, however, were running two to one for punishing North Korea.

It was late afternoon when Harward finally managed to get some time with the president, and they huddled in the Oval Office's small conversational area. The secretary of defense and the chairman of the Joint Chiefs of Staff had briefed the president on a range of retaliatory options the day before. Now he needed to make a decision.

"Trevor, the secretary and the chairman laid out a good range of options, but I have to tell you I'm torn about whether we should act at all."

"I could sense you were uncomfortable during the briefings, Mr. President. To tell you the truth, I'm torn also. On the one hand, North Korea attacked our ship on the high seas with the intent of capturing our crew and holding them hostage, and we lost many good sailors and several airmen in our A-10s because of their actions. But on the other hand, we took everything they threw at us, got our people safely out of there, and inflicted a high cost on their military. I don't think it's lost on anyone the North Koreans aren't a first-rate military power. We can hurt them as bad as we'd like and there's nothing they can do about it, short of invading the South."

"I take your point, Trevor. But the American people seem to be inclined to extract a price for this."

"Yes, I know they are. Now, here is an option you may not have considered," Harward replied, as the two men lapsed into an extended conversation.

Aaron Bleich knew the situation between the United States and North Korea was still fluid, and he had his entire Geek Tank focused on that nation and especially on communications into and out of the various military headquarters in Pyongyang. He had divided the monitoring responsibilities for those networks across his entire team and had tuned up the automated collation algorithms to focus on a few key threads.

Now he waited. Would it be one of his Geek Squad rock stars or his prized machines that alerted them to any North Korean moves? No one had left the Geek Tank for the last twelve hours and takeout containers and plastic sports-drink bottles littered their crowded subterranean warren. Bleich was scrolling through a number of databases he had assigned himself to monitor when his question was answered with the door to his office springing open. It was Hasan Khosa.

"Aaron, I've got an intercept that may be something."

"Okay, Hasan, whatcha got?"

"It's North Korea. Someone there must have screwed up and made a transmission on an unencrypted cell phone. They have what I believe is a terrorist element in New York, and they intend to attack the United Nations."

Khosa briefed Bleich on the text of the intercept, and soon the two of them were headed directly for Chase Williams's office.

The call from his handler startled Seung Min-jae. As planned, the instructions from the man were short and cryptic. "Put your plan in motion and execute it tomorrow at the prearranged time and place."

"It will be done," Seung replied, and he clicked off his phone. But after he rang off, he immediately asked himself, *Can we make final preparations this quickly?* No matter, he had his orders.

Seung's immediate reaction was to gather the others. But he paused to work out the plan in his own mind first. *Calm down, Min-jae, there really is no more planning that needs to be done; this is simply execution of the mission in a compressed time frame.* Still, now that it was "real," Seung began to step through what needed to be done to see if there were any last-minute flaws with the plan or holes he needed to plug. He reflected back on their painstaking preparations and allowed himself a bit of self-congratulation. He knew they were ready and had no doubt of their success. Yet it would have been good to be given more time for the final staging of the explosives.

Once the decision had been made to attack the United Nations by exploding a van loaded with C-4 in the parking garage of the U.N. building, they had painstakingly put together a plan. Seung and the other members of his team had taken turns watching the entry of the U.N. garage early in the morning. They learned the names of all the vendors that delivered food and beverages to the United Nations each morning. There were almost a dozen of them, since there were thousands of workers to feed every day. Seung had recommended one vendor to his handler at the U.N., one that used a van just like theirs to make their deliveries. The handler had approved his selection and sometime later told him where to have the van painted. A few days ago, Seung and one of the others had followed one of that company's vans back to their food store to determine its location. Several days after that, they mugged one of that company's van drivers as he left work and headed home. It was staged to look like a simple robbery. They took his wallet, watch, and all other valuables, and, most important, his company identification, which allowed him access to the U.N. garage. That was enough for them to have an expert forger make badges for Seung's entire team. Once that was done, they were ready, and had been for some time. Satisfied their plan was sound and there was nothing that needed immediate attention, Seung Min-jae decided it was time to gather the others.

* * *

At Op-Center, it was anything but restful. As soon as his two Geek Tank stars had told their story to Chase Williams, the Op-Center director called the watch commander and had him do a recall of the entire Op-Center team. Immediately, phones throughout the Northern Virginia, suburban Maryland, and greater Washington, D.C., area began to ring, and scores of cars rolled onto highways headed for Fort Belvoir North.

Once he finished giving instructions to Bleich and Khosa, Williams had two more things on his immediate list. First, he called Allen Kim's number. The conversation was brief and to the point; he put the CIRG team on mission alert. That done, Williams texted a quick POTUS/Eyes Only memo and launched it on the secure circuit. He followed this with a call to the Situation Room watch floor. With that, all he could do was wait until his team converged on Op-Center.

Seung Min-jae gathered his team together in their tiny apartment. "We have received our orders, and the attack will happen tomorrow morning at the prearranged time." This was met by smiles around the table. "Now, we had previously thought that we would have several days' advance notice, but now we have to move more quickly than that. Yet we still have ample time to make our final preparations. Here is what I want us to do . . ."

A short time after Seung met with his team over their kitchen table, Chase Williams had his team assembled in his office. Anne Sullivan, Roger McCord, Brian Dawson,

Duncan Sutherland, Rich Middleton, Jim Wright, and a few others filled every seat in his small office. Dawson had arrived in Washington only an hour ago, having flown across multiple time zones and experiencing numerous airborne refueling rendezvous on the Air Force's fastest jets, which Op-Center had whistled up to bring him back from Okinawa.

"All right, thank you all for coming in," Williams began. "Roger's Geek Tank has done a fantastic job and alerted us about this probable attack. I briefed the president a half hour ago, and he'd like me to come over to the Oval later this morning. As you know, Allen Kim and his team are saddling up and getting ready to move north to a forward operating position in the greater New York City area. We're still evaluating precisely where. We are fairly certain there's going to be an attack on the United Nations building, but that's about all we are sure of right now. I know you all haven't had much time to think about this, but what do you have for me thus far?"

Roger McCord spoke first. "Boss, armed with what we do know, Aaron and his team are focusing all their collation architectures and anticipatory intelligence to try to narrow down where this attack will come from and how it will be carried out. I don't need to tell you the options cover a pretty wide spectrum, but they're working hard on narrowing it down."

"You've engaged Adam Putnam's folks at the National Counterterrorism Center?"

"We have. We can count on his full cooperation, and he's throwing all his resources at this."

Williams continued working through his mental checklist. "Homeland Security? Attorney General? New York City officials?"

"All in play," Dawson replied. "I've already spoken with one of the deputies at Homeland Security, and the secretary will likely be calling you later this morning. We anticipate they'll be fully on board with our CIRG team leading this and will support us in whatever we need from them. Jim Wright is on the phone with New York's mayor to bring him fully up to speed. It's their city, and of course they want to be involved, but once Jim lays out our capabilities and our mandate, I think we'll be working closely with them. They get it and have practiced for such events. More to follow, and Jim will come in and brief you as soon as he gets off the phone with the mayor."

There was an uncomfortable silence, and Williams could sense Dawson was struggling to frame what he was about to say. He could also sense why. "And the attorney general, Brian?"

"Ah, boss, we're still working that one. I called their watch commander myself about two hours ago and got a call from the deputy AG about ten minutes after that. Mind you, he had just been woken up early in the morning and was likely still processing what he had been told, but his initial response wasn't, well, it wasn't encouraging. They don't share our sense of urgency."

"Just what did he say?"

"He said, 'He failed to see why Op-Center needed to be involved so soon.'"

"I see. I'll call the AG myself later this morning

before I head over to the Oval Office to ensure he has the full picture, or at least shares our concerns."

"Boss," Richard Middleton said, "we haven't had a lot of time to study this, but we think the most important thing to do in the next few hours is narrow the options regarding how this attack might occur. Until we do that, we may never get Allen and his team in position in time to intervene. And short of completely evacuating the United Nations and cordoning off a several-block radius around the building, which is what I'd do if I were the New York mayor, we're at a disadvantage. Until we can narrow the attack options regarding whether this attack will come from land, sea, or air, the CIRG team may not get there in time. And it would be nice to know if this planned attack is chem-bio, explosive, or whatever. You know the range of possibilities we need to consider."

"That's why I have my A team here in this room," Williams replied. "Now let's put our brains together and do just what you suggest." Then, turning to Roger McCord, he continued. "Roger, please ask Aaron to come on in. I think we need him to be part of this process."

A minute later, Aaron Bleich arrived, and Williams's brain trust began their work.

Allen Kim looked up from his desk at the CIRG building at Quantico and motioned for his visitor to sit down. He had most of his team in motion and was now going over his personal checklist to ensure he was ready to lead his team north to thwart the anticipated attack.

"Sandee, do you know why I called you in here?"

Actually, I don't, Sandee Barron wanted to say. But as the junior pilot in the CIRG's air arm, her professional instincts told her it was better to just listen.

"We're about to move out and do our first operation with Op-Center. I need to bring only A players. You haven't been here that long. Are you up for this assignment?"

Hell, yes, I'm up for it, Sandee heard herself thinking. *I may be the junior pilot in this outfit, but I've got more hours in the H-60 than anyone else. I've studied my ass off and trained like I'm going to fight. I know I'm ready.* "Yes, sir," was all she said.

"When I met with Op-Center's JSOC team leader a while ago, he said you two worked together on an op and you were the kind of pilot I wanted with me on a tough assignment. I've taken that advice under advisement, but if I take you, I leave a pilot who has been with my team for years behind here. Trust me; no one wants to stay behind. Are you *really* ready?"

"You've seen me in training, sir. You're gonna have to make that call."

Kim considered this. He was looking for a reason *not* to take Barron and was waiting for her to pitch him on taking her north. But she didn't do that. She was willing to let her performance speak for itself. *Moxie*, Kim thought, *this pilot has moxie, and that's what I'm going to need for this operation.*

"Saddle up, Barron. Let's get moving."

Seung Min-jae was professional to the core. He told himself with all the planning and rehearsals they had done, he didn't need to overmanage his team regarding how they were going to conduct this attack. That said, the combination of pent-up nervous energy and adrenaline rush pushed him to walk through the plan with his team several times so they had it just right.

"So, just humor me," he smiled. "One more time, and then we'll be at rest until late this evening."

There was one sigh, and several eyes rolled. He ignored their grumbling and moved ahead.

"We know this neighborhood pretty much shuts down by about ten P.M. We'll begin then. You'll go to the garage and get the van a half hour before that and have it in front of our apartment at ten sharp."

The driver nodded ascent.

"We'll work individually and begin carrying the explosives down to the van in large garbage bags. It will look like we're bringing material back to the company. Wear your company badges, and in the unlikely event a passerby says anything, just say, 'Big party.' Got it?"

Heads nodded around the table.

Looking toward the driver again, he continued. "You'll take the van back to the garage and lock it up once we have it loaded. Then we'll wait."

"Do we begin in the morning just like we practiced, at the same time?" one of the men asked.

Seung looked mildly annoyed that the question came up. "Yes. Just like we practiced. Beginning at four thirty A.M., three of us will head to the garage at ten-minute intervals." Looking at the driver, he said, "You will drive, and I'll be in the passenger seat." Now, looking at the team's only woman, he added, "You will ride on the floor right between us. We'll begin driving at five fifteen and arrive at the U.N. garage soon after it opens for vendor deliveries at five thirty. We'll park right next to the freight elevators, where all of the vendors park." To the driver, "The two of us will get out of the van, grab the bags of food, and head to the freight elevators with any other vendors that are there that early. Once we get out of the elevators, we'll leave the building and dispose of our bags in a Dumpster. You will walk back here to the apartment, and shortly after that I'll use the remote detonator to blow up the van."

After the driver nodded that he understood, Seung turned to the woman. "And you know your job?"

"Yes. After you two are gone, I'll get out, lock the van, and, when no one is passing by, spill the contents of my purse next to the van's right rear tire. Then, when I'm certain no one is looking, I'll puncture the tire, then put the spare tire, tire iron, jack, and other material on the ground next to the van . . ."

"And put the paper on the windshield. 'Flat tire, back in ten minutes'?"

"Yes, just as we have practiced," she replied.

Seung turned to the other two men. "You two know what to do. We've gone over it often, so I know you won't fail. You will begin immediately after the rest of us go to the van. Take all the material needed to make meth amphetamine that we've collected and stage it in the kitchen, just like we've discussed. Wipe down this apartment thoroughly so there are no fingerprints or anything else that could tie us to this place. Then incinerate the apartment so it looks like our meth lab exploded. After that, steal one of the cars in the long-term section of the Quik Park over on East Thirty-fourth Street and meet us at the prearranged place south of the United Nations at six forty-five sharp. From there, we drive to Newark Airport. We'll have ample time to catch a flight to Buffalo just before noon."

"And from there we fly to Tokyo and then to Pyong-yang?" one of the men asked.

"Yes," Seung hissed, "just as we have planned." Seung Min-jae paused to remind himself why he was leading this group, not one of the others.

Yet even with these final talk-throughs, Seung was uneasy. The key to what they were about to do was precision—the kind of precision that comes only with thorough rehearsal. The original plan had them rehearsing each portion of the plan, followed by a full dress rehearsal without explosives. But he was not given the time for this. His superiors in North Korea seemed to think they were like rifle shells that could simply be loaded and fired. So with the order to attack immediately, he would have to be satisfied with these kitchen-table drills.

Chase Williams arrived in the Oval Office a few minutes late for their scheduled meeting. As Williams entered the Oval, he could see the president and his national security advisor were in a somber mood, and he understood why. The nation had endured two major domestic attacks on his watch, and now a third seemed imminent. Coming on the heels of the LCS crisis, Williams wondered how much the president could endure. And Williams could feel the pressure himself. After the last domestic attack, Williams had convinced the president to give Op-Center control of an FBI CIRG team. Now he had what he wanted, and he knew his president was looking to him for answers.

"Chase, what do you have for us?"

"Mr. President, first, my apologies for being late. I have my entire team mobilized to try to narrow down options as to where this attack might be coming from."

"Yes, I know that. But I have to tell you, we don't seem to be making a lot of progress."

"I wish I could tell you we've narrowed things down with some certainty, Mr. President, but we haven't. We are deploying our CIRG team to New York, and they are staging at the old Coast Guard base on Governors Island. The helo-borne elements should be arriving there in"—Williams paused to look at his watch—"in about ninety minutes. Other elements are traveling north from Quantico by ground."

"Have you all been able to sniff out anything about where the attack might be coming from?"

"Mr. President, first of all, while you asked Op-Center to lead this effort, we're not flying solo. Trevor has mined the best talent on his national security staff, and Adam Putnam has the entire national intelligence community in overdrive to provide us with everything we've asked for. I spoke with the attorney general, and he's agreed to have the FBI director mobilize their CIRG elements to back us up." Williams neglected to mention that he had to all but threaten the AG to get his cooperation.

"And your intelligence tells you this attack is certain, Chase?" Harward asked. "At least that's the gist we got from the two memos you sent the president."

"As certain as we can be. And we're playing it out just that way."

"But have you narrowed down where it is coming from, Chase?" Midkiff asked.

"Only by conjecture, Mr. President. We know the intercepts that initiated this came from North Korea. We also know that North Korea has said it will make its case at the United Nations. We know they are aware the president will be addressing the United Nations General Assembly. That much we know. And while we don't know with certainty whether this attack will come from the land, the sea, or from the air, we think we understand their capabilities and limitations."

"We're listening, Chase," the president prompted.

"We'll start with an air attack, Mr. President. We've ruled that out because we protect our commercial flights so well now and also because we can clamp down a no-takeoff mandate on all private airports within a large radius around the city. And they know we can scramble fighters to shoot down any aircraft that approaches the U.N., so we think an air attack is an extremely low probability."

Williams paused to frame his thoughts. "As far as attack from sea, from the East River, we think that's a nonstarter as well. Between the Coast Guard and the

New York City Police Department, we have total control of the East River and no boat could breech those defenses. So we've all but ruled out that possibility."

"That leaves the land," Harward said, "and there are a number of possibilities there."

"You're right, Trevor, but here's how we've narrowed the list. One option is a lone shooter armed with a semi-automatic or other weapon who gets past the building security personnel. Possible, but not likely, and also an unlikely choice as one gunman could inflict only so much damage. Or they could be planning an attack from near the U.N. with something heavier like RPGs or a similar weapon. Again, not a likely option, as it would do only limited damage. That brings us to what we think is the most likely option. If their goal is to poke the international community in the eye at the United Nations, we think they'll try to conduct a major attack. But such an attack will have to let them have some degree of plausible deniability. They will want to do something dramatic but leave us unable to prove they did it. If they don't, they know they'll invite retaliation; even the Chinese won't be able to protect them. So it will have to be well thought out and clandestine. We think they're going to try a Timothy McVeigh–type attack. He killed over one hundred and fifty people and injured almost seven hundred others when he attacked the Alfred P. Murrah Federal Building in Oklahoma City back in April nineteen ninety-five. And he almost got away. We think that's the kind of attack they want to conduct."

"So we could cordon off all the streets in New York

leading to the United Nations, couldn't we, Chase?"
Harward asked. "We're not defenseless against something like this, especially now that we know an attack
is coming almost for certain."

"You're right, Trevor. That's certainly one option. Yet
I understand we've already discussed that with New
York's mayor, right Mr. President?"

"I have, Chase, and I think he and I are on the same
page. We are balancing the need to take those measures
against causing widespread panic throughout the city,"
the president replied. "That and the business of the U.N.
has to go on; it can't be stopped because of a terrorist
threat."

"We are on the same page as well, sir. Our goal is to
work outward from the United Nations building and dis-
cover where this attack vehicle is and nip this entire
attack in the bud—"

"But this truck or whatever they're planning to use
could be coming from anywhere," Harward blurted. "At
this very moment, it might be outside Manhattan or outside the city altogether."

"You're right, Trevor, and all this is only our best
educated guess at the moment, but we've got to start
somewhere. And, frankly, while we're all doing our
best, we're also hoping for a break."

As the president considered this, Williams continued.
"Mr. President, I'm mindful you're scheduled to deliver
a speech at the United Nations tomorrow afternoon.
Needless to say, your safety is an equal concern to our
finding these conspirators before they attack."

"I discussed this with New York's mayor, Chase. I'll

not change my plans and leave that building and his city to take a hit. If we don't find these terrorists before tomorrow afternoon when I'm scheduled to speak, I can cancel my appearance then. But the building and the surrounding area will be evacuated at the same time. The mayor assures me there are well-thought-through plans as to how to do that and he's confident it can be done quickly and without wholesale panic."

"Yes, Mr. President," Williams replied. "That sounds like the prudent course of action."

"But hear me out, both of you," Midkiff added. "If I cancel my speech at the United Nations—a speech that is widely anticipated to be a strong condemnation of North Korea—because I'm afraid to go to the United Nations in the face of a possible North Korean terrorist threat, then they've won, haven't they? I'm not cavalier about my safety, but I am mindful of ensuring the international community knows the United States stands for something."

"Yes, Mr. President," Harward replied. "I think Chase and I get it."

The three men continued their earnest conversation, knowing they needed to blunt this attack at all costs. For Trevor Harward, he would continue to offer the president his best counsel—he was a patriot above all else. But, deep down inside, he knew Chase Williams now owned this problem.

At Op-Center, Aaron Bleich had his Geek Tank humming like a Google marketing team. They had focused their collection efforts on Manhattan Island figuring the control-centric North Koreans would want their team ready to assault the United Nations on a moment's notice and would brook no delays. They also assumed whoever was coordinating this attack would receive orders directly from somewhere in Pyongyang, most likely KPA military headquarters, and he focused his team and his beloved computers on phone, e-mail, and text messages coming into or going out of Manhattan. In other words, he had taken every measure to cover the range of likely possibilities to narrow down the location of whoever was going to carry out this attack.

That was the good news. The bad news was over a million and a half people lived in Manhattan's twenty-three square miles, and it was likely that anyone over the age of twelve was calling, texting, and e-mailing every day. Yet Aaron Bleich was not one to shrink from a challenge, and he, his team, and his computers were bent to the task. And, almost as an afterthought, the logical Aaron Bleich did admit he needed a bit of luck.

On Governors Island, the rapidly growing Op-Center/ CIRG team was up and running under the capable eye of Allen Kim. Jim Wright and Brian Dawson were on scene with them and had set up a secure communications link with Op-Center as well as with the New York City Police Department command center.

Their team on the island was bolstered by assets they had borrowed from other FBI CIRG units at Quantico, especially air assets. There were four dedicated Op-Center–CIRG H-60 Blackhawk helos. One of those ready-service helos was flown by Sandee Barron. As part of their rapid-action planning, Allen Kim and his team were mindful of how gridlocked Manhattan could become. They understood if their team was on the ground in Manhattan trying to intercept the assault before it reached the U.N., they would need to move quickly—and that meant by air.

Another option would have been to stage CIRG-SWAT elements on the ground near the United Nations, hidden but ready to make an interdiction on the U.N. grounds. After consultation with New York City's mayor, that option was rejected. They were all mindful of the damage McVeigh's ammonium-nitrate-fertilizer-laden Ryder truck had done in Oklahoma City. The city's mayor was fearful if the attackers saw a goal-line defense near the United Nations, they would attack another nearby building in the area, causing equal or worse damage and loss of life.

So Kim and his CIRG element waited on Governors Island, their helos preflighted and ready for launch, their SWAT teams suited up and on hair-trigger alert. They could cover the less than five miles to the United Nations building in half as many minutes. Like most of the rest of the CIRG pilots, Sandee Barron felt most comfortable not near but inside the cockpit of her H-60.

It was not lost on Paeng Min-ju that she was the only woman on the team. She always felt her four male companions were looking at her. It wasn't because she was pretty, since she knew she was not, but because they resented her being on the team. They never said it. But, at twenty-six, she was not naive and recognized that North

Korea, in addition to being a totalitarian state, was also a male-dominated society. Her four comrades did not see the value of having her on the team, and no matter how hard she had worked or how obedient to Seung Min-jae she had been over the past months, they didn't consider her an equal but a second-class citizen who'd been inflicted on them by the higher-ups for appearance's sake or to serve as the team's servant.

Because of her desire to prove herself, let alone her conditioning to obey without question, she had wrestled with her decision for some time. But in the final analysis, two considerations dominated her thinking. One was the fact that she was not as sanguine as Seung Min-jae that they would ever leave America. She knew how the Americans reacted to attacks on their homeland and how they retaliated. They would never get out of New York alive, she thought. The second consideration concerned someone on the other side of the world, someone living alone on the outskirts of Pyongyang. Her mother was a widow and was dying of cancer. She wanted, no needed, to say good-bye. The day before, when she had been sent to the market to buy food, she had furtively bought a disposable cell phone as well as an international calling card. Now she waited until it was morning in Pyongyang, when her mother would be awake.

CHAPTER TWENTY-FIVE

November 17, 0330 Eastern Standard Time

Anne Sullivan planned for eventualities like the full Op-Center staff hunkering down in their basement building for an extended period. No one would leave, nor could she make them, but she could make them comfortable. It was the unfulfilled mother in her. She had a large quantity of high-end futons stashed for just such eventualities, along with a supply of light blankets and pillows. She also made arrangements through the National Geospatial-Intelligence Agency deputy director to have the NGA gym remain open so the staff could shower as their stay there wore on.

About a third of the staff was bedded down already when Maggie Scott sat bolt upright in her chair. She had previously been a star employee at Amazon, and Aaron Bleich had assigned her to monitor phone calls between Manhattan and North Korea. As the calls hit the Op-Center servers, a translation algorithm changed the words to English and displayed them on one of the monitors on Maggie's desk. Of the many calls, most were of no interest to the goth-clad Scott because they involved business transactions or routine calls between North Korean visitors and their families in North Korea. But one call on her feed had caught her attention. She noticed the call had been placed about ninety minutes ago and was just now coming up in the queue. She replayed it twice:

> *Mother, I am sorry I missed you. Please take care. You know I am on an important assignment. Before he died, you and father agreed this was a worthwhile undertaking. I cannot tell you much, but we have been called to action. It is an endeavor that he would have been proud of and I hope to make you proud as well. I think I will be all right, but I am unable to say for certain. Please remember I love you.*

Convinced she might have stumbled onto something, she sent the file to Aaron Bleich and made a beeline for his small office. She needed Aaron to trace the location of the call.

Bleich was asleep on his futon, but Maggie didn't hesitate a second. "Aaron, wake up. Get on your computer and open the file I just sent you."

Groggy to the point of incoherence, Bleich half-walked, half-crawled to his desk. He maneuvered his mouse and clicked on the file.

Maggie could see him reading it through a second

time. Then Bleich let out a long, slow whistle. "This looks like the real deal, Maggie. There are some trigger words in there."

"Can you trace it from this workstation?"

"I think so," Bleich replied as he opened a program on his desktop. An unintelligible series of numbers flashed across his screen, and soon a map appeared in the background.

"There. The Murray Hill section of Manhattan. That's where it came from. I don't have an exact location. We need our triangulation algorithm to run for a while, but I think I have it nailed to a several-block radius." He grinned, but with more than a hint of smugness. "These throwaway phones are just so tedious."

"Where is that? Where is Murray Hill?" the California-born-and-raised Scott asked.

"Only several blocks from the United Nations," Bleich replied, and took off running toward Chase Williams's office, pausing only briefly for a shout into Roger McCord's office.

Jim Wright was in their makeshift command center on Governors Island, feeling in his gut they might be called into action at any time. Yet he also knew he needed to be prepared for a long ordeal. He wanted to pace himself but knew he couldn't. He knew adrenaline could carry him for a while, but perhaps not the whole way. His watch stander called out to him.

"Mr. Wright, I have Mr. Williams on the line. He wants to talk to you, and then he wants to talk to Mr. Dawson."

"I'll take it right here," Wright replied. "Wake up Dawson and ask him to come in here pronto."

"Boss, what do you have for me?"

"Jim, we think we've located the North Korean cell that plans on bombing the United Nations," Williams began. "Aaron's folks have traced a call made from the Murray Hill neighborhood on Manhattan's east side." As Williams spoke, Wright looked at a large map of Manhattan they had posted in their command center.

"That's damn close to the United Nations, boss. If the attackers are that close, we need to move and move fast. Wait one, sir." Turning to his watch stander, he shouted, "Call Mr. Kim and tell him we're moving. Get his on-deck team aboard the standby helo and get that bird turning. We need to go now!"

At the team rest area near the makeshift command center, Allen Kim answered his cell phone on the second ring. After exchanging a few words with Jim Wright, Kim swung into action. He alerted his teams, and they moved swiftly. He could already hear the Blackhawks spooling up, knowing the flight crews were quickly pushing through their prelaunch checklists.

While his on-deck team piled onto the two lead helos, the backup team boarded the second two. Kim huddled his fire-team leaders and command pilots at the edge of the pad. "Okay, listen up. This is the real deal. We're gonna mount up in four Blackhawks and head north along the East River at dash speed. We think this attack is going to come from somewhere in the Murray Hill area and then head directly for the United Nations.

Our job is to stop it before it gets going." He looked
at the pilots and team leaders. They nodded in understanding.

He paused to bring up a map of Manhattan on his
secure iPad and then scrolled up toward the East Side
around Thirty-fourth Street. "All right. We're mounting up all four birds. I want the first bird—that's yours,
Fred—to drop a fire team off right here at St. Vartan's
Park, between Thirty-fifth and Thirty-sixth Streets.
That's the heart of the Murray Hill neighborhood.
They'll have the best chance to surprise these terrorists, or whoever the hell they are, before they can get
moving." Turning to command another pilot, he said,
"Zack, I want you to take your fire team and drop them
right here at Robert Moses Playground. You can see it's
between Forty-first and Forty-second Streets and hard
by the East River. These locations'll be our goal-line
defense. Once you drop your fire teams, I want both of
you to hold right here at the southern end of Roosevelt
Island in case you have to pick up your fire teams and
move them."

The two pilots and the two fire-team leaders all nodded assent.

"Marty and Sandee, that leaves you two and your fire
teams. You'll be our on-call units if these attackers
aren't where we think they might be. I want you to hold
right here at one hundred feet off the water and at best
fuel-conservation airspeed," he said, pointing at tiny
Belmont Island in the middle of the East River. "You'll
be up on several nets, but I also want you to carry Iridium satellite phones and stay in contact with me in real

time." He paused to look around. "The idea is for the teams on the ground to flush the game so one or the other or both the remaining fire teams can move to intercept them. I'll be aboard Sandee's chopper with that team and will coordinate from there."

Kim paused a moment, looking for any signs of confusion or hesitation. He saw none, only purpose. "All right. Time hack. On my mark 0426 . . . mark." *Now I've got to pull this off. Have I made the right decisions?*

As Allen Kim boarded the third helo, Brian Dawson and Jim Wright were on their phones alerting all the other players.

As they had planned, Paeng Min-ju was the first one to leave the apartment and begin walking toward the garage where their van was parked. As she walked the deserted streets, she wrestled with her guilt. Not guilt that she had disobeyed their strict orders to avoid communicating with anyone while they were on this mission, but guilt about the message she'd left for her mother. How would her lonely mother take it? Would she worry? Of course she would. She vowed she would use the calling card and the disposable cell phone to again call her mother once their mission was complete. She would tell her not to worry, that all would be well. That would put her mind at rest.

While it was nothing compared to the bitter-cold Pyongyang winters, there was a bite to the chilly November morning air as she trudged toward the parking garage. A few days ago, one of the men had asked Seung Min-jae why he chose to park their van in a parking garage so far away, almost ten blocks south of their apartment. But Seung had bitten his head off, so she knew better than to ask. She just lowered her head and plodded south along Second Avenue toward the parking garage.

Chase Williams had established a strong working relationship with the FBI director, and he, in turn, was accommodating to Williams's requests to equip "his" CIRG element with the most modern technology, technology the other CIRG units had yet been equipped with. It was a delicate balance, since the director did not want his teams to feel they were being underequipped while Op-Center's CIRG element got everything they wanted. They had finally worked out an arrangement where the Op-Center's CIRG element would test prototype gear, and, if it was found useful, the entire FBI CIRG would consider adopting it. And it helped that the upgrades came out of the Op-Center's budget.

One piece of gear they were beta testing was the upgraded remote-control drone. In commercial use for years, the tiny, battery-powered, four-bladed unmanned drone had been upgraded to military standards. The mini-heli drone was equipped with a high-resolution camera and sophisticated communications gear. Kim had two of these drones flying over, as well as north of, the Murray Hill area looking for anything out of the ordinary. It wasn't the best arrangement, but it was the best shot they had. They viewed the video in real time in their command center on Governors Island, and the same video feed was piped to Op-Center in real time. A skillful controller could fly the little drone through doorways and into parking garages, but it had yet to be tested operationally.

The other two flight crews had dropped their fire teams off as instructed at St. Vartan's Park and at Robert Moses Playground and now held in a tight racetrack at the southern end of Roosevelt Island. There was no need for night-vision goggles as the lights of Manhattan, Queens, and Brooklyn, as well as a crisp horizon, made for easy flying.

On the ground, the fire teams set up overwatch stations. They wore blue coveralls, not unlike those of New York's finest, and tried to blend in as best they could while awaiting events to unfold. Brian Dawson had coordinated with the New York City Police Department, and they had put up barriers on the streets surrounding both parks to keep vehicles from approaching. They had also posted patrol cars strategically to keep looky-loos away. Now all the SWAT teams could do was to wait for a break. If nothing broke soon, Dawson would put another team on the ground to patrol the area—again, hoping to flush out the game. But for now, they did what they could to maintain tactical surprise.

At Op-Center, Hasan Khosa was assigned to monitor the radio-controlled drone feed. Something had caught his attention, so he played it back on one screen at four times the speed while he monitored the live feed on another screen. A woman had emerged from an apartment in Murray Hill and walked a long way to a parking garage, but no car came out of the garage. He pulled up a file and found several parking garages closer to the apartment she emerged from. Curious. Then a man left that very building ten minutes later and walked to the same garage. Still no car. When a third man came out of the building and started walking in the same direction, it was too much of a coincidence for Khosa. First he called Jim Wright on Governors Island. Then he called Aaron Bleich.

Bleich was there in thirty seconds. "What's up, Hasan?"

"Here, look at this." Khosa ran the playback at sixteen times the speed. "Three people, leaving the same building, walking past several garages, and all ending up at the same garage, but no car has come out of the garage since the first person arrived. And the building is close to where Maggie picked up that cell-phone call hours ago."

Bleich considered this for a moment. "Call Brian and Jim back and get them to anchor one of the drones over that garage—and get them to play back the same segment you showed me. And get Allen Kim into the loop. I think he's going to want to have one of his fire teams roll in on that garage."

Chase Williams and Brian Dawson had a short but intense phone conversation. Williams made it a point not to second-guess his senior leaders, especially when they were on scene and he was at Op-Center headquarters. Dawson knew this, but he also knew the stakes involved, and he welcomed the dialogue. Both knew if there was going to be an attack on the United Nations, that attack was imminent, and there was a better than even chance it would be launched from the South Plaza garage at the intersection of Second Avenue and East Twenty-sixth Street. Dawson had free rein to use his CIRG element to investigate and to take out the threat. Williams took the assignment to keep the president, AG, and FBI director appraised.

Like Chase Williams, Brian Dawson was not wont to megamanage those working for him. He had handpicked Jim Wright as his domestic crisis manager; it was in his hands. Wright now focused on stopping whatever vehicle came from the South Plaza garage and approached the United Nations building. Wright had control of all the Op-Center CIRG assets. Dawson would coordinate with the New York City Police Department.

Jim Wright reached Allen Kim on his bird's secure link. "Allen, I think your units on the ground are still in the right places. How do you want to handle intercepting the vehicle we think is going to pop out of that garage and head for the U.N.?"

Kim considered this for a moment. He was still turning over the options in his mind as he monitored the map of Manhattan on his laptop screen. "If the truck, or whatever they're driving, comes out of the garage here and they head directly for the U.N., they'll likely drive south a half block and turn west on East Twenty-fifth Street, then head straight up Third Avenue, or go further south to East Twenty-third Street and drive east to First Avenue. Not much traffic this hour of the morning on either of those avenues, and the drones will keep an eye on them. As soon as the vehicle starts moving north, I'm going to redeploy the fire team at St. Vartan's Park and have them take up a blocking position either here at Third Avenue and Thirty-fifth Street or at First Avenue and Thirty-fifth Street. I'm gonna ask you to co-ordinate with Brian and have the New York police block traffic from flowing onto either First or Third Avenue, depending on what route they pick."

"Good, Allen. How about your two backup fire teams?"

"They're my insurance policy. Once we see the vehicle emerge from the parking garage and it heads north on whatever route it takes, I'll have both Blackhawks in loose formation trailing about six to eight blocks behind them. If they break through my fire team at Thirty-fifth Street, I'll have one of the helos dash ahead and fast-rope a team on the ground and block them from moving north."

It was shortly after 0500 when Kim addressed his two backup Blackhawks. "Marty, Sandee, here's the plan . . ."

Seung Min-jae arrived at the garage at five ten, right on time, and joined the others in the van. They had over-filled the Honda Odyssey's tires to support the weight of the C-4 that filled every square inch of the van behind their seats. The rear rows of seats had been removed a week ago, and it was all cargo space now. Their bags of produce were jammed on the floor at their feet.

Seung looked at Paeng Min-ju. "You look nervous, sister. Don't worry. Our plan is well thought out." He tried to sound more confident than he felt. "It will be over soon, and we'll be on an airplane before lunchtime."

"I'm not nervous. I know my assignment."

Seung looked at the driver. "Are you ready?"

"Yes."

"Good. Turn south out of the garage and then west on Twenty-fifth Street. We'll drive north on Third Avenue as we discussed."

Sandee Barron and Marty Axelson were anchored in a tight racetrack orbit at five hundred feet, just south of the intersection of Second Avenue and Fourteenth Street. Marty was the senior pilot of the two—he had been with the CIRG almost three years and, subject to Allen Kim's instructions, would direct the airborne operations. He called Sandee on the tactical net. "We got a good brief from Allen, Sandee. Any questions from your perspective?"

"No. I think I've got it, Marty. If they go up First Avenue, you will follow them, and I'll fly trail. If they go up Third, I'll follow as lead with you in trail."

"That's affirm. If they get past our fire team on Thirty-fifth Street, there's still the team at Robert Moses Playground, but that's damn close to the U.N., too close for my money. One of us will be asked to put our team on the ground and take them out, if they get past the first fire team."

"Roger that, Marty, but still no weapons free, right?"

"Right. Allen says the New York police have told them the city is waking up by now. Too many people already on the streets, which makes the possibility of collateral damage too high. As the vehicle approaches Thirty-fifth Street, we'll be following a block or two behind. We'll either fast-rope our SWAT teams onto the avenue ahead of them, or, if the traffic's clear, we'll land, and they can jump out."

"I like the landing option better," Sandee replied. "Faster than fast-rope."

"Roger that. But we'll have to make that call in real time. How's your fuel?"

"I've got one plus four-five. You?"

"About the same. For now, we wait."

The heavily laden van emerged from the garage and headed south. Seung Min-jae had told the driver to move at five miles per hour less than the speed limit. The last thing they needed to do was attract the attention of the New York City police. They had planned well, and now they were close to success. *It was the little things,* Seung reminded himself. They did not want to have a patrol car pull them over.

The van turned right on Twenty-fifth Street as planned and then, one block later, turned north on Third Avenue. They were headed north and would arrive at the United Nations' garage as planned at five thirty sharp.

Jim Wright and Allen Kim were watching the drone feed from their respective perches—Wright in the command center, Kim airborne. They saw the van nearly simultaneously. "Allen, there—our van just came out of the garage, made two turns, and is on Third Avenue, moving north. I'm having my operator maneuver the drone to get a look at the logo on the side of it."

The drone operator sitting in front of Jim Wright maneuvered the little bird skillfully. At his bidding, the little quadro-copter dropped to street level and came alongside the van. "It says, 'Angelo's Produce,'" the man said over the tactical net, "but I can't read the address or any of that. What would a produce van be doing parked in a residential parking garage?"

"No reason I can think of, at least no good one," Kim replied. "Let's treat them as a target. I'll talk to Brian, and he'll get the New York police to cordon off all the streets leading to Third Avenue. Let's stop these guys now!"

"Sandee, I just heard from Jim on the tactical net. Your target is moving north along Third Avenue. Move into close trail. I repeat, move into close trail." As he spoke, Allen Kim shucked his seat belt and moved up between Sandee and her copilot. He wanted a real-time view of their prey.

Sandee Barron needed no further urging. As briefed, she headed up Third Avenue to give chase. And as they had prebriefed, Marty paralleled her course and was back several hundred yards, but along First Avenue in case the van jogged that way. In the back of both helos, the CIRG-SWAT operators waited patiently, each hoping that his team would get the call to action.

"I'm heading north on Third Avenue at ninety knots," Sandee calmly reported over the net, "crossing Eighteenth Street now. Tell me what street the van's crossing; I don't want to overrun this guy."

"It's approaching Thirtieth Street, Sandee," Hasan Khosa chimed in, as if he were flying formation with her and Marty, which in many ways he was. There were advantages to just monitoring the drone's feed and not having to fly it—you could analyze what you saw dispassionately. "You can kick it ahead. Our fire team will intercept it at Thirty-fifth Street."

"Roger. Tell me what I'm looking for. What does this guy look like?"

"It's a white Honda Odyssey van with 'Angelo's Produce' painted on the side—red lettering. It's moving at just under the speed limit."

"And if our ground team can't stop them," Jim Wright interjected, "Get your people on the ground ahead of it."

"Understood, control."

"You copy, Allen?"

"Roger that, Jim."

On the ground, Jack Duffy had his men splayed across Third Avenue. While all signs pointed to this van's being a hostile target, they couldn't be sure, so deadly force wasn't authorized—yet. The CIRG-SWAT team was armed with light wands to signal the van to stop in the predawn hours. If the van ran their barrier, they were ready. A half block north, they had laid out spike strips across the entire avenue. They would blow the van's tires and bring it to a screeching halt.

* * *

As the driver crossed Thirty-third Street and looked ahead, he did a double take. "It looks like armed men ahead. They look like policemen."

Seung Min-jae sat bolt upright in his seat. "Don't slow down. Speed up."

"They are waving us over," the driver said, now past Thirty-fourth Street and only a few hundred yards from the armed men.

"I said speed up, speed up! Floor the accelerator!"

The driver followed Seung's instructions as Paeng Min-ju, crouched between the van's two seats, just hung on. The van picked up speed and was now approaching sixty.

The fire-team leader was waving the lighted wand insistently, signaling the van to slow down and pull over. But it was speeding up! He needed to make an instantaneous decision: Use deadly force to stop the van or let it pass and count on the spike strips to do their job.

"Clear the street," he shouted as he picked the second option. His men all scattered up onto the sidewalks.

On seeing the SWAT-clad men scatter, something triggered for Seung Min-jae. This was too easy.

"Sidewalk," he yelled to the driver.

No reaction.

"SIDEWALK!" he shouted, but the man sat mute, uncomprehending, still pointing the van straight ahead in the middle lane of Third Avenue.

Seung leaned over, grabbed the wheel, and jerked it to the right. The van's tires squealed, and it tilted, and they bounced up on the sidewalk.

"Keep driving straight on the sidewalk until you

reach Thirty-sixth Street, then turn right. They planned this ambush, and there'll likely be another one up ahead. We'll head north on Second Avenue."

"But that's one way heading downtown," the driver protested.

"I know. It's the one street they're likely not covering."

The driver knew better than to argue with Seung. He wheeled right on Thirty-sixth Street and then took a hard left onto Second Avenue. The New York City Police Department had cleared First and Third Avenues of traffic, but not Second. Oncoming cars beeped their horns but swerved to avoid the speeding van, now barreling ahead at close to seventy miles per hour.

Airborne, Marty Axelson and Sandee Barron watched all this play out and knew that, other than the fire team at Forty-first Street, they were all that stood between the van and the U.N. Sandee was only two blocks behind the van when it broke through the fire team on the ground. She immediately dropped down to one hundred feet and moved up to fly right behind the van. For his part, Marty saw no value in remaining on First Avenue and made his own maneuver. In order to see ahead, Allen Kim had all but crawled into the cockpit with Sandee Barron.

For the first time since he had taken this assignment, Seung Min-jae was losing faith in his ability to carry out his mission. It was already clear they'd not be able to park their van in the United Nations' garage, calmly walk away, and detonate their C-4 remotely.

Once the iron gates of the U.N. garage were open in

the morning, there was no lifting-arm gate at the entry booth to slow down vehicles. He knew they could blow through there without stopping; the guard at the booth was just a badge checker and not armed. Maybe they could drive into the garage, stop the van, and then run out the way they came in. He could use his remote detonator once they were safely away. Maybe, just maybe, they could still escape in the confusion of the explosion.

When he heard the whap, whap, whap of the Blackhawk's blades coming up from behind, he recognized that option was wishful thinking.

"Faster, faster," he shouted, urging the driver forward.

Instincts took over for Sandee Barron. She was now flying at fifty feet off the deck, just a few yards behind the van, as she kept it in her chin bubble. She was multitasking, watching the van and looking for obstacles. Those in the van had to know she was there, and it didn't look like the vehicle was going to slow down. There wasn't enough time to sprint ahead and deploy her fire team, and there was no way to turn obliquely so one of her fire-team members could take a shot; she'd impale herself on a building along Second Avenue.

Sandee took the helo down until she was directly over the van. Once there, she jerked the collective down a fraction of an inch and jerked it up again.

Inside the van, the driver had a death grip on the steering wheel as the main landing gear of Sandee's eleventon helicopter smashed into the top of the van. The impact was massive, and he barely kept control of his vehicle.

"Faster, faster," Seung urged.

Again the landing gear smashed into the van's roof, this time even harder. The three passengers were near panic but still determined to carry out their deadly mission. Seung went into his mental map of the target area. He decided they would turn hard right on Forty-fourth Street and approach the UN building head-on.

As the van passed Fortieth Street, Seung Min-jae and his two fellow travelers looked up ahead. To their horror, a helicopter was hovering just a few feet off the ground several blocks ahead. It was turned sideways, and they could see the barrels of weapons pointing at them.

Airborne over the van, Sandee Barron saw Marty Axelson's helicopter just as the assassins in the van saw it. Then she heard Marty's voice. "Sandee, pull up, pull up now!"

She was less than thirty seconds from broadsiding Marty's bird and needed no further urging. She pulled the cyclic into her lap and yanked an armload of collective, and the Blackhawk leapt into the sky. She kept the engines near redline until they had climbed to a thousand feet. In the back, the SWAT troopers held on for dear life.

Seung Min-jae was dedicated to his cause but knew the Blackhawk hovering ahead was about to blow his van to bits. His mission would be a complete failure, and his family would be shamed. Huge buildings housing the wealthy and their wares loomed up on either side of them. He was dead anyway. With scarcely a thought to what might await him in the next life, he activated the detonator.

Even anchored overhead at a thousand feet, well above the skyscrapers below, Sandee Barron felt the shock wave as the van's C-4 registered a massive explosion. She knew they had stopped the assassins, but she looked down in horror as she saw Marty Axelson's Blackhawk blown out of the sky. Allen Kim, leaning out the side of the Blackhawk, felt as if he'd been stabbed in the heart. One of his fire teams was now entombed in the hulk of what had been the Blackhawk.

CHAPTER TWENTY-SIX

OP-CENTER HEADQUARTERS, FORT BELVOIR NORTH

November 29, 0900 Eastern Standard Time

In what was becoming a tradition, Chase Williams gathered his Op-Center team soon after they had all returned home and hosted a modest victory celebration. In this case, they were celebrating two victories—rescuing the LCS crew and blunting the attack on the United Nations. The staff had taken over the National Geospatial-Intelligence Agency's atrium cafeteria for this quiet, late-afternoon event. There had been no long speeches, just a quiet recounting of their success and an unspoken but profound recognition of how much they depended on each other.

When he did offer a few words, Williams reminded his staff of the enormous degree of autonomy they enjoyed, something found nowhere else in government. This autonomy, he pointed out, came with a great deal of responsibility. He complimented them on their mastery of an increasingly diverse skill set. He praised them for protecting Americans and American interests abroad. And they had now shown they could do that at home as well. Williams had not minced words when he reminded them these missions were not without risk. For the first time, they had lost comrades in arms.

In the days following this impromptu celebration, Williams and his senior staff had begun attending the memorial services of CIRG team members who perished when Marty Axelson's helicopter was lost during the mad chase to keep the North Korean assailants from reaching the United Nations. They had attended three memorial services already, and there were more to come in the days ahead. Not all of them could attend every service, but no member of the CIRG-SWAT team was laid to rest without at least one senior member of the Op-Center staff in attendance. Allen Kim was not surprised when the director of Op-Center himself turned up at the graveside service of one of his junior operators.

Now Williams was meeting with his senior staff: Anne Sullivan, Roger McCord, Brian Dawson, Duncan Sutherland, Rich Middleton, Hector Rodriguez, and Jim Wright. This was to be their first detailed hot washup, and it promised to be an all-day affair. Williams did not like to surprise his staff, nor did he entertain recriminations when things had not gone as planned or an alternative course of action might have proved more successful. Over the past week, he had told his senior leaders what he wanted from this meeting so they could come prepared for an informed discussion. He tasked

Anne Sullivan to come up with an agenda that would support this important after-action review.

Williams began with only a short preamble. "Ladies and gentlemen, thank you all for carving out this time to meet collectively. I trust you each had a good Thanksgiving holiday with your families and our suspension of operations for a few days facilitated that. I think it's important we do this hot wash early on, while the events of the past several weeks are still fresh in our minds. We were successful in our efforts and accomplished our mission, but we also lost comrades. Our success is tempered by those losses. I've asked Ms. Sullivan to put together a tight agenda to keep us moving through the morning and perhaps into the afternoon. Anne, what do you have for us?"

"Sir, you wanted to discuss three things. First, how things transpired back here at Op-Center and what techniques and procedures might we change to better handle the headquarters function. Associated with that is what hardware and software we might need to better execute our command, control, and communication responsibilities. Roger and Rich will lead that discussion. Next, you wanted to explore the detailed mechanics of the rescue of the LCS crew to include our surge into theater and our command relationships with all the players in that theater. Part of this in-theater review is a candid look at the performance of our JSOC team and the equipment they have at their disposal. Brian, Hector, and Duncan will lead that discussion. Finally, you wished to discuss our takedown of the van during their mission to attack the United Nations. You wanted to address the working relationship with our FBI-CIRG element, our coordination with the FBI and local officials, and the tactics employed by Allen Kim's team. Brian and Jim will lead that part of the discussion. Did I miss anything, sir?"

"Thanks, Anne. I think you have it about right. And I also want to review how and when I communicate and interface with senior government leaders, including the president. I wish this to be a no-holds-barred discussion. If there's a better way to handle information, prosecute key intelligence, manage tactical data, streamline internal procedures, or facilitate interagency cooperation, I want to know about it. This is not about turf or ego; it's about efficiency and performing at a higher level. And I count on you all to give it to me straight. Fair enough?"

All nodded in agreement. Williams and his staff lapsed into an extended discussion that would go through the afternoon and into the early evening. When they were done, they had agreed on a series of procedural and operational changes. These changes would require time, money, and a great deal of effort, but they would make Op-Center better prepared to deal with the next crisis.

EPILOGUE

January 17, 1000 Pacific Standard Time

A crisp sea breeze snapped the flags at the Broadway Pier in San Diego, California. The pier was a favored location for both civilian and military ceremonies. San Diego was a diverse and cosmopolitan city, but it was still a Navy town. The many hundreds awaiting the proceedings had only to look around. To the west there were two nuclear aircraft carriers moored at Naval Air Station North Island. And but a few hundred yards south, the aircraft carrier USS *Midway* (CV-41), veteran of almost forty years of conflicts, now served as a floating naval museum.

Moored to either side of the pier were the first two ships of the littoral-combat-ship class, USS *Freedom* (LCS-1) and USS *Independence* (LCS-2). Admiral Ben Curtis, the commander of the Navy Region Southwest and the unofficial "Navy mayor of San Diego," paced nervously at the end of the pier, waiting for the presidential motorcade to arrive. His aide broke the tension as he pointed south to where a line of black sedans and SUVs drove into view. Following a flurry of handshakes and official greetings, Admiral Curtis escorted President Wyatt Midkiff to the podium at the end of the pier. Directly in front of him, Commander Kate Bigelow and her crew stood at attention in their dress-blue uniforms. Behind them were their families, friends, and a great many San Diego residents who simply loved their Navy.

President Midkiff began. "Ladies and gentlemen, friends and family, and most importantly, the gallant crew of USS *Milwaukee*. We are gathered here today to award the Presidential Unit Citation to USS *Milwaukee*. Those of you in uniform know, but many of our civilian guests may not know, this high honor is awarded to units of the United States Armed Forces for extraordinary heroism in action against an armed enemy. Few units are even considered for this award. The unit must display gallantry, determination, and esprit de corps in accomplishing its mission under extremely difficult and hazardous conditions. USS *Milwaukee* has distinguished itself in this regard." The president turned to Admiral Curtis and said, "Admiral, please read the citation."

Curtis read the citation. When he was finished, the crowd erupted in thunderous applause. Then the president stepped off the dais and walked up to Kate Bigelow with the Presidential Unit Citation pennant in his hand. Bigelow rendered a sharp salute, and Midkiff handed her the blue, yellow, and red striped pennant.

"Captain, please accept this with the grateful appreciation of our nation."

"Thank you, Mr. President. I accept this award on behalf of my crew, both those you see standing here with me today and those who we lost in combat. I can only hope this award will bring some measure of comfort to those whose loved ones are not physically present, but are with us in spirit."

Midkiff was moved and grasped Bigelow's hand in both of his, shaking it for an extended time. Then he went completely off script and walked through the ranks of *Milwaukee*'s crew and shook each crew member's hand. The crowd rose to its feet and sustained its applause until the president was finished. His parting words to Kate Bigelow were, "And I will look forward to seeing you in Washington in a few weeks."

Once the LCS crew was safely back on American soil and after the North Korean attack on the United Nations was blunted, the president's national security team went to work. They began the complex task of working to ensure North Korea was put in a box and effectively stripped of its power to attack American or friendly interests in the future. The key to that effort was China. There were weeks of intense, secret negotiations between the world's two most powerful nations. Ultimately, the two leaders met face-to-face, and President Midkiff and his Chinese counterpart had a remarkably open and candid discussion. China's premier was forthright with his apologies for indulging North Korea's territorial ambitions, but he was also candid about that nation's claim to the oil and gas reserves on the seabed floor. A great deal of these reserves *were* in North Korean waters, and all of these resources were in what China claimed as its sphere of influence.

The two men hammered out a pact where North Korea would exploit only those waters where they had legal claims recognized by the international community. The oil and gas under other portions of the Yellow Sea would be tapped by an international consortium administered by the United Nations through the International Maritime Organization. China would pay North Korea for the energy they recovered with food, medicine, and nonmilitary assistance. The United States pledged to respect the energy dealings between North Korea and China on a most-favored nation-status, ensuring China could meet its energy needs for the foreseeable future. It was not a perfect solution by any means, but it would have to do for now.

President Midkiff's cryptic remark to Commander Kate Bigelow that he would "see her in Washington in a few weeks" played out in a ceremony in the Rose Garden. Flanked by her parents, a few close friends, and the chief of naval operations, the president awarded her the Navy Cross, the nation's second highest decoration for bravery.

Following the short ceremony, President Midkiff drew her to one side. "Commander, sadly USS *Milwaukee* is no more. You were the last to command the vessel, but your time in command was cut short, was it not? Do you know what's next for you with the Navy?"

Kate Bigelow's life had been consumed in dealing with the aftermath of the final days of *Milwaukee*. This involved after-action reports, personnel issues, and meetings with senior Navy officials. And several publishers had contacted her about the book rights to her story. She had yet to come to a decision on the what-next question. She started to form an answer, only because the president was standing there and she had to say something, when the chief of naval operations spoke up.

"If I may, sir, we have an opening for the commander in the Pentagon on the Joint Staff right now. But we won't keep her ashore for long, and as soon as her short tour in the Pentagon is over, I know we'll have an Aegis cruiser in San Diego that needs a good skipper to take the helm."

The president smiled and nodded while Kate Bigelow tried to suppress more than just a modest smile.

As the meeting was breaking up, a tall urbane man crisply turned out in a Brooks Brothers suit found Kate Bigelow and quietly offered her his congratulations. "I think you have a great future in the Navy, Commander. We need people like you in uniform who aspire to senior leadership positions."

The man looked vaguely familiar, but she couldn't place him. But his manner was so soft and reassuring that she couldn't help herself.

"Thank you, sir, but past command at sea, I'm not sure if I'll want to stay in the Navy."

He smiled in understanding. "Well, at least keep an open mind. The Navy needs people like you. But if it doesn't work out, give me a call."

He handed her a card and stepped away. The card had but a name and single phone number. It was the name that arrested her: Chase Williams—no title, no blue pennant with four stars signifying his former rank, nothing. When she looked up, she noticed he was now in close consultation with the president.

Within a week after the attempted attack on the United Nations, the National Security Staff, the National Intelligence Community, and the Pentagon were united in their assessment regarding the attempted attack on the United Nations. They agreed the perpetrators of the attack were all North Korean students placed in U.S. colleges over the past several years for the sole purpose of being available to attack America should they be ordered to do so by their masters in Pyongyang.

But that was all they knew. This sleeper cell of young North Korean men and women in America could have included only the five involved in this attempt—the three who were incinerated in the van and the two caught trying to cross the Canadian border just outside Buffalo—or all of those in the United States. There was simply no way of knowing, and aggressive days-long questioning of the two caught at the border yielded no hint of which scenario was correct.

The number of students they were dealing with was not insignificant. Under the auspices of the Choson Exchange, a well-funded nonprofit organization founded by Harvard, Yale, and the University of Pennsylvania, over eighty North Korean students had been placed in colleges throughout the United States. Most were the sons and daughters of North Korea's elite, who knew better than their nation's purposely uninformed masses how poor the Hermit Kingdom's higher education system was.

While some in the Justice Department questioned the wisdom—let alone the legality—of rounding up every North Korean student in the United States, deporting them in mass, and thus destroying a program that had been established to initiate at least a small dialogue and opening with North Korea, the president was adamant. The threat to the security of the United States was just too great if even one potential dedicated assassin remained on U.S. soil. He signed the presidential executive order without trepidation or regret.

Three days after the executive order was signed, after an exhaustive search of all databases containing the locations of these students, agents of the Immigration and Naturalization Service and the FBI—assisted by local police—rounded up every North Korean student in America, escorted them to waiting aircraft, and abruptly cut short their stay in America.

The crew of USS *Milwaukee* was granted a liberal amount of leave after returning to the United States. Following their return to duty, they were provided with counseling and debriefing sessions not unlike those reserved for prisoners of war. As their ship was no more, the Navy's personnel bureau worked to reassign each crew member to a new command, accommodating their professional and personal preferences where they could.

Commander Jack O'Connor was one of those, but his

situation was different—and not an easy one. While Kate Bigelow had nearly completed her command tour, the loss of *Milwaukee* left him waiting in the wings for command. O'Connor had done an enormous amount of soul searching and had reached out to Kate Bigelow. At his request, they had met to discuss his future. O'Connor had taken himself out of consideration for command at sea. She was surprised he would give up the chance for a sea command, since for her it was so very important—no, more than important; it was everything. And she was relieved, since she could never have recommended him for command. Jack O'Connor had elected to take a lateral transfer to the Navy Acquisition Corps. He was offered an assignment in the Naval Sea Systems Command in the Littoral Ship Program Office, where he would have a role in bringing additional LCS-class ships into the Navy fleet.

Several weeks later, President Wyatt Midkiff and his national security advisor met in the Oval Office. Midkiff had just returned from his favorite vacation spot—Sun Valley, Idaho—and was relaxed and refreshed. The weeklong ski vacation had been a tonic the exhausted chief executive had sorely needed. Trevor Harward had instigated the vacation by convincing the first lady the president needed—sorely needed—this break.

The president was a good enough leader that he paid attention to the behind-the-scenes work of loyal subordinates. "Trevor," he began, "it's not lost on me the first lady didn't come up with the idea of this Sun Valley vacation all on her own. I appreciate you caring about my health, both my physical and emotional health, as much as about my ability to do my job and lead our nation."

"Guess you can sniff out even the most well-planned conspiracy, Mr. President," Harward replied, smiling. "Looks like we'll have to up our game in the future to try to keep our little secrets secret. But I think if you'll look back on the days since you took the oath on the Capitol steps, you've had more crises to deal with than perhaps any president since FDR."

"I'm not so sure about that, Trevor, but let's leave it at I'm glad to be back in the saddle and getting back to work. We still have a lot to do to keep the promises we made to the American people during our campaign."

"We do, Mr. President. But before we get too deep into the things on our domestic agenda, there's something we should talk about that's going on beyond our shores because it's something that could reach us well before we're ready to deal with it."

The president shifted uneasily in his chair as Harward powered up his secure iPad and brought up a map.

Read on for an excerpt from

TOM CLANCY'S
OP-CENTER:
SCORCHED EARTH

Created by Tom Clancy and Steve Pieczenik
Written by George Galdorisi

Available in August 2016 in trade paperback
from St. Martin's Griffin

CHAPTER ONE

SOUTHEAST OF AL BUKAMAL, SYRIA

March 3, 0930 Eastern European Time

Alan Burton's head slammed into the overhead of the Humvee with eye-watering force. Nearly stunned by the impact, he dropped back into his seat, feeling his scalp for signs of blood. "Damn; that hurt!"

General Bob Underwood suppressed a smile and held out a Kevlar battle helmet to his aide. "Try this. It's harder than your skull."

Burton accepted the helmet and put it on, just in time to cushion his head's next collision with the roof of the heavily armored vehicle.

The ride in the army truck was rough as it stormed across the Syrian farmland that lay hard by the Euphrates River and close to the Iraq border, en route to the Syrian city of al Bukamal. Their convoy had crossed the unguarded Iraqi/Syrian border a half hour ago. One Humvee led the one Underwood and his aide were riding in, while one trailed them. A total of eight special operations Rangers from the 75th Ranger Regiment provided security for Underwood and Burton.

While Underwood and his aide were attired in much the same way as their Ranger Regiment escorts—Interceptor Body Armor bullet-resistant vests, MICH TC-2000 Kevlar Advanced Combat Helmets, M9 Beretta side arms and the rest—there was one distinct difference. Underwood had last hung up his Marine Corps uniform almost two years ago when he retired as the Commander of the United States Central Command—or CENTCOM.

Now, he was back on familiar territory as the Special Presidential Envoy for the Global Coalition to Counter ISIL—the Islamic State of Iraq and the Levant. In his six months in this assignment, Underwood had spent time in Iraq, Jordan, Lebanon, Syria, Turkey and Yemen. He was in Syria again because the Syrian refugee crisis was worse now than at any time since it began in the wake of the 2010 Arab Spring uprisings. The president had dispatched him to Syria to try to broker a cease-fire between the Syrian government and the forces opposing it—Hezbollah, ISIS, the Free Syrian Army, and a number of fringe rebel groups. Underwood didn't fancy his chances of success forging an agreement between and among the warring parties. Still, to Underwood, a presidential order was a presidential order.

"How much longer until we get to al Bukamal, Sergeant?" Underwood asked the driver.

"About fifteen minutes, General."

"Thanks. Ask our lead vehicle to slow down after

we make the next turn. Last time we ran this route we almost took out a herd of cattle."

"I remember, sir, and wilco."

Underwood returned his attention to the ruggedized Panasonic CF-29 laptop as his aide scrolled through their agenda for the meeting. "General, here are the players from the Free Syrian Army we'll—"

The sound of the rocket-propelled grenade hitting the side of their Humvee was ear-splitting and shook their three-ton truck violently. Flames shot along the side of their vehicle. Underwood and his aide hung on as their driver tried to steady the burning Humvee.

Seconds later, there was a deafening sound as an improvised explosive device detonated under the lead vehicle. Underwood and his aide both looked up in horror as the lead Humvee leapt into the air just yards ahead of them and crashed down on its side and then rolled over on its back. Fire began to consume that truck as thick black smoke billowed into the air.

Their driver immediately started to take well-rehearsed evasive action and gunned his V-8 turbo-diesel engine as he tried to drive around the destroyed truck in front of them. Suddenly, Underwood's aide cried out, "Look out!" as an AMZ Dzik "Wild Boar" infantry military vehicle barreled straight for the right side of their Humvee. It was too late. The Polish-designed truck the Iraqi Army had once owned hit them square-on as Underwood and his aide tried to grab on to any available handhold.

Gravity took over and their vehicle teetered—then landed on its left side with a sickening thud. The last thing Underwood remembered before passing out was their driver's head hitting the bulletproof glass on the left front door, his helmet popping off, and blood gushing from his skull as it rebounded from the glass before hitting it again.

The Rangers in the trailing vehicle did precisely what they'd been trained to do—they converged on Underwood's Humvee, dismounted, and quickly deployed in a protective ring around it, their gun muzzles pointed in different directions, searching for threats.

"Command, this is unit Mike-Hotel, taking fire from unknown hostiles approximately one-five klicks southeast of al Bukamal!" the senior man in the trail vehicle shouted into his Motorola XTS5000R secure UHF radio. "One vehicle destroyed, one disabled. Hawk down, repeat Hawk—" the first lieutenant, the senior Ranger still alive, started to say. But his voice was quickly silenced as well-aimed shells from Browning MEHB heavy machine guns, fired from converging American-made M117 Guardian Armored Security Vehicles, ripped through him and also cut down his fellow Rangers.

With all the Americans in the lead and trail American trucks dead or dying, the men in the attacking vehicles converged on the Humvee carrying Underwood.

"Major, I just got a radio call from Mike-Hotel, the 75th Ranger Regiment element providing security for General Underwood. Sir, it was a partial transmission—"

The watch commander cut him off in midsentence. "What did you hear, Staff Sergeant?"

"Sir, he said they were southeast of al Bukamal and that Hawk was down—"

The Army major standing the duty watch at the former Victory Base complex near Baghdad International Airport converged on the staff sergeant's console and immediately barked, "Play it back now!"

Every man and woman in the command center stood transfixed as they listened to the frantic call from the convoy as it was replayed twice.

The watch commander turned to another man and said, "Call CENTCOM Headquarters on the command net. Tell them Hawk is reported down and request air cover."

"Yes, sir. Major, where should I request they get the air cover?"

"Just tell 'em, damn it!"

But the watch team knew there would be no air cover. The United States had pulled out of Iraq years ago. A skeleton U.S. military force remained in Iraq to train the Iraqi army as well as provide security to people like the Special Presidential Envoy for the Global Coalition to Counter ISIL. However, they had little more than a few dozen vehicles like the now-destroyed Humvees, a handful of helicopters, and a few crew-served weapons in addition to their personal weapons. The Americans in the convoy were on their own.

As soon as Underwood tried to move, he realized his left arm was broken. With the Humvee on its left side, his brain was in overdrive as he hung suspended by his lap belt and harness and looked out the smoke-blackened right-side windows of the smashed truck. What had just happened? They were attacked—but by who? He thought he knew, but he tried to banish the thought from his mind.

"Sir, are you OK?" Burton said as he struggled to free himself from his belt and harness and come to Underwood's aid.

"I . . . I think so, Alan. Our driver is dead. What about the Ranger in the front passenger seat?"

His aide looked into the front seats and replied, "I'm afraid they're both dead, sir."

"My arm's bunged up; help me unstrap. We've gotta get out before this truck explodes," Underwood said, as he groped for his Beretta with his right hand.

Just then, they heard loud voices and felt heavy thumping on their Humvee. They jerked their heads and looked as the right-side back door was yanked open. Several pairs of arms reached into the vehicle as first Underwood, and then Burton, were lifted out of the truck and roughly dropped to the ground. Other men grabbed them and dragged them a short distance away from their broken vehicle.

A crowd of men surrounded the two Americans and began kicking them while shouting in a language neither understood. Suddenly, another man pushed his way to the front of the group and stood over Underwood. He held a tablet in his hand. He looked at Underwood, then looked at the tablet, then looked at him again.

"That's him," the man said, drawing a pistol from his belt, as the other men nodded in agreement.

Underwood looked on in horror as the man raised the pistol, took aim, and put a bullet in Burton's forehead.

The Presidential Special Envoy recoiled in horror as blood, bone, and brain tissue from his aide's shattered skull landed on him. Then he looked up at the flag flying from the nearest Guardian Armored Security Vehicle. It was the unmistakable black flag with white Arabic writing. It was the flag flown by ISIS.

Underwood cried out in agony as two of the men grabbed him, bent both his arms back, hog-tied him, and threw him into the Guardian ASV. Then the ISIS vehicles sped away.

"The Presidential Special Envoy?"

"Yes, sir!"

"His convoy was attacked?"

"Yes!"

"Where?"

"Southeast of al Bukamal, Syria."

The Air Force colonel conducting the interrogation was the watch commander at the CENTCOM command center at MacDill Air Force Base in Tampa, Florida. The report by the Navy chief petty officer manning the command net on their watch floor was far from complete. She knew only as much as the sketchy report she'd heard from the soldier at the former Victory Base complex in Baghdad. It was still well before sunrise in Tampa and they were two of only five watchstanders in the command center. The partial report was enough to rouse the colonel to action.

He turned to the Army master sergeant at the console on his left.

"Call Beale. We need eyes-on at that location—*now*! Tell 'em to get a Global Hawk moving in that direction. We'll give 'em updated position information when we get it."

The rest of the watch team sprang into action as chat windows opened and questions—but few answers—streamed back and forth between Baghdad and Tampa. Meanwhile, flash messages rocketed up several chains of command. Soon, other watchstanders, those manning the National Counter-terrorism Center, the National Military Command Center, the White House Situation Room, and other command centers processed what they heard and began to notify key seniors. In the Sit Room, the National Security Council senior staffer leading the watch team picked up the phone and called the president's national security advisor, Trevor Harward.

Bound and gagged and with a sack over his head, Underwood tried not to let the sheer terror of the moment overwhelm him. As a Marine Corps first lieutenant, he had led men in combat in Operation Desert Storm. He had served in other conflicts in the ensuing decades and had numerous tours as a commander in Iraq as well as in Afghanistan. He had never feared his enemy—but he feared those holding him now.

The Guardian ASV bounced along near its maximum speed of sixty miles an hour. Underwood tried to keep track of time to somehow gauge how far he was traveling, but random large bounces shot shards of pain into his broken arm that almost overwhelmed his senses. He became almost numb to the pain and tried to think through what over three decades of military training had taught him about how to react in a crisis.

It was morning in Washington, D.C., when Trevor Harward entered the Oval Office. He had called President Wyatt Midkiff in the family quarters shortly after the president's normal wake-up time and told him the news, promising to bring him up to speed in the Oval later that morning.

The president had worked with Harward long enough to know his national security advisor was giving him every detail he knew, but the lack of information about the situation still frustrated him. And there was a personal element. Midkiff had worked closely with Underwood when the general commanded CENTCOM and was especially cheered when he had accepted the position as Special Presidential Envoy for the Global Coalition to Counter ISIL. He knew Underwood had dedicated his life to the Marine Corps, had served almost continuously in the Middle East and South Asia for the latter third of his career, and was a devoted family man who looked forward to spending more time with his wife, his children, and his grandchildren when he retired and came home to Great Falls, Virginia. But the man's unique credentials made him the consensus choice to serve in this capacity, and the president and his wife had courted the Underwoods—especially Mrs. Underwood—to entice the general to take on this assignment. Now he was missing and very likely kidnapped.

"Trevor, I've listened to what you told me over the phone and I read your memo. I'm less interested in what's happened than I am in what we're going to do to find Bob Underwood."

Harward paused. He knew what the president wanted to hear: that the U.S. national and military intelligence agencies had located Underwood's position and that a combat search-and-rescue mission was being mounted to snatch him away from his captors. That was not the case—far from it.

"Mr. President, we got eyes-on with a Global Hawk about two hours ago. General Underwood's convoy was ambushed in what appears to have been a well-orchestrated attack. All of the vehicles in the convoy are still there and are either damaged or destroyed. There were ten personnel in the convoy, counting General Underwood and his aide. The Global Hawk picked up what we think are six bodies surrounding the vehicles."

"But we can't see inside the Humvees, right?"

"Right, Mr. President. We have two channels in work to try to do just that—"

"How . . . how will we do that?" the president interrupted.

"We have operatives working with the Free Syrian Army. The closest ones are in—" Harward paused to look down at his secure iPad "—Deir ez-Zur. It's about one hundred and thirty kilometers—eighty miles— north-northwest of al Bukamal. Our people there don't have air assets, so they're driving toward al Bukamal, but it's rough terrain and slow going."

"The other channel we have is with the Iraqi Army," Harward continued. "The CENTCOM Commander is working with the Iraqi military to try to get some of our 75th Rangers aboard Iraqi helicopters and get to the site ASAP—"

"Iraqi helicopters?" the president interrupted again. "Don't we have any American helicopters there?"

"We do, but they're attack helicopters, with very little space for troops. We need bigger birds that can haul more men out to the site."

"All right, I get it. But you said, 'working with' the Iraqi military. Are there any issues? With all the damn blood and treasure we've poured into that country and the way we're still propping them up now, they'd better treat this like a five-alarm fire and give us everything they've got. Do I need to call the Iraqi president?"

"No, sir. I made it clear to General George that if he needed our help, he'd get it. The Iraqi military has a pretty good inventory of American, French, and Russian helicopters. It's just a question of picking ones that can make the two-hundred-plus-mile round trip carrying the Rangers and all their gear."

"I want to know immediately when those helos are en route."

"Yes, Mr. President."

"Anything else you need to tell me about this mess?"

"There is one more thing. We won't know this for certain until we have eyes at the site; the Global Hawk can only pick up so much detail. But we think there's an ISIS flag planted in the ground at the ambush site."

The normally controlled president lost it. "Damn it!" Midkiff shouted. "Find Bob Underwood. I don't care how we do it, just do it!"

"Roger . . . Aaron?" Chase Williams said as his intelligence director and the intel director's networks assistant appeared in his doorway. Op-Center's director was reading a report and sipping his Sumatra dark roast coffee from his Navy mess-decks mug. Williams put the report aside and motioned the two men to sit down.

Now in his third year as the leader of Op-Center, Williams had helped his president deal with crises across the globe, as well as at home. He was recruited—hard—by Op-Center's former director, Paul Hood, when the president decided to reestablish the organization.

Williams brought just the right qualities to the job. A retired Navy four-star, he was a former Combatant Commander for both Pacific Command and Central Command. He had proven his mettle in uniform, and now, as director of the National Crisis Management Center—as Op-Center was officially known—Williams enjoyed the president's complete trust and confidence. He had saved American lives at home and abroad and used his international and domestic Op-Center assets as precision instruments.

Roger McCord began, "Boss, you've read our reports and have likely seen the network news feeds, so you know the convoy carrying the President's Special Envoy was attacked. You also know there are at least six KIA and the CENTCOM Commander is trying to get eyes on the ground to see if General Underwood is there."

"Bob Underwood's a good man," Williams said. "He did a phenomenal job at CENTCOM under tough circumstances—much tougher than I ever faced. What else we got?"

McCord, a former Marine who previously commanded the Intelligence Battalion at the Marine Special Operations Command, or MARSOC, had been one of Williams's first hires when he took over Op-Center. With a Ph.D. from Princeton, magna cum laude in international affairs, McCord was a former infantry Marine who transferred to Marine Corps intelligence when he was wounded in Ramadi. He was in many ways Williams's alter ego. Williams trusted him without question, but what he liked best about McCord was that his intelligence director never guessed and always gave it to him straight.

"Aaron has mined ISIS's social media and also hacked into the transmissions bouncing off some of the cell phone towers near their compound in Mosul. I'll let him tell you more, but from what we can figure, it looks like ISIS has General Underwood and has taken him well away from the ambush site."

Williams had suspected as much, but hearing it from McCord caused him to sag in his chair. "Aaron?" he asked.

Aaron Bleich's official title was Intelligence Directorate, Networks Assistant. But that title so understated his role in the organization that Williams kept asking

McCord to change it. Widely regarded as the intelligence director's MVP, Bleich had been recruited via a gaming company front at the annual Comic-Con International Convention in San Diego, California. "Chief hacker" sounded like a too-judgmental title, but that was the long and short of what Bleich did so well.

Bleich was the architect behind the data mining and anticipatory intelligence programs that made Op-Center hum and that put its analysis abilities on a level above—likely far above—any other intelligence collection efforts in or out of government. Bleich ensured that Op-Center had access to all the information collected by each of the sixteen U.S. intelligence agencies. More importantly, he had carefully built the automated collation and analytical programs to make sense of the mountains of data Op-Center ingested. Big data didn't worry the Geek Tank leader; he embraced it and put it to use. Bleich had built his Geek Tank around machines and people—and the people were the best and the brightest minds, hired away from companies like Google, Amazon, Salesforce, and eBay.

"It's like this, sir," Bleich replied. "ISIS has only dribbled out a little bit into social media, but they've been burning up the cell phone circuits. They definitely have General Underwood. We're all but certain he's out of Syria and into Iraq. Beyond that, there's not much more we can say with any certainty."

"But what's your anticipatory intelligence suggesting?" Williams prodded.

Bleich looked towards McCord before continuing. He had overstepped his bounds with his immediate boss before and had been gently nudged back into line. McCord just nodded, so he continued.

"Well, the President's Special Envoy for Countering ISIL is a prize for any terrorist organization, but perhaps more so for ISIL because his very existence suggests we intend to take the fight to them. Most of the cell phone conversations we're picking up are carefully worded—we suspect ISIS is well aware of our monitoring capabilities—but my . . . umm . . . our analysis suggests there's little drama in their calls. It's more like whoever has him is just reporting in to someone at the top of their food chain."

"Mabad al-Dosari is still their leader," McCord interjected.

"You're saying the ISIL fighters who snatched him aren't operating independently. You think they've grabbed him at al-Dosari's behest and are bringing him to their compound in Mosul?"

"That's right," Bleich added. "And you know that area is no-man's-land for the Iraqi Army. They don't even make a pretense of controlling it."

"Do you think what you're picking up and what you're analyzing will alert us once they have him there in Mosul?" Williams asked.

"We're pulling out all the stops to ensure it'll do just that," McCord interjected. "Aaron will keep us posted on a real-time basis. You want us to send the ops folks in, Boss? You thinking of sending our JSOC unit downrange?"

"No, not yet," Williams replied. "Give me a minute to let the president know what we know. Once I do that, we'll get the rest of the staff together and see if there's anything we can do to help."

As soon as McCord and Bleich left, Williams sat in front of his computer and composed one of his short, cryptic memos to the president. It was in the format of Williams's own design for communications that were strictly between him and President Midkiff. The infrequent communiqués were initially labeled, "President of the United States/Op-Center Eyes Only" which Williams later abbreviated to, "POTUS/OC Eyes Only."